THE SPACE AMID SECONDS

LOGAN BUTTERFIELD

For information, address: logan.r.butterfield@gmail.com

ISBN PRINT: 9798303846548

Cover Design by Bicao Butterfield and Logan Butterfield
Printed in the United States of America.

To Bicao and, by extension, 妈妈 (Mom) & 爸爸 (Dad)—
for without whom this,
and I, would and could not be.

Contents

CHAPTER 1

THE MORNING AFTER

Olivia Chén always set her phone to Do Not Disturb at exactly 10:47 PM. The precision wasn't conscious—like most of her habits, it had evolved from the residue of someone else's preferences. Marcus had needed exactly thirteen minutes to brush his teeth, check his calendar, and send his last work email before bed at 11:00 PM. She'd started silencing her phone to give him those thirteen minutes of focus, and now, three months after their break-up, her thumb still found the crescent moon icon at 10:47 every night.

Which was why, when she woke to forty-seven notifications at 6:13 AM on a Sunday morning, her first thought wasn't about the messages themselves, but about how she must have forgotten to set Do Not Disturb for the first time in two years, four months, and nine days.

Her second thought, as her sleep-blurred vision began to focus on the preview text, was that she was still dreaming:

Rebecca Liú is engaged to Marcus Cài!

The timestamp showed 11:42 PM. Her notifications had started exactly fifty-five minutes after her nightly ritual, as if the universe had been waiting for her to lower her defenses. Each message land-ed like the tick of her grandfather's metronome—steady, relentless, marking time in the worst possible way.

She sat up in bed, her silk pillowcase sliding away with a whis-per that sounded too much like *finally*. The morning light through her east-facing window cast bony shadows across her phone screen, lines like the bars of a cage. Or perhaps like the spokes of a wheel, she thought, remembering her grandfather's voice: *Every mechanism has its breaking point, Ā-Xīn. The trick is knowing whether it's meant to be fixed or transformed.*

Her ex-best friend and her ex-boyfriend. The two people who had most shaped her daily rhythms over the past three years, who had separately left her life in the past six months, had somehow found their way to each other. Rebecca, who had stopped speaking to her after a fight about time—about how Olivia never had enough of it, about how she was always calculating it, parceling it out like a miser with coins. And Marcus, who had ended things because their timing was off, because she was "still trying to live life like it's a for-mula when it's really jazz."

The notifications kept coming, each one a small percussion against her measured life. WhatsApp messages from her mother's mahjong group. WeChat updates from distant cousins in Shanghai. Instagram tags from college friends. Email alerts from mutual con-nections. Each one a tooth in a gear, turning, connecting, meshing with the next to drive home a single truth: while she had been care-fully maintaining her routines, life had spun wildly forward without her.

She watched the number climb to forty-eight, forty-nine, fifty. Her thumb hovered over the first message—from her mother, of course, sent at 11:43 PM: *Did you know about this? Why didn't you tell me? Call me!*

The real question, Olivia thought, wasn't whether she knew. It was whether she should have known, whether there had been signs in the measured spaces of her days, in the careful borders she drew around her hours. Had she been so focused on keeping time that she'd forgotten to watch it?

Her room filled with the soft, steady tick of the wall clock—her grandfather's first successful repair, given to her on her tenth birthday. She'd never noticed before how the sound echoed slightly, each tick returning as a gentle ghost of itself, like a choice and its consequence, a moment and its memory.

Fifty-one notifications. Fifty-two.

Olivia Chén, who had never been late to anything in her life, who measured coffee grounds to the gram and her steps to the meter, who had inherited her grandfather's love of precision and her father's fear of waste, looked at the time: 6:27 AM. In exactly thirty-three minutes, she would begin her Sunday morning routine with a visit to the farmers' market. She had exactly thirty-two minutes to decide whether to maintain the rhythms that had defined her life, or to finally let them break.

The fifty-third notification arrived like a strike of a hammer against a bell: Rebecca had tagged her in the engagement photo. She hadn't opened it yet, but she knew, with the same certainty that guided her fingers across watch mechanisms, that the photo would be timestamped at 10:47 PM.

At 7:00 AM, Olivia joined the stream of early risers flowing into the farmers' market at the border of North Beach and China-town. The morning fog hung like gauze over Telegraph Hill, softening the edges of buildings her grandfather had once used as markers to test his repaired watches. *When the minute hand touches the top of the campanile,* he would say, *the ferry horn should sound. If it doesn't, we adjust again.*

She moved through her usual pattern—past the flower vendor setting out peonies, around the elderly couple arranging their mushrooms in precise concentric circles, between the twin sisters who sold sourdough still warm from midnight baking. Her feet knew this dance by heart, could trace its steps even as her mind circled endlessly around the number fifty-three, around the timestamp 10:47, around the way time seemed to bend and fold until every moment pointed back to Marcus.

The coffee stand appeared through the thinning fog like a ship emerging from memory. For thirty-seven Sundays, she had stood in this line, reciting the same order: dark roast beans, single-origin Ethiopian Yirgacheffe, whole not ground. She'd memorized the details after the third time Marcus had sighed and explained why it was the only coffee worth drinking, how the high elevation and precise processing created notes of bergamot and jasmine that no other bean could replicate.

"The usual?" The vendor reached for the familiar bag, his movements as automatic as her arrival.

Olivia opened her mouth to say yes, but stopped. In the pocket of her coat, her phone vibrated—notification fifty-four, or perhaps fifty-five. She hadn't checked since leaving her apartment. The weight of it against her ribs felt like her grandfather's old metronome, counting beats she no longer needed to keep.

"Actually," she said, the word falling into the space where her habitual 'yes' should have been, "what would you recommend?"

The vendor—she realized she'd never read his name tag before—paused, hand hovering over the Ethiopian beans. "For you specifically? Or for what you usually make?"

"For me," she said, and was surprised to find she didn't know what that meant. She tried to remember the last time she'd chosen coffee for herself, before Marcus had inserted his preferences into the architecture of her days. The memory surfaced slowly: her grandfather's kitchen, a tin of dark Chinese coffee thick enough to stand a spoon in, the way he would add a single dried orange peel to each cup while telling her stories about Xiamen.

"I used to drink my coffee strong," she said, the words feeling like translation. "Strong enough to hold all the things you're not ready to say."

The vendor—James, his name tag read, though something about the way he wore it suggested it wasn't quite right—smiled with one corner of his mouth. "Ah," he said, turning to a different shelf. "You're looking for something honest."

Her phone vibrated again. In the distance, a ferry sounded its horn, the sound rolling through the fog like a question seeking its answer. She thought of all the mornings she'd stood here, checking the time against the tower clock, making sure she maintained the precise rhythm of Sundays with Marcus. But the tower was hidden in the fog now, and for the first time, she realized she didn't need to see it to know the time was changing.

"Yes," she said, watching as James reached for a small batch of beans she'd never noticed before. "I think I am."

The beans James selected were darker than Marcus's precious Yirgacheffe, almost black in the weak morning light. He measured them with hands that moved like her grandfather's—precise but unhurried, as if accuracy and speed were distant cousins who preferred not to acknowledge each other.

"Vietnamese coffee," he said, "roasted with butter and a touch of vanilla. But the secret—" he held up a small sachet that smelled of smoke and memory,"—is that we age it with cassia bark from an old family recipe."

Olivia inhaled, and suddenly she was eight years old again, watching her grandfather repair a nineteenth-century pocket watch while drinking coffee from a glass cup that had survived three generations and two revolutions. He would let her smell the coffee but never taste it, saying, *Some pleasures need to wait for the right moment, Ā-Xīn. Time makes them sweeter.*

"The French left Vietnam," James continued, his voice carrying the same careful cadence as his movements, "but their coffee stayed, transforming into something entirely new. Like time itself—it changes everything it touches, but also gets changed in return."

Her phone buzzed again in her pocket. She imagined the notifications climbing past sixty now, each one a small weight added to the morning. But for the first time since waking, the vibration felt distant, as if it belonged to a different version of herself—one who still measured her life in other people's preferences.

James wrote her total on a receipt with handwriting that seemed to flow like calligraphy, each number placed with deliberate care. But instead of tearing it off immediately, he paused, pen hovering over the paper. "You know," he said, "my grandmother used to say that the best moments in life happen in the minute pauses from one second to next—when we're not watching the clock, but truly living the time we have."

He added something at the bottom of the receipt before hand-ing it to her along with the coffee. Under the total, in that same flowing script, he had written: *Time is not a river flowing one way, but an ocean moving in all directions at once. Choose your tides wisely.*

The quote tugged at something in her memory—a line from one of her grandfather's journals perhaps, or maybe something he'd once said while working on a particularly difficult repair. She looked up to ask James about it, but he had already turned to help another customer, his movements once again measured and sure.

The fog was beginning to lift as she left the market, the sun slicing through in sharp angles that reminded her of light through her grandfather's magnifying glass. The coffee beans shifted in their bag with each step, their weight different from what she was used to carrying. Different, she realized, but not wrong—like the difference between who she had been at 10:47 last night and who she was becoming in the changing light of morning.

Her phone vibrated one more time, but instead of reaching for it, she found herself pulling out the receipt, reading the quote again. The ink seemed to shimmer slightly, as if the words themselves were floating in time rather than fixed on paper. She thought of Marcus's insistence on precision, on doing things the "right" way, and wondered if perhaps she'd been looking at time all wrong—not as an ocean of possibilities, but as a narrow channel that only flowed in one direction.

Olivia saw a clock in the midst of the bustling street, its face catching the strengthening sunlight. For the first time in years, she didn't check her phone against it.

The morning sun had fully claimed the day by the time Olivia returned to her apartment, casting long rectangles of light across the stack of boxes she'd been avoiding for eight months, three weeks, and two days. Her grandfather's boxes. They had arrived the day after the funeral, carefully packed by her mother with labels in both English and Chinese Hanzi: *"Tools/*工具*,"* *"Books/*书籍*,"* *"Memories/*回忆*."*

She set her new coffee beans on the kitchen counter, the receipt's ink catching the light like the face of a watch. The quote about time being an ocean seemed to ripple as she moved past it, drawing her attention to the boxes the way a tide pulls at the shore.

For months, she'd arranged her life around these boxes without actually touching them. They had become part of her apartment's geography—landmarks she navigated between while maintaining the careful rhythms of her days. Marcus had called them her "cardboard elephants," too big to ignore but too heavy to move. Now, watching the sunlight trace their edges, she wondered if perhaps they had really been hourglasses all along, waiting for the right moment to turn.

The first box opened with a sigh of cardboard and memory. The scent that emerged was instantly familiar: clock oil and metal, paper and time. Her grandfather's tools lay nested in their wooden case like an alphabet of possibility—each piece worn smooth in exactly the right places, telling the story of decades spent healing the wounded hours of strangers' lives.

She lifted out a loupe, remembering how he would let her look through it when she was small. *Everything changes when you look closely enough*, he would say. *Even time has texture if you know how to see it.* The lens caught the light, projecting a tiny rainbow onto her palm like a piece of fractured time.

Beneath the loupe lay his favorite screwdriver, its wooden handle polished by years of use to the warm sheen of well-loved jade.

She had watched him use it hundreds of times, his movements so precise that the tool seemed to disappear into his hands, becoming an extension of his will. Now, holding it herself, she felt the weight of inheritance—not just of objects, but of understanding.

Further down, wrapped in silk that had once been bright red but had faded to the color of sunset, she found his collection of balance wheels. They nested together like a family of mechanical moons, each one calibrated to measure time at a slightly different pace. *Because sometimes,* he had told her, *a watch needs to run a little faster or slower to tell the truth of its owner's life.*

Her phone hummed again in her pocket—a reminder, she knew without looking, of all the messages she still hadn't answered. But its mechanical vibration seemed hollow compared to the quiet elegance of the tools before her, each one designed to measure time in ways more meaningful than minutes.

At the bottom of the case, tucked into a velvet pouch that still held the shape of its contents, she found a silver pocket watch. Not one she recognized from his collection, but one that made her breath catch with its unfamiliarity. It was heavier than it looked, its case engraved with patterns that seemed to shift in the changing light—clouds or waves or perhaps both, moving around the edges like the border between sea and sky.

When she opened it, the face was unlike any she had seen in her grandfather's shop. Instead of numbers, it bore characters that might have been Hanzi mixed with something that looked like Sanskrit, but certainly something altogether different than she had seen before, arranged not in a circle but in spirals that drew the eye inward. The hands were still, but something about their position suggested not death but pause—as if the watch was merely waiting, like her grandfather's boxes, for the right moment to begin moving again.

A piece of paper fluttered from the pouch, covered in her grandfather's distinctive handwriting—English and Hanzi intertwined like twin streams flowing into the same sea. But before she could read it, a sharp crack of silence cut through her apartment. Her own bedside clock, the one he had given her so long ago, had stopped.

The silence from her bedside clock seemed to amplify another absence—the constant vibration in her pocket had stopped. Olivia reached for her phone, finding it dark and unresponsive, its screen a perfect mirror reflecting her own startled expression. She pressed the power button with the same instinctive urgency she'd once seen in patients coding on her mother's hospital rounds: clear, compress, shock, repeat. But the screen remained obstinately black, as if it had decided to join her grandfather's mysterious pocket watch in its timeless pause.

For the first time in six years, she couldn't check the exact time. The knowledge struck her like a missed step on a familiar staircase— that peculiar vertigo of finding emptiness where certainty should be. Her kitchen clock read 10:17, the microwave displayed 10:22, and her grandfather's stopped clock simply held its hands like a shrug at 10:47. Which one told the truth? She thought of James's words about time moving in all directions, and wondered if perhaps they all did.

The phone repair shops wouldn't open until eleven—or was it noon on Sundays? She had always relied on her phone to know such things, its calendar a precise map of urban rhythms. Now that map was gone, along with her contacts, her photos, her carefully curated playlists for every mood and moment. Gone too were the fifty-something notifications about Rebecca and Marcus, though their weight lingered like phantom limb pain.

She turned back to her grandfather's tools, scattered across her kitchen table like constellations waiting to be named. The loupe caught a ray of sunlight, sending it spinning across the walls in prismatic arcs. Time, she realized, looked different through each lens—the way it had when she was small, before phones had turned it into something to be tracked rather than experienced.

Her mother would be waiting for a response to those midnight messages. Rebecca might be wondering about her silence. Marcus... what would Marcus think of her digital disappearance? Once, he had challenged her to go phoneless for a day, betting she couldn't survive without her calendar alerts. She had declined, calling it an unnecessary exercise in chaos. Now chaos had found her anyway, arriving not with the bang of broken glass but with the softer, more permanent silence of a dead battery.

She picked up her grandfather's mysterious pocket watch again, studying its spiraling symbols with new attention. Without her phone's constant tether, the weight of it felt different in her palm—more present, somehow. The strange characters caught the light like ripples on water, and she remembered something else her grandfather used to say: *A broken clock is right twice a day, but a watch that shows no time at all might be telling the most truth.*

The sun had shifted while she sat there, the kitchen's shadows rotating like hour hands around her still figure. She could feel time moving differently now, no longer parceled into notification pings and calendar alerts, but flowing more like the ocean James had described—deep and vast and full of unknown currents.

A sound drew her attention to the window: the campanile was striking the hour, its bells rolling through the city like waves. She counted eleven tones, each one distinct, each one a moment that couldn't be paused or rewound or captured in digital memory. The last note hung in the air like a question, and Olivia found herself reaching not for her dead phone but for her grandfather's watchmaking tools, her fingers closing around the worn wooden handle of his favorite screwdriver.

Some things, she realized, could only be fixed by first letting them break completely.

The second box yielded its secrets more reluctantly than the first, sealed with packing tape that had yellowed at the edges like old photographs. "*Books/* 书籍," her mother's explicit script declared, though when Olivia finally worked the box open, she found something more intimate than mere books. These were her grandfather's journals, notebooks, and repair logs—the paper trail of a life measured not in years but in movements restored and moments preserved.

The notebooks were arranged chronologically, their spines creating a timeline from bottom to top. The earliest ones bore dates from Xiamen, filled with diagrams of movements she'd never seen and characters written in a younger, more urgent hand. She remembered him describing the watchmaking district there, where ancient timepieces would arrive via silk roads both old and new, carrying stories in their worn gears and weathered cases.

But it was a different volume that caught her attention—one bound in indigo cloth that had been wrapped separately in silk, tucked between two repair ledgers as if hiding. The fabric held the same shade as the traditional indigo-dyed clothes her grandfather had described from his childhood in Fujian, when fabric makers would judge the depth of color not by sight but by the number of times they had submerged the cloth. Seven dips for everyday wear, nine for special occasions, eleven for pieces meant to last generations.

This book had the weight of eleven dips, though its pages were only partially filled. Opening it released a scent of ink and tea, and something else—osmanthus flowers, perhaps, the same ones her grandfather used to dry between the pages of his important documents. The first page bore no date, only a single line in his distinctive blend of English and Hanzi:

时间不以分钟计算，而是以决定之间隙而计算 *(Time isn't measured in minutes, but in the spaces between decisions)*

Below this, in smaller script:

For when you're ready to understand, 阿昕 *(Ā-Xīn).*

Her hands trembled slightly as she turned the page, recognition blooming like ink in water as she saw her family's nickname for her stamped on the page in her grandfather's hand. This wasn't just another journal—this was the memoir he'd mentioned in fragments over the years, the one he'd always said he was "still living his way into." She had assumed it was merely another of his philosophical metaphors, like his saying that every watch told two stories: the one marked by its hands and the one carried in its gears.

The text alternated between English and Hanzi, not in translation but in conversation, each language carrying parts of the story the other couldn't quite hold. She caught glimpses of Xiamen's nar-

13

row streets, of workshops lit by paper lanterns, of a young apprentice learning to measure time by the pulse in his fingertips. But there were gaps too—unoccupied places between paragraphs that felt deliberate, as if her grandfather had been leaving room for truths he wasn't yet ready to commit to paper.

A loose sheet slipped from between the pages, covered in technical drawings of the pocket watch she'd just found. The margins were filled with calculations and notes in multiple hands—some she recognized as her grandfather's, others unknown yet somehow familiar, as if she'd seen their echo somewhere before. The drawings showed the watch's curious face from multiple angles, its spiral patterns resembling both astronomical charts and ocean currents.

In the corner of the sheet, a small note caught her eye: *Some mechanisms aren't meant to be fixed alone.* Next to it, in different handwriting: *Time shared is time multiplied.*

The campanile struck again outside—noon already, though it felt both longer and shorter than the hour that had passed. Olivia looked up from the memoir to find her apartment transformed by midday light, the shadows of her grandfather's tools overlapping with the scattered pages like the hands of multiple clocks converging on a single moment.

The memoir's next page was blank, waiting. Her grandfather's voice seemed to whisper from the void: *Every story has its own timing, Ā-Xīn. The trick is learning to trust the pauses as much as the movement.*

Olivia traced her grandfather's words with her fingertip, feeling the slight indentations in the paper where his brush had lingered between strokes. *Time isn't measured in minutes, but in the spaces between decisions.* The sentence seemed to pulse with new meaning now, like a heartbeat felt rather than heard.

She thought of all the decisions that had led to this moment: Marcus choosing his precise Ethiopian beans, Rebecca choosing silence, her grandfather choosing to leave this memoir unfinished. And her own choices—to maintain routines that no longer served her, to measure her days by others' rhythms, to keep these boxes sealed like time capsules of grief.

The empty pages that followed that first line felt less like an absence now and more like an invitation. Her grandfather had always treated omission as an active choice in his designs, explaining how the gaps between gears were as crucial as the teeth that connected them. *Without some freedom for a degree of movement,* he would say, adjusting a balance wheel with infinite care, *even the most perfect mechanism will tear itself apart.*

She returned to the mysterious pocket watch, holding it beside the open memoir. The spiraling symbols on its face seemed to echo the way her grandfather's languages spiraled together on the page, each one reaching for truths the other couldn't quite grasp. Time shared is time multiplied, the unknown hand had written. She wondered what multiplication meant when applied to the unknown—how many futures might spiral out from a single changed choice?

The sunlight had shifted again, afternoon gold replacing the clinical clarity of noon. Her dead phone lay forgotten on the kitchen counter, its black screen no longer reflecting her face but absorbing light like the surface of still water. The notification count that had seemed so overwhelming at dawn now felt like a measurement from another life—as irrelevant as Marcus's coffee preferences, as distant as Rebecca's carefully curated intimacy.

In the quiet of her apartment, surrounded by the ghosts and gifts of her grandfather's craft, Olivia made her first unmeasured decision of the day. She opened her laptop—not to check her messages or update her calendar, but to order a set of watchmaking tools of her own. Her fingers hesitated over the trackpad as she realized she didn't know the precise specifications, the exact measurements that Marcus would have insisted on researching. Instead, she found herself choosing by instinct, selecting pieces that caught her eye and sparked memories of her grandfather's hands at work.

The campanile marked the half-hour, its single note hanging in the air like the end of an unfinished sentence. Olivia looked at the empty pages of the memoir, then at the expanse on her kitchen table where she'd unknowingly begun arranging her grandfather's tools in a pattern that mirrored his old workbench. The afternoon light caught the loupe's lens, sending another rainbow spinning across the walls, landing atop her grandfather's memoir.

She picked up a pen—not her usual precise ballpoint, but an old fountain pen from her grandfather's collection. The ink flooded the nib like time rushing into absence, and she began to write in the blank pages he'd left behind: *The space between decisions is where we learn to trust our own timing.*

The words felt both completely her own and somehow inherited, like the patina on well-loved brass or the smooth wood of a handle shaped by generations of careful hands. Outside, fog was rolling back in from the bay, softening the edges of the afternoon. Yet, inside, everything was coming into focus with the sharp clarity of a watch crystal finally wiped clean.

CHAPTER 2

OUT OF SYNC

Monday morning arrived with the kind of fog that turned San Francisco's grid into a maze of memories and maybes. Olivia navigated by the ghost-shapes of buildings, her grandfather's pocket watch a warm weight in her coat pocket, her dead phone a lighter one in her bag. The repair shop she'd found— or rather, the one her neighbor's ancient Thomas Guide had led her to—sat at the intersection of Grant and Sacramento, where Chinatown's lanterns gave way to the Financial District's steel and glass.

The shop occupied the ground floor of a narrow Victorian, wedged between a dim sum restaurant and a fortune teller's parlor. Its window display caught her eye first: instead of the expected wall of phone cases and tablet screens, vintage timepieces filled antique wooden trays, their hands moving in what looked like synchronized choreography. A sign in elegant copperplate script read "Malhotra Electronics & Watch Repair," though the "Electronics" part appeared to be a more recent addition.

The bell above the door chimed in perfect B-flat—she recognized the note from her grandfather's tuning exercises—as she entered. The interior was an anomalous fusion of past and present:

sleek phones and tablets lined one wall, while the other housed a collection of clock faces that ticked with subtle syncopation. The air smelled of clock oil and silicon, an oddly compelling combination that reminded her of her grandfather's stories about Xiamen's watchmaking district, where tradition and innovation had danced their own complex duet.

"I'll be with you in exactly one minute and forty-three seconds," called a voice from behind a beaded curtain that separated the front of the shop from what sounded like a workshop. The precision of the statement made her smile—it was the kind of thing she would have said, before her phone's death had begun teaching her about the flexibility of time.

She wandered to the wall of clocks, each one marking time slightly differently. One tracked the moon's phases, another showed the tides, and a third displayed what looked like astronomical movements in delicate golden lines. Her attention caught on a pocket watch that bore an uncanny resemblance to the one in her coat—the same spiral patterns around the edge, though these moved clockwise while her grandfather's moved counter-.

"One minute and forty-three seconds," said the same voice, now directly behind her. "As promised."

She turned to find a man about her age, wearing a watchmaker's loupe pushed up on his forehead like an extra eye. His hands bore the same kind of careful calluses as her grandfather's—marks of work that required both strength and delicacy—but there was something else familiar about him that she couldn't quite place.

"Aarav Malhotra," he said, extending a hand that smelled faintly of vanilla and... cassia bark? "Though most people just call me the guy who fixes things that tell time."

The recognition clicked: his handwriting on the coffee receipt, the quote about time being an ocean. "You're James," she said, then immediately felt the color rise in her cheeks. "I mean, you were James. At the farmers' market."

His smile had the same asymmetrical quality it had worn behind the coffee stand, though now it was accompanied by a raised eyebrow. "And you're the one who was ready for honest coffee," he said. "Though I suspect that's not why you're here today."

Olivia reached for her phone, but her hand brushed the pocket watch instead. She felt its warmth against her fingers, as if it had been keeping secrets rather than time. "My phone," she said, drawing out the dead device instead. "It stopped working yesterday morning. Just after—" She paused, realizing she was about to measure time by someone else's engagement announcement again.

"Just after you decided to change your coffee?" Aarav suggested, his eyes crinkling at the corners in a way that suggested he understood more than he was saying. "Interesting timing."

The word caught her like a gear tooth: *timing*. Not time, with its rigid measurements, but timing—that mysterious space between intention and action that her grandfather's memoir had hinted at. The pocket watch seemed to grow warmer in her pocket, as if responding to the thought.

"How long will it take to fix? By end-of-day today? Tomorrow, perhaps? " she asked, falling back on the familiar comfort of quantifiable time.

Aarav held her phone up to the light, turning it with the same care she'd seen her grandfather use with particularly delicate mechanisms. "That depends," he said, "on whether you want it fixed quickly or fixed right." He glanced at the pocket watch peeking from her coat. "Some things are worth taking time with, wouldn't you say?"

The wall of clocks ticked around them, each one marking the moment slightly differently, as if suggesting there might be more than one way to measure the distance from now and to what came next.

Aarav began filling out a repair ticket, his pen moving across the paper in the same flowing strokes that had transformed her coffee receipt into a message about oceanic time. Now, in the clear light of his shop, she could see how each character seemed to pull the next along, like waves drawing themselves across sand.

"The warranty information goes here," he said, tapping a blank space on the form, "though I suspect you're like me when it comes to keeping receipts."

Olivia reached into her bag, past the dead phone and her grandfather's memoir, to retrieve the coffee receipt she'd saved—not filed away in her usual meticulous system, but carried like a talisman. She unfolded it carefully, the paper soft at its creases from being opened and closed throughout yesterday's strange, clockless afternoon.

His handwriting rippled across both papers now, creating a kind of cartography of coincidence. The same subtle flourish marked the beginning of each capital letter, like the way her grandfather would always pause before starting a new repair, gathering intention before action.

"Most people don't notice handwriting anymore," Aarav said, his eyes moving between the receipt and her face. "They're too busy with digital fonts and predictive text. But every hand tells a story—pressure points, hesitations, the gaps between letters. Like mechanical watches, each one has its own signature rhythm."

She thought of the unknown handwriting in her grandfather's notes, its confident curves somehow familiar now as they sat beside Aarav's script. "Your grandmother," she said, the words emerging before she could measure them. "Was she a watchmaker too?"

Something shifted in his expression—subtle as the change in a watch's escapement, there and gone in a fraction of a second. "She was. In Mumbai first, then here. Though most people didn't expect to find a woman fixing watches in either place." He picked up the coffee receipt, studying his own words as if seeing them differently. "She used to say that writing and watchmaking were the same art—both about capturing time between movements."

The wall of clocks seemed to tick more thinly, as if lending pause to the memory. Olivia found herself pulling out her grandfather's pocket watch, its case warm against her palm. "My grandfather used to say something similar about the space between decisions."

Aarav's hands stilled on the repair form, his pen hovering over the signature line like a compass needle searching for true north. The morning fog pressed against the shop's windows, turning the world outside into a soft-focused dream of itself, while inside, time seemed to pool around them like still water.

"May I?" he asked, gesturing to the pocket watch with a watchmaker's restrained eagerness. She hesitated only a moment before placing it in his outstretched hand, noting how his fingers curled around it with practiced care, like someone handling a bird's egg or a precious memory.

His sharp intake of breath was barely audible, but in the quiet shop, it rang like a bell.

"This isn't just any pocket watch," Aarav said, his voice carrying the same careful modulation he'd used when explaining the Vietnamese coffee's heritage. He turned the watch over in his hands, fingers tracing the spiral patterns as if reading braille. "The case design alone—I've only seen work like this once before."

"In your grandmother's collection?" Olivia asked, watching how the morning light caught the edges of the pattern, making them seem to move like waves under his touch.

His eyes lifted to meet hers, dark and suddenly intent. "Your phone's data recovery will take at least a week. Possibly two." The shift in topic felt deliberate, like the precise adjustment of a balance wheel. "That kind of wait seems to be unbearable for some, well, many."

"I'm learning to appreciate different measures of time," she said, thinking of her morning navigating the city without digital assistance, how each street had seemed to reveal itself only when she was ready to find it.

"Then perhaps," he said, setting the pocket watch down between them on the counter, "we might arrange an exchange of sorts. Your grandfather's watch needs restoration—not repair, there's a difference—and you have his tools." He gestured to the leather case visible in her bag. "I could teach you how to use them properly."

The offer hung in the air like the wait from a tick to the tock. Through the window, Olivia could see the fog beginning to lift, revealing glimpses of the city's tangled geometries. Time moved differently here in Aarav's shop, she realized, more like the ocean in his coffee receipt quote—deep and full of hidden currents.

"Most of my students," he continued, when she didn't immediately respond, "come looking for quick fixes. They want to know how to change a battery or set a digital alarm. But traditional watchmaking..." He picked up a loupe from the counter, holding it so the light created a perfect circle on the wooden surface. "It's about learning to see time differently. To understand it as a conversation between pieces that each move to their own rhythm, yet somehow create harmony together."

The wall of clocks ticked around them in their subtle syncopation, as if emphasizing his point. Olivia thought of her grandfather's memoir, of the empty pages waiting for continuation, of the mysterious second handwriting in the margins that seemed to dance with his across decades.

"When would we start?" she asked, surprised by the eagerness in her own voice.

Aarav smiled, the asymmetrical quirk of his lips now accompanied by a warmth in his eyes that reminded her of afternoon light through amber. "Time is the one thing I have in abundance," he said, reaching beneath the counter to retrieve a worn leather apron that could have been the twin of her grandfather's. "Though I should warn you—my grandmother taught me that every lesson begins with tea. She believed certain blends helped tune the hands to different types of movements."

He held out the apron, and Olivia noticed that its leather bore the same rich patina as the strap of her grandfather's watch case. "Your first lesson," he said, "will be learning to feel time rather than measure it. Sometimes the break amongst seconds is where the real work happens."

The morning light had shifted again, casting their shadows at an angle that seemed to point toward the beaded curtain and the workshop beyond. Somewhere in the city, a cable car's bell rang out, its tone merging with the shop's chorus of ticking clocks. Olivia reached for the apron, and as her fingers brushed against Aarav's, she felt something shift in the rhythm of her own internal timing—like the subtle click of gears finally finding their proper alignment.

The osmanthus tea Aarav brewed filled his workshop with a fragrance that pulled at Olivia's memories like silk unraveling—autumn afternoons in her grandfather's shop, the sweet scent mixing with clock oil and brass polish as he taught her to identify different movements by sound alone. Now, seated at Aarav's workbench with her grandfather's loupe in hand, she found herself inhabiting a similar moment, though the light fell differently here, catching on unfamiliar tools and casting new shadows.

"The first thing to understand," Aarav said, placing a simple pocket watch between them, "is that every timepiece has two hearts—the balance wheel that measures the moments, and the perceptible, not-quite-stop between oscillations that gives those moments meaning."

His hands moved as he spoke, graceful and precise as a conductor's, demonstrating how to hold the loupe at exactly the right angle to see both hearts at once. Olivia leaned forward, trying to match the angle of his wrist, when the shop's bell chimed—not in B-flat this time, but with a discordant jangle that suggested someone had pushed the door open too forcefully.

"陈诺昕 (Chén Nuò Xīn)! I've been calling you all morning!"

Her mother's voice carried her full name, reserved only for exceptional moment of ire, through the beaded curtain with the inevitable force of a mainspring unwinding. Olivia's hand jerked, sending the loupe skittering across the workbench like a startled water strider across a pond.

"Māma?" She turned to find Helen Chén sweeping into the

workshop, elegant as always in her surgeon's precision and her carefully curated casual weekend wear. Behind her followed a young man in a slate gray suit that probably cost more than all the watches on Aarav's front wall combined.

"Your phone's been going straight to voicemail," Helen continued, her eyes taking in the workshop, the leather apron, Aarav's presence, and apparently finding all three wanting. "Dr. Shī's son David has been trying to reach you about coffee." She gestured to the suit behind her as if presenting evidence in a medical conference.

Time seemed to stutter, like a watch with a damaged escapement. Olivia felt the memory of fifty-three notifications press against her consciousness—how many of those had been from her mother, orchestrating this very moment?

"Actually," Aarav's voice cut through the tension with the same quiet authority he'd used to explain watch mechanisms, "we're in the middle of something rather delicate." He lifted the pocket watch from the workbench, holding it so the light caught its open movement. "Timing is crucial at this stage."

Helen's expression shifted microscopically—the kind of shift Olivia had learned to read as a child, when her mother's expectations and reality failed to synchronize. But before she could speak, David Shī stepped forward, his interest apparently genuine.

"Is that a Lange & Söhne movement? The finish on the plates looks like their work from the 1890s." He leaned closer, and Olivia noticed Aarav's hands tighten slightly around the watch, though his smile remained professionally pleasant.

"You have a good eye," he said, "but this is actually something much rarer. A hybrid design that combines European precision with Chinese artistry. It was quite common in certain workshops in Xiamen during the late Qing dynasty, though few examples survive."

The words seemed to ripple through the workshop's warm air, carrying echoes of her grandfather's voice from the memoir: *Some mechanisms aren't meant to be fixed alone.* Olivia found herself reaching for her grandfather's pocket watch, its weight in her pocket suddenly significant.

"Olivia helps me with these special pieces," Aarav continued, his voice carrying the same careful measure as his hands. "She has a natural talent for understanding complex movements."

The compliment settled in the rests between heartbeats, genuine as gravitational force. Helen's eyes narrowed slightly, reading the room with the same precision she used in surgery. David shifted his weight, his expensive suit rustling like autumn leaves.

"Perhaps we could discuss the movement over dinner?" he suggested, directing the question to Olivia but glancing at her mother for approval.

The workshop's many timepieces ticked onward, their synchronized rhythms suddenly emphasizing the asynchronous nature of this moment—her mother's careful plans colliding with the unexpected gravity of Aarav's workspace, where time moved like osmanthus-scented tea spreading through water, finding its own path between the leaves.

Olivia looked down at her hands, still wearing her grandfather's worn leather apron, and felt the weight of choice settling into her bones like heritage finding its proper home. "I'm afraid," she said, surprised by the steadiness in her voice, "my schedule is rather full at the moment. I'm learning to repair time."

After her mother's departure—a process that involved three separate attempts at rescheduling coffee with David and one pointed comment about the dust on Aarav's window displays—the workshop settled back into its rhythm of synchronized ticking. But something had shifted in the quality of the silence of lapsed sounds, like the subtle change in air pressure before rain.

"Your grandfather," Aarav said, polishing the demonstration watch with careful strokes, "was Chén Wĕi Míng?"

The question carried weight beyond its syllables. Olivia looked up from where she'd been readjusting her loupe, catching an expression in his eyes that reminded her of the way light refracts through crystal—sharp angles softened by transmission.

"Yes," she said, then, remembering the unknown handwriting in the memoir's margins: "Did you know him?"

"Not directly." Aarav's hands stilled on the watch case. "But my grandmother spoke of him often. They were...contemporaries." He reached beneath his workbench, producing a leather-bound album that bore the same patina of age as her grandfather's tool case. "Perhaps you should see this."

The album opened to a newspaper clipping from 1978, its edges foxed but the text still clear: "RIVAL WATCHMAKERS SPLIT PRIZE AT PACIFIC HOROLOGICAL EXHIBITION." Below the headline, two figures stood before a display of timepieces—a younger version of her grandfather, his posture already carrying the precise dignity she remembered, and beside him, a woman whose stance mirrored his own, though her smile held a challenge that the camera had caught like lightning in a bottle.

"My grandmother, Neha Malhotra," Aarav said softly. "They were the only Asian watchmakers invited to compete. The judges couldn't decide between their pieces, so they divided the grand prize—something unprecedented at the time."

Olivia studied the photograph, noting how her grandfather and Neha stood exactly the same distance apart as the watches they'd created, as if they too were mechanisms calibrated to maintain perfect tension. "What were they competing with?"

"That's the interesting part." Aarav turned to another page, where a detailed sketch showed two pocket watches, their cases bearing spiral patterns that seemed to move even on paper. "They each designed a watch that challenged traditional chronometry. My grandmother's piece tracked lunar cycles in relation to ocean tides. Your grandfather's mapped stellar movements against human heartbeats." He paused, his finger hovering over the drawings. "The judges said the watches seemed to be in conversation with each other, like two halves of a single idea."

The memory of her grandfather's unfinished memoir stirred in Olivia's mind—the designed emptiness between paragraphs, the mysterious second handwriting that now seemed achingly familiar. She reached for her coat pocket, withdrawing his pocket watch with hands that suddenly felt like they belonged to someone else.

"Like this?" she asked, placing it beside the sketch.

Aarav's breath caught audibly. With the deliberate movements of someone handling nitroglycerin, he reached beneath his collar and withdrew a chain. At its end hung a pocket watch that could have been the twin of her grandfather's—or perhaps, she thought as he laid it beside hers, its reflection in some unparalleled mirror.

"My grandmother's final piece," he said. "She never sold it, never showed it to anyone outside the family. She said it was half of a promise that time hadn't been ready for."

The watches lay between them on the workbench like paired compasses pointing to a truth that had been ticking away beneath the surface of their lives. In the afternoon light, their spiral patterns seemed to reach for each other across the weathered wood, creating a new design in the distance between—a pattern that spoke of decisions made and unmade, of time flowing not like a river but like an ocean, with depths and currents that could carry secrets across generations.

"There's more," Olivia said, thinking of the memoir waiting in her bag, of the pages filled with two different hands sharing a single margin. "I think they were more than rivals."

The wall of clocks ticked onward, each one marking time slightly differently, as if suggesting that some stories needed multiple rhythms to be properly told.

The evening light was turning golden when Helen returned, this time without David Shī but carrying something heavier than matchmaking intentions. Olivia recognized the shift in her mother's energy before she spoke—it was the same careful modulation she used before delivering difficult news to patients' families.

"I thought I'd find you still here," Helen said, her eyes taking in the scattered tools and open watches with the same clinical assessment she gave X-rays. But there was something softer in her expression too, like sunlight catching on an old photograph's edges. "We need to talk about Wàigōng's house."

The words fell into the workshop's peaceful rhythm like pebbles into still water. Aarav, who had been teaching Olivia the delicate art of cleaning pivot points, quietly excused himself through the beaded curtain, though not before catching her eye with a glance that somehow conveyed both support and space.

"The market's strong right now," Helen continued, settling onto the worn wooden stool that had, until moments ago, been Ol-

THE SPACE AMID SECONDS

ivia's learning perch. "The realtor thinks we could close by the end of the month."

"Close?" The word felt wrong in Olivia's mouth, like tea brewed for too long turned bitter. "You're selling the house?"

Her mother's hands—surgeon's hands, precise and certain—smoothed invisible wrinkles from her silk blouse. "It's been empty since the funeral, měi. We've been paying property taxes on memories."

But they weren't just memories, Olivia wanted to say. They were moments caught in chromatics: the workshop where she'd learned to hear the difference between a Swiss lever escapement and a Chinese duplex, the garden where her grandfather had taught her to measure time by the angle of shadows falling across his sundial, the kitchen where he'd brewed orange-peel coffee on Sunday mornings while telling stories about the watch shop his father had run in Xiamen.

"What about his tools?" she asked instead, gesturing to the workbench where her grandfather's leather case lay open like a book mid-sentence. "His collection?"

"You have what you need here," Helen said, her gaze drifting to the paired pocket watches still lying on the bench. Something flickered across her face—recognition, perhaps, or a memory she hadn't expected to encounter. "The rest we can sell with the house. There's a collector interested in the whole estate."

Olivia's hand found her grandfather's watch, its weight anchoring her as the world seemed to shift beneath her feet. Through the workshop window, she could see the fog rolling in again, turning the street into a parallel universe where time moved both more swift and slow, disinterested. She thought of the memoir in her bag, of the mysterious conversation between her grandfather and Aarav's grandmother playing out in shared margins and private vacuum.

"There's more in that house than just tools," she said, thinking of all the boxes she hadn't yet opened, all the stories still waiting to be found. "There's history."

"History," Helen said, with the gentle firmness she used when explaining why a treatment couldn't wait, "doesn't pay property taxes, měi." But then she paused, her hand hovering over one of the pocket watches as if drawn by some invisible force. "Though I remember this. Your grandfather was working on it the day I told him I'd been accepted to medical school. He said some workings take generations to complete."

The workshop's many timepieces ticked onward, their synchronized rhythms now seeming like a countdown. Olivia looked at the paired watches, at their spiral patterns reaching across what can be perceived by but few, at the story they were trying to tell through their silent movements.

"Give me a month," she heard herself say. "Before you list it. There's something I need to find."

Helen's eyes met hers, and for a moment Olivia saw past the surgeon's precision to the daughter who had once watched her own father work miracles with time. "Two weeks," she said finally. "That's how long it takes to prepare the listing anyway." She stood, straightening her blouse with habitual precision. "But Olivia? Letting go is how we move forward."

As her mother's footsteps faded, Olivia remained at the workbench, watching the fog swallow the last of the day's light. Behind her, Aarav's quiet return was marked only by the gentle touch of a tea cup being placed at her elbow—osmanthus again, but this time with an undertone of something deeper, like time itself had been steeped in the leaves.

The osmanthus tea had grown cold, untouched, when Aarav noticed something catching the last fragments of daylight in Olivia's grandfather's tool case. Between layers of worn leather and velvet dividers, a glint of metal winked like a star seen through moving clouds.

"There's something else here," he said softly, his hands already moving with the deliberate grace of someone accustomed to handling fragments of time. From beneath a false bottom—so cleverly constructed that only a watchmaker would recognize the seam—he withdrew an object wrapped in silk the color of midnight in Xiamen.

Olivia set down her cooling tea, drawn by the reverence in his movements. The fog had fully claimed the street outside, transforming the workshop windows into mirrors that reflected their forms bent over the workbench like figures in an old daguerreotype.

The silk fell away in waves, revealing a timepiece unlike either of their grandparents' watches. Where the paired pocket watches bore spiral patterns that reached toward each other, this one's case was etched with interlocking circles that seemed to fold into themselves, creating a seemingly infinite regression of curves that drew the eye ever inward.

"I've never seen anything like this," Aarav breathed, turning the piece carefully in the fading light. "The case design—it's neither Chinese nor Indian, but somehow both. And neither." His fingers traced the patterns with the sensitivity of a safe-cracker reading tumblers. "It's as if someone took our grandparents' styles and..."

"Merged them," Olivia finished, reaching for her grandfather's memoir. She flipped to the technical drawings she'd found earlier, spreading them beside the mysterious watch. The similarities were unmistakable—the same impossible geometry, the same suggestion of motion caught in metal—but the drawings showed only components, never the complete piece.

"Look at this," Aarav said, his loupe catching the last ray of natural light. "The maker's mark—it's two sets of initials intertwined: WMC and NM."

"Chén Wěi Míng and Neha Malhotra," Olivia whispered, the names settling into place like perfectly matched gears. "They made this together."

Aarav's hands stilled on the case. "My grandmother once told me that true innovation in watchmaking is found in-between traditions. She said some mechanisms can only be created when different rhythms learn to move as one." He looked up, meeting Olivia's eyes with an intensity that seemed to bend time around them. "I always thought she was speaking metaphorically."

With movements that felt both careful and inevitable, they opened the mysterious watch's case together, their fingers brushing like hour and minute hands passing at midnight. The mechanism inside caught the workshop's warm light and held it, seeming to pulse with a life of its own. Instead of traditional hands, it bore three rings of different metals—brass, silver, and something darker that might have been oxidized steel—each rotating independently yet influencing the others' movements through some hidden mathematics of attraction.

"It's a love letter," Olivia realized, watching the rings dance their precise orbit. "Not just between two watchmakers, but between two traditions. East and West, old and new, Apollonian and Dionysian." She thought of her grandfather's memoir, of the absence of marks left between paragraphs, of margins filled with two different hands sharing a single conversation across time.

"Look," Aarav said suddenly, pointing to where the rings aligned momentarily. In that brief convergence, characters became visible in the spaces between—Hanzi and, what Aarav identified as, Marathi Balbodh Devanagari merging to form words that seemed to shift even as they read them: *Some mechanisms are meant to be discovered together.*

The workshop's many timepieces ticked onward in their evening rhythm, but this new watch moved to its own measure, tracking not seconds but the something between them, where all possibility lived. Outside, fog pressed against the windows, trying to peer in on what they'd found.

Olivia looked at her two weeks' deadline, at the mystery unfolding between their inherited tools and traditions, at Aarav's hands still steady beside hers on the workbench. "We need to go to my grandfather's house," she said. "Tonight. Before the fog gets any thicker."

Aarav was already reaching for his coat, his movements sure. "Time," he said, echoing both their grandparents' hidden message, "has its own way of bringing mechanisms together."

CHAPTER 3

WINDING DOWN

The Financial District measured lunch breaks in market fluctuations and calendar alerts, but in Aarav's workshop, time flowed to the rhythm of tiny screwdrivers and the soft click of gears finding their homes. Olivia had begun arriving at precisely 12:27 each day, giving herself three minutes to change into her grandfather's apron before their lesson began at 12:30. The routine had established itself as naturally as the oscillation of a balance wheel, each day adding another layer to their shared understanding of mechanisms both mechanical and personal.

"The trick with a chronograph," Aarav explained on a fog-wrapped Tuesday, his hands steady as he demonstrated the delicate art of calibrating a stop-second function, "is understanding that it measures the intervals between events, not the events themselves." The watch beneath his loupe was a 1950s Seiko, its case bearing the gentle patina of decades spent marking moments that mattered to someone now unknown.

Olivia leaned closer, breathing in the familiar blend of clock oil and osmanthus tea that had become the scent of these afternoon interludes. Their investigation of her grandfather's house had yielded more questions than answers—boxes of letters in coded references, drawers with false bottoms, and mechanical components that seemed to belong to timepieces that shouldn't exist. But here, in the quiet sanctuary of the workshop, those mysteries settled into the background like the steady tick of the wall clocks, waiting for their moment to align.

"Like the space between decisions," she murmured, thinking of her grandfather's memoir and its half-finished stories. Her fingers found their position on the tiny lever Aarav had indicated, muscle memory already developing from days of practice.

"Exactly." His smile carried the same asymmetrical quality it had worn behind the coffee stand, though now it held layers of shared understanding. "Your grandfather and my grandmother understood that. It's why their watches didn't just measure time—they measured intention."

The merged timepiece they'd discovered lay between them on the workbench, its mysterious rings continuing their endless dance even when unwound. They'd agreed to proceed slowly with its examination, treating it like an archaeological find that required patience and context to fully understand.

A strand of hair fell across Olivia's vision as she adjusted the chronograph's clutch lever. Without thinking, Aarav reached over to tuck it behind her ear, his fingers carrying the same precise care he used with the most delicate watch parts. The moment stretched like a spring being wound, full of potential energy.

The workshop's many timepieces ticked onward, each marking the second slightly differently, creating a subtle syncopation that seemed to echo the beating of her heart. Through the window, she could see office workers hurrying past with takeout containers and phones pressed to their ears, living in a different kind of time alto-gether.

"Tell me about the first watch you remember," Aarav said soft-ly, his hands returning to the demonstration piece but his attention still holding her like a jewel bearing.

She thought of market mornings in her grandfather's work-shop, of light falling through dusty windows onto brass and steel. "It was a music box watch," she said, the memory unwinding like a carefully maintained spring. "A wedding gift my grandfather was repairing. When it chimed the hour, it played 'Jasmine Flower,' but something in the mechanism had begun to drift, making the notes hang too long between beats."

"Creating new music in the drops," Aarav observed, his voice carrying the same warm resonance as well-maintained clockwork.

"Yes." Olivia smiled, remembering. "My grandfather said sometimes mistakes create their own kind of perfection. He adjusted the timing just enough to keep the melody recognizable while pre-serving its unique rhythm. The owner cried when she heard it—said it was more beautiful than when it was new."

Their hands moved in parallel now over the Seiko's move-ment, making minor adjustments that would add up to perfect tim-ing. Outside, the fog began to lift, sending shapes of light dancing across their workbench like the shadows of time itself passing by.

It wasn't until Wednesday that the pattern revealed itself, emerging like a watchmaker's mark under proper magnification. Ol-ivia had just finished reassembling her first pocket watch movement when her stomach growled, the sound almost lost beneath the work-shop's symphony of ticking. Aarav glanced at the wall clock—1:47 PM, well past their usual lesson time.

"We lost track," he said, that asymmetrical smile playing at the corners of his mouth. "Though perhaps 'lost' isn't the right word for time well spent."

Olivia reached for her coat, her hands still carrying the muscle memory of fitting tiny screws into corkingly precise holes, when she noticed the date on Aarav's desk calendar. Wednesday. Duck noodle soup day at Lucky Fortune, where she and Rebecca had met every Wednesday at 1:15 for the past three years, splitting an order of xiaolongbao and trading stories about their respective offices' politics.

The realization struck her like a mainspring unwinding too quickly—she hadn't thought about those lunches once since her phone died, hadn't noticed their absence in the same way she hadn't noticed being bound by their rhythm. Even after Rebecca had stopped speaking to her six months ago, she had continued going to Lucky Fortune every Wednesday, ordering for two out of habit, watching the second soup grow cold while pretending to check emails.

"What is it?" Aarav asked, noticing her stillness. He had begun preparing a fresh pot of tea—chrysanthemum this time, his grandmother's preferred blend for afternoons when time needed gentle redirection.

"I just realized I've been haunting my own life," Olivia said, the words feeling like confession. "Following patterns I didn't even know I was making."

Through the workshop window, she could see Lucky Fortune's red awning two blocks down, the lunchtime crowd already thinning. Rebecca would be there now, probably sharing soup dumplings with Marcus, their new rhythm already established while Olivia had been keeping time with ghosts.

Aarav set the teapot down, its ceramic surface catching the afternoon light like a watch crystal. "My grandmother used to say that habits are like watch hands—they keep moving in their set pattern until something stops them completely." He paused, studying her face with the same careful attention he gave to complex mechanisms. "Maybe, a dead phone can be that something."

The workshop's many timepieces ticked onward, each marking the moment slightly differently, as if suggesting there were infinite ways to measure the span between who she had been and who she was becoming. The muscle memory in her fingers had already begun to change, replacing the automatic reach for her phone with the deliberate grip of watchmaking tools.

"There's a dim sum place around the corner," Aarav said, his voice carrying the same gentle exactness he used when teaching her to handle delicate components. "The owner collects mechanical calculators. She lets me repair them in exchange for soup dumplings that she swears are better than Lucky Fortune's."

The invitation hung in the air like a pendulum paused at the crest of its swing. Olivia thought of all the Wednesday lunches she'd spent maintaining appearances, calculating conversations, keeping time with expectations instead of intentions. She looked down at her hands, still wearing the careful calluses of her morning's work, and made a decision as deliberate as selecting the right tool for a repair.

"I'd like to test that claim," she said, watching as Aarav's smile shifted from asymmetrical to full, like a watch face finally catching the perfect beam of light.

As they stepped out into the afternoon, the fog had lifted enough to reveal the city's varied architectures—Victorian cornices alongside modern glass, Chinese tiles meeting Italian stonework, each keeping its own integrity while somehow moving together. Rather than turn toward Lucky Fortune's familiar awning, Olivia found herself following Aarav down an alley she'd passed a hundred times but never explored, where steam rose from basement kitchens in spiral patterns that reminded her of their grandparents' watches.

The muscle memory of her old routine tugged once, gently, then released—like a mainspring finally allowed to find its natural rest.

Mrs. Guō's dim sum shop occupied a narrow existence between past and present, its walls lined with mechanical calculators in various states of repair. As Olivia watched the lunch crowd ebb and flow through the steamy windows, she noticed something that her phone-occupied days had hidden—the meticulous choreography of modern life, as methodical as any watch movement.

"Look," she said to Aarav, gesturing with her chopsticks toward a group of office workers across the street. "They're all checking their phones at exactly forty-five-second intervals, like a synchronized escapement."

Aarav followed her gaze, his watchmaker's eye catching the pattern instantly. "The corporate world's version of a repeater mechanism," he observed. "Though less elegant than the ones we repair."

She saw it everywhere now—the mechanized preciseness with which people moved through their lunch hours, each action timed to invisible but insistent rhythms. A woman in a charcoal suit paused every twelve steps to check her screen, the movement as automatic as breathing. Two men in identical blue shirts walked past, their arms swinging in perfect opposition like the pendulums of synchronized clocks.

"I used to move like that," she realized, remembering how her days had been measured in notification pings and calendar alerts. "We all did, at the investment firm. Fifteen minutes for coffee, thirty for lunch, five-minute breaks between meetings—all of it scheduled down to the second."

Through the window, she watched a young couple at a nearby table, both staring at their phones while their tea grew cold between them. They reminded her of the paired pocket watches they'd found, but with their movements frozen, unable to reach across the separation between.

"There's a term in watchmaking," Aarav said, deftly catching a xiaolongbao before it could break, "for when a mechanism runs perfectly but without purpose. We call it 'empty precision.'" He gestured toward the calculators on the wall, their gears visible through glass cases. "These machines could compute complex equations, but without human intention, they're just intricate arrangements of metal."

Mrs. Guō appeared at their table with a pot of oolong that smelled of mountain winds and hope. She moved with a different rhythm altogether—each gesture flowing into the next like a well-maintained calendar watch tracking the phases of the moon.

"Your grandmother," Mrs. Guō said to Aarav in Mandarin that carried the lilt of Shanghai – quickly and keenly translated by Olivia, "used to say that machines should serve life, not the other way around." She set down the teapot with a precision that spoke of decades of practice. "But nowadays, everyone wants to become a machine."

Olivia thought of her grandfather's mysterious timepiece, with its rings that moved independently yet influenced each other. She

41

watched Mrs. Guō navigate between tables, her movements adapting to each guest's rhythm while maintaining her own—like a complex mechanism that could harmonize different timekeeps without losing its essential nature.

"I think," she said, lifting her tea cup more deliberately than she once would have, "that's why our grandparents created watches that measured more than minutes. They wanted to remind people that time isn't just something that passes—it's something we create together."

Through the window, the fog had begun its afternoon advance from the bay, softening the edges of the mechanical parade outside. A woman hurried past, her phone-checking pattern interrupted by a child's laughter. She looked up, blinked as if awakening, and for a moment her movements became her own again—organic, unpredictable, alive.

"The most complex watch configuration," Aarav said, his eyes meeting Olivia's with an intensity that made time seem to pool around them, "is worthless if it forgets its purpose is to serve the human heart."

The calculators on the wall clicked their agreement, their gears turning like thoughts finding new pathways. Outside, the city's rhythms continued their programmed dance, but now Olivia could see little lapses—where lived was waiting like an unwound spring to be released.

Walking back to the workshop through the gathering fog, Olivia and Aarav passed a group of tourists photographing the same storefront simultaneously, their phones raised in identical gestures like an automaton ballet. The sight prompted Aarav to pause beside a century-old street clock—one of the few remaining in the city that still kept perfect time.

"I have a theory," he said, watching the minute hand move with the deliberate grace of well-maintained brass, "about why phones have changed more than just how we communicate." His voice carried the same measured quality he used when explaining particularly complex mechanisms. "They've fundamentally altered our relationship with time itself."

Olivia thought of her dead phone, now living in Aarav's workshop while its data underwent careful recovery. "Because they make everything instant?"

"Partly." He traced the clock's weathered numerals with his eyes, a watchmaker's habit of reading time through observation. "But it's more about how they've eliminated the separation of moments. Not really a physical separation, but the slots that are not actually empty nor really filled with time, but with the timing of others where discord can merge into harmony. In the age of mechanical watches, time moved like poetry—each tick creating a natural pause, a breath, a break for reflection. Digital time flows like prose, uniform and uninterrupted."

A cable car rumbled past, its bell marking their conversation with uneven music. Through the fog, its passengers were visible only as silhouettes, each outlined by the preoccupied blue glow of phone screens.

"When my grandmother first came to America," Aarav continued, "she was fascinated by how different cultures measured time. In Mumbai, she said, time moved like a river with many tributaries—religious time, family time, market time, all flowing together but maintaining their distinct rhythms. Here, she found everyone trying to synchronize to a single digital beat."

They resumed walking, their pace unconsciously adjusting to match the street clock's second hand. "My grandfather used to say something similar about Xiamen," Olivia said, remembering passages from his memoir. "He talked about how each neighborhood had its own time, marked by temple bells and tide changes rather than minutes and hours."

"Exactly." Aarav's hand brushed hers as they navigated around a cluster of people waiting for the light to change, all staring at their phones like sundial readers awaiting shadow. "Phones promise to make us more connected, more efficient, but they've actually compressed time into a single dimension. Everything becomes urgent and immediate, leaving no room for the natural pauses that used to shape our days."

Olivia added, "For me, it's the lack of flexibility. Almost as if time will forget you or you might even forget it, if you stop tracking it."

"It's a form of persistent anxiety." replied Aarav.

Shaking her head in agreement, Olivia continued, "Definitely. Though I can't quite say that caring about time or using phones in this way is wrong. You?"

"Definitely not. But," Aarav hesitated, "left uncalibrated – things, or rather, people..." he paused.

"...can become unwound." Olivia completed his thought to nodding from Aarav. "However, people are not watches." Both chuckled as she uttered the sentence. "So who calibrates people?" she opened the question not really expecting an answer.

"Fortunately, or maybe unfortunately, that comes down to each and every one of us, I suppose."

They reached the workshop door, its weathered brass handle

warm despite the fog's chill. Inside, the wall of clocks continued their synchronized yet distinct rhythms, each marking time in its own voice.

"Watch this," Aarav said, moving to his workbench. He took out their grandparents' mysterious timepiece, its triple rings still dancing their endless orbital pattern. "See how each ring moves at its own pace, yet they're all influenced by each other? That's how time used to feel—personal and universal at once, like jazz musicians playing together but maintaining their individual expressions."

Olivia leaned closer, watching the rings catch the afternoon light. "But phones make everyone play the same note at the same time."

"And that's what our grandparents were pushing against with their designs." He opened a cabinet, revealing a collection of timing devices spanning centuries—hourglasses, sundials, water clocks, each one measuring time through different natural rhythms. "They understood that true innovation in horology wasn't about perfect synchronization, but about finding harmony between different ways of experiencing time."

The workshop's many timepieces ticked in their subtle syncopation, as if demonstrating his point. Outside, the fog had thickened enough to muffle the city's digital pulse, creating a pocket of space where time could move at its own pace.

"Maybe that's why my phone died," Olivia said, the thought emerging like being woken from a light slumber at the tender sound of a far-off chiming. "Not just to lead me here, but to remind me there are other ways to move through time."

Aarav's smile caught the light like a well-polished crown wheel. "Some mechanisms," he said, echoing their grandparents' hidden message, "need to break before they can be transformed."

The discovery came as Olivia was cleaning her grandfather's loupe collection, each lens revealing a different facet of the afternoon light. The first had seemed innocent enough—a folded piece of rice paper tucked into the velvet lining of a brass magnifier's case. But as she unfolded it, she recognized her grandfather's distinctive blend of English and Hanzi characters, the ink still carrying a ghost of osmanthus scent:

Time moves differently in Xiamen's rain. Each drop creates its own moment, separate yet connected, like the beads of a merchant's abacus. It was during such a rain that I first saw her—the woman who would teach me that some mechanisms require two hearts to keep proper time.

"Aarav," she called softly, her voice carrying the same careful modulation she used when handling delicate gear trains. He looked up from the chronograph he was adjusting, catching something in her tone that made him set down his tools with deliberate precision.

The next fragment came forth from inside a hollow screwdriver handle, the paper so fine it was almost translucent: *She arrived with the monsoon winds, carrying a box of tools I had never seen—Indian implements adapted for Chinese movements. "Time is a language," she said, "and every culture speaks it differently." Her name was Neha, and she moved like someone who had learned to dance with time rather than measure it.*

Together, they began examining every tool in her grandfather's collection, finding pieces of the story hidden like secrets in a watchmaker's puzzle box. A chapter about their first shared repair nestled in the false bottom of a parts organizer. Notes about late-night discussions of horology and heritage curled inside a broken balance staff marker. Each discovery felt like turning another page in a book that had written itself in the breaks between ticks.

The Western watchmakers laughed when we proposed combining traditions, read a passage tucked behind the crystal of a defunct shock absorber gauge. *They said time could only be measured one way. But Neha understood what I had always suspected—that true innovation comes from the places where different rhythms meet.*

"My grandmother never talked about Xiamen," Aarav said, carefully extracting a sheet folded into improbably small squares from inside a hollow pivot burnisher. "But she kept a jar of osmanthus flowers on her workbench until the day she died."

The fragments began to form a pattern, like gears arranged before assembly. Each tool seemed to hold the piece of the story it had helped create—the development of their hybrid mechanisms described in the very implements used to build them. It was a romance told in technical specifications and philosophical asides, in the precise language of watchmaking and the flowing script of personal revelation.

We worked in secret, revealed a note hidden in the rim of a case opener, meeting in the hours before dawn when the city kept different time. Each morning, we would separate our tools and return to our respective traditions, but the mechanisms we created together kept counting the moments until we could meet again.

The afternoon light shifted through the workshop windows as they uncovered more pieces, each one adding depth to the story of their grandparents' collaboration. Some passages were in Neha's hand, her Balbodh Devanagari intertwining with Wěi Míng's Hanzi ones like the rings in their mysterious timepiece.

Time isn't just a measurement, read one joint entry, the two scripts intertwining like lovers' hands, *it's a conversation between past and future, tradition and innovation, heart and mechanism. Some conversations take genera-*

tions to complete.

"Look at this," Aarav said, holding up a timing machine calibrator that had clearly been modified by both their grandparents. Inside its altered case, they found a series of technical drawings showing the evolution of their shared designs, each sketch dated and annotated in both hands.

The workshop's many timepieces ticked onward as they pieced together the story, their steady rhythms providing accompaniment to a tale that had waited decades to be fully heard. Outside, fog gathered at the windows as though it were aiming to get a surreptitious glance of the unweaving inside.

"They weren't just creating watches," Olivia realized, studying a passage about the mathematics of love disguised as gear ratio calculations. "They were writing their story into the mechanisms themselves, knowing someday someone would know how to read it."

Aarav's hand reached for hers across the workbench, warm and steady as a well-maintained movement. "Maybe," he said softly, "special functions are meant to be discovered together."

At the close of Aarav's lips and precisely as Olivia was leaning in to adjust a particularly delicate lever escapement, Helen Chén's third "accidental" visit of the week occurred. The workshop door chimed its B-flat warning just as Aarav's hands were covering hers, prepared to guide her through the subtle pressure needed to align the pallet fork.

"I was just passing by," Helen announced, her clinical disposition somehow making even coincidence sound carefully calibrated. "On my way to that new dim sum place everyone's talking about." She paused, taking in their shared workspace with the same analytical eye she used in operating theaters. "The one that's actually three blocks in the opposite direction."

Olivia felt Aarav's hands withdraw from hers with watchmaker's care, though the warmth of his touch lingered like the aftereffect of summer sunlight on skin upon entering shade. The escapement beneath her loupe suddenly seemed to mirror her own internal orientation—poised between action and hesitation, waiting for the right moment to advance.

"Dr. Chén," Aarav said, his voice carrying the same measured courtesy he used with his most particular clients. "Would you like to see what your daughter has accomplished this week?"

It was a masterful redirection, Olivia thought—as elegant as the hybrid movements they'd been discovering in their grandparents' notes. Her mother's objective distance wavered slightly as Aarav began explaining Olivia's progress, his description of technical achievements somehow making them sound like poetry.

"She has her grandfather's hands," Helen said unexpectedly, watching Olivia resume work on the escapement. Something in her tone carried an echo of memory, like a bell's toll heard through fog. "The same way of holding time still while working with it."

The observation held in the workshop's warm air like motes in sunlight. Olivia looked up to find her mother studying the wall of clocks with an expression she hadn't seen since the funeral—something between longing and recognition.

"Wàigōng used to let me watch him work," Helen continued, more to herself than to them. "Before medical school, before everything became about efficiency and precision..." She trailed off, her hand unconsciously touching the watch she wore—a sleek digital piece that seemed suddenly out of place among the workshop's deft industrial chorus.

"Perhaps," Aarav suggested, with the careful timing of someone used to calibrating delicate mechanisms, "you'd like to see the piece we discovered in his tools? The one he worked on with my grandmother?"

Helen's intake of breath was subtle but distinct. "Neha Malhotra," she said, the name carrying weight she seemed surprised to find she could still bear. "I remember her. She would bring osmanthus tea when she visited his workshop. I always thought..." She stopped, professional composure reasserting itself like a regulator returning to rhythm.

"Thought what, Māma?" Olivia prompted, sensing something crucial hovering in the pause betwixt what was and yet remained unsaid.

"Nothing important," Helen said, but her eyes lingered on the mysterious timepiece with its three rotating rings. "Just a child's observation about the way time moved differently when they worked together." She straightened her silk blouse with habitual propriety. "I should go. I have a surgery scheduled at—" She checked her watch, then smiled faintly at the irony of the gesture. "Well, soon."

But instead of leaving, she moved closer to the workbench, studying the array of tools laid out with surgical fastidiousness. "David Shī's mother called again," she said, her tone attempting casualness but achieving something closer to a poorly regulated movement. "Apparently, he's quite impressed with your knowledge of vintage timepieces."

Olivia exchanged a glance with Aarav, catching in his eyes the same understanding that had passed between their grandparents across workbenches and cultural divides. "Some parts," she said carefully, "require exactly the right pairing to function properly."

Helen's lips curved in what might have been the beginning of genuine amusement. "Is that what we're calling it now?" She turned to leave, then paused at the door. "Your father's mother would have approved, you know. She always said the Chén family kept time differently from everyone else." With that, she slipped out into the fog-enveloped afternoon, leaving behind a silence filled with the workshop's steady ticking and the weight of things almost said.

"She'll be back tomorrow," Olivia said, returning to the escapement with renewed focus. "Probably with another 'urgent' message from someone's son."

"Time and mothers," Aarav observed, his hand finding its way back to hers with unambivalent inevitability, "both move in cycles we're still learning to measure."

The realization arrived like the solution to a complex theorem—not in a sudden flash, but in the gradual alignment of previously unseen patterns. Olivia was cleaning the workshop's display cases, each timepiece reflecting the late afternoon light differently, when she found herself examining a watch Marcus had once admired: a 1960s Longines with a precise but unremarkable movement.

"He said it was elegant," she remembered aloud, the words carrying less weight than they once had. "But he meant predictable."

Aarav looked up from where he was documenting another fragment of their grandparents' story, his pen paused mid-character. "Sometimes we don't recognize a mechanism has stopped until we try to wind it again."

The truth of it settled into her bones like the workshop's steady ticking. She thought of all the ways her relationship with Marcus had wound down long before their final conversation—how they had become like a watch whose mainspring had gradually lost its tension, each interaction carrying less energy than the last until even the appearance of movement became an illusion.

"I kept perfect time for him," she said, watching glimmers of escaping sun dance between display cases. "Adjusted my rhythm to match his, regulated my decisions to his preferences. Ethiopian coffee, exactly thirteen minutes for bedtime routine, premium phone insurance renewed every eleven months..." She traced the edge of the display glass, leaving a clean line through the gathering dust. "But a watch that only keeps someone else's time isn't really keeping time at all, is it?"

Through the window, she could see couples passing on the sidewalk, some moving in sync, others in their own distinct rhythms. One pair caught her eye—an elderly couple walking arm in arm, each step adjusted to accommodate the other's pace without either losing their essential tempo.

"My grandmother used to say that true partnerships are like duplex escapements," Aarav said, moving to stand beside her. "Each part maintains its own swing while supporting the other's movement. The moment one tries to force synchronization, the whole system fails."

Olivia thought of the fragments they'd discovered in her grandfather's tools—how his relationship with Neha had flourished precisely because they'd crystalized their distinct approaches while creating something new together. Their love hadn't been about perfect alignment but about the harmony possible between different traditions, different rhythms, different ways of measuring what mattered.

"The night Marcus left," she said, the memory's sharp edges

being filed down in the workshop's soft light, "he said I was too concerned with precision. But that wasn't really it, was it? I was precise about the wrong things—trying to calibrate myself to his expectations instead of understanding my own timing."

The wall of clocks ticked their various rhythms, each one valid, each one true to its own design. She thought of Rebecca and Marcus's engagement announcement—how it had felt like a collision but shouldn't have been. They had always shared the same rhythm, the same way of moving through time, while she had been winding herself tighter and tighter trying to match a beat that was never truly hers.

"Look at this," Aarav said delicately, holding up their grandparents' mysterious timepiece so it caught the late sun. The three rings moved in their endless dance, each following its own path while influencing the others. "Some systems only work because of their differences, not in spite of them."

His hand found hers with the natural gravity of well-balanced gears meeting their wheels. The contact sent warmth spreading through her fingers like oil through a movement, making everything flow more smoothly, more naturally. This, she realized, was what time felt like when you weren't forcing it—when you allowed it to move at its own pace, following its own truth.

"I think," she said, watching their joined shadows stretch across the workshop floor like hands on a sundial, "I'm finally running on the right time."

The fog outside had begun its evening advance from the bay, easing the city's edges while forging its essentials. In its gentle obscurity, past and present seemed to merge like the languages in their grandparents' notes—distinct yet harmonious, each enriching the other without losing itself.

The workshop's timepieces marked the moment in their various voices, like an orchestra finding its theme. Some mechanisms, Olivia thought, had to wind down completely before they could be rewound with new purpose, new energy, new truth. The trick wasn't in preventing the unwinding, but in recognizing when it was time to begin again.

Chapter 4

Counter-Clockwise

Time moved differently in her grandfather's house. Olivia felt it the moment she and Aarav crossed the threshold, as if they'd stepped through a semi-permeable membrane between present and previous. Minute particles of fine fabric and repair residue from long ago performed a ballet in the morning light like seconds made visible, each one carrying a memory that had waited patiently to be rediscovered.

"His workshop was through here," she said, leading Aarav down a hallway where framed technical drawings mapped the evolution of horological innovation. But instead of moving forward, they found themselves drawn to the kitchen, where a calendar still hung on the wall, frozen on the month of her grandfather's passing. An empty cup sat beside the sink, a thin film of oxidized tea marking its last use like the rings of a tree recording time's passage.

Aarav moved through the space with the same deliberate grace he applied to watchmaking, his presence somehow both foreign and familiar in this sanctuary of timekeepers. His fingers traced the edge of a cardboard box marked "Tools/工具" in Helen's precise handwriting, the touch reverent as if he could read the history contained within through his fingertips alone.

"Start with this one?" he suggested, his voice carrying the same gentle resonance that had drawn Olivia to his coffee stand that fateful morning. The question loomed in the air between them, weighted with the understanding that opening these boxes meant more than just sorting through possessions.

Olivia nodded, settling beside him on the floor. The hardwood was warm from the sun, its heat seeping through her jeans like time itself rising up to meet them. As she reached for the box's seal, her sleeve pulled back to reveal her grandfather's watch on her wrist – still marking time in its own unique rhythm, unconcerned with the digital precision that had once governed her life.

They worked in companionable silence, creating careful piles: keep, donate, consider. Each item emerged from tissue paper like a butterfly from its chrysalis, carrying stories in its worn edges and polished surfaces. A brass loupe still bore the impression of her grandfather's thumb, its lens catching sunlight and throwing rainbow arcs across Aarav's cheek.

"Look at this," he said softly, holding up a watchmaker's notebook. The leather cover had aged to the color of well-steeped oolong, its pages rippling with what appeared to be decades of notations. But as he opened it, something fluttered to the floor between them – an envelope, yellowed with age, addressed in handwriting that made Olivia's breath catch.

"That's not my grandfather's writing," she said, though something about the elegant strokes tugged at her memory like a half-forgotten melody.

Aarav picked up the envelope with watchmaker's care, his expression shifting like light through crystal. "No," he agreed quietly.

56

"It's my grandmother's."

The revelation settled between them like the gap between tick and tock. Olivia watched as Aarav's fingers traced the characters of the address – a mixture of English and Hanzi that mirrored her grandfather's own bilingual notations. The envelope had never been sealed, its flap merely tucked in like a secret waiting to be discovered.

"Read it?" she suggested, her voice barely above a whisper. The sunlight had shifted, creating a perfect spotlight on the aged paper in Aarav's hands.

He nodded, carefully withdrawing a single sheet covered in the same elegant script. As he read, his voice took on the cadence of waves against a shore:

Dear 伟铭 (Wěi Míng),

The mechanism you suggested for the lunar phase calculation is elegant beyond words. I've been testing it against the Mumbai tide tables, and it holds true even during the monsoon's chaos. Perhaps you were right – some movements can only be perfected when traditions flow together like rivers meeting the sea.

I've enclosed my modifications to the escapement design. The notations might seem foreign to your eyes, but I trust your hands will understand what my words cannot fully express.

Until our next exchange,

Neha

The letter's date placed it in 1975, years before their grandparents' public collaboration at the exhibition. Olivia thought of the paired pocket watches they'd discovered, how their patterns seemed to reach for each other. "They were corresponding in secret," she realized. "Trading innovations through letters while maintaining their separate traditions in public."

"Like watchmakers' Romeo and Juliet," Aarav mused, "but

with happier engineering." His smile caught the light, transforming his usual asymmetrical quirk into something warmer, more intimate.

As they continued unpacking, more letters emerged from unexpected places – tucked into tool rolls, pressed between pages of technical manuals, hidden in false bottoms of parts boxes. Each one revealed another layer of their grandparents' relationship, a love story told in gear ratios and escapement designs.

"Your spring mechanism may be efficient," Olivia read from one, laughter coloring her voice, "but it lacks elegance. Try again." She looked up to find Aarav watching her with an expression that made time seem to condense around them like honey in winter's early morning light.

"My grandmother's favorite criticism," he said softly. "She used it like others use terms of endearment."

They worked through the afternoon, the piles around them growing like the phases of the moon their grandparents had so carefully tracked. The 'keep' stack rose steadily, each item chosen not for its practical value but for the stories it contained, the connections it revealed.

The sun was setting by the time they reached the bottom of the first box, painting the room in shades of amber that reminded Olivia of aged watch crystals. In the fading light, she found herself studying Aarav's hands as he carefully rewrapped a set of precision screwdrivers – the same careful movements she'd seen in old photographs of her grandfather, the same reverence for tools that contained worlds of possibility.

"We should continue tomorrow," he suggested, though his tone carried a reluctance that matched the weight in her chest at the thought of leaving this cocoon of discovery.

Olivia nodded, but neither of them moved. The house creaked gently around them, settling into evening like a well-loved vehicle finding its rest. Through the window, fog was beginning to roll in from the bay, softening the city's edges while somehow making this room feel sharper, more real.

"There are certain things," she said finally, her fingers brushing against another unopened letter, "that take exactly the right amount of time to discover."

Aarav's smile in response was like watching a perfect gear train engage – each element falling into place with inevitable grace. "Tomorrow, then," he agreed, standing and offering her his hand. As she took it, the contact sent warmth spreading through her fingers like oil through a movement, making everything flow more smoothly, more naturally.

They left the room exactly as it was – piles of sorted treasures catching the last light like islands in a sea of the joyful unexplored, each one waiting to reveal more of the story that had brought them to this moment, in this place, together.

The fog followed them down the steps and into the evening, its cool touch a reminder that between clarity and shadow exists bounty, in the moments when time itself seems to pause and listen.

*****

The morning fog had retreated to the bay by the time Olivia found herself standing before Borderlands Books, its Victorian facade catching the midday sun like a watch crystal awaiting polish. The familiar bell above the door – tuned to a perfect D-minor that had once made Marcus lecture about sound frequency and productivity – now seemed to chime with a different resonance, as if her recent past had changed not just her perception of time but of sound itself.

Inside, the bookstore wrapped around her like a well-worn coat, its narrow aisles and towering shelves creating a labyrinth of beckoning excavation. The air carried its eternal mixture of paper, leather, and the subtle metallic tang of aging bindings – scents that reminded her of her grandfather's technical manuals, of margins filled with two different hands sharing a single conversation across decades.

She had avoided this place since the breakup, letting its significance fade like an unwound clock. But now, with the weight of her grandfather's letters in her bag and the memory of Aarav's hands carefully sorting through history, she found herself drawing strength from its familiar chaos.

"Olivia?" The voice carried across the shop floor like a discordant note in a familiar symphony. "Oh my god, I was just thinking about you!"

Rebecca stood by the newly arrived section, her presence as precisely curated as ever. Everything about her – from her carefully distressed designer jeans to her artfully messy bun – spoke of the same deliberate casualness that had once made Olivia feel perpetually out of sync.

"The engagement party," Rebecca continued, her smile carrying the same practiced warmth that had once seemed so genuine. "We're having it here. Next Saturday. I was going to email you the invitation, but..." She gestured vaguely, perhaps remembering the rumors of Olivia's digital disappearance that must have been circulating through their old social circle.

Time seemed to compress and expand simultaneously, like a ice under pressure. Olivia felt the weight of their shared history –

three years of Wednesday lunches, countless weekend brunches, the careful construction of a friendship that had seemed unshakeable until it wasn't. She thought of the way Rebecca had always checked her phone during conversations, measuring their interactions in digital increments rather than moments of genuine connection.

"Here?" The word emerged softer than intended, carrying none of the sharp edges she might have once honed it to. Through the window, she caught a glimpse of her reflection overlaid on the street scene beyond – her grandfather's apron still tied around her waist, small brass shavings catching light in her hair like stars in early evening.

Rebecca's expression shifted, perhaps catching something unexpected in Olivia's response. "It was Marcus's idea, actually. He said it's where we first..." She trailed off, seemingly realizing the weight of what she was about to say.

But the revelation didn't land with the impact it might have weeks ago. Instead, Olivia found herself noticing the way Rebecca's hands moved as she spoke – quick, precise but thoughlesss movements, like someone scrolling through time rather than experiencing it. So different from Aarav's deliberate grace or her grandfather's measured precision.

"It's perfect," Olivia said, surprising them both with her sincerity. "This place deserves to hold happy stories."

She moved past Rebecca to the philosophy section, her fingers trailing along spines that had once been as familiar as the days of the week. There, between Camus and de Beauvoir, she found what she hadn't known she was looking for – a worn copy of "One Hundred Years of Solitude" misplaced among the existentialists like time itself had arranged this moment.

Opening it released the scent of aged paper and possibility. A note fell from between its pages, the handwriting now as familiar as her own heartbeat: "To find yourself in time, you must first lose yourself in stories."

Aarav's message caught the light like a secret finally ready to be discovered. She thought of their morning sorting through her grandfather's letters, of the way time had pooled around them like light through stained glass. The book's weight in her hands felt like an anchor, not to the past but to a present that was finally moving at its own perfect pace.

"Are you... okay?" Rebecca's voice carried genuine concern now, perhaps seeing something in Olivia's expression that didn't fit her expectations of how this encounter should unfold.

Olivia looked up, really seeing her former friend for the first time since everything had changed. Rebecca stood haloed by the afternoon light streaming through the shop's windows, her perfectly coordinated appearance suddenly seeming less like armor and more like a costume – something worn to play a part that perhaps didn't fit as well as it once had.

"I'm learning to tell time differently," Olivia said, the words emerging with quiet certainty. She held up the book with its hidden message. "Revisiting old books with a new mind sometimes helps with understanding."

The statement stuck in the air between them like the gap between tock and tick. Through the windows, fog was beginning to reclaim the afternoon, disappearing the city's edges while somehow highlighting others.

"I should go," Rebecca said, her hands already reaching for her phone with unconscious urgency. "There's so much planning still to do..."

Olivia nodded, but her attention had already returned to the book in her hands, to the promise of stories within stories, of messages hidden between lines like her grandfather's letters tucked between tools. As Rebecca's footsteps faded toward the front of the store, Olivia found herself walking to the register, the decision to purchase this particular copy feeling as natural as the progression of hours.

Outside, the fog had begun to paint the street in watercolor washes, transforming the familiar neighborhood into something just outside of memory. Olivia tucked the book into her bag alongside her grandfather's letters, feeling the weight of different kinds of stories settling against each other like gears finding their proper alignment.

The walk back to Aarav's workshop seemed to measure itself in heartbeats rather than steps, each one bringing her closer to a rhythm that felt increasingly like her own. The book's presence against her side felt like a key waiting to unlock another layer of understanding, allowing for openness between moments where truth had been waiting to be found.

The workshop's afternoon light painted copper highlights across the scattered tools as Olivia entered, the familiar scent of clock oil and osmanthus tea wrapping around her like a welcome. Aarav looked up from his workbench, his asymmetrical smile deepening as he caught sight of the book cradled in her arms.

"Successful hunting?" he asked, setting aside the delicate balance wheel he'd been adjusting. The afternoon sun caught in his loupe, still perched on his forehead like a third eye, sending prismatic patterns dancing across the worn wooden surfaces around them.

"You could say that." Olivia approached the bench, drawing out the copy of "One Hundred Years of Solitude" with the same care she now used handling delicate watch mechanisms. "Though I think perhaps it found me."

She opened the book to where his note still marked its place like a pressed flower between pages: "To find yourself in time, you must first lose yourself in stories." The paper had relaxed at its creases from being read and refolded throughout the afternoon, each examination revealing new depths to the careful strokes of his handwriting.

"Ah," Aarav said softly, recognition warming his voice like a candelabra in an otherwise cool room. "One of my wandering thoughts found its way home."

"You leave notes in books?" The question carried more weight than its simple syllables suggested, like a watch that told more than just time.

"Stories get lonely sitting on shelves," he replied, his hands moving to prepare a fresh pot of tea – oolong this time, its leaves unfurling like memories awakening. "Sometimes they need conversation, marginalia that reminds them they're part of something larger than their own bindings."

The workshop's many timepieces ticked in subtle harmony as Olivia settled onto her usual stool, the leather of her grandfather's apron creaking gently. "Like letters hidden in tool cases?"

"Exactly." Aarav's smile caught the light like a well-polished crown wheel. "Our grandparents understood that some messages need to wait for the right moment to be found. They left their story in the margins of manuals, in the evidently unoccupied areas of mechanisms. I leave mine in books, hoping they'll find their way to readers who need them."

He placed a cup of tea before her, its surface reflecting the afternoon light like a still pool waiting to be disturbed. "Books are time capsules," he continued, his voice carrying the same measured cadence he used when explaining particularly complex movements. "A note in the margin is a way of leaving a part of yourself for someone else to find, when they're ready to discover it."

Olivia traced the edge of her teacup, watching ripples form and dissolve like moments passing into memory. "What if we did that?" The words emerged before she could measure them, carrying all the spontaneity she'd once feared. "Left notes for each other in books we share?"

Aarav's expression shifted, the way light changes when passing through water. "A private conversation in public margins?"

"Our own kind of letters," Olivia agreed, thinking of their grandparents' hidden correspondence. "Something that exists in-between stories, in-between pages."

Aarav reached beneath his workbench, producing a leather-bound volume she hadn't seen before. Its cover bore no title, but the way he handled it spoke of significance. "Then perhaps we should start with this."

The book opened to reveal pages of technical diagrams, each one annotated in multiple hands – some she recognized from their grandparents' letters, others unknown yet somehow familiar. Between the drawings of escapements and gear trains, margins bloomed with conversations carried out across decades.

"My grandmother's personal notebook," Aarav explained, his finger tracing a line of Balbodh Devanagari that danced alongside Hanzi. "She kept it as a record of her innovations, but it became something more – a dialogue between traditions, between hearts trying to find their own rhythm."

The afternoon light shifted as they bent over the pages together, their shoulders touching with the same congruous inevitability that drew planets into orbit. Each turn revealed new layers of conversation: technical observations that became poetry, mathematical formulas that read like love letters when you knew how to decode them.

"Sometimes," Aarav said softly, his voice close enough that Olivia could feel its warmth, "the most important things can only be said about not what we're supposed to be discussing."

His hand brushed hers as they both reached to turn a page, the contact sending electricity spreading through her fingers. The workshop's various timepieces seemed to tick more discretely, as if lending privacy to the moment unfolding between them.

"Here," Olivia said, reaching for her newly acquired book. She opened to a random page, the paper carrying that particular scent of decay that conotes life that only well-read books possess. Taking out her grandfather's fountain pen – the one she'd found in his tool case, still carrying a cartridge of sepia ink – she began to write in the margin: "Time isn't something we measure, but something we create between moments of understanding."

Aarav watched the ink flow across the paper, his expression holding the same focused appreciation he gave to particularly elegant clockwork. When she finished, he took the pen with deliberate care, his script flowing beneath hers like a river finding its course: "And some moments are meant to be discovered together."

The words seemed to shimmer on the page, as if the ink was still determining its final form. Outside, fog had begun to gather at the windows, transforming the late afternoon light into something amorphus and permeable. Inside, time moved like tea leaves unfurling, each moment opening to reveal new depth, new scent.

They spent the remaining hours of daylight trading the book back and forth, each margin becoming a floating place of resort where thoughts could bloom without pressure of immediate response. Some notes were philosophical, others playful, all carrying the weight of truth found in unexpected places.

As the last direct sunbeam faded from the workshop, Olivia looked at their shared marginalia with the same wonder she'd felt discovering her grandfather's letters. Each note was a small mechanism of connection, keeping time in its own unique way.

"Books really do get lonely on shelves," she said softly, watching Aarav inscribe one final thought before the light grew too dim. "They need someone to remind them they're part of a more expansive story."

His smile in response held all the warmth of the fading day, all the promise of pages yet to be turned. "What's written between what's already been said," he replied, "provides new light."

The workshop settled into evening's quiet rhythm, their shared books and inherited tools keeping company like old friends finally introduced. Outside, the fog continued its gentle advance, but inside, clarity had never felt more present.

The two moved upstairs, where the attic air moved carefully with decades of accumulated stillness, illuminated only by the beam of their flashlights. Here felt like the inside of a pocket watch – enclosed, intimate, holding secrets in its crafted darkness. She and Aarav had made their way up here after discovering another letter that mentioned a hidden workspace above her grandfather's main study, where the evening light was "perfect for detailed escapement work."

"Here," Aarav said softly, his voice carrying that watchmaker's precision that somehow made even whispers feel like proclamations. His flashlight beam caught something metallic tucked between two roof beams – an old toolbox, its brass fittings tarnished to a subtle green that spoke of years of patient waiting.

Olivia moved carefully across the attic's floorboards, each step measured as if she were adjusting a delicate mechanism. The toolbox bore no markings save for a subtle pattern etched into its lid – interlocking spirals that echoed the design of their grandparents' mysterious timepiece.

"It's locked," she observed, fingers tracing the keyhole's worn edges. But even as she spoke, Aarav was already reaching into his pocket, producing a key that caught their crossed flashlight beams like a star in darkness.

"Found it this morning," he explained, "hidden in the false bottom of my grandmother's old parts cabinet. The pattern matches." His hands, steady as ever, fitted the key into the lock. It turned with a sound like time itself being unwound.

Inside, beneath a layer of silk that had once been red but had faded to the color of sunset, they found a blueprint. The paper had yellowed at its edges, but the technical drawings remained crisp – precise lines mapping out a mechanism unlike anything Olivia had seen in her grandfather's other works.

"Look at these annotations," she breathed, holding her flashlight closer. The margins were filled with two distinct hands – her grandfather's familiar blend of English and Hanzi dancing alongside what she now recognized as Neha's elegant Balbodh Devanagari script. They weren't just notes about the mechanism; they were conversations, questions posed and answered across the span of years.

"'The moon phase calculation needs to account for emotional tides as well as oceanic ones,'" Aarav read from one margin, his grandmother's handwriting flowing like water across the page. "'Time moves differently when the heart is involved.'"

Beside it, in her grandfather's more measured strokes: "'Perhaps that's why we measure it in beats rather than seconds.'"

The blueprint itself showed something extraordinary – a watch design that seemed to fold space within space, using three interconnected rings to track multiple forms of time simultaneously. As they studied it closer, Olivia realized with growing wonder that it matched the mysterious timepiece they'd found, but showed it in an unfinished state, with modifications and possibilities sketched in both their grandparents' hands.

"They were creating something entirely new," Aarav said, his voice colored with revelation. "Not just combining their traditions, but inventing a whole new way of measuring time." His finger traced a particularly complex gear train marked with both Hanzi characters and Balbodh Devanagari. "Look – this isn't just about tracking hours and minutes. They were trying to create a mechanism that could measure meaning, the space between decisions."

A soft thud made them both start. A leather-bound journal had fallen from where it had been wedged between the blueprint's folds, its pages splaying open like wings catching air. Inside, they found more than just technical notes – they found the story of a collaboration that had bloomed into something deeper.

"'Today N. suggested that time flows differently in shared spaces,'" Olivia read from one entry dated 1976. "'Her hypothesis about non-linear emotional chronometry seems impossible to prove through traditional methods, yet when she's here, I find myself agreeing. Hours pass like minutes, yet each minute holds the weight of days.'"

Their flashlight beams crossed again as Aarav turned to a later page, creating a pool of light that seemed to concentrate around another entry: "'W.M. understands what I've always known – that the best innovations come from the places where different rhythms meet. We're creating more than just a timepiece; we're building a bridge between ways of seeing the world.'"

The attic creaked gently around them, settling into the night's cooling air like an old mechanism finding its rest. Through a small window, fog was visible creeping across the city, obscuring boundaries between buildings just as their grandparents' collaboration had attempted to do the similar between traditions and thoughts.

"This wasn't just a watch they were designing," Olivia realized, the truth emerging like a perfectly balanced wheel finding its pivot. "It was a love letter written in gears and springs, a way of proving that different approaches to time could create something more beautiful together than apart."

Aarav's hand found hers in the dimness, warm and steady as a well-maintained movement. "Some effort can't be realized alone," he said softly, echoing words they'd found written in both their grandparents' hands across various margins and notes.

They spent hours in that attic, flashlight batteries growing dim as they pieced together more of the story through blueprints and journal entries. The complicated dance of secrecy and innovation, of professional rivalry transforming into something profoundly personal, unfolded before them like the petals of an mechanical flower crafted by four hands working as two.

When they finally descended, the fog had claimed the city entirely, turning the world outside the windows into a soft-focused dream of itself. But inside, everything felt more distinct, entangled– as if understanding their grandparents' shared past had somehow brought their own present into perfect focus.

The blueprint, carefully rolled and tied with faded silk ribbon, felt like both a key and a compass in Olivia's hands. Whatever their grandparents had been trying to create with their impossible time-piece, its completion seemed to have been waiting not just for the right moment, but for the right inheritors to understand its true purpose.

"Time shared is time multiplied," Aarav quoted softly from one of the margin notes they'd found, his voice carrying all the weight of generations of watchmakers learning to measure what mattered most.

In response, Olivia felt something shift in her own internal timing – like the subtle click of gears finally finding their proper alignment, like the entirety of her expanding to hold all the existence of what was yet to come.

***

The evening had barely settled into Olivia's apartment when her mother arrived, unannounced as always, her surgical intrusions stealing seconds away from time that never occurred. Olivia had just finished arranging the day's discoveries on her kitchen table – the blueprint, the journal, fragments of a love story told in technical specifications and marginal notes.

Helen Chén's entrance carried with it the scent of hospi-tal antiseptic barely masked by expensive perfume, a combination that had always reminded Olivia of time measured in heartbeats and monitor beeps rather than gears and springs. She paused in the doorway, her eyes conducting the same thorough assessment she gave to preoperative patients.

"You haven't been answering your phone," Helen said, though her tone suggested this wasn't really why she'd come. Her gaze settled on the blueprint spread across the table, something flickering behind her professional composure like light catching an imperfection in crystal.

"It's still being repaired," Olivia replied, watching her mother's carefully maintained facade shift almost imperceptibly. "But you knew that, didn't you? Since you've been checking on me at the workshop almost daily."

Helen moved further into the apartment, her Louboutin heels clicking against the hardwood like a metronome marking particularly precise seconds. She stopped at the table, one manicured finger hovering over the blueprint's edge where Hanzi swirled alongside Balbodh Devanagari notations.

"I remember this," she said softly, the words carrying a weight Olivia had rarely heard in her mother's voice. "Your grandfather would work on it late at night, when he thought everyone was asleep. But I used to watch from the stairs, counting the hours by the sound of his pencil on paper."

The admission hung in the air like dust in sunlight, each particle a memory waiting to be examined. Olivia studied her mother's face, seeing perhaps for the first time the ghost of a young girl who had once measured time by her father's movements rather than operative procedures.

"Tell me about them," Olivia said gently, pulling out a chair.

"About Wàigōng and Neha."

Helen's composure wavered for a moment, like a magnet under the influence of two opposite poles. She sat with uncharacteristic heaviness, her perfect posture softening as if decades of carefully maintained equilibrium were finally allowed to rest.

"They were two different types of designs," she said, her voice taking on a quality Olivia had never heard before – something almost lyrical. "Wàigōng moved like a Swiss movement – every action measured, every decision precise. But Neha..." A smile touched her lips, transforming her face into something younger, more vulnerable. "She was like a tidal clock, flowing between traditions and expectations with natural grace."

Outside, fog pressed against the windows, turning the city's lights into soft halos that seemed to pulse with the rhythm of memory. Inside, time moved with disparate grace, measured now in the fractures within Helen's carefully chosen words.

"I used to bring them tea," she continued, her fingers tracing the blueprint's intricate gear trains. "Late at night when they worked on this. They never sent me away, just shifted their papers so I could sit and watch. Sometimes Neha would tell me stories about Mumbai while Wàigōng adjusted tiny mechanisms I couldn't even see."

"Why didn't you ever mention her before?" Olivia asked, thinking of all the years she'd wondered about her grandfather's mysterious innovations, never knowing they'd been born from such an extraordinary collaboration.

Helen's laugh held the same bitter notes as over-steeped tea. "Because I watched it end. Watched them choose tradition over..." She paused, selecting her next words with pained care. "Over what could have been. They let other people's expectations become the escapement that regulated their movements."

The weight of this revelation settled around them like 2:00 a.m. fog, seeping into what had been said and what remained hidden. Olivia thought of the mysterious timepiece with its three interconnected rings, wondering if it had been meant as more than just a mechanical innovation – if perhaps it had been an attempt to create a mechanism that could transcend the very traditions that kept its creators apart.

"And now," Helen said, her clinical tone returning like armor being reinstated, "you're spending your days in another watchmaker's shop, learning to measure time in ways recognizable as legitimate."

The observation carried no judgment, only a kind of weary recognition that made Olivia's heart ache. She thought of Aarav's hands guiding hers through delicate repairs, of margins filled with conversations that flowed between professional and personal like time itself moving through multiple dimensions.

"At times," Olivia said softly, "it is worth the risk of disrupting tradition."

Helen's eyes met hers, sharp as surgical steel but holding something softer beneath – perhaps understanding, perhaps regret, perhaps both. "Just remember," she said, standing with restored precision, "that time moves forward regardless of how we choose to measure it." She smoothed her silk blouse with habitual care. "Which reminds me – we need to discuss the house. The market won't wait forever."

But even this return to practical matters couldn't completely mask the shift that had occurred. As Helen moved toward the door, she paused, her hand resting on the frame like a balance wheel at the apex of its swing.

"Your Năinai would have understood," she said, almost too quietly to hear. With that, she absconded into the fog-shrouded evening, leaving behind a silence filled with the weight of histories both revealed and still invisible.

Olivia remained at the table, watching the blueprint's lines blur in the growing darkness. Each character, whether Hanzi or Balbodh Devanagari, seemed to pulse with new meaning now – not just technical specifications for an improbable timepiece, but the carefully coded diary of a love story that had never fully wound down.

Outside, the fog had thickened, disappearing the city's gaze, moderating the night inside. Olivia felt something shift in her understanding of both past and present – like the subtle adjustment of a timing lever that changes everything about how a mechanism measures the moments that matter most.

The night had deepened to the shade of well-oiled brass by the time Olivia settled into her reading chair, her grandfather's book warm in her lap like a sleeping cat. The fog outside had transformed the city's usual nighttime chorus into something muted and intimate, creating a pocket of silence perfect for the kind of mental wanderings and creations that only emerge in the hours between midnight and dawn.

Around her, the apartment held its breath in the peculiar stillness that comes with profound revelation. The blueprint from the attic lay carefully rolled on her desk, its edges catching the soft lamp light like the rim of a watch crystal. Beside it, her grandfather's journal waited, its pages still holding the warmth of her mother's unexpected memories.

Olivia opened "One Hundred Years of Solitude" to where she

and Aarav had begun their margin correspondence, their shared notes creating a parallel narrative that wound through García Márquez's prose like time itself moving through multiple dimensions. In the quiet of her lamp-lit corner, she uncapped her grandfather's fountain pen, its nib catching the light like a star about to fall.

"What if time isn't something we move through," she wrote in the margin, her words flowing with the same deliberate grace she'd learned to use with delicate watch mechanisms, "but something we carry with us? Like memory, or hope, or the weight of decisions we haven't yet made?"

The ink dried slowly, each character seeming to pulse with possibility. She thought of her mother's revelation about watching her grandfather and Neha work late into the night, of traditions becoming boundaries that contained rather than sustained. The pen moved again, adding beneath her first note: "When some mechanisms break, it was necessary and true so that we can build anew from their pieces."

Tomorrow, she would return the book to Aarav, adding another layer to their growing conversation in margins. But for now, she let herself sink into the clouded range residing between reading and writing, between memory and musing, between the measured tick of her grandfather's repaired wall clock and the softer rhythm of her own heartbeat.

The fog pressed closer against her windows, its presence transforming the city lights into distant stars seen through layers of time. Inside, surrounded by the inherited tools of timekeeping and the newly discovered stories of love transcending tradition, Olivia felt something shift in her understanding of how moments could be measured.

She turned to a fresh page, the paper crisp with possibility. In the margin, she began to write what felt like both a question and an answer: "Perhaps the space between seconds is where we learn to trust our own timing – not the rhythms we've inherited or the patterns we've been taught, but the natural movement of hearts finding their way to what matters most."

The night deepened around her as she continued writing, each note a small calibration of understanding. Time moved differently in these late hours, measured not in staccato but in the flow of ink across paper, in the opening between marks, in the quiet certainty that some stories can only be told in the margins of other tales. Olivia wrote until her pen ran dry, until the fog began to pale with approaching dawn, until each page held some new understanding of how love and time could wind together like the perfect marriage of gear and wheel.

As the first hint of morning began to soften the night's edges, she closed the book gently, feeling its weight like a promise in her hands. Tomorrow would bring more discoveries, more shared margins, more moments of connection measured not by any clock but by the steady accumulation of understanding between two hearts learning to beat in complementary rhythm.

The fog was already beginning to retreat as she finally sought sleep, carrying with it the weight of old traditions and leaving behind the lighter air of potential. In the last whiffs of waking before dreams claimed her, Olivia thought of mechanisms and margins, of time shared and multiplied, of between seconds where love had always waited to be found.

Her grandfather's watch ticked softly on her nightstand, its rhythm now sounding less like the passing of time and more like gentle encouragement: Some stories, it seemed to say, can only be told in the spannable distance between what we think we know and what we're aware and prepared to discover. Some mechanisms take generations to complete, not because they're complicated, but because they're waiting for the right hearts to understand their purpose.

The dawn arrived like the turning of a page, each moment holding the weight of both ending and beginning, each second creating space for new stories to be written in the margins of time itself.

CHAPTER 5

TIME ZONES

L AX sprawled before Olivia like a mechanical watch laid bare, its terminals extending like gear trains into the morning haze. She sat at gate 73, her grandfather's pocket watch heavy in her coat pocket, its warmth a constant reminder of all she was carrying with her across the Pacific. The liquid crystal displays overhead blinked their relentless digital countdowns, marking time in stark contrasts to the analog wisdom nestled against her hip.

Without her phone, the airport felt both more immediate and more distant, as if she were viewing it through her grandfather's loupe – each detail crystalline but somehow removed from its usual context. Travelers flowed around her in practiced patterns, their movements synchronized by invisible digital pulses from devices she no longer possessed. She watched a businessman check his watch, then his phone, then his watch again, as if hoping for different answers from competing timekeepers.

The book Aarav had lent her lay open in her lap, its margins blooming with his annotations like flowers pressed between pages. His handwriting carried the same careful precision he used when adjusting balance wheels, each character weighted with intention.

She traced one note with her fingertip, feeling the slight indentation in the paper: "Time zones are humanity's attempt to organize chaos – but chaos has its own rhythm, if we learn to listen."

A child's laughter cut through the terminal's white noise, drawing Olivia's attention to a young girl spinning in place, her arms outstretched like the hands of a clock gone wonderfully wrong. The girl's mother reached for her phone, presumably to capture the moment, then stopped, choosing instead to simply watch. The scene stirred something in Olivia's memory – her grandfather explaining how some moments resist mechanical measurement, how joy moves to its own tempo.

From her bag, she withdrew the travel guides and maps he'd used decades ago, their creases softened by time and use. Their pages carried a different kind of information than her defunct phone had provided – not just routes and schedules, but histories, textures, the accumulated wisdom of countless travelers who had navigated by paper and intuition rather than GPS. Between two pages, she found a pressed cherry blossom, its delicate form preserved like a moment frozen between seconds.

The boarding call came in waves – first in English, then Japanese, each announcement creating its own lineament ripple through the waiting crowd. Olivia gathered her belongings with deliberate care, but before joining the line, she pulled out a postcard she'd chosen specifically for its image: a long-exposure photograph of LAX at night, plane lights creating streaks across the sky like time made visible.

On its blank side, she wrote:

Time feels slower at the airport, like it's waiting to catch up. I wonder if it's the same for you in the shop, surrounded by so many different rhythms trying to synchronize. The woman next to me keeps checking two watches — one set to LA time, one to Tokyo. But I think of your grandmother's notes about emotional chronometry, and I wonder if perhaps we need a third watch entirely, one that measures the space between where we are and where we're meant to be.

   - O

She didn't write Aarav's address — not yet. Something about the unmailed postcard felt right, as if this message needed to mature with nuance and experience like empathy or fine vinegar before finding their recipients. She tucked it into her copy of "The Wind-Up Bird Chronicle," between pages where Murakami wrote about time moving like water underground.

As she boarded the plane, Olivia felt the weight of her grandfather's watch like an anchor to a past that was somehow also the passage to her future. The pocket that had held her phone felt conspicuously light, but her bag was heavy with paper maps and handwritten recollections. Somewhere over the Pacific, she would cross the International Date Line, that imaginary seam in time's fabric where today touches tomorrow. But for now, she settled into her seat and watched Los Angeles recede through the window, its grid-pattern streets fading into the morning light like the lines of a technical drawing being gently erased.

Tokyo emerged from the pre-dawn haze like a watch face illuminated by degrees — first the bright points of skyscrapers, then the flowing lines of elevated trains, finally the intricate mesh of streets that seemed to operate on multiple temporal planes simultaneously. Olivia stood at the intersection of tradition and modernity in Shibuya, her grandfather's maps spread before her like mechanical diagrams, their aged creases creating new pathways across the city's living geometries.

The crosswalk's countdown ticked away in crisp digital certainty, while beside her, an ancient ginkgo tree swayed to rhythms unchanged since her grandfather had first walked these streets. Above, massive video screens projected time-warped advertisements into the morning mist, their light catching in the droplets like memories refracting through daydreams. Yet beneath this modern cascade, tiny shrines nestled in unexpected corners, their burning incense measuring time by scent rather than sight.

The investment firm's Tokyo office occupied the forty-seventh floor of a glass tower in Marunouchi, its windows offering views of the Imperial Palace gardens where time moved in seasonal cycles unchanged for centuries. Her colleagues had been surprised when she declined a company phone for the trip, even more surprised when she pulled out her grandfather's pocket watch during the morning meeting.

"Analog in the age of digital?" her Tokyo counterpart, Tanaka-san, had asked, his eyes catching the watch's unusual spiral patterns with quiet interest. "Like choosing to write with a brush when keyboards are available."

Without her phone's constant tether, she found herself tracking herself through senses – the gradual warming of tea in ceramic, the length of shadows across temple steps, the changing cadence of footsteps as office workers gave way to afternoon shoppers. A group of schoolchildren passed, their yellow caps bright against the gray morning, their choreographed chaos a reminder of what her grandfather had written about synchronized randomness. In his journal, he'd described Tokyo as "a city where multiple times exist simultaneously, each operating according to its own internal logic." Standing here now, watching salary men rush past elderly women carefully arranging their shop displays, she understood what he'd meant.

Near a vending machine that sold both ancient herbal teas and modern energy drinks, she found a traditional tea house tucked away like a secret between epochs. The sliding door whispered across its wooden track with a sound unchanged since the Edo period. Inside, time rose and landed like the steam rising from cast iron kettles — slow, deliberate, yet impossible to grasp.

Each day unfolded according to multiple chronologies: meetings timed to the second, lunch breaks that seemed to exist outside normal hours in tiny restaurants where chef's movements marked time like perfectly tuned escapements, tea ceremonies that transcended thirst to art and immersion, evenings when the city's lights transformed modern architecture into something ancient and mysterious. Shifting her time between work, self explorations, and somewhere in-between the two, her grandfather's pocket watch kept its own counsel in her coat, ticking away moments that seemed to expand and contract like the bellows of an accordion.

"The first cup is for the eyes," the tea master told her in careful English, her motions sedulous as a watch's escapement. "The second for the mind, the third for the heart." Each pour marked time not in minutes but in degrees of understanding, in the kind unpacking of steeping leaves that had been waiting decades for this specific moment.

Enraptured, Olivia followed the tea master's hands move through positions refined by centuries of practice, and she began to sketch mentally her first letter to Aarav:

Tokyo exists in temporal layers, like the strata of Earth revealing different ages simultaneously. I find myself thinking of your workshop, how each clock marks time slightly differently, creating a symphony of seconds. Here, time moves in rhythms — sometimes a rush, sometimes a pause. It's not just a measurement; it's a mood.

I visited a shrine where they still use water clocks, each drop marking time with the same patience as falling snow. The monk told me that in ancient Japan, they divided the day differently in summer than in winter, making hours longer or shorter to match the sun's journey. I wonder what our lives would be like if we still measured time by natural rhythms rather than atomic precision.

The tea master here uses movements passed down through generations, each gesture a connection to countless moments before. It reminds me of how you hold your tools — not just with precision, but with reverence for all the hands that have shaped them.

There's a type of incense they burn that measures time by scent and quality — each stick precisely crafted to burn for a specific duration; each variety measures a different quality of moment—sandalwood for meditation, cherry bark for celebration, ancient pine for remembering. The ash falls like snow in slow motion, each particle a moment made visible. I find myself wondering if perhaps time isn't something we measure, but something we experience, like music or the lack of pulse from heartbeat now and heartbeat then.

She paused in her writing, watching as a young woman in a business suit knelt at the tea house's threshold, carefully removing her shoes before entering this pocket of slower time. The woman's digital watch blinked insistently, but once inside, she seemed to shed her contemporary urgency like a coat no longer needed.

Returning to her letter, Olivia added:

In one of the books you lent me, you wrote in the margin about how some moments can only be understood in retrospect. I'm beginning to think that maybe some moments can only be understood from half a world away, viewed through the lens of distance like light through your grandmother's prized crystal loupe.

The city is waking up now, each district moving to its own, tailored peri-

odicity — temple bells mixing with train announcements, ancient wood creaking against glass and steel. It's beautiful in its contradiction, like the way your workshop manages to exist both in and out of time.

I carry your coffee's taste in memory, a chronometer of sorts marking my time away from, yet evermore toward, you. The tea master here says that every cup of tea is unique because it captures a specific moment that can never be replicated or repeated. I wonder if the same is true of time itself — if each second is unique not because of what it measures, but because of who we share it with.

The paper lanterns outside began to glow as afternoon light faded, their shadows dancing across her pages like the hands of countless clocks marking different measures of the same moment. Olivia folded the letter carefully, tucking it into her grandfather's notebook where his own observations about Tokyo's temporal nature awaited conversation with hers.

Standing to leave, she caught her reflection in the tea house's ancient mirror — her image overlaid with the calligraphy behind her, creating a palimpsest of past and present, of here and there, of what was and what might be.

"Your watch," Tanaka-san whispered as they stretched through the bubble of the tea house, "it reminds me of something I once saw in an old shop in Yanaka. Your absence of phone, this watch, and after observing you these past few days, leads me to think ou to navigate oddly...not in a negative way — but off from our usual colleagues from foreign offices."

Olivia merely inclined the left side of her mouth in a subtle smile, thanked Tanaka-san, and departed. She thought of Aarav's asymmetrical smile, how it seemed to exist in its own temporal space, unbound by conventional measurements of moment or memory.

Outside, Tokyo's evening rushed past in streams of light and shadow, each intersection a convergence of multiple times – digital, analog, natural, mechanical – all flowing together like rivers meeting the sea. Her grandfather's watch kept its steady pace against her hip, marking not just the passage of time, but its deepening.

Materialized from Tokyo's back streets like a memory taking physical form, the workshop Olivia sought emerged – a narrow two-story building wedged between modern apartments, its wooden facade darkened by decades of patient waiting. The air carried traces of lacquer and time-softened metal, a scent so familiar it made Olivia's throat tighten. A wind chime crafted from old clock parts marked her arrival with a chorus of tiny bells, their rhythm as precise as any masterfully tuned clock.

Yamamoto-san, her grandfather's apprentice, stood in the doorway as if he'd been expecting her all along. Time had shaped him like water shapes stone – gradually, unyieldingly, but leaving the essential nature unchanged. His hands, when they clasped hers in greeting, carried the same careful calluses she'd begun to develop under Aarav's tutelage.

"Chén-sensei's granddaughter," he said, his English carrying the same measured cadence as his movements. "You have his hands." He gestured to where her fingers had automatically moved to touch a half-dismantled pocket watch on his workbench, drawn to its exposed mechanism like a pianist to keys.

The workshop's interior unfolded like a Chinese puzzle box, each surface revealing new layers of horological history. Wooden drawers labeled in her grandfather's distinctive handwriting stood alongside Yamamoto's more angular script, their contents cataloging decades of shared innovation. Light filtered through windows hazed by years of metal dust, creating an atmosphere that seemed

86

to exist outside conventional time.

"He was different here," Yamamoto said, retrieving a leather-bound album from beneath his workbench. "Away from the weight of tradition, he allowed himself to experiment." The photos inside showed a younger version of her grandfather, his usual steadfastness softened by the joy of discovery. In one image, he bent over a workbench alongside a woman whose elegant hands seemed to dance above a disassembled movement – Yamamoto's wife, perhaps, or another watchmaker drawn to this sanctuary of alternative chronometry.

"Here," Yamamoto continued, leading her to a glass-fronted cabinet in the workshop's rear. Inside, nestled on a bed of faded silk, lay an unfinished watch unlike anything Olivia had seen in her grandfather's collection. Its case bore traces of both Chinese and Japanese design elements, the back etched with patterns that seemed to move in the workshop's shifting light.

"His last project here," Yamamoto explained, opening the cabinet with ceremonial care. "He called it 'Time's Conversation' – an attempt to create a movement that could track multiple temporal philosophies contemporaneously." The unfinished mechanism inside revealed glimpses of extraordinary complexity – wheels within wheels, each designed to move according to different cultural interpretations of time's passage.

Olivia's hands trembled slightly as she accepted the watch, its weight somehow both more and less than expected. Through her loupe, she could see her grandfather's distinctive touch in each hand-finished component, but there was something else too – an underlying geometry that echoed the mysterious timepiece she and Aarav had discovered.

"He never completed it," Yamamoto said softly. "Said some mechanisms need to wait for the right movement – or perhaps the right hands." His eyes held hers meaningfully, and Olivia felt the weight of inheritance settling into her bones like oil seeping into well-used gears.

That evening, in her hotel room, she wrote to Aarav:

I think I've been carrying a smaller version of him in my mind. Here, he feels larger, like time expanded him. The workshop remembers him differently – not as the scrupulous master maintaining tradition, but as an innovator who understood that time itself could be reinvented.

Yamamoto-san showed me an unfinished piece that shares design elements with the watch we found. It's as if they were having a dialogue across continents and decades, each watchmaker adding their own understanding to a shared vision of how time might be measured differently.

There's a photo of him here, laughing as he adjusts a movement that by all traditional standards shouldn't work. It reminds me of how you look when you're testing the boundaries of conventional chronometry – that same light in your eyes that suggests time itself might be more flexible than we've been taught to believe.

The workshop feels like a shrine to possibility – each drawer containing fragments of dreams that were too expansive for their era. Yamamoto-san says my grandfather used to speak of a future where time would be measured not just in minutes and hours, but in the unmarked places without current understanding and wonder.

She paused in her writing, watching Tokyo's lights create patterns on her ceiling like the trajectories of multiple possible futures. The city hummed below, its rhythms both foreign and strangely familiar, like a movement she'd known all along but was only now learning to read.

I'm beginning to understand why he spent so much time here, in this realm between traditions. There's a freedom in the margins of maps, in the blind spots among established measures. Perhaps that's what he and your grandmother were reaching for – not just a new way to track time's passage, but a way to honor its mysteries.

The unfinished watch sat on her desk, its presence as potent as a question waiting to be asked. In its incomplete state, it seemed to embody all the possibilities that lay between conception and creation, between one heart's rhythm and another's response.

Through her window, she could see a temple's ancient timekeeper lighting lanterns as he had every evening for decades, each flame marking time's passage not in seconds but in the eternal dance of light against darkness. She thought of Aarav's workshop, of how he moved through his days guided by both particularity and poetry, and felt the distance between them shift from geographical to something more complex – a measurement for which no conventional measurement or measurer would suffice.

Night pressed against Olivia's hotel window like time itself seeking entry. The room's dimensions felt both vast and intimate – fostering compressing solitude yet somehow being expanded by the weight of discovery. Through the floor-to-ceiling glass, Tokyo's lights performed their nightly choreography, each building's illumination timed to beats she was only beginning to understand.

A package from Aarav had arrived that morning, wrapped in brown paper that bore coffee stains and smelled faintly of osmanthus. She'd carried it with her throughout the day, its presence in her bag like a second heartbeat, waiting until this quiet hour when Tokyo's pulse slowed to a meditation.

Now, cross-legged on the too-large bed, she unwrapped it with the same intentional care she'd learned to use when handling delicate mechanisms. Inside, nestled in layers of tissue paper, lay a small brass component – a bridge from a pocket watch movement, its surface bearing the kind of patina that only decades of patient existence could create.

The letter accompanying it was written on paper that matched the pages of their shared margins, as if Aarav had torn it directly from their mutually told stories:

Olivia,

This bridge comes from a movement your grandfather once repaired in my grandmother's shop. She kept it all these years, saying some mechanisms carry memories in their metal. I found it in her personal effects, wrapped in a note that read: "For when time needs a crossing."

The workmanship is extraordinary – look at how the beveling catches light from any angle, how each screw hole is perfectly countersunk. But what fascinates me most is the slight modification to the traditional design. Your grandfather added a subtle curve to the upper flank, something that would be invisible to anyone not looking for it. My grandmother's notes say this adjustment allowed for a deeper engagement between wheels, creating a more intimate connection between components.

I've been studying our families' shared history through the artifacts they left behind. Each discovery feels like finding another piece of a movement we're only now learning to assemble. Their collaboration wasn't just about combining traditions – it was about creating something entirely new in the area without established methods.

The watch you described from Yamamoto-san's workshop sounds like it might accept this bridge. Perhaps that's what it's been waiting for all these years – the right connection between past and future, between here and there.

Olivia lifted the bridge to catch the city's light, watching how the brass seemed to come alive under Tokyo's electric glow. Through her grandfather's loupe, she could see what Aarav meant — the subtle alteration that would have gone unnoticed by anyone not trained to see beauty in microns and degrees.

She placed the component beside the unfinished watch from Yamamoto's shop, the two pieces seeming to speak to each other in a language of angles and intentions. With hands steadied by weeks of practice, she began to test the fit, feeling rather than hearing the moment when metal recognized metal.

The bridge slipped into place with the kind of register that feels like destiny — not the harsh click of forced alignment but the buoyant sigh of pieces finding their long-awaited home. The watch's movement, previously frozen in possibility, stirred beneath her fingers like a sleeping creature beginning to wake.

Her response to Aarav poured onto paper with the same unbridled naturalism:

The bridge fits as if it were made for this space — or perhaps this space was made for it. I'm reminded of something Yamamoto-san said about how every watchmaker leaves room in their work for future conversations. Did they know, our grandparents, that we would be the ones to continue their dialogue?

Tokyo at night feels like the inside of a timepiece — all these tiny lights moving in attentive patterns, each one keeping its own rhythm while contributing to a larger motion. From my window, I can see at least three different kinds of time being measured: the ancient temple clock marking the hours with incense, the digital displays counting down train arrivals, and the silent passage of stars behind the city's glow.

The watch seems different now, more purposeful. With the bridge in place, I can see how the wheels want to move — not in the regular circular motion we're used to, but in a complex pattern that reminds me of the way tea leaves swirl in a cup, finding their own path to meaning.

Your grandmother was right about mechanisms carrying memories. When I hold this piece, I can feel the echo of other hands that have shaped it, other eyes that have studied its curves. It's like finding a note in the margin of being itself, written in a language only watchmakers can read.

She reached for her grandfather's tool roll, selecting a fine brush to clean the newly united components. As she worked, Tokyo's lights painted her hands in shifting patterns, creating a dance of shadow and gleam that reminded her of the way Aarav's eyes caught the afternoon sun in his workshop.

A final note flowed from her pen:

Sometimes I think time isn't something that passes, but something that accumulates – like the patina on brass or the wisdom in margins. Each moment adds another layer to who we are, who we might become. This bridge, this watch, these letters we exchange – they're not just objects moving through time, but time itself taking physical form, waiting for the right hands to wind it back to life.

She sealed the letter in an envelope that still carried traces of coffee and clockwork, addressing it to the workshop where Aarav would receive it in a future she was still learning to measure. Outside, Tokyo's rhythm shifted as night deepened toward dawn, each pulse of light and shadow marking time not in minutes but in revelations.

The watch on her desk ticked softly, its newly bridged movement speaking in a voice that seemed to carry echoes of all the hands that had shaped it – her grandfather's rigor, Yamamoto's patience, Aarav's insight, and now her own emerging understanding of how time could be both measured and set free.

The temple garden unveiled itself in layers, each step down the moss-covered path revealing new dimensions of stillness. Olivia had found it by following one of her grandfather's hand-drawn maps, its margins filled with notes about a place where "time moves like water over stones – inevitable but never the same twice." The afternoon air swayed decorated with incense and the whispered conversations of wind through ancient maples and their youthful leaves.

She settled on a worn stone bench, its surface softened by centuries of contemplation. Before her, carefully raked gravel formed patterns that seemed to shift with each change of light, creating ripples that measured time in texture rather than increment. In the distance, wind chimes crafted from temple bronze marked the breeze's passage with tones that her ear recognized as perfectly pitched to F-sharp minor.

"Your grandfather used to sit there," a voice observed, its English carried on careful syllables. The temple historian emerged from the shadows like a figure stepping out of memory, his indigo robes the same shade as the sky between clouds. "He said it was the perfect spot to understand how the ancient timekeepers learned to measure what cannot be held."

Yoshida-sensei, as he introduced himself, settled beside her with the fluid grace of someone who had transcended conventional time. His age was impossible to guess – his face bore the kind of wisdom that came from observation rather than years. "You've brought his watch," he noted, nodding to where her grandfather's timepiece rested against her hip.

"And his questions," Olivia added, thinking of the unfinished mechanism waiting in her hotel room, its newly bridged movements suggesting possibilities she was only beginning to grasp.

"Ah," Yoshida smiled, the expression rippling across his face like stones dropped in still water. "Then perhaps you should see this." From his sleeve, he withdrew a wooden box worn smooth by countless hands. Inside, nestled on faded silk, lay what appeared to be a timing device unlike any Olivia had encountered in her studies.

"Wadokei," he explained, lifting the object with reverent care. "A Japanese time-keeper from the Edo period. It measures time according to the natural world rather than arbitrary divisions. The hours stretch and contract with the seasons, like a heart responding to joy or sorrow."

Olivia leaned closer, her watchmaker's eyes catching the incredible complexity of the mechanism. Unlike the rigid precision of European chronometers, this device seemed to embrace variation – its scales adjusting to mirror the organic rhythms of daylight and darkness.

"Your grandfather spent many hours studying this," Yoshida continued, his fingers tracing patterns on the device's case that echoed the gravel garden's design. "He was fascinated by how it reconciled the mechanical with the natural. Like your work with young Malhotra-san, yes?"

The question caught her off guard, though perhaps it shouldn't have. "You know about Aarav?"

"Time has its own way of connecting stories," he replied, his smile suggesting layers of understanding that transcended simple knowledge. "When your grandfather and Malhotra-san visited this garden, they spoke of creating timepieces that could honor multiple truths simultaneously. Their grandchildren working together now – this is not coincidence, but rhythm."

A gust of wind stirred the garden, sending maple leaves spinning like hands on countless invisible dials. Olivia thought of Aarav's latest letter, still crisp in her pocket, where he'd written about discovering similar conversations hidden in his grandmother's notebooks.

"I think I've been measuring time in the wrong way," she said, watching shadows trace paths across the gravel like indicator hands marking unmapped increments. "It's not about controlling it—it's about moving with it."

"Now you begin to understand what your grandfather discovered here," Yoshida nodded, returning the wadokei to its box with careful precision. "Time is not a river flowing one way, but an ocean moving in all directions at once. The mechanical clock is just one way of placing buoys on that ocean."

He rose, adjusting his robes with good grace. "There is a saying among temple timekeepers: 'The space between moments is where wisdom grows.' Your grandfather added his own observation: 'And where hearts learn to beat in harmony.'"

The afternoon light had begun to soften, taking on the quality of bloomed kinmokusei. Olivia withdrew her notebook, its pages now carrying traces of Tokyo's varied rhythms. As Yoshida departed as quietly as he had appeared, she began to write:

I think I've been measuring time in the wrong way. It's not about controlling it—it's about moving with it. The temple historian showed me a timekeeping device that changes with the seasons, like a heart adapting to love. I wonder if that's what our grandparents were trying to create – not just a new way of tracking time, but a way of honoring its mystery.

The garden here doesn't fight against time's passage but embraces it. Each falling leaf, each shift of shadow becomes part of its beauty. Even the gravel patterns, so carefully maintained, are designed to be altered by rain and wind. There's something profound in that acceptance – a recognition that permanence isn't about remaining unchanged, but about finding grace in transformation.

I carry your letters like coordinates mapping a journey I didn't know I was taking. Each one marks a point where understanding deepens, where distance becomes less about space and more about the beautiful complexity of timing itself.

The wind chimes sang their F-sharp minor song as darkness began its gradual claim on the garden. Olivia watched the shadows lengthen time to be visible, thinking of all the ways different cultures had tried to measure the immeasurable, harness the beyond-ethereal. Her grandfather's watch kept its steady rhythm against her hip, while somewhere across the Pacific, Aarav's hands were probably adjusting another movement to its own perfect tempo.

The mystery wasn't in how to control time, she realized, but in how to move with it gracefully – like the temple's ancient timekeepers, like leaves on water, like hearts learning to beat in complementary rhythm.

Its concentric circles of activity flowing with the precision of a well-maintained movement, Tokyo Station spread before Olivia like a mechanical mandala. She found a wooden bench worn smooth by decades of waiting passengers, its patina recording countless moments of transition and pause. The morning light filtered through the station's historic dome, creating patterns that tracked time in shadows across the marble floor.

Her notebook lay open on her lap, its pages catching the same light that had illuminated her grandfather's work all those years ago. The time difference between Tokyo and San Francisco stretched across the Pacific like a gear train, each hour marking not just distance but the strange elasticity of existing in multiple moments simultaneously.

She watched a station attendant adjust a massive clock mounted above the Shinkansen platforms – not by changing its hands, but by carefully cleaning its face with practiced reverence. The man's movements echoed the same care she'd seen in Aarav's hands when he polished watch crystals, that peculiar tenderness reserved for objects that measured life's passing.

"Time is different here," a voice observed in English tinged with the musicality of multiple languages. An elderly woman had settled beside her, her silver hair arranged in traditional style that spoke of hours measured by ritual rather than convenience. "You feel it too, yes? How it bends around the station like your gaze is through water?"

Olivia nodded, recognizing in the woman's eyes the same knowing gleam she'd seen in Yamamoto-san's workshop. "It's as if every time zone exists here at once," she replied, watching as travelers moved through their carefully choreographed passages, each keeping time to rhythms carried from distant shores.

"Ah," the woman smiled, her face creasing like a continually-added-to note from a lover. "You speak like someone who repairs time rather than just measuring it." Her gaze dropped to Olivia's hands, noting the calluses that marked her as a watchmaker's apprentice. "My husband used to say that train stations are where time admits its true nature – neither linear nor circular, but spiral, like your thoughts when you miss someone."

The observation settled into Olivia's consciousness like oil seeping into a movement's jewels. She thought of Aarav, probably just ending his day as hers began, their lives operating on keepers geared to different but complementary rotations. Reaching for her pen, she began to write:

It feels like we're on different timelines, but somehow that brings us closer. It's like leaving a note for someone to find in the future – each word carrying the weight of hours waiting to be discovered. The station attendant here cleans the clock faces with the same care you use on watch crystals, as if time itself might run more smoothly when treated with veneration.

The elderly woman watched her write, a knowing smile playing at the corners of her mouth. "When I was young," she offered, her voice carrying a hearth of well-forged memories, "we had a word for the time between sending a letter and receiving its reply. We called it 'kokoro no ma' – the space where hearts learn patience."

Through the station's vast windows, Olivia watched a pair of bullet trains arrive incisively simultaneously on parallel tracks, their synchronization a testament to Japan's mastery of measured moments. But between the tracks, in a small garden seemingly forgotten by the station's mechanical precision, an ancient cherry tree bloomed according to its own calendar, its petals marking time in natural rhythm.

I see an older couple on the platform, she continued writing, *holding hands as they wait for the 11:47 to Kyoto. They move together with the kind of synchronization that comes not from watching clocks but from decades of shared moments. It reminds me of how the watches in your shop all tick slightly differently but somehow create harmony.*

The elderly woman stood, adjusting her kimono with practiced grace. "Time differences," she said, her words carrying the weight of personal experience, "are not obstacles to be overcome, but spaces to be appreciated. Like the gap between rain clouds – without it, we would never see the sky."

As if in response to her words, the station's enormous clock began to chime the hour, its tone resonating through the building like ripples through water. Olivia felt each vibration in her chest, remembering how Aarav had taught her to diagnose a movement's health by its sound rather than its appearance.

The station master here sets his pocket watch to the atomic clock in Tokyo Tower, she wrote, *but also keeps a water clock in his office that measures time by ancient rhythms. When I asked him why, he said, 'Some moments need scientific precision, others need the wisdom of water.' I think of your workshop, how you balance digital timing machines with your grandmother's handmade tools, and I understand what he means.*

A child raced past, his laughter cutting through the station's measured rhythms like a melody through metronomic beats. His mother followed more slowly, her pace governed not by schedules but by the natural tempo of nurturing. Olivia watched them disappear into the crowd, thinking about how time moved differently for each person, each age, each type of love.

Perhaps that's what time difference is in reality, she continued her letter. *Each shrine, each intersection, each tiny workshop, each vending machine, each garden, each rail station in its own time. They don't apologize for moving slower or faster than the worlds around them, for being disparate yet concurrent. They simply remain true to their nature, like perfectly regulated movements following their own truth.*

I'm learning that accuracy and authenticity aren't the same thing, she wrote. *A watch can be precisely wrong if it's calibrated to the wrong time. I'd become accustomed to measured me by how well I synchronized with external rhythms.*

Maybe I'm not learning to keep better time, but learning to trust my own timing, your own, our own timing, other's own timing. Though our time difference is physical absence it's more akin to the gap between tick and tock – not an absence that harms, but the very thing that gives the sound its meaning.

As she sealed the letter, the morning light had shifted, painting the station in new patterns that seemed to suggest different interpretations for measuring the confluence of heart and mind, where the distinction dissolves to less sensible. The elderly woman had vanished into the flow of travelers, but her words remained, settling into

Olivia's thoughts like the slow accumulation of wisdom given only to watching, patient trees.

Through the station's historic arches, Tokyo continued its adept dance of past and future, each moment a negotiation between tradition and progress. Olivia touched her grandfather's watch, feeling its steady pulse against her palm, and understood that some distances couldn't be measured in hours or miles, but only in the enduring accumulation of shared understanding.

Existing in suspension, Narita International Airport and its massive forms measured departure and arrival in indifferent equality. Olivia sat at her gate, surrounded by the gentle chaos of transitions, her grandfather's watch marking time alongside the digital displays that counted down to takeoff. The morning fog had rolled in from Tokyo Bay, transforming the runways outside into suggestions rather than certainties, like memories still forming themselves into permanence.

Her final postcard to Aarav lay before her, its blank side awaiting words that seemed to resist conventional expression. The image showed the ancient temple clock she'd visited, photographed at the moment when morning light first touched its bronze face. Around her, travelers checked phones and watches with particular desire, but she found herself measuring this moment by heartbeats instead of minutes.

You were right, she wrote, the ink flowing like time itself across the paper, *Time is more than what we make of it. It's what makes us. In Tokyo, I learned to read it differently – not just in the precision of atomic clocks or the gentle arc of shadows across temple stones, but in the spaces between understanding.*

I carry back more questions than answers, but perhaps that's the point.

Our grandparents knew that some mechanisms require mystery to function properly. The watchmakers here have a term for it: 'ma' – the pregnant pause between moments, in which meaning grows without tampering.

The gate's digital display ticked down another minute, its red LEDs reflecting off the window where morning fought with fog. Olivia touched the bridge piece in her pocket, its brass warm from proximity to skin, like a secret keeping itself. The unfinished watch from Yamamoto's shop lay carefully wrapped in her carry-on, its newly completed movement speaking in harmonies she was only beginning to understand.

The temple historian showed me a timekeeping device that changes with the seasons, she continued writing, *and I couldn't help but think of your workshop, how each clock marks time slightly differently, creating a symphony rather than a single note. Perhaps that's what we're really repairing – not just the mechanisms themselves, but our understanding of what they're trying to tell us.*

A child's laughter cut through the terminal's measured rhythms, drawing her attention to a family saying goodbye. The scene struck her with peculiar force – not for its sorrow, but for its suggestion of time's circular nature. Every departure contained the seeds of return, every ending curled around itself to touch beginning.

Yamamoto-san said something just before I left that I'm still turning over in my mind, like a particularly complex gear train that reveals new patterns with each rotation. He said our grandparents weren't just watchmakers – they were time weavers, creating patterns from the threads of different traditions. Looking at their unfinished work now, I think I understand what he meant.

The fog outside had begun to lift, revealing glimpses of morning sun that caught the metal of waiting aircraft like blazing silhouettes. Olivia found herself thinking of time zones not as divisions but as connections – invisible lines drawing hearts together across distance and duration.

The watch we're working on, she wrote, her pen moving with new-found certainty, *isn't just a mechanism for measuring moments. It's a dialogue between past and future, between East and West, between hearts learning to beat in harmonious rhythm. Every time I adjust its balance, I feel like I'm tuning an instrument that plays notes we're only beginning to hear.*

The boarding call came in waves of language – Japanese, English, Mandarin – each announcement creating its own unique vibration through the waiting crowd. Olivia gathered her belongings with deliberate care, each movement measured not by the clock on the wall but by the weight of what she was carrying home.

Tomorrow for me is already your yesterday, she concluded, *and perhaps that's perfect. Like the ma between noise and not, between question and answer, between sending a letter and receiving its reply – these gaps aren't empty time but fertile ground where understanding takes root.*

As she sealed the postcard, her grandfather's watch chimed softly against her hip – not its usual sound, but something slightly different, as if it too had been transformed by crossing time zones and traditions. The fog had lifted completely now, revealing a horizon where sky met city in a line as fine as the edge of a well-crafted wheel.

The last passengers were boarding as Olivia added a final note in the margin of her travel journal, its pages now rich with the accumulated wisdom of borrowed time: *Some journeys measure distance not in miles but in understanding. Some mechanisms need to be discovered rather than invented. And some hearts learn to keep time not by counting seconds, but by trusting the space betwixt them.*

She joined the queue, each step forward marking not just progress toward home but toward a future that seemed to tick with new possibility. As the plane lifted into morning sky, Tokyo receded below like a dream resolving itself into memory, its countless timepieces marking moments that would continue to resonate long after she'd crossed the date line's invisible threshold.

Somewhere over the Pacific, tomorrow would become yesterday, time would fold back on itself like a möbius strip, and two hearts would continue their careful calibration across hours and horizons. The mystery, Olivia realized, wasn't in how time moved, but in how it moved us – like the steady sweep of a perfect escapement, like love finding its own perfect rhythm.

The sun caught her grandfather's watch one last time as Japan disappeared beneath clouds, its face reflecting light in a pattern that somehow suggested Aarav's asymmetrical smile. Time, she thought, wasn't something to be mastered but to be understood – not a river flowing one way, but an ocean moving in all directions at once, carrying hearts like well-crafted ships toward shores both known and still to be discovered.

CHAPTER 6

BROKEN MECHANISMS

The evening light filtered through the dusty windows of Aarav's shop, casting long shadows across the wooden workbench where countless timepieces had found renewed life. Tonight, however, the usual symphony of ticking clocks felt more like a funeral dirge, each mechanical heartbeat measuring out the growing distance between two people who had, until recently, found synchronicity in their shared silence.

Olivia hesitated at the threshold, her hand lingering on the brass doorknob. The bell above hadn't chimed—it hadn't needed to. She'd been coming here so often that her presence had become as natural as the scent of metal and clock oil that perpetually hung in the air. But tonight, something felt different. The distance between seconds seemed to stretch longer, more leaden.

Aarav hunched over his workbench, his usually precise movements lacking their characteristic grace. Before him lay the mysterious timepiece that had become their shared obsession, its gears exposed like an open wound. He didn't look up when she entered, though his shoulders tensed slightly—a detail that wouldn't have been noticeable to anyone who hadn't spent hours studying the subtle language of his body at work.

"I brought coffee," Olivia said, setting down a cup near his elbow. She'd switched from her usual hazelnut blend to a darker roast recently—a small act of rebellion against her own patterns that somehow felt significant. "Though it seems like you might need something stronger."

Aarav's hands stilled over the timepiece. In the wan light, she noticed the shadows under his eyes, the slight tremor in his usually steady fingers. "Thanks," he muttered, but didn't reach for the cup. Instead, he picked up his loupe, examining a gear with unnecessary intensity.

"That bad, huh?" Olivia leaned against the workbench, close enough to feel the warmth radiating from his body, far enough to respect the invisible barrier he'd erected.

"My father called." The words fell between them like dropped tools. "He has a contact at Microsoft. Says there's a position opening up in their Mumbai division."

The implications hung in the air, heavy as storm clouds. Olivia watched as Aarav's fingers moved over the timepiece's mechanism, his movements growing increasingly aggressive. "And what did you tell him?"

"That I'd think about it." He adjusted a gear with more force than necessary. "He says I'm wasting my education here. That this—" he gestured around the shop, at the countless timepieces that lined the walls like silent witnesses, "—is a relic. That I'm holding onto something that doesn't exist anymore."

"And you believe him?" The words came out sharper than intended, carrying the edge of her own recent wounds—her mother's casual dismissal of her grandfather's legacy, the impending sale of their family home.

"I believe that I'm tired of disappointing people." The gear slipped under his tools, catching wrong. A small snap echoed through the shop, followed by Aarav's sharp intake of breath.

"Let me see," Olivia reached for the timepiece, but Aarav pulled it away.

"I've got it." His voice had grown cold, professional. "Maybe you should go home, Olivia. It's getting late."

"So that's it? You're just going to push everyone away because your father thinks he knows what's best for you?" She stood straight, anger and hurt warring in her chest. "You're not the only one dealing with family expectations, Aarav. But at least you have the choice to keep what matters."

"Choice?" He laughed, a sound devoid of humor. "What choice? Between disappointing my family and watching this business slowly die? Between holding onto the past and actually building a future?" He finally looked up at her, his dark eyes intense. "Not all of us have the luxury of living in between moments, Olivia. Some of us have to exist in real time."

The words struck like physical blows, each one finding the soft spaces between her carefully constructed defenses. She thought of her phone-free existence, of her grandfather's memoir, of all the ways she'd been trying to find meaning absent timing. Had it all been just another form of running away?

"Real time?" Her voice trembled slightly. "Is that what you think this is about? Time management? This shop isn't just about fixing watches, Aarav. It's about understanding that some things are worth preserving, even if they don't fit into your father's definition of progress."

He turned back to the timepiece, his silence more devastating than any response could have been. In the gathering darkness, the distance between them seemed to expand, becoming its own kind of time zone.

Olivia waited for a moment longer, hoping he might say something, anything. But there was only the sound of his tools against metal, the steady ticking of the clocks around them, each second carrying her further from the connection they'd built.

The bell above the shop door chimed weakly as Mrs. Patel from the Indian restaurant next door poked her head in, the scent of cardamom and clove following her like a fragrant shadow. Her usual cheerful expression faltered at the tension crackling between Olivia and Aarav.

"Bad time?" she asked, her shrewd eyes taking in the scattered tools, Aarav's rigid posture, Olivia's barely contained emotions.

"No, I was just leaving," Olivia said quickly, gathering her bag. She could feel Aarav's gaze burning into her back but refused to turn around.

"Shame," Mrs. Patel clicked her tongue. "I brought samosas. Fresh from the kitchen. And news about that developer who's been sniffing around the block." She set down a paper bag that immediately filled the shop with its tempting aroma. "Three more businesses sold this month. That fancy tech startup is offering double market value."

Aarav's hands tightened on his tools. "The Bangalore-based one?"

"The very same. Same company your father consults for, no?" Mrs. Patel's innocent tone carried a weight that made Olivia pause at the door. "Such timing, wouldn't you say?"

The revelation hung in the air like the dust in the shop's porous light. Suddenly, Aarav's father's insistence on the Mumbai position took on a different color. Olivia turned back, catching Aarav's expression as understanding dawned.

"He tends to move like this," Aarav said quietly. "He likes to help without telling me all the information. I know it's his love but... I really wish I had his trust."

"You want to talk about it? Make a plan of some kind?" Olivia searched, with hope he might open up.

"No." he replied a little too quickly.

"You know where to find me," she said finally, "when you're ready to talk about what's really breaking." She turned and walked out, the shop's bell finally chiming, marking her departure like a clock striking midnight.

Behind her, in the growing darkness, Aarav stared at the damaged timepiece, its broken gear a perfect metaphor for the evening. He reached for the coffee she'd brought, now grown cold, and took a sip. It was darker than usual, bitter. Something about that detail made his throat tighten unexpectedly.

Outside, the street lamps were beginning to flicker on, their light catching the first few drops of an approaching storm. Time continued its relentless march forward, heedless of the hearts trying to find their rhythm in its wake.

***

The house that had sheltered three generations of Olivia's family now stood half-emptied, its rooms echoing with the hollow sounds of approaching departure. Cardboard boxes lined the hallways like sentries, each labeled in her mother's painstaking hand: "Donate/捐," "Storage/存," "Keep/留." The familiar scent of lemon wood polish couldn't quite mask the musty smell of old papers and memories being disturbed after years of quiet rest.

"Olivia? Is that you?" Her mother's voice drifted down from upstairs, carrying that particular tone of forced cheerfulness that had become her trademark since the divorce. "I'm in Wàigōng's study."

Olivia paused at the bottom of the stairs, her hand resting on the bannister where, decades ago, her grandfather had carved tiny notches marking her growth. Each groove told a story—the summer she shot up three inches, the year she'd stopped growing entirely. She traced one with her thumb before ascending, her footsteps creating hollow echoes against the wooden stairs.

Helen Chén stood in the middle of what had once been an organized chaos of horological tools and manuscripts, now reduced to neat stacks and labeled containers. She wore one of her real estate showing outfits—a cream blazer and pencil skirt that seemed desperately out of place among the dust and cardboard—and held a crystal paperweight in her manicured hands.

"I thought we could start with the bookshelves," she said, not looking up from the paperweight. "The estate sale people are coming on Thursday, and we need to decide what's worth keeping."

"Worth keeping," Olivia echoed, the words tasting bitter on her tongue. She moved to the window, where her grandfather's workbench still stood untouched. Afternoon light filtered through the dusty glass, creating patterns that reminded her of the way light played across Aarav's workbench. Her throat shortened uncomfortably.

"Honey, we've talked about this." Helen set down the paperweight with a soft clink. "The market's hot right now, and this house is too big for one person. Besides," she added, her voice taking on that careful, therapeutic tone she'd adopted since starting dating her previous therapist, "sometimes letting go is the healthiest choice we can make."

Olivia ran her fingers along the workbench's scarred surface, remembering countless hours spent watching her grandfather work, his hands steady and sure as they brought dead timepieces back to life. "Is that what you told yourself when Dad left?"

The silence that followed was sharp enough to cut.

"That's not fair." Helen's voice had lost its practiced smoothness. "Your father made his choices. I'm making mine. And frankly, Olivia, I'm worried about you making any at all."

"What's that supposed to mean?"

"Look at you." Helen gestured vaguely. "You quit your job, you threw away your phone, you spend all your time in that little watch shop downtown... It's like you're trying to freeze time instead of moving forward."

"I'm not freezing anything," Olivia protested, though the words felt hollow even to her. Hadn't Aarav accused her of something similar just hours ago? "I'm just trying to figure things out."

"Figure what out? How to hide from real life? You're twenty-eight, Olivia. No career direction, no relationship prospects—"

"I have prospects," Olivia cut in, then immediately regretted it as her mother's eyebrows rose with interest.

"Oh? Would these prospects have anything to do with that young man at the watch shop?" Helen moved closer, her heels clicking against the hardwood floor. "The one whose family used to compete with your grandfather?"

Olivia turned back to the workbench, opening drawers at random to avoid her mother's knowing gaze. "Aarav is just teaching me about watch repair. It's not—" She stopped abruptly as her hand brushed against something in the bottom drawer. Pulling it out, she found herself holding a photograph, its edges worn soft with age.

In the image, her grandfather stood at his workbench, much younger than she'd ever known him. But it was the figure in the background that caught her eye—a young woman in a sari, her dark eyes bright with something that might have been challenge or might have been amusement. She was beautiful in a fierce way, her presence commanding even in the faded photograph.

Olivia turned it over. On the back, in her grandfather's precise handwriting: "Some mechanisms only work when they are together."

"What's that?" Helen asked, moving to look over her shoulder.

"Nothing," Olivia said quickly, slipping the photo into her pocket. "Just an old receipt." She turned to face her mother, suddenly feeling very tired. "Look, I know you're worried about me. But I'm not hiding from life. Maybe I'm just trying to understand it better."

Helen's face softened slightly. "Life isn't a watch, sweetheart. You can't take it apart and put it back together until it works the way you want it to."

"No," Olivia agreed, thinking of Aarav's frustrated movements over the broken timepiece, of her own attempts to piece together the fragments of her life. "But maybe understanding how things break is the first step to fixing them."

Her mother sighed, reaching out to touch her cheek in a rare gesture of affection. "Just don't forget that some things are meant to change. That's how we grow."

Olivia leaned into the touch for a moment before pulling away.

"I should go. I have some writing to do." She headed for the door, then paused. "Mom? That woman in Dad's old photos—the ones from before you met. Did you ever feel like you were competing with a ghost?"

Helen was quiet for a long moment, her hand resting on a box labeled "Photos/照片 - 1980-1995." Finally, she said, "The hardest part wasn't competing with the ghost. It was realizing that sometimes, no matter how much you love someone, you can't make them choose you over their past."

Olivia nodded, her grandfather's photograph burning in her pocket like a secret. As she left the study, she could hear her mother beginning to sort through more boxes, the soft sounds of the past being categorized and contained floating down the hallway behind her.

The photograph's message echoed in her mind: "Some mechanisms only work when they are together." She thought of Aarav, of the growing distance between them, of all the things that seemed to be breaking apart in her life. Perhaps it wasn't about choosing between past and future at all. Perhaps it was about finding a way to make them work together, like the intricate gears of a well-crafted timepiece.

But first, she had to understand what was broken.

Night had settled over Olivia's apartment like a heavy blanket, bringing with it the kind of silence that makes one's thoughts sound too loud. The refrigerator hummed its monotonous song—a sound she'd never noticed when her phone used to fill every quiet moment with its digital chatter. Now, each small noise seemed to carry weight: the occasional car passing outside, the settling of old pipes, the soft tick of the wall clock she'd rescued from her grandfather's study.

She sat at her small writing desk, a cup of chamomile tea growing cold beside her. The steam had long since stopped rising, much like her ability to find the right words for the letter she'd been trying to write to Aarav for the past hour. The blank page stared back at her, its emptiness a mirror to the hollow feeling in her chest.

Her grandfather's leather-bound memoir lay open before her, its pages worn soft with handling. She'd found herself returning to it more frequently lately, as if his words might offer some cipher for decoding her own tangled emotions. Tonight, she'd discovered a chapter she hadn't noticed before, tucked between pages that had stuck together. The paper was different here—older, more delicate—as if these thoughts had been added years after the original writing.

There is a peculiar agony, she read, *in watching passion calcify into principle. Today, I argued with N. again about the future of our craft. She sees automation as evolution; I see it as erosion. We've had this argument so many times that the words have become ritual, each of us playing our assigned parts with stubborn precision.*

Olivia paused, her finger tracing the letter N. Could it be? The woman in the photograph—Aarav's grandmother—her name would have been Neha. The timing fit.

But tonight, as I watched her leave the workshop, her shoulders rigid with righteous anger, I realized something that thirty years of watchmaking never taught me: sometimes the most precise mechanisms are the ones most likely to break. One gear, set slightly too tight against another, doesn't allow for the natural give and take that keeps time flowing smoothly.

She reached for her tea, finding it cold but drinking anyway. The bitter taste matched her mood.

Perhaps that is why N. and I could never find our rhythm, despite—or because of—our shared passion. We were too similar, too unwilling to allow for imperfection in our pursuit of excellence. Now, looking back, I wonder if what we called principle was really just fear dressed in finer clothes. Fear of change, yes, but more than that: fear of admitting that neither of us held the complete truth.

Olivia set down the cup and pulled out a fresh sheet of paper.

Dear Aarav, she wrote, then stopped. How could she explain that she understood his struggle because she was living it too? That maybe they were both so afraid of breaking what they had that they were forcing it to be more perfect than any human connection could be?

The letter took shape slowly, in fits and starts:

I found a photograph today, of our grandparents. They're both so young, caught in a moment before their passion for precision turned them into rivals. There's something in the way they're looking at each other—not directly, but aware, so aware of each other's presence. It made me think about us, about how we're letting our fear of imperfection create the very breaks we're trying to avoid.

She paused, pen hovering over the paper. The words felt too raw, too honest. Would he even want to hear them? The memory of his cold dismissal at the shop made her hesitate.

Maybe that's what scares me most about watching you consider leaving the shop, she continued, the words flowing now despite her doubts. *Not that you might choose a different path, but that you might choose it for the wrong reasons. That like our grandparents, we might let our principles become prison cells, keeping us safe but separate.*

A car passed outside, its headlights sweeping across her walls like searching fingers. In that brief illumination, she caught sight of her reflection in the window—tired eyes, hair slightly disheveled, looking very much like someone in the middle of understanding something important but difficult.

But I'm learning, she wrote, *that maybe to measure from one second to the next isn't about perfect timing. Maybe it's about the courage to exist in the*

114

uncertain passing, to let ourselves be works in progress rather than finished pieces.

She stopped there, the rest of the page remaining blank. The letter felt unfinished, but then again, maybe that was the point. Some things needed undisturbed but checked time to develop, like photographs in a darkroom, like feelings in the quiet hours of night.

Olivia folded the letter carefully and placed it in her desk drawer, next to the photograph. Whether she would ever give it to him remained uncertain, but the act of writing it had clarified something for her: sometimes the most important connections were the ones that happened in the silent union of what we say and what we mean.

The wall clock chimed softly, marking another hour's passage. She looked at the drawer containing the letter, then at her grandfather's memoir, still open to the chapter about S. Outside, the city had grown quiet, as if holding its breath, waiting to see what the next moment might bring.

In that stillness, Olivia realized that maybe her grandfather had left her more than just his tools and his writings. He'd left her a map for navigating the delicate machinery of human hearts—not by showing her how to avoid mistakes, but by revealing how even broken connections could lead to understanding, if only we were brave enough to examine the damage without flinching away.

She closed the memoir gently, but left the drawer with the letter slightly ajar—a small act of hope, a door left open to possibility.

The following day arrived wrapped in an unusual silence. Aarav's shop, typically alive with the synchronized symphony of dozens of timepieces, seemed to hold its breath. Several clocks had stopped overnight, their arrested hands casting accusatory shadows across the walls. Even the afternoon light, filtering through dust-speckled windows, felt different—thinner somehow, as if the very air had grown weary of carrying so much unspoken weight.

Olivia stood outside longer than necessary, the photograph burning in her pocket like a small sun. Through the window, she could see Aarav's silhouette, his movements lacking their usual fluid grace. The bell above the door remained stubbornly silent as she entered—it had finally broken yesterday, she realized. Another small death in a day full of them.

"I found something," she said by way of greeting, her voice sounding too loud in the muted space. Aarav didn't look up from his workbench, but his hands stilled over the disassembled timepiece. The same one from yesterday, she noted. Still broken.

When he didn't respond, she approached slowly, each step measured like the ticking of a clock. The photograph felt heavy as she placed it on the workbench, carefully avoiding the scattered gears and tools. Its aged surface caught the light, revealing two young faces frozen in a moment of unguarded connection.

"They weren't always rivals," she said softly, watching as Aarav's eyes finally lifted to study the image. His expression shifted minutely—surprise, recognition, something else she couldn't quite name.

"Where did you find this?" His voice was hoarse, as if he hadn't used it all day.

"My grandfather's study. We're packing it up." She swallowed hard against the admission. "There's something written on the back."

Aarav turned the photograph over with watchmaker's precision, his thumb tracing the faded inscription. *Some mechanisms only work when they are together.* She watched his face carefully, searching for some sign that the words meant as much to him as they had to her.

But when he looked up, his eyes were distant, guarded. "Thank you," he said formally, pushing the photograph back toward her. "But I should get back to work."

"Aarav—"

"The timepiece isn't going to fix itself." He reached for his tools, but his hands weren't steady. The tremor was subtle—anyone else might have missed it—but to Olivia, who had spent innumerable hours watching those hands work their magic on broken things, it was like watching a master pianist lose their touch.

"Let me help," she offered, moving closer. The familiar scent of clock oil and metal filings wrapped around her, achingly familiar. "We can figure it out together."

For a moment, something flickered in his expression—a crack in the careful mask he'd constructed. Then he nodded, shifting slightly to make room for her at the workbench.

They worked in silence, passing tools back and forth with the unconscious synchronicity of long practice. The timepiece lay between them like an open heart, its gears and springs exposed to their careful ministrations. Olivia found herself holding her breath as Aarav attempted to fit a particularly delicate gear into place.

His hands shook again. The gear slipped.

A sharp snap cut through the silence, the sound of metal giving way under too much pressure. They both froze, staring at the broken spring that had just skittered across the workbench.

"Some things can't be fixed." Aarav's voice was barely a whisper, but in the quiet shop, it carried the weight of a shout.

Olivia felt something inside her crack. "That's not true. You're just afraid to try."

"Afraid?" He laughed, a harsh sound that didn't suit him at

all. "I've been trying my whole life. Trying to keep this shop alive. Trying to honor tradition while everyone around me sprints toward the future. Trying to—" He cut himself off, turning away.

"To what?" She pressed, even as part of her warned against pushing too hard. "To feel something real? To connect with someone who understands?"

"You don't understand." He stood abruptly, his chair scraping against the wooden floor. "You're playing at this, Olivia. Experimenting with a simpler life, reading your grandfather's philosophical musings about time and connection. But for me? This is everything. And I'm watching it slip away, piece by piece."

The words hit her with unbridled force, each one finding its mark with devastating accuracy. She stood too, anger and hurt warring in her chest. "Playing at this? You think that's what I'm doing?"

"Aren't you? You'll go back to your phone, your corporate job, your comfortable life. But this—" he gestured around the shop, at the silent clocks, the broken timepiece, the curated chaos amid one to the other, "—this is my life. And I can't afford to pretend anymore."

Olivia stared at him, really looked at him, seeing the shadows under his eyes, the tension in his jaw, the way he held himself like a spring wound too tight. In that moment, she understood something that all her grandfather's writings hadn't quite prepared her for: perhaps love wasn't enough to bridge the gap between two people's fears.

Without a word, she turned and walked out of the shop. The bell didn't ring to mark her departure—it didn't need to. The silence said everything.

Behind her, Aarav stood motionless at his workbench, staring at the broken timepiece and the photograph that still lay beside it. In the fading light, the young faces of their grandparents seemed to watch him with a mixture of understanding and reproach. He picked up the photograph again, really looking at it this time.

There was something in their expressions he hadn't noticed before—a kind of tension, yes, but also a profound connection. Despite their rivalry, despite their differences, they had shared something essential: a deep understanding of how delicate the balance was between preservation and progress, between holding on and letting go.

The realization came too late. Outside, the sound of Olivia's footsteps had already faded into the gathering dusk, leaving him alone with his broken mechanisms and the stale air of the breaking sentences he wished he could take back.

Above him, a single clock suddenly resumed its ticking, the sound echoing through the empty shop like a reminder that time, regardless of human drama, keeps moving forward. Whether we choose to move with it—that's the choice we all have to make.

The park near Olivia's apartment had always been a refuge of sorts, a pocket of green stillness amid the city's relentless motion. Now, as she sat on a weathered bench beneath a canopy of maple leaves, the overcast sky seemed to mirror her internal landscape— heavy with unspoken words, threatening to collapse at any moment.

In the distance, children played on the aging carousel, their laughter carrying across the autumn air in sharp contrast to her mood. The sound reminded her of herself at that age, spinning on her grandfather's work stool while he explained the delicate art of timing. *Life*, he'd said, adjusting his loupe with careful precision, *is like a perfect escapement. The trick isn't in avoiding the stops and starts, but in finding the rhythm within them.*

She pulled her grandfather's memoir from her bag, its leather cover soft and worn beneath her fingers. The passage about his argument with Sana seemed to find her without effort now, as if the book had memorized its own wounds:

The greatest irony of watchmaking is that we spend our lives pursuing perfect time, yet perfection itself is the enemy of true connection. A watch that keeps perfect time is rigid, unyielding. It cannot adapt to the natural variations in the world around it. Perhaps that is why N. and I could never find our way forward—we were too committed to our own versions of perfection to allow for the beautiful imperfection of human connection.

A child's cry of delight pierced the air, followed by a parent's answering laugh. Olivia looked up to see a young father teaching his daughter to ride a bike, his hands hovering protectively near her shoulders as she wobbled forward. The scene blurred unexpectedly, and she realized she was crying.

"Damn it, Aarav," she whispered to the empty air beside her. How had they managed to break something that had barely begun? She thought of his trembling hands over the timepiece, of the way his voice had cracked when he said, *"Some things can't be fixed."* Had he been talking about the watch at all?

Meanwhile, across town in his dimly lit shop, Aarav sat alone at his workbench, staring at the photograph she'd left behind. His grandmother's fierce expression seemed to challenge him across the decades. He remembered her stories about the rivalry with Olivia's grandfather—how it had started as respect, grown into competition, and finally calcified into something that kept them both from moving forward.

Never let pride make your choices for you, she'd told him once, near the end. *It's the heaviest weight a heart can carry.*

He picked up the broken spring from the timepiece, turning it over in his hands. The metal had snapped cleanly—too much pressure applied too quickly. Magnetically, his mind snapped to the thought of Olivia and the words he'd said.

Back in the park, Olivia ran her fingers over another passage in the memoir, one she'd read so many times the pages were starting to thin:

Time is not a linear path but a series of moments that echo and repeat, like the oscillations of a balance wheel. Each generation faces the same fundamental choice: to remain fixed in place, perfectly correct and perfectly alone, or to risk the messiness of real connection. The trick lies in understanding that true precision comes not from rigidity, but from finding the perfect amount of give.

The sky finally released its held breath, fat droplets of rain beginning to fall. Parents called their children in from play, the carousel slowed to a stop, and still Olivia sat, letting the rain soak into her clothes, her hair, the pages of the memoir. She thought about patterns—how her grandfather and Sana had let their shared passion become a wall between them, how she and Aarav were dancing around the same possibility of loss.

But perhaps there was another way to read their story. Perhaps the photograph, with its captured moment of connection before rivalry took hold, wasn't just a record of what was lost but a map to what could still be found. The inscription on its back seemed to whisper a truth that went beyond mere mechanics: *Some mechanisms only work when they are together.*

She closed the memoir carefully, protecting it from the strengthening rain. The answer wasn't in its pages—not really. The answer was in the interludes between what was written, in the courage to acknowledge that sometimes the most precise calculations couldn't account for the wild variables of the heart.

Standing, she took one last look at the empty playground, the abandoned carousel, the rain-slick paths leading in all directions. She thought of Aarav's hands, steady when working with the most delicate mechanisms but trembling when faced with the possibility of real connection. She thought of her own fears, masked as principles, her need for perfect timing preventing her from taking any real risks.

It was time, she realized, to stop waiting for the perfect moment. Time to understand that sometimes the intervals betwixt the perceived, right time and all other wrong times was where the real story lived—not in the precise tick of ordered time, but in the messy, beautiful gaps where life actually happened.

The rain continued to fall, each drop marking another moment passing, another chance to choose differently. Around her, the park slowly emptied, but the rhythm of the world continued—imperfect, unpredictable, and all the more precious for being so.

The day had bled into evening by the time Olivia found herself back at Aarav's shop. The streetlights had just begun their nightly vigil, casting pools of amber light that seemed to pulse with the rhythm of her heartbeat. Through the window, she could see him working by a single lamp, its glow creating a halo around his hunched form. The scene reminded her of a Hopper painting—all shadows and solitude, beautiful in its loneliness.

The door was still unlocked. She hesitated, her hand on the handle, feeling the cool brass beneath her rain-dampened fingers. The broken bell above hung silent, a mute witness to her return. Inside, the usual chorus of ticking clocks had diminished to a sparse handful of survivors, their synchronized rhythm now more like a chamber ensemble than a full orchestra.

Aarav didn't look up when she entered, but his hands stilled over the workbench. The broken timepiece lay between them like a casualty of war, its gears scattered across the wooden surface in a constellation of brass and steel.

"I overreacted," she said into the silence. The words felt inadequate, but they were a beginning.

He remained still for a long moment, then set down his tools with deliberate care. "So did I." His voice was rough, as if he'd spent the hours since she'd left engaged in an argument with himself.

Olivia moved closer, noting the way the lamplight caught the edges of the photograph, still lying where she'd left it. In the dim light, their grandparents' faces seemed to hold different expressions—less challenging, more wistful.

"Do you think we could—" she gestured at the broken timepiece, letting the question hang unfinished in the air between them.

Aarav finally looked up, his dark eyes carrying shadows she hadn't seen before. "Start again?"

"Start anywhere," she amended, reaching for a spare stool. "Even if it's from broken pieces."

He watched her settle beside him, close enough that their elbows nearly touched. The familiar scent of clock oil and metal shavings mingled with the lingering petrichor she'd brought in from outside. "The spring's completely shattered," he said, picking up the broken piece. "We'd need to fabricate a new one."

"Then that's where we start." She pulled her grandfather's memoir from her bag, its pages still damp from the rain. "He wrote about something similar once—about finding the right tension. Not too rigid, not too loose."

"Like relationships," Aarav murmured, almost to himself. Then, more clearly: "I've been thinking about what you said. About playing it safe."

"And I've been thinking about what you said about pretending." She opened her tool roll, selecting a fine-gauge wire. "Maybe we were both right. And both wrong."

They worked in companionable silence for a while, their movements tentative but synchronous. Olivia shaped the wire while Aarav calculated the precise tension needed. The lamp threw their shadows against the wall, where they merged and separated like dancers learning a new rhythm.

"My father called again," Aarav said suddenly, his hands steady as he tested the new spring's flexibility. "I told him I needed more time."

Olivia nodded, understanding what it must have cost him. "Time seems to be the one thing we're all running out of," she said, thinking of her mother's empty house, of stopped clocks, of moments that couldn't be recaptured.

"Or maybe," he replied, fitting the spring into place with surgical precision, "we just need to learn how to measure it differently."

The timepiece lay between them, still broken but somehow more honest in its disarray. They had named its wounds now, acknowledged its fractures. It was a start.

Outside, the city continued its nocturnal transformation. The shop windows reflected their bent heads, the lamp's glow creating a small universe of shared focus and possibility. A clock on the far wall suddenly chimed the hour, making them both jump slightly.

"It might not work," Aarav said softly, and they both knew he wasn't just talking about the timepiece.

"No," Olivia agreed, reaching for her loupe. "But maybe that's not the point."

He looked at her then, really looked at her, as if seeing past the careful walls they'd both constructed. "What is the point?"

She thought of the photograph's inscription, of her grandfather's words about imperfection, of all the moments that had led them here. "Maybe it's about finding the courage to try anyway."

The new spring gleamed under the lamplight, waiting to be tested. Around them, the few remaining working clocks kept their steady rhythm, marking out the ostensibly polar uncertainty and hope between broken and healing, between ending and continuing.

They bent together over the workbench, their shadows merging once more on the wall behind them. The night stretched ahead, full of possibilities and pitfalls, but for now, in the warm circle of lamplight, they had found something worth preserving—a fragile peace, a tentative understanding, a chance to rebuild what had been fragmented.

Nevertheless, outside, the city's pulse continued, comfortably indifferent to the small dramas playing out within its bounds. But in Aarav's shop, time seemed to move differently, marking itself not in seconds or minutes, but in the careful exchange of tools, in shared breaths, in the delicate work of two people learning to trust the breaks between certainties.

The broken timepiece waited patiently for their attention, its scattered parts like a map to somewhere new, somewhere they might find their way to together—if only they were brave enough to follow where it led.

CHAPTER 7

BETWEEN HANDS AND STARS

The morning light filtered through the shop windows in thin, dusty beams, each one illuminating countless specks of brass and steel that hung suspended in the air like stars in a mechanical observatory. A heap of mail sat in a neat stack on his workbench, mostly bills and catalogs, their mundane presence a stark contrast to the delicate timepieces awaiting his attention. But amid the everyday correspondence, an envelope caught his eye—cream-colored paper bearing his aunt's distinctive Devanagari script, the characters flowing across the surface like lava over stones.

His hands, usually so steady when manipulating his watches, shook slightly as he opened the letter. The paper carried the faint scent of incense and cardamom, instantly transporting him to childhood summers spent in Pune, where time moved to the rhythm of temple bells rather than mechanical ticks.

My sweet nephew Aarav, the letter began in Marathi, the words carrying the weight of mountains in their careful strokes. *The family home misses you. Each room holds memories of your father's childhood, your grandmother's teachings, the legacy that flows through your veins like the sacred waters of the Mutha River. The family speaks of you often, wondering when you will return to walk these halls again.*

He settled onto his workbench stool, the letter continually trembling in his hands. Around him, the shop's timepieces continued their steady march forward, each tick a reminder of moments not spent in another home.

Your cousin Avinash has taken over your uncle's software company, his aunt continued, her words carrying a gentle but unmistakable pressure. *He asks after you, wondering why someone of your intelligence chooses to remain bound to the past when the future offers such promise. But I remember how your grandmother spoke of you—her chosen heir, the one who understood that some traditions carry wisdom modern minds have forgotten.*

Aarav's eyes drifted to the photograph of his grandmother that hung above his workbench. Her stern expression belied the warmth he remembered, the way her eyes would crinkle at the corners when she approved of his work. In her final practicing years, she'd spent hours teaching him not just the mechanics of watchmaking, but its philosophy—the delicate balance between preservation and progress that had defined her life's work.

His aunt proceeded: *I have enclosed something I think you should see—a verse from the Amrutānubhava that your grandmother marked in her personal copy: "Do not see duality in the world. What you fight and what you embrace are but two hands of the same body."*

His fingers traced the quoted words, feeling the slight indentations in the paper where his aunt's pen had pressed with particular emphasis. The morning light caught the metal shavings scattered across his workbench. Each shaving represented a moment of careful work, of choosing this path despite the growing pressure to abandon it. One in particular caught the light in his eye – momentarily illuminating and blinding him.

His aunt continued, carrying echoes of conversations he'd had countless times before: *The world changes, dear nephew, but change need not mean abandonment. Your grandmother understands this well—how to hold the past and future in perfect balance, much like bereavement whilst maintaining quotidian joy. Perhaps it is time for you to find your own balance, to understand that honoring tradition doesn't mean refusing to grow.*

A customer's bell chimed in the front of the shop, its clear tone cutting through his reverie. Aarav carefully refolded the letter, tucking it into his waistcoat pocket where it pushed against his heart like a question waiting to be answered. As he rose to greet whoever had entered, his eyes fell on the mysterious timepiece he and Olivia had been studying—its unconventional mechanism a testament to the possibility of bridging seemingly opposing forces.

The morning light had strengthened, burning away the last traces of dawn's uncertainty. Yet Aarav felt the weight of his aunt's words, of his grandmother's marked passage, settling into his bones like fine metal dust after a day's work.

He touched the letter through his pocket once more, feeling the crispness of its edges, the solidity of its presence. Then, squaring his shoulders, he moved toward the shop's front room, carrying with him all the questions stirred up by ink and memory, by duty and desire, by the ever-present tension upon him.

The clocks ticked on, their steady rhythm a reminder that even in moments of deepest doubt, time moved forever forward, carrying all things—tradition and progress, past and future, resistance and surrender—in its relentless flow.

Evening had settled over the city like a silk shawl, transforming the sharp edges of Aarav's apartment into something softer, more contemplative. The space reflected his distinctly dual nature—minimalist furniture arranged with mathematical precision, yet the walls held frames of intricate Warli art his mother had insisted he take when he'd moved out. The traditional tribal figures danced in eternal circles, their simple forms telling complex stories of community and continuity.

His aunt's letter lay open on the kitchen counter, its presence drawing his eyes even as he moved through his evening routine. The familiar scents of cardamom and clove filled the air as he prepared his evening chai, following the precise measurements his grandmother had instilled in him since childhood. Three-quarters of a cup water, one-quarter milk, five green cardamom pods crushed just so, two cloves, and tea measured to the exact gram—a recipe that was equal parts science and ceremony.

The phone felt heavy in his hand as he dialed, each number a deliberate choice he could no longer postpone. His mother answered on the second ring, her voice carrying across thousands of miles with characteristic clarity.

"Aarav." Just his name, but laden with everything that remained unsaid between them. She continued in Marathi, their mother tongue flowing between them like a river finding its ancient course. "I was beginning to think you'd forgotten how to use a phone."

"Namaskāra, Aai," he replied, the familiar greeting carrying the weight of ritual. "I received Masi's letter."

A pause, filled with the soft bubbling of his chai reaching its precise temperature. "Ah," his mother said, and in that single syllable he heard decades of careful navigation between duty and desire. "And what did you think of the Amrutānubhava passage?"

Aarav lifted the pot from the heat with practiced timing, watching the deep amber liquid swirl as he poured it through a strainer. "I think Masi isn't subtle in her messaging."

"Since when has your Masi ever been subtle?" His mother's laugh carried a hint of steel beneath its warmth. "But she isn't wrong, Aarav. You cannot keep straddling two worlds forever. Even a perfectly balanced wheel must eventually turn in one direction or another."

The chai's steam rose in delicate spirals, reminding him of the mechanisms he spent his days repairing—each component affecting the others in ways both subtle and intrinsically. "Is that what father did? Chose a direction?"

The silence that followed felt thick enough to cut. When his mother spoke again, her voice carried the careful measure she used when searching for him to understand rather than respond. "Your father fought the world, but in doing so, he lost the rhythm of his heart. Do not let that happen to you, mulagā."

"I'm not fighting the world, Aai," Aarav protested, though the words felt hollow even as he spoke them. "I'm working to save something valuable."

"Are you?" The question held motionless between them like incense in still air. "Or are you hiding behind your grandmother's legacy because you're afraid to create your own?"

He sank into his reading chair, the leather scrunching in release beneath him. Through the window, city lights blurred in the gathering dark, each undistinguished point a life unknown yet perceived by him. "I don't know how to be what everyone wants me to be."

"Oh, mulagā." His mother's voice modulated with understanding. "Have you forgotten what your Nani always said? The most precious timepieces aren't the ones that keep perfect time, but the ones that keep true time."

The chai had cooled to drinking temperature. Aarav lifted the cup, letting its assuasive warmth seep into his hands. "And what is my true time, Aai?"

"That's what you must discover. But remember—you carry the weight of where you come from in your blood. It's not something you can forget, no matter how far you run."

He thought of Olivia then, of how she moved through his shop with growing confidence, her presence somehow making his home feel both different and more itself. "What if I'm not running from something," he said slowly, "but toward something I don't yet understand?"

His mother was quiet for a long moment, and he could picture her in her Mumbai apartment, perhaps sitting near the window cross-legged on the floor drinking her own cup of chai she'd prepared for herself while gazing into the world were thousands of vendors could have more easily and swiftly prepared the similar drink for her – as was his mother's greatest strength, at least when she desired to do so, balancing so effortlessly in the between. "Then perhaps," she said finally, "you are more like your father than either of us thought. But hopefully wiser."

The conversation turned to other matters—family gossip, his cousin's upcoming wedding, the changes in their old neighborhood. But beneath the ordinary exchange ran a current of deeper understanding, of questions that couldn't be answered in a single phone call.

When they said goodbye, the evening had deepened into true night. Aarav sat in the gathering darkness, his empty chai cup motionless yet somehow still warm beside him. The Warli figures on his walls seemed to move in the shadows, their eternal dance a reminder of cycles that had turned long before him and would continue long after.

His aunt's letter still lay on the counter, its edges catching the city light that filtered through his windows. The quote about duality echoed in his mind: "What you fight and what you embrace are but two hands of the same body."

Outside, traffic moved in its endless flow, each vehicle carrying its own story, its own purpose. Inside, Aarav felt not a quite resolution surface, but perhaps the beginning of one. He reached for his phone again, this time to text Olivia about a particularly unremarkable repair he'd been considering. Some mechanisms, he was learning, required more than one pair of hands to achieve their true potential.

***

In the city's older quarter that seemed to exist in its own sphere of time, existed a small Marathi temple tucked away with weathered stone steps worn smooth by decades of faithful feet. Aarav hadn't planned to come here—his feet had simply carried him, seeking something he couldn't quite name after the weight of his mother's words. The morning fog had begun to lift, but traces of it still clung to the temple's carved eaves like fragments of dreams reluctant to fade.

Sandalwood incense threaded through the air, its familiar scent triggering memories of childhood visits to Pandharpur with his grandmother. She would sing abhangas as they climbed the temple steps, her voice trembling with emotion as she shared the devotional poetry of saints like Janabai and Muktabai. Now, removing his shoes at the temple's threshold, Aarav found himself remembering one particular line: "Let me carry water to you with broken hands, for only in serving do I find myself whole."

The temple's interior held that particular quality of silence that seems to vibrate with accumulated prayers. A few early morning worshippers moved quietly through their devotions, each lost in their own communion. Before the statue of Vitthal, Aarav settled cross-legged on the cool stone floor, letting the familiar posture arrange his thoughts like the tools on his workbench.

The deity's image stood serene, hands on hips in the characteristic pose that had solaced generations of devotees. In the fog-tinged morning light, the traditional brass arti lamps cast moving shadows that reminded Aarav of watch hands marking secret hours. He closed his eyes, sensing rather than seeing the world upon him, feeling the weight of tradition and expectation pressing against his skin like humid air before rain.

His grandmother's voice seemed to echo in the quiet: "Even the simplest mechanism has its sacred geometry, nātū. The space between tick and tock is where divinity dwells." She had taught him to approach his work as a form of worship, each repair an act of devotion to something larger than himself.

A priest moved near, his bare feet silent against the ancient stone. Without opening his eyes, Aarav could smell the sacred tulsi leaves and feel the subtle shift in the air that accompanied the man's presence.

"You carry a weight," the priest observed in Marathi, his voice carrying the same gentle authority Aarav remembered from temple priests in Pune. "It bends your shoulders like a bridge trying to span too wide a river."

Aarav opened his eyes, meeting the priest's knowing gaze. "I'm trying to understand my path," he admitted, the words coming easier in his mother tongue. "Everyone seems to see it so clearly except me."

The priest's smile held the wisdom of years spent watching souls wrestle with eternal questions. "To surrender is not to lose," he said, preparing to offer a blessing. "It is to gain what cannot be grasped."

The words settled into Aarav's consciousness like oil seeping into wood, revealing deeper patterns beneath the surface. He thought of Olivia, of how her presence in his shop had somehow made everything both more complex and more clear. Of how watching her learn to trust her hands with delicate repairs had awakened something in him he hadn't known was sleeping.

"But how do we know," he asked, his voice barely above a whisper, "what we're meant to surrender to?"

The priest paused in his preparations, considering the question with the same care Aarav gave to his most dear timepieces. "The heart knows," he said finally. "Like water finding its level, like thought finding its mind. The difficulty isn't in knowing, but in trusting what we know."

Morning light had begun to stream through the temple's high windows, creating patterns on the stone floor that reminded Aarav of the technical drawings he and Olivia had been studying—geometries that somehow made sense when viewed from the right angle. The other worshippers had begun their morning arti, their voices rising in ancient rhythms that seemed to make the very air pulse with devotion.

Without conscious thought, Aarav found himself reciting one of his grandmother's favorite abhanga verses: "The path is narrow, the passage steep, but every step brings me closer to truth." The fa-

miliar words spoke not only of spiritual journey but of all the choices that shaped a life.

The priest smiled, recognition flickering in his eyes. "Saint Tu-
karam," he nodded. "He understood that surrender requires more
courage than resistance." He began to move away, then paused,
adding softly, "And that sometimes the truest path isn't the one we're
expected to take, but the one our heart cannot help but follow."

The blessing, when it came, felt like a key turning in a lock Aarav hadn't known was there. The priest's hands, weathered by years
of service, moved through the ancient gestures with the same precision Aarav used when working in his shop. Each motion seemed to
carry centuries of accumulated wisdom, passed down through generations like his grandmother's tools.

As he left the temple, stepping back into the now more glow-
ing morning light lifting the lingering fog, Aarav felt lucent too. The
weight of his aunt's letter, his mother's words, his own doubts—they
hadn't disappeared, but perhaps they had begun to arrange themselves into a pattern he could begin to read.

The city was fully awake now, traffic moving in its complex
dance of intention and accident. But Aarav carried with him a pocket of temple quiet, a space where questions could exist without demanding immediate answers. His phone buzzed in his pocket. He
let it wait, giving himself these few moments to hold the morning's
revelations like precious stones, turning them over in his mind to
catch their different edging glints.

The temple stood behind him, its ancient stones holding the
lives of those seeking and finding, losing and gaining, surrendering
and succeeding. Aarav took a fragment of this wisdom held and began to sense a path that belonged uniquely to him. Whether it led

toward or away from what others expected remained to be seen. But for now, the simple act of acknowledging its existence felt like its own kind of worship.

***

The Chaha Katta Café buzzed with its luncheon rush, the clash of cups and conversation creating a proverbial symphony of intermingled and indifferent public life that contrasted sharply with his morning's temple tranquility. Aarav sat across from Sameer, his oldest friend in the city and fellow Marathi immigrant, watching steam rise from an untouched masala chai. The drink, perfectly spiced and prepared with apparent dedication, somehow failed to offer its usual comfort.

Sunlight cast through the café's wide windows, catching on the copper fixtures and turning them to liquid fire. The repurposed edifice occupied that careful balance between modern and traditional that seemed to define so much of their immigrant experience—exposed brick walls decorated with vintage Bollywood posters, industrial lighting hanging above tables made from reclaimed temple wood.

"You can't be serious about keeping the shop analog forever," Sameer was saying, his Harvard MBA confidence wrapped around him like expensive armor. He gestured with his phone, its onyx resin surface catching the light. "Look at this app I'm developing—it can diagnose watch problems through machine learning. The algorithm is already more accurate than most human experts."

Aarav traced the rim of his cup, feeling the subtle imperfections in the ceramic. "There's more to repair than diagnosis," he said quietly. "Some things can't be reduced to ones and zeros."

"That's precisely the kind of thinking that's holding our community back." Sameer leaned forward, his voice taking on the inten-

sity he usually reserved for venture capital pitches. "We have a re-
sponsibility to protect and advance our culture, Aarav. But clinging
to outdated methods isn't preservation—it's calcification."

The words struck uncomfortably close to his mother's warning
about fighting the world. Aarav watched a barista craft elaborate
latte art, her hands moving with the same careful precision he used
when adjusting balance wheels. "What exactly are we preserving,"
he asked, "if we abandon the very practices that define us?"

Sameer's smile carried a hint of condescension. "Our identity
isn't tied to mechanical watches any more than it's tied to bullock
carts or hand-ground spices. Culture evolves. You're young, talented, with a degree in mechanical engineering. You could be revolu-
tionizing the industry instead of, well, hibernating in it."

Outside, a group of tech workers hurried past, each one seemingly connected to their devices like modern devotees to digital gods.
Aarav thought of the temple priest's words about surrender and
courage, about paths that hearts cannot help but follow.

"The philosophy of Hindutva," Sameer continued, warming
to his subject, "teaches us that we must fight to protect what we are.
The world won't wait while we wind watches by hand." He paused,
studying Aarav's expression. "Why do you cling to a past that demands surrender? We must fight to protect what we are."

"Is it really protection," Aarav countered, drawing on his read-
ings of Dnyaneshwar, "if it hardens us? The poetry of our saints
teaches us to flow, not to calcify. Even the Gita speaks of finding
dharma through action aligned with nature, not against it."

As their conversation became heavier, the afternoon light began to shrink behind wispy veils in the sky, painting fainter shadows
across their table. Sameer's expression softened slightly, showing the

THE SPACE AMID SECONDS

friend beneath the businessman. "I worry about you, yaar. You're too talented to become a relic. The digital wave is here, whether we ride it or not."

"Maybe it's not about riding or resisting," Aarav said, thinking of his grandmother's way of adapting techniques while maintaining their essence. "Maybe it's about finding a third path—one that honors, even enhances, traditions and other approaches."

Sameer's laugh held more concern than humor. "The market doesn't care about third paths, my friend. You'll have to choose: do you fight for your place in the world, or do you fade into it?"

The question swept in like a cold front local to the cafe, freezing the steam of the cups around them dense with implications neither of them could grasp entirely. Aarav thought of Olivia, of how she approached each repair with a blend of respect and curiosity that somehow made the work feel both ancient and new.

"Perhaps," he said finally, "the real question isn't about fighting or fading, but about understanding what's truly worth preserving." He met Sameer's gaze steadily. "The poetry of our saints lives on not because we fixed it permanently in time, but because each generation finds new truth in it."

The café had begun to empty, the lunch crowd dispersing back to their offices and obligations. Sameer checked his phone—the gesture automatic, unconscious—before gathering his things. "Just... think about what I said. The world's moving forward, Aarav. Make sure you're not the only one still counting backward."

After Sameer left, Aarav remained at the table, watching the play of light through his half-empty cup. The chai had grown cold, its spices settled into patterns like the sediment fortune tellers read. He thought of his grandmother's workbench, of the way she would adapt modern tools to long-standing techniques, creating something that was neither old nor new but timelessly true.

His phone buzzed—a message from a client inquiring if her watch would be ready for collection today, as she had a date that evening. The modern device carried her distinctly analog question with appropriate an juxtaposition that, somehow, felt right – like the meeting point of two necessary truths.

The café's ambient music shifted to classical Indian fusion—ancient ragas played on electronic instruments. Aarav smiled at the synchronicity, gathering his things to head back to his shop where perhaps someone would be waiting with questions that made his inherited world feel both more real and more full of potential inspiration.

Stepping onto the pavement he was bathed in warm afternoon light and the oddly soothing impassivity of the cars and shoes, alike, rushing past him. Sameer's words echoed in his mind: "You'll have to choose." But perhaps, Aarav thought, the real choice wasn't between dichotomy, but in finding the courage to create something that actually created harmony, at least a bit of it, among the discord.

By the time he made it, a light blanket of night had settled over the workshop like gravity on a three-day-old balloon, transforming the set of storied walls into something more intimate, almost confessional. Aarav worked by the warm glow of a single desk lamp, its light creating a small universe of brass and steel around him. The day's conversations—with his mother, the priest, Sameer—seemed to hover in the shadows beyond the circle of light, each one adding its weight to the quiet.

A pocket watch lay open before him, its rusted components spread across his workbench like artifacts from some mechanical archacology. He'd found it during his morning walk, half-buried in a box of discarded items outside an antique store. Something about its abandoned state had called to him, demanding attention despite—or perhaps because of—its broken condition.

The workshop's numerous timepieces marked the late hour with their synchronized symphony, but Aarav barely registered their familiar chant. His entire world had narrowed to the delicate task before him, each corroded component telling its own story of neglect and hope.

"You've seen better days," he murmured in Marathi, carefully removing another layer of oxidation from a gear tooth. The metal beneath revealed hints of its original luster, like truth emerging from beneath accumulated assumption. His grandmother had always encouraged him to talk to his projects, insisting that mechanisms, like people, responded better to gentle understanding than force.

The work required complete presence, cultivating a vacuum for the doubts that had plagued him throughout the day. Each cleaning, each adjustment, each careful realignment demanded the kind of focused attention that felt like meditation. His hands moved with inherited wisdom, following patterns learned through years of patient observation and practice.

As he worked, memories surfaced like bubbles in still water. His grandmother teaching him to feel a mechanism's rhythm, to diagnose problems through touch as much as sight. His father's rare visits to the workshop, wearing success like a shield against the life he'd left behind. His mother's careful balance between respecting tradition and embracing change, albeit in a more bellicose fashion than was worn by his grandmother.

The watch's balance wheel was particularly challenging, its

staff bent almost beyond repair. Aarav studied it through his loupe, considering options. A modern replacement would be easier, more practical. But something about the original component's handcrafted quality demanded special retention.

"It's not perfect," he said to the empty workshop.

Hours passed in the focused flow of detailed work. Outside, the city's pulse slowed to its nighttime rhythm, but inside the workshop time moved according to different rules, bending to the needs of the mechanism.

When the watch finally ticked again, the sound carried all the triumph of a first breath after too long underwater. Aarav held it to his ear, listening to its unique voice emerge from beneath years of silence. The rhythm wasn't perfect—couldn't be, given the compromises necessary for preservation—but it carried its own kind of truth.

He thought of what Sameer had said about progress and protection, about the necessity of choosing sides in the war between past and future. The watch in his hands seemed to offer a different perspective—not unchanged, but revived.

His phone sat on the workbench, its screen dark yet accusatory. Earlier, he'd received another message from his aunt, this one with photos of the family's Ganesh Chaturthi celebrations. The images showed his cousins in their modern apartments, traditional diyas sharing space with LED displays, WhatsApp messages carrying ancient blessings across digital distance.

The repaired watch ticked steadily in his palm, its warmth seeping into his skin like a truth finally acknowledged. Perhaps this was what his grandmother had tried to teach him—that the real art was in finding the balance between what must be kept and what could be reimagined.

Dawn had begun to paint the workshop's windows with pale light when Aarav finally set down his tools. The watch's steady rhythm had joined the workshop's chorus, adding its beautifully peculiar notes to the ensemble. He thought of Olivia, of how she approached each repair with both reverence and innovation, somehow making the work feel both passsive and active.

As he cleaned his workspace with efficiency, the choice before him repositioned. It wasn't between preservation and progress, between surrender and resistance—like repairing a watch not to erase its history, but to allow its story to continue.

The day would bring its own challenges, its own questions. But for now, in the gentle transition between night and morning, Aarav felt the watch tick on, neither against nor at the behest of time – but within it.

***

First light varnished Aarav's apartment in shades of pale, yet there, possibility. He sat at his desk, the surface cleared of its usual technical manuals and repair notes, a single sheet of cream-colored paper before him. The fountain pen—a gift received from his grandmother—felt both awkwardly familiar in his hand, its weight a reminder of connections that transcended generations.

His apartment seemed to refuse to exhale, almost contingent on what he would do. A stick of sandalwood incense traced delicate patterns in the air, its scent mingling with the metal dust that clung to his clothes from the night's repair work. The repaired pocket watch sat beside him, its steady ticking a quiet encouragement.

Dear Olivia, he began, then paused, watching the ink dry like moments crystallizing on paper. The characters flowed from his pen

142

with deliberate grace, each one carrying weight beyond its simple shape:

I've spent my life fighting to find my place, but perhaps I need to learn when to let go. Time, like many things I'm coming to find, cannot always be controlled. It must sometimes be trusted to move as it will.

He thought of the temple priest's words about surrender requiring more courage than resistance, of his mother's gentle warning about losing the rhythm of one's heart, of Sameer's challenge about choosing sides amongst the being done and the been done. The pen moved again, finding its own truth:

In our work, we speak often of precision, of the necessity of exact measurements and perfect alignments. But lately I've been thinking about the moments that can't be captured by any mechanism, no matter how finely crafted.

Through his window, he could see the city awakening, each early commuter carrying their own story, their own measure of time. The morning light caught on his grandmother's photograph, softening her stern expression into something closer to understanding.

There's a verse from Saint Dnyaneshwar that my grandmother used to quote when I was struggling with a particularly difficult repair: "The heart knows its own timing, like water knows its own level." I never fully understood what she meant until recently. Until I watched you approach our work with both reverence and curiosity, somehow making everything feel both ancient and new.

He paused, letting the ink dry while considering his next words. His revitalized pocket watch kept its steady rhythm beside him, patently cheering life onward.

Last night, I repaired a watch that by all practical measures should have been replaced. Its components were corroded, its alignment distorted by years of neglect. Modern wisdom would say it's not worth the effort, that progress demands we discard what's broken in favor of what's new and efficient. But as

143

I worked through the night, cleaning each piece, preserving what could be saved while carefully modifying what couldn't, I began to understand something about value that can't be measured by practical standards alone.

The incense had burned down, leaving a thin trail of ash like a calendar of consumed holidays. Outside, the morning had fully arrived, bringing with it the city's familiar goings-on. But Aarav remained at his desk, letting the words flow like oil into worn gears:

There's a saying in Marathi: "जे व्हायचं ते होणारच" (What will happen will happen). Not as resignation to fate, but as recognition that some patterns emerge naturally, like the wear marks on well-used tools or the patina on beloved mechanisms. I'm beginning to think that perhaps our work together—your presence in my shop, the way you've helped me see familiar things with new eyes—is such a pattern.

A car horn sounded in the street below, its harsh note a reminder of the modern world waiting beyond his window. Aarav thought of Sameer's warnings about progress and protection, but the words that came to his pen spoke of different truths:

The mystery isn't in how time moves, but in how it moves us. Like the delicate balance between tick and tock, between tradition and innovation, between surrender and growth. My grandmother understood this—how to hold seemingly opposing forces in perfect tension, creating something that moves past simple measurement.

The sun had fully risen now, transforming his desk into an island of warm light. He could hear his neighbors beginning their day, their muffled movements creating a curiously human backdrop to his thoughts.

I don't yet know where this path leads, what pattern we're creating together. But I'm learning to trust what is between the certainties, the moments that can't be measured by any mechanism we've yet devised. Perhaps that's what my grand-

mother meant about true time—not the unyielding marking of minutes, nor the ever yielding marking either, but the dynamic acknowledgment of what matters.

He signed the letter with careful strokes, watching the ink dry one final time.

The pocket watch ticked steadily beside the finished letter, its rhythm a reminder that some moments can't be forced into existence through rigid patterns. Like water finding its level, like hearts finding their rhythm, some things had to be allowed to find their own way forward.

Soon he would see Olivia, would watch her move through his shop with growing confidence, would feel the familiar tightness in his chest when she smiled. But for now, he let the letter rest on his desk, its words a bridge between what was and what might be, between the careful measure of tradition and the wild possibility of change.

The morning light strengthened, burning away the last traces of dawn's pallid hue. Aarav rose, preparing for another day of detailed work and toward delicate balance, carrying with him all his questions and revelations. His letter, whether delivered, served to bridge the span from one heart and to another, even if that heart was merely his own.

CHAPTER 8

TANGLED THREADS

Olivia sat like standing water in her grandfather's workshop, baked in thick strands of pale and weary afternoon light and long shadows across the weathered wooden workbench. Now, surrounded by cardboard boxes marked "Personal/ 个人物品" in her mother's precise handwriting, the container that hosted uncounted fond memories for her felt both smaller and infinitely more vast than she remembered.

Aarav knelt beside her, his presence a steady anchor as they sorted through the detritus of her grandfather's life. His fingers, so precise in their handling of delicate watch parts, moved with equal care through the yellowed papers and forgotten photographs.

"Look at this," Olivia murmured, pulling free a bundle of letters bound with faded twine. The paper had aged to the color of weak tea, but the ink remained sharp and clear. Her breath caught as she read the signature on the first envelope. "These are from your grandmother."

Aarav's hands stilled on the box he'd been examining. "To your grandfather?"

"Yes." Olivia carefully untied the twine, handling the letters as if they might crumble away at any moment. The first one was dated spring of 1962, the handwriting elegant but assertive, each stroke keen and fine.

My dear Rival,

Your latest creation has caused quite a stir among our mutual acquaintances. While the craftsmanship is, as always, impeccable, I cannot help but notice the striking similarity to the escapement design I showed you at last month's horological society meeting...

"She certainly didn't pull her punches," Olivia said, a surprised laugh escaping her. The letter continued in the same vein, a masterful blend of compliments and subtle digs, admiration wrapped in thorns.

Aarav shifted uncomfortably beside her. "Maybe we shouldn't—"

"Look at this one," Olivia interrupted, already deep into the second letter. *Your stubbornness rivals only your talent, which I suppose is saying something...* She glanced up at Aarav, finding his expression troubled. "What's wrong?"

He ran a hand through his dark hair, a gesture she'd come to recognize as a sign of internal conflict. "These are private thoughts, Olivia. What if we learn things we can't unlearn? About them, about our families?"

The dust motes swirled between them, catching the dying light like suspended stars. Olivia looked down at the letters in her hands, feeling their weight—not just physical, but historical, emotional. "I think we owe it to them," she said finally. "To understand. They left these for a reason."

Aarav's resistance softened, but his eyes remained uncertain. "All right," he conceded. "But let's be careful with what we uncover."

They read through the letters chronologically, watching the relationship between their grandparents evolve through carefully chosen words and subtle shifts in tone. The professional rivalry remained constant, but underneath it grew something else—a current of understanding, of shared passion, of happenings never quite acknowledged.

The final letter in the stack made Olivia's heart skip. Unlike the others, it was unfinished, the last line trailing off mid-thought: *I fear this endeavor will destroy us both...*

"What endeavor?" Aarav asked, leaning closer to examine the incomplete sentence. His shoulder brushed against hers, and Olivia found herself acutely aware of the contact, of the way time seemed to slow in his presence.

"I don't know," she said softly, "but I think we need to find out."

The workshop had grown dim around them, the sun nearly set. As Aarav reached past her to switch on the old desk lamp, its warm glow catching the planes of his face, Olivia felt the weight of their own unspoken words, their own careful dance around truth and consequence. In the short space between them gathered all the questions they hadn't yet dared to ask, all the happenings they hadn't yet dared to acknowledge.

The letters lay between them like a bridge or a barrier—she wasn't sure which. But as she carefully retied the twine, Olivia knew with certainty that they had crossed some invisible threshold. Whatever secrets their grandparents had left behind, whatever truths lay waiting in the shadows of the past, would change everything—for better or worse.

The drive to Aarav's family home was quiet, the letters a tangible presence in Olivia's lap. Through the car window, she watched the transformation of their small town's architecture from the Victorian storefronts of downtown to the mid-century homes that spoke of a different era's aspirations. Aarav's hands were tight on the steering wheel, his usual calm demeanor disturbed by small tells—a muscle working in his jaw, the occasional tap of his finger against the leather.

"She might not want to talk about it," he said finally, breaking the silence as they turned onto Maple Street. The row of ancient trees created a natural tunnel, their leaves casting dappled shadows across the windshield. "My grandmother... she keeps certain doors firmly closed."

Olivia touched the letters through her bag. "Like the door to your grandfather's old workshop?"

His slight wince told her she'd struck a nerve. They both knew the small building behind his family's house remained perpetually locked, a repository of unspoken history that no one dared disturb.

The house itself stood as a testament to accumulated time— not grand, but well-loved, with window boxes full of marigolds and a wraparound porch that had hosted three generations of watchmakers. Mrs. Neha's rocking chair still commanded the corner spot, though she rarely sat there now.

They found her in her usual place: the oversized armchair by the living room window, surrounded by the gentle ticking of dozens of clocks. The sound had always reminded Olivia of a heartbeat, as if the house itself were alive. Today, it felt like a countdown.

"Nani," Aarav said softly, touching his grandmother's shoulder. She looked up from her book, her dark eyes still sharp despite her frail appearance. A half-finished cup of chai sat cooling on the side table, the spices perfuming the air.

"Ah, my two young horologists," she said, her accent more pronounced in her age. Her gaze fell immediately to the bag in Olivia's hands, and something flickered across her face—recognition, perhaps, or apprehension. "You've been exploring old ghosts."

Aarav knelt beside her chair while Olivia perched on the ottoman, creating an intimate triangle. The afternoon light caught the silver in Mrs. Neha's hair, illuminating her like a figure in a classical painting. When Aarav withdrew the letters, his grandmother's hands trembled slightly before she clasped them in her lap.

"Just old arguments," she said, waving dismissively. "Nothing worth disturbing the peace over."

"Nani," Aarav pressed gently, "these aren't just arguments. There's something here that feels unfinished." He hesitated, then added, "Like the watch in the locked workshop."

The mention of the workshop changed something in Mrs. Neha's posture. She sat straighter, and for a moment, Olivia saw the young woman from the letters—proud, passionate, uncompromising.

"Some things," she said carefully, "are better left unfinished." But Olivia recognized the tone from her own grandfather's voice whenever he spoke of regret disguised as wisdom.

"Please," Olivia said quietly. "My grandfather never spoke of this, and now I'll never hear his side. But maybe understanding the past could help us understand..." She trailed off, not quite ready to articulate what she and Aarav might need to understand about their own present.

Mrs. Neha studied her for a long moment, then reached for her chai. The cup rattled slightly against the saucer. "It wasn't supposed to be a rivalry at all, you know. Not at first." She took a sip, gathering her thoughts. "Your grandfather and I, we shared a vision. The others, they were content to make watches that simply kept time. But we... we wanted to capture something more elusive."

"What was that?" Aarav asked.

"The space amid seconds," she replied, her eyes distant. "The moment when possibility becomes reality. We thought if we could measure that, contain it somehow..." She shook her head. "But we were young, and proud. What began as collaboration became competition. We both believed we could achieve it alone, that we didn't need..." She stopped, setting down her cup with a final-sounding clink.

"Need what?" Olivia prompted softly.

Mrs. Neha's smile held decades of conscientiously preserved sorrow. "Each other," she said simply. "We didn't realize that what we sought couldn't be captured in gears and springs alone. It lived in the moments we shared over cups of tea, in late-night debates about escapement mechanisms, in..." She stopped again, then reached for a key she wore on a chain around her neck. "The rest is in here. But it may not be what you want to hear."

From a drawer in the side table, she withdrew a leather-bound journal, its pages thick with inserted notes and diagrams. "Your grandfather's last letter is in there too," she told Olivia. "The one I never answered."

As she handed the journal to Aarav, their fingers brushed, and Olivia saw him recognize the weight of the gesture—not just of the book itself, but of the trust, the permission to understand.

"Time," Mrs. Neha said softly, "doesn't heal all wounds. Often it just teaches us to carry them more gracefully." She looked between them, her gaze knowing. "But perhaps you two will be wiser than we were."

The clocks ticked on around them, marking the moments between words, between heartbeats, between realizations. Outside, the afternoon light began to fade, casting long shadows across the floor like the hands of some cosmic timepiece, measuring out the somewhere able to fasten upon what was and what might have been— what might still be.

***

The Heritage Day Festival transformed Carlton Park into a kaleidoscope of motion and color, strings of Edison bulbs crisscrossing overhead like constellations waiting for dusk. Olivia moved between the vendor stalls, clipboard in hand, checking off items with mechanical precision—anything to keep her mind from dwelling on the weight of Mrs. Neha's journal, still untouched in her messenger bag.

The late afternoon sun cast long shadows across the grass, and the air carried the mingled scents of kettle corn and autumn leaves. She paused to adjust a banner that had come loose, its letters proclaiming "Celebrating 150 Years of Community" in bold serif font. The irony wasn't lost on her—how many of those years had been shaped by the unspoken story she now carried?

"The sound system's acting up again," came a call from the main stage. "Something about the timing being off between speakers."

Olivia smiled despite herself. Even the technology seemed determined to remind her of temporal disconnects today. She was halfway to the stage when a familiar laugh cut through the festival noise, stopping her mid-stride.

Marcus.

He stood by the artisan booths with Rebecca, his fiancée, both of them looking like they'd stepped out of a lifestyle magazine. Rebecca wore a cream cashmere sweater that probably cost more than Olivia's rent, while Marcus sported the same easy confidence he'd worn throughout their relationship—the confidence that had made her feel simultaneously special and somehow never quite enough.

"Olivia!" Rebecca's voice carried past them, calculatedly friendly and precise as a metronome. "The festival looks amazing!"

Trapped by social convention, Olivia forced her feet forward. Each step felt like moving through honey, time stretching and contracting around her. "Thanks," she managed. "The whole committee worked hard."

"We saw the write-up in the Register," Marcus said, his smile carrying that hint of approval that once would have made her glow. Now it just made her aware of a dull ache, like pressing on a bruise to test if it still hurt. "Pretty impressive for a first-year event coordinator."

"Second year," she corrected without pause, only to wonder why she bothered.

Rebecca touched Marcus's arm in that unconsciously possessive way that spoke volumes about security and insecurity. "Oh, we should tell her about the gallery opening!"

But Olivia's attention had shifted. Aarav stood at the entrance to the park, looking simultaneously out of place and exactly where he belonged. He wore dark jeans and a charcoal sweater that emphasized the breadth of his shoulders, but it was his expression that caught her—intense, uncertain, carrying the weight of everything they'd learned in his grandmother's living room.

He made his way toward them, each step deliberate, like a

man crossing a bridge he wasn't sure would hold. The festival noise seemed to dim around them, creating a pocket of silence that held just their four bodies and all their tangled histories.

"Aarav," she said, too softly, then louder: "I didn't expect you tonight."

"I thought you might need..." he hesitated, glancing at Marcus and Rebecca. "A hand with anything."

"Right, Aarav—the watch guy," Marcus said, snapping his fingers as if placing a minor character in a story. "Olivia mentioned you've been teaching her the trade. Must be fascinating, keeping that dying art alive."

The words landed with the weight of pebbles thrown at glass—small impacts threatening larger fractures. Olivia watched Aarav's jaw tighten, saw the subtle shift in his posture that spoke of years navigating similar dismissals.

"It's not dying," Aarav said, his voice quiet but carrying an underlying strength that made Marcus blink. "It's evolving. There's a difference between obsolescence and transformation." He paused, then added, "The best crafts don't just measure time—they connect us to it. To each other. To that which matters."

The words hung in the air between them, heavy with unspoken meaning. Olivia felt something expand in her chest—pride, certainly, but also a deeper recognition. Here was someone who understood value beyond market trends, who saw beauty in the distance in the understood and less than.

"How... philosophical," Rebecca offered into the awkward silence, her tone suggesting she meant something else entirely.

A burst of feedback from the sound system made them all wince, breaking the moment. "I should check on that," Olivia said quickly. She turned to Aarav, finding his eyes already on her. "Walk with me?"

They left Marcus and Rebecca behind, moving through the crowd that seemed to part organically around them. The string lights had begun to glow as dusk settled in, creating beacons of warming coziness in the gathering darkness.

"I'm sorry," they both said at once, then laughed, the tension easing slightly.

"You have nothing to be sorry for," Olivia insisted. "That was... what you said was perfect."

"I shouldn't have come without warning you. I just..." He ran a hand through his hair, a gesture she was coming to recognize as a sign of emotional turbulence. "After this afternoon, I couldn't stop thinking. About time. About choices. About how we measure the moments that change us."

They reached the stage, but neither moved to address the sound system. Around them, the festival continued its choreographed chaos—children chasing each other with glow sticks, vendors calling out their wares, music weaving through it all. But they stood in their own pocket of time, suspended amidst as-is and as-could-be.

"The journal," Olivia said finally. "Have you...?"

"Not yet. It didn't feel right, reading it alone."

The admission carried more weight than its simple words suggested. Olivia touched her bag where the journal lay waiting, feeling its presence like a compass pointing toward some truth they weren't quite ready to face.

"Later?" she suggested, and saw the relief in his eyes.

"Later," he agreed, and somehow it felt like a promise of more than just reading together.

Above them, the festival lights swayed gently in the evening breeze, casting shifting shadows that danced like the hands of a hundred clocks, all marking time to their own rhythm. In the distance, the sound system crackled again, but neither of them moved to fix it. That is, Olivia was finding more and more that perfectly existed in instances that were imperfectly their own.

***

The shop after hours held a different kind of silence than during the day—less expectant, more contemplative. Moonlight filtered through the front windows, casting long shadows across the workbenches where hundreds of timepieces marked the seconds with their synchronized whispers. Olivia sat cross-legged on the worn leather armchair in the corner, while Aarav occupied his usual spot at the main workbench, the journal lying between them like a bridge across time.

The desk lamp created a warm oasis of light that seemed to isolate them from the world outside, transforming the shop into something closer to a confession booth than a place of business. The leather cover of the journal bore the marks of frequent handling, its spine cracked in places that suggested favorite passages revisited.

"Should you do the honors?" Olivia asked, her voice barely above a whisper, as if speaking too loudly might dispel the intimate atmosphere they'd created.

Aarav's fingers traced the edge of the cover, a watchmaker's touch—gentle, precise, respectful of delicate things. "Together," he said, opening to the first page.

The handwriting was different from the letters—less formal, more urgent. Where the letters had been composed with public consumption in mind, these pages held the raw truth of private thoughts:

October 15, 1962

It happened again today. That moment when time seems to stop, when the stretch of seconds begins to reach further than is putative – like honey in new year's moonlight covering the same distance as your eyes doing in that moment. W.M. understands—I see it in his eyes when we work together. There's something more to time than its measurement. We're not just building watches; we're trying to capture the infinite in the finite, to hold a moment in mechanical form...

Olivia leaned forward, her shoulder brushing against Aarav's as they read. The contact sent a small current through her, like the jump of a second hand marking a significant moment.

"Your grandmother," she said softly, "she wasn't just talking about horology, was she?"

Aarav shook his head, turning the page. Diagrams filled the margins—complex arrangements of gears and springs, but with notes that spoke of philosophy more than mechanics: *The escapement must breathe with the moment. Time isn't linear; why should its measurement be?*

They read on, watching the collaboration between their grandparents unfold through technical sketches and passionate debates documented in hurried script. The project they'd undertaken seemed concertedly impossible and perfectly logical: a timepiece that would mark not just the passing of seconds, but the weight of them.

"Look at this," Aarav said, pointing to a particular passage. *The challenge isn't in measuring time's passage, but in capturing its essence. How do we quantify the difference between a minute spent in joy and one spent in sorrow? Between a second of anticipation and one of regret?*

"They were trying to create something impossible," Olivia mused, but there was wonder in her voice rather than dismissal.

"Were they?" Aarav turned to face her, their proximity suddenly acute in the lamp's intimate glow. "Or were they just ahead of their time, understanding something about moments that we're only now beginning to grasp?"

The journal continued, documenting late nights and break-through moments, shared cups of tea and heated disagreements. But as the entries progressed, a tension began to build. Professional ambition clashed with personal connection. Pride began to over-shadow partnership.

March 3, 1963

W.M. insists we can achieve mechanical precision while maintaining emotional resonance. But his approach feels too rigid, too bound by tradition. There must be room for innovation, for breaking free of established patterns. We argued again today. The worst part is seeing in his eyes the same fire I feel in my heart. We're too alike, perhaps. Too stubborn. Too afraid of what might happen if we admit that this project has become about more than just watchmaking.

"Too afraid," Aarav repeated quietly, the words holding in the air between them like a curse made manifest.

They found technical specifications for the watch they'd been developing—a revolutionary design that would have required both of their expertise to complete. The mechanism was intricate, almost living in its complexity, with components that seemed to draw from both Eastern and Western horological traditions.

"This is brilliant," Aarav breathed, his professional admiration evident in every word. "The way they integrated the traditional escapement with these modified complications... it's like a conversation between two different approaches to time itself."

The final entry was dated just weeks before their collaboration ended:

April 17, 1963

We were so focused on measuring the space amid seconds that we forgot to mind the space amid us. Pride has built walls where bridges should be. The watch sits unfinished in my workshop, a testament to what happens when fear overwhelms possibility. W.M. says we should abandon the project—that some dreams are better left as dreams. But how do we abandon something that has become the very measurement of our connection?

"Your grandmother never finished it," Olivia said, realization dawning. "The watch in the locked workshop..."

"It's their watch," Aarav confirmed, his voice quilted with emotion. "The physical expression of everything they couldn't say to each other."

They sat in silence for a moment, surrounded by the mild ticking of timepieces that suddenly seemed inadequate to measure the weight of this revelation. When Aarav spoke again, his voice was barely audible over the synchronized chorus of seconds passing.

"Maybe it's not just about fixing what's broken," he said, closing the journal with cautious reverence. "Maybe some things need to stay unfinished to remind us of what we've lost."

Olivia reached out, her hand covering his where it rested on the journal's worn cover. "Or maybe," she countered, feeling the warmth of his skin against hers, "finishing it is how we honor them. How we learn from their mistakes."

The moonlight had shifted, casting new shadows across the workbench, but neither of them moved to break the connection. Around them, the watches kept their steady rhythm, marking time in a world that suddenly felt full of possibility—and second chances.

They found their way to the roof through the narrow stairwell behind Aarav's shop, the journal's revelations still echoing in their minds. The night had brought with it a gentle breeze that carried the promise of rain, and the city spread out before them like a constellation of earthbound stars. Three stories up, the world felt both infinitely vast and intimately close.

Olivia settled onto the ancient wooden bench that Aarav's father had installed years ago, its weathered slats telling their own story of time's passage. The cushions were still damp from an earlier shower, but neither of them seemed to mind. Above, clouds shifted across the face of the moon, creating an ever-changing play of blanketing shadow and chilling light.

"I come here sometimes," Aarav said, breaking their comfortable silence, "when I need to remind myself that time isn't just something we measure in the shop." He leaned forward, elbows on his knees, hands clasped as if in prayer or confession. "The city has its own pulse up here. Different from watches. Less precise, maybe, but more honest."

Olivia watched his profile in the diffused moonlight, noting how the tension he usually carried in his shoulders had transformed into something else—something closer to the weight of recognition. "What are you afraid of?" she asked softly, the height and the hour making way for dangerous questions.

He laughed, but the sound held no humor. "Currently? Everything." His hands unclasped, one running through his hair in that familiar gesture of emotional turbulence. "I'm afraid of becoming my grandmother—so dedicated to craft that I forget to live. Afraid of letting down a legacy I'm not sure I ever fully understood until today." He paused, turning to look at her. "Afraid of history repeating itself in ways I'm only beginning to recognize."

A distant train whistle cut through the night, its mournful sound echoing off buildings before fading into memory. Olivia pulled her knees to her chest, making herself small against the vastness of the sky. "I understand fear," she said. "After Marcus... I thought I was afraid of losing someone again. But maybe what really terrifies me is the possibility of building something real. Something that matters."

"Like the watch they tried to create?"

"Like anything that forces us to admit we can't control the march forward of life—we can only choose what we during that march." She unfurled slightly, letting her shoulder brush against his. "I spent so many years trying to keep perfect time with everyone else's expectations. My mother's career aspirations for me, Marcus's idea of who I should be, even my own rigid plans for the future. But sitting in your shop, learning to repair watches... it's the first time I've felt like I'm moving to my own rhythm."

Aarav shifted beside her, and she felt the moment his hand found hers in the darkness—not grabbing, not claiming, just resting beside it with the possibility of connection. "There's a concept in watchmaking," he said, his voice taking on the quality it had when he shared the secrets of his craft. "Movement compatibility. Two mechanisms that seem perfect on paper can be subtly misaligned in reality. The art isn't in forcing them to fit, but in understanding how they naturally want to work together."

The breeze tickled them both underneath the chin, carrying with it the first petrichor hints of the approaching rain. Olivia turned her hand over, letting their palms meet, feeling the calluses on his fingers that spoke of years of detailed work. "And how do you know?" she asked. "When something is naturally compatible?"

"You listen," he said simply. "Not just with your ears, but with everything you are. Every instinct, every doubt, every hope. The mechanism will tell you if you're paying attention."

A drop of rain landed on their joined hands, then another.

Neither moved. "What is this telling you?" Olivia whispered, barely audible over the growing rhythm of the rainfall.

Aarav's response was to intertwine their fingers, the gesture somehow both tentative and certain. "That some patterns are worth breaking," he said. "That some risks are worth taking. That maybe..." he took a breath, "maybe we don't have to choose between honoring the past and creating our own future."

The rain was falling steadily now, but they remained on the bench, protected by the building's overhang. Below, the streets gleamed like rivers of light, and the air was filled with the symphony of water meeting concrete, metal, glass—each surface creating its own unique percussion.

"I'm not her," Olivia said finally. "I'm not your grandmother, and you're not my grandfather. Their story doesn't have to be ours."

"No," Aarav agreed, his thumb tracing absent patterns on her palm. "But maybe we can learn from it. Maybe we can find what they couldn't—the balance between passion and partnership, between tradition and growth."

Thunder rolled in the distance, a bass note under the rainfall's steady rhythm. They should have gone inside, away from the growing storm, but neither moved. There was something too perfect about the moment—the rain, the darkness, the quiet truth of their joined hands.

"We should look at the watch," Olivia said suddenly. "The one in your grandmother's workshop. Not to fix it, necessarily, but to understand it. To see what they were trying to create."

Aarav was quiet for so long that she thought he might refuse. When he finally spoke, his voice carried the weight of generations of careful decisions. "Tomorrow," he said. "We'll look at it tomorrow."

The word rested between them like a promise, like the hold between lightning's strike and thunder's crack—charged with potentiality and the understanding that some, faithful moments, once set in motion, cannot be undone.

The rain continued to fall, and they continued to sit, their hands linked, their hearts beating in a rhythm that no watch could quite capture. Above them, the clouds parted briefly, revealing a sky full of stars that had been there all along, waiting to be noticed by those who knew how to look up from their careful measures and trust in something less precise but infinitely more true.

Dawn painted the workshop in much the way dreams do—colored but somehow disparate, with superb vibrance—the early morning light filtering through windows still beaded with last night's rain. Olivia arrived to find Aarav already there, his pressed shirt and perfectly combed hair betraying his nervousness about what they were about to do. The contrast with her windblown appearance—she'd barely slept, spending hours re-reading her grandfather's old notes—made her smile despite her own anxiety.

"Ready?" she asked, knowing the question carried more weight than its single syllable suggested.

He held up a key that looked too delicate for its purpose, its brass surface etched with intricate patterns that spoke of another era's attention to detail. "Nani gave it to me this morning. She was waiting when I arrived, as if she knew."

The walk to his grandmother's workshop felt ceremonial, each step measured against the weight of history. The small building stood apart from the main house, its weathered red brick softened by decades of ivy growth. Morning glory vines wrapped around the door frame, their purple blooms just beginning to open to the day.

The key turned with surprising ease, as if the lock had been recently oiled. Inside, time stood still in a different way than in Aarav's shop. Where he commingled with the rhythm of daily work, this room felt preserved—a museum of memory more than a workspace.

"There," Aarav said softly, pointing to a workbench beneath the window.

The timepiece sat in a shaft of morning light, its partially assembled form resembling a mechanical flower caught mid-bloom. Brass and steel components gleamed with the patina of age, but the craftsmanship was immediately apparent. Olivia recognized elements from the journal's diagrams, but seeing them realized in metal and glass took her breath away.

"It's glorious," she whispered, afraid to disturb the room's delicate atmosphere.

Aarav moved to the bench with practiced grace, his watchmaker's instincts overpowering his hesitation. "Look at how they integrated the escapement," he said, voice brimming with professional admiration. "The way the wheels interact... it's like they created their own language of motion."

They bent over the piece together, their shoulders touching as they studied the mechanism. The design was unlike anything Olivia had seen in her grandfather's other work or in her studies with Aarav. It seemed to flow rather than tick, each component leading naturally into the next like poetry rendered in metal.

"Here," Aarav said, pointing to a tiny space near the center of the movement. "This looks like..."

"A compartment," Olivia finished, reaching for her loupe. The magnification revealed what they'd missed: a minuscule latch, nearly invisible to the naked eye.

With movements that spoke of years of handling delicate mechanisms, Aarav carefully triggered the release. The compartment opened with a whisper of metal on metal, revealing a small brass plaque no larger than a fingernail.

The engraving was fine enough to require the loupe to read: *To measure time is to measure love.*

"Oh," Olivia breathed, the simple words striking further within her than any technical manual or philosophical treatise.

"There's more," Aarav said, carefully turning the plaque over. On the reverse, in equally delicate script: *For those who understand that some moments cannot be measured, only treasured.*

They stood in silence, letting the weight of the discovery settle around them. Outside, birds began their morning chorus, their song filtering through the ivy-covered windows like nature's own time-keeping.

"They never finished it," Olivia said finally, "because it was already complete in its incompletion. The space they left... it was intentional."

"A reminder," Aarav agreed, "that some things can't be contained in gears and springs." His hand found hers, continuing their connection from the previous night. "Some things need room to breathe, to grow, to transform."

The morning light had strengthened, casting their shadows on the workbench where they merged into a single shape. The time-piece caught the light differently now, its unfinished state no longer seeming like failure but like potential—a pause between tick and tock, holding all the prospect of what might be.

"We could finish it," Olivia suggested, but her tone held a question.

Aarav studied the mechanism for a long moment, his expression thoughtful. "I think," he said carefully, "that some stories need to write their own endings."

As if in response, a breeze stirred through the open door, carrying the scent of rain-washed morning and blooming morning glories. The timepiece sat between them, not just a relic of the past but a gateway to the future—their future, if they were brave enough to claim it.

"Besides," Aarav continued, a smile touching his lips, "I think we have our own story to write."

Olivia looked at their joined hands, at the timepiece that had brought them here, at the room full of memories that somehow felt less like a museum now and more like a commencement. "Yes," she said simply, feeling the truth of it in her bones. "We do."

They left the workshop as they'd found it, the timepiece still caught in its eternal moment of becoming. But they carried with them something that their grandparents had perhaps understood all along: that the most precious moments in life are not the ones we can measure, but the ones that measure us—our courage, our hearts, our capacity for love.

The morning glory blooms framed the doorway as they left, their purple petals fully open now to embrace the day. Aarav locked the door with the same care he'd used to open it, but something had shifted. The key no longer felt like a burden of history but a present—permission to honor the past while creating their own future, one unmeasured moment at a time.

CHAPTER 9

UNWRITTEN MARGINS

The afternoon light slanted through Olivia's apartment
windows, casting long shadows across the scattered books
that had become her companions in recent weeks. She sat cross-
legged on her hardwood floor, surrounded by volumes borrowed
from Aarav, their spines cracked and pages dog-eared with use. A
cup of green tea—she'd abandoned coffee—grew cold beside her as
she traced her fingers along the margins of a worn copy of "Until
August."

Aarav's handwriting filled the margins like delicate clockwork,
each letter neat and defined yet somehow organic. His notes turned
the technical into the philosophical: *The escapement mechanism in a
watch is like the minute stop between breaths—it's what gives time its rhythm.*
Something about his words made her chest tighten, as if he'd written
them knowing she would find them, knowing she would understand
the deeper meaning beneath the mechanical allegory.

She reached for her fountain pen—another recent change, es-
chewing the digital for the tangible—and hesitated above the pris-
tine margin beneath his note. The nib hovered there, a droplet of
ink threatening to fall, before she finally wrote: *Perhaps we're all just*

looking for the right mechanism to keep us ticking forward.

The words felt both insufficient and too revealing. She'd spent years crafting careful text messages and curating social media posts, but here, in these margins, she found herself writing with an honesty that startled her. Without her phone—lost now for weeks—she could no longer hide behind carefully filtered photos or strategically timed responses. The margins had become her confession booth.

She turned to a fresh page in her notebook, the paper heavy and cream-colored, another gift from Aarav. The letter began forming itself before she could second-guess the impulse:

Dear Self,

What if I stopped measuring time by what I've lost and started counting what I've gained? The betrayal that sent me spiraling—Rebecca's casual decimation of our friendship—now feels like the first domino in a sequence I needed to fall. Maybe time isn't linear at all. Maybe it's more like the gears in the clocksmith workshop, everything connecting back to itself in ways we can't see until we're ready to look.

I used to think precision meant control. I scheduled my life in fifteen-minute increments, as if I could somehow contain time itself within the boxes of my calendar app. But there's something about watching Aarav work, seeing how he handles even the most precise mechanisms with a kind of reverent tenderness, that makes me wonder if I've misunderstood more than my these thoughts, more than what I see and feel and claim to know around me.

The grandfather I thought I knew left behind more than just his memoir—he left questions that feel like answers in disguise. His voice echoes in the tick of every clock in Aarav's shop: Time is not meant to be measured, but experienced.

She paused, pen hovering once again, aware of how the quality of light in the room had shifted. The shadows had lengthened, the day slipping away while she sat surrounded by other people's words and her own tentative responses. In the margin of her letter, she added a final note: *The missing moments in time is where we actually actually experience our own.*

A door slammed somewhere in the building, the sound jolting her from her reverie. She looked down at the books scattered around her like fallen leaves, each one marked with conversations she and Aarav had yet to have aloud. Their dialogue, conducted in ink and margins, felt more intimate than any late-night text conversation she'd ever had.

She gathered the books carefully, knowing she would return them to Aarav tomorrow. Each one felt heavier now, weighted with unspoken words and half-formed realizations. As she stacked them on her coffee table, a loose page fluttered to the floor—a diagram of a watch movement, annotated in Aarav's precise hand. In the corner, barely visible, he'd written: *Every series of pieces have their breaking points. The art is in knowing how to rebuild.*

The words settled over her like the fog rolling in with the fading light, and she found herself reaching for another blank page, ready to respond to a conversation that was only beginning to take shape.

***

The morning light filtered through the weather-worn windows of Aarav's workshop, creating halos around the hundreds of timepieces that lined the walls. Each clock marked time at its own pace, their collective ticking forming an arrhythmic symphony that had become as familiar to Olivia as her own heartbeat. The air carried the metallic whisper of brass polish and the earthier notes of aged wood, a scent she'd begun to associate with possibility.

Aarav stood at his workbench, his dark hair catching the sunlight as he bent over a Victorian carriage clock. His movements were precise, almost meditative, as he manipulated tiny gears with hands that seemed too strong for such delicate work. He didn't look up when the bell above the door announced Olivia's arrival, but she caught the slight upturn of his lips, the momentary suspension in his breathing that acknowledged her presence.

"I brought your books back," she said, setting the stack on the counter with deliberate care. The sound seemed to ripple through the workshop, disrupting the mechanical chorus. A few loose pages shifted, threatening to spill their marginalia onto the aged wooden surface.

Aarav placed his tools down with the same attention he gave to everything—each movement measured, intentional. When he finally turned to face her, his eyes held that familiar mix of intensity and restraint that made her chest tighten. "Did you find what you were looking for in them?"

The question perched between them, heavy with unspoken meaning. Olivia ran her fingers along the spine of the topmost book, buying time. "I found more than I expected," she admitted. "Your notes... they're like finding pieces of you scattered through the pages."

He moved closer, reaching past her to open one of the books. His sleeve brushed against her arm, and she caught the faint scent of sandalwood and metal that seemed to cling to him. "Like this one?" His finger traced a line she'd written in response to his note about escapement mechanisms. "You wrote that time isn't what we measure, but what measures us."

"I was thinking about my grandfather when I wrote that," she said, though they both knew it wasn't entirely true. "About how he used to say that watches don't tell time, they tell stories."

Aarav's hand lingered on the page. "Speaking of stories..." He turned away, moving to a cabinet behind his workbench. From inside, he retrieved the mysterious timepiece they'd been puzzling over for weeks. Its case gleamed dully in the morning light, the intricate engravings catching shadows like secrets. "I think I found something."

He set it between them on the counter, then reached for a pair of delicate tweezers. "Here," he said, offering them to her. Their fingers brushed in the exchange, and Olivia felt that familiar jolt of awareness that seemed to accompany every accidental touch.

"The mechanism," he continued, his voice taking on the careful tone he used when explaining particularly complex repairs, "it's not broken in the way we thought. Look." He guided her hand to the inner workings of the piece, where dozens of tiny gears nested together like a mechanical puzzle. "See how the teeth on this wheel are worn differently? It's as if..."

"As if it was designed to wear this way," Olivia finished, leaning closer. Her shoulder pressed against his as they both bent over the timepiece. "But why would anyone design something to fail?"

"Maybe not to fail," Aarav mused, and she could feel his osmanthus scented breath on her cheek. "Maybe to change. Look how delicate these components are. The slightest pressure could shatter them, but they've survived decades."

"The strongest things are often the most fragile," Olivia quoted, remembering a line from one of his margin notes. "You just have to handle them right."

The words balanced in the air between them, charged with meaning neither of them was ready to acknowledge. Aarav's hand stilled over the timepiece, and for a moment, the ticking of the clocks seemed to fade into silence.

"Exactly," he said finally, his voice barely above a whisper. He straightened up, creating space between them that felt both necessary and painful. "It's like your grandfather wrote in his journal— sometimes the most precious things are the ones that could break at any moment."

Olivia set the tweezers down, aware of how her hands had begun to tremble. "Is that why we're so careful?" The question emerged before she could stop it, laden with implications she hadn't meant to reveal.

Aarav turned to face her fully then, his dark eyes searching her face. The morning light caught the flecks of gold in his irises, and Olivia found herself holding her breath, waiting for an answer that might change everything.

Instead, he reached for another tool, his movements deliberately measured. "Sometimes," he said, "being careful is the only way to keep something precious from falling apart." He paused, then added more softly, "And sometimes being careful is what keeps us from truly seeing what we have."

The workshop filled again with the sound of ticking clocks, each one marking moments that seemed to stretch and compress like the springs they spent their days repairing. Olivia picked up the tweezers again, focusing on the delicate mechanism before them, aware that they were both navigating something far more fragile than any timepiece.

***

The late afternoon sun cast long shadows through her grandfather's study, turning the frozen air debris in the room into drifting constellations. Olivia stood in the doorway, cardboard boxes scattered around her feet like fallen dominoes. Each one represented a category of his life: books, tools, photographs—all the physical remnants of a man who had understood time better than anyone she'd known.

The house had that peculiar stillness unique to worlds where someone once lived but no longer does. Even the air felt different, heavier more with memory than oxygen. Her mother had been pushing to list the property, but Olivia kept finding reasons to delay. *Just one more weekend*, she'd say. *There might be something important we've missed.*

Today, she focused on the workbench tucked into the corner, its scarred surface still bearing the marks of decades of careful work. Her grandfather's tools lay exactly as he'd left them, arranged with the precision of a surgeon's instruments. As she ran her fingers along their worn handles, she could almost hear his voice: *Tools remember the hands that hold them, Ā-Xīn. They too hold the memory of every repair.*

The old toolbox beneath the bench was the last thing left to sort. Its metal surface was cool against her hands as she lifted it, the weight surprising her. Inside, beneath layers of smaller tools and spare parts, she found a leather-bound notebook she hadn't seen before. The pages were yellow with age, the binding cracked but holding. Her grandfather's handwriting filled the pages with the same fastidiousness she now recognized in Aarav's annotations.

She settled onto the floor, her back against the wall, and began to read:

June 15, 1978

It is not the ticking that defines a clock, but what occurs when those ticks are not. Those are where its resilience lies. Today I watched young Thomas Miller bring in his father's pocket watch, handed down through three generations. The piece was beautiful—a Waltham from 1892—but it hadn't run in years. As I opened it, I found the problem wasn't in the gears or the springs, but in the areas without them. Time and neglect had filled those crucial gaps with dust and debris, each particle a tiny obstacle to the flow of time.

I wonder if relationships aren't the same way. It's not the moments of connection that define them—rather, the silences we allow to fill with misunderstanding, the gaps we let widen until they become chasms closeness. Margaret asked me yesterday why I spend so many hours in the shop, and I couldn't find the words to explain that every repair is an act of redemption, a chance to right what time has wronged.

The words blurred as tears welled in Olivia's eyes. She thought of all the Sunday dinners she'd skipped in the months before his death, the calls she'd let go to voicemail because she was too busy with work or too caught up in her own drama with Rebecca. The immensity of the passing between their last interactions now felt like canyons she could never cross.

She pulled out her phone—a new one, still strange in her hands—and opened the folder of saved voicemails she hadn't been able to bring herself to delete. Her grandfather's voice emerged, slightly tinny but unmistakable:

Ā-Xīn, I found something interesting in an old Elgin today that made me think of you. Stop by when you can. There's always time for family, even if we think there isn't.

She'd never made that visit.

The toolbox sat open beside her, its contents gleaming dully in the fading light. Among the precision screwdrivers and tiny files, she spotted something that made her breath catch—a small brass key, similar to the one they'd found in the mysterious timepiece at Aarav's shop. She held it up to the light, noting the unusual pattern of its teeth.

Her phone buzzed with a text from her mother: *Realtor wants to schedule photos next week. Time to let go, honey.*

Olivia looked around the room, at the lifetime of careful work and patient dedication represented in every tool and manual. The answer she typed surprised her with its clarity:

Not yet. There's something I need to repair first.

She placed the newly discovered notebook and key carefully in her bag, then began to sort through the tools with renewed purpose. Each one she selected was chosen with the same care she'd watched Aarav use in his shop, understanding now that some inheritances weren't just about objects, but about the patience and dedication they represented.

As she worked, her grandfather's words echoed in her mind: *"Those are where its resilience lies."* Perhaps that's what she'd been learning all along—that resilience wasn't about avoiding breaks or preventing wear, but allowing for understanding and openness for repair and renewal.

The sun had nearly set by the time she finished, casting the room in shades of blue and gray. She stood in the doorway one last time, the weight of the toolbox solid against her hip. Tomorrow, she would show Aarav what she'd found, but tonight, she allowed herself to feel the full weight of what she was finally ready to repair.

***

The Bartlett Street library's reading room existed in a perpetual state of twilight, regardless of the hour. Ancient oak shelves rose like cathedral spires, their uppermost reaches lost in shadow. The air hung heavy with the perfume of aged paper and furniture polish, a scent that reminded Olivia of her grandfather's study. She'd arrived early, claiming a table in the far corner where brass reading lamps cast pools of warm light onto the polished wood.

Aarav appeared precisely at two, his footsteps echoed against the stone-carved, vaulted ceilings. He carried a leather messenger bag that she recognized from his shop—the one he used for his most delicate tools. Without speaking, he settled into the chair beside her, close enough that she could detect the familiar notes of sandalwood and metal that seemed to follow him everywhere.

She slid a piece of paper across the table: *Found something in Grandfather's study yesterday. The marginalia in his notebook mentions a specialty materials supplier from the 1970s — M. Blackwood & Sons.*

Aarav's eyes flickered as he read, then he reached for his own notebook. His response, written in his characteristic precise hand, made her lean closer: *The same supplier appears in my grandmother's ledger. She ordered custom springs from them between 1975-1979. Too specific to be coincidence?*

The scratch of pen on paper became a quiet dialogue between them, each note carrying layers of meaning beneath the words:

Olivia: *Also found this.* She sketched the brass key she'd discovered.

Aarav's response came quickly, his usually meticulous writing showing a hint of excitement: *The teeth pattern matches the lock mechanism in our timepiece. Your grandfather must have known.*

Known what? She wrote, her hand brushing against his as she passed the note.

He began to respond but paused as a small commotion drew their attention. At a nearby table, a young girl—no more than seven—struggled with a wooden puzzle, her frustration evident in the set of her small shoulders. The puzzle pieces scattered across the table like autumn leaves, refusing to fit together.

Without conscious thought, Olivia rose and approached the child's table. She knelt beside her, keeping her voice at a library whisper. "Sometimes the pieces make more sense if you look at what exists between them," she said, gently turning one piece over. "See how this edge has a shadow? That tells you something about where it belongs."

The girl's face brightened as understanding dawned. Together, they began sorting the pieces, Olivia guiding with subtle gestures rather than words. From his seat, Aarav watched the interaction with an expression Olivia couldn't quite read—something between tenderness and recognition.

When she returned to their table, a new note waited for her: *You remind me of my grandmother. She used to say that patience was the only tool that never needed sharpening.*

The observation made her chest grip, yet lighten. She responded: *Tell me about her.*

Their notes became more personal, straying from the technical into memory:

Aarav: *She had a way of seeing through problems to their core. Said every mechanical failure was just a misunderstanding between parts that were meant to work together.*

Olivia: Grandfather used to say something similar about relationships.

A pause, then: *Maybe that's why they were rivals. They saw the same truths from different angles.*

The afternoon light shifted as they worked, their research punctuated by these increasingly intimate exchanges. When Aarav finally found the reference they'd been searching for, his hand trembled slightly as he wrote: *M. Blackwood's workshop still exists. It's on the outskirts of town. The grandson runs it now.*

Olivia felt her pulse quicken: *We should go.*

Their eyes met over the paper, and Aarav added one more note: *Together?*

The word grew larger on the paper between them, blooming with possibility. Olivia reached for her pen, but instead of writing, she simply nodded, the gesture small but decisive. Around them, the library's hushed atmosphere seemed to deepen, as if the books themselves were holding their breath.

A librarian began making her rounds, adjusting the reading lamps as afternoon surrendered to evening. Olivia gathered their notes—a paper trail of cautious revelations and careful hopes. As she slipped them into her bag, her hand brushed against her grandfather's notebook, and she felt the weight of unfinished stories pressing against her fingers.

Aarav stood, offering her his hand as she rose. The touch was brief but deliberate, like the precise movement of watch hands marking a significant hour. As they walked toward the exit, their footsteps synchronized naturally, another unspoken dialogue in the language they were slowly creating together.

Outside, the evening air carried the invitations of autumn. Olivia paused on the library steps, watching as Aarav checked his pocket watch—a habit she'd come to find endearing. He looked up, catching her gaze, and smiled in that way that made her wonder if time could actually pause, just for a moment.

"Tomorrow?" he asked, breaking their silence at last.

"Tomorrow," she agreed, understanding that they were planning more than just a visit to a workshop. They were taking another step into the realm that occupied between their separate histories, where answers—and perhaps something more profound—waited to be discovered.

The workshop of M. Blackwood & Sons materialized out of the morning mist like a forgotten memory. Located at the end of a gravel drive lined with ancient oak trees, the Victorian-era building wore its age with dignity—pockmarked bricks and clouded windows suggesting secrets rather than decay. Olivia's hand found Aarav's instinctively as they approached the heavy wooden door, its brass handle patinated with decades of use.

Micah Blackwood Jr. met them in a space that seemed to exist outside of conventional time. Sunlight filtered through high windows, catching dust motes that danced like golden particles of frozen time. Workbenches lined the walls, each supporting projects in various stages of completion—gleaming brass mechanisms and half-assembled movements that reminded Olivia of mechanical organisms caught mid-metamorphosis.

The craftsman himself appeared to have been cast from the same material as his workshop—weathered but precise, with eyes that held the sharp focus of someone who had spent a lifetime studying the minute details of existence. His steel-gray hair was swept back from his forehead, and his hands, when he reached for the mysterious timepiece, moved with the deliberate grace of a conductor.

"Ah," he said, his voice carrying the texture of aged, but well-tended-to wood. "I wondered if this would find its way back here." He turned the piece over in his hands, his fingers tracing the engraving with familiar reverence. "Your grandparents were rather insistent about the specifications."

Olivia and Aarav exchanged glances. "Both of our grandparents?" Aarav asked, his hand tightening almost imperceptibly around Olivia's.

Micah nodded, reaching for a jeweler's loupe. "They came together, you see. Quite the pair—competitors in public, but here..." He adjusted the light over his workbench. "Here, they spoke the same language. They understood something about time that few others grasp."

He opened the case with practiced ease, revealing the intricate mechanism within. "This spring," he said, indicating a nearly invisible component, "was their masterpiece. Your grandmother's design," he nodded to Aarav, "and your grandfather's implementation," he smiled at Olivia. "It was meant to last a lifetime, but not remain unchanged."

"The wear patterns," Olivia breathed, leaning closer. "They're intentional?"

"Indeed." Micah's eyes crinkled with appreciation. "The spring was designed to stretch and contract over decades, adapting to the stresses rather than resisting them." he added, looking meaningfully at their still-clasped hands. "Rigid things break. Flexible things endure."

Aarav released Olivia's hand to examine the mechanism more closely, but the ghost of his touch lingered. "But why create something so complex just to measure time? There are simpler ways."

Micah straightened, his expression softening with what might have been nostalgia. "Who said it was meant to measure time?" He reached beneath his workbench and withdrew a leather-bound journal, its pages yellow with age. "Your grandparents didn't want to measure time—they wanted to measure moments. The shared ones. The ones that matter."

He opened the journal to a carefully marked page, revealing technical drawings annotated in two distinct hands. "See here? The mechanism doesn't mark regular intervals. It responds to usage patterns, to the presence of human interaction. It's meant to record the moments when people come together, when they choose to be present with each other."

Olivia thought of her grandfather's workshop, of all the Sunday dinners she'd missed. "So when it stopped working…"

"It wasn't broken," Micah finished gently. "It was waiting. For the right moment. For the right people to understand its purpose." He began gathering tools with methodical purpose. "I can recreate the spring, but it will take time. Weeks, perhaps."

"We can wait," Aarav said, his eyes meeting Olivia's with quiet intensity.

As Micah disappeared into his storeroom to check his materials, Olivia found herself drawn to a workbench where a partially dismantled pocket watch lay in organized chaos. Without thinking, she reached for Aarav's hand again, the gesture as natural as breathing.

"Our grandparents," she said softly, "they knew each other better than anyone realized."

Aarav's thumb traced small circles on her palm, each movement like the tick of a second hand. "It seems they understood that calculated distances can develop their conscientious rhythms."

The morning light had strengthened, burning away the last of the mist outside. Through the windows, the oak trees stood like patient guardians, their leaves beginning to turn the color of old brass. This place seemed to permit a different time movement too, flowing in shared heartbeats, in held breaths, in the gentle pressure of intertwined fingers.

Micah returned with a small wooden box, its surface marked with the patina of ages. "Your grandparents left this," he said, placing it carefully on the workbench. "They asked me to keep it until the timepiece found its way home." He paused, studying them both. "I believe that time has come."

The box sat between them, both invitation and challenge. Olivia felt Aarav's pulse quicken through their joined hands, matching the acceleration of her own heart. Whatever lay within would change things—had already changed things, simply by existing. The question was whether they were ready for what those changes might provide.

In the hush of the workshop, surrounded by the booming backdrop of ticking timepieces, they stood together in the wait between this moment and the next.

***

Aarav's apartment existed in perfect counterpoint to his crowded workshop—a study in intentional minimalism that made Olivia think of purpose-driven, curated museum displays. Yet, this display was a decidedly introverted one—sure of itself, and for a select few. The evening light filtered through bare windows, casting long shadows across hardwood floors that had been worn smooth by time. A single photograph of his grandmother commanded one wall, her stern expression softened by the hint of a smile that seemed reserved for the camera alone. Beneath it, a shelf displayed a collection of antique watchmaking tools, each one positioned with care.

The wooden box from Micah's workshop sat unopened on Aarav's kitchen counter, a quiet presence that seemed to alter the gravity of the room. They moved around each other in his small kitchen, preparing dinner with the unconscious synchronicity of dancers who had somehow learned each other's steps without realizing it. Olivia chopped vegetables while Aarav measured spices for his grandmother's curry recipe, their movements creating a domestic symphony of knife against cutting board, metal against metal, breath against breath.

"It's strange," Olivia said, watching as he added cardamom pods to the simmering pot, "how some scents can hold entire histories." The aroma reminded her of stories he'd told about Sunday mornings in his grandmother's kitchen, of lessons learned between stirs of a wooden spoon.

Aarav's hand paused over the pot, his profile outlined in steam. "Like metal polish and old books?" he asked, glancing at her with understanding. They both carried these sensory memories now—his workshop, her grandfather's study, the world where their separate histories had begun to interlace.

After dinner, they settled on cushions on the floor, surrounded by books and the remnants of masala chai. The box sat between them now, its presence both invitation and boundary. Olivia traced the grain of the wood with her fingertip, feeling the subtle variations that time had carved into its surface.

"I've been afraid," Aarav said suddenly, his voice low and careful, "of letting anyone too close to the work. To this." He gestured vaguely at the apartment, the tools, himself. "My family expects me to modernize, to make the business more 'efficient.' But the work requires slowness, attention. Like reading between the lines."

Olivia reached for her notebook—the one she'd been carrying since losing her phone—and opened it to the letter she'd written to herself days ago. Her hands trembled slightly as she held it out to him. "I think I understand something about that now."

He took the notebook with watchmaker's hands, handling it as carefully as he would a delicate hinge on a neglected pocket watch. His eyes moved over her words, pausing at certain phrases as if cataloguing them for future reference. When he reached the end, he picked up a pen from the floor beside him.

In the margin of her letter, he wrote with his characteristic precision: *Time doesn't fix things; people do.*

The simplicity of the statement caught in Olivia's throat. She watched as he continued writing, each word measured and deliberate:

My grandmother used to say that a watchmaker's greatest skill isn't in knowing how to fix what's broken, but in recognizing what's worth preserving. I think perhaps she wasn't just talking about timepieces.

Olivia leaned closer, drawn by the intimacy of his handwriting, the way his letters leaned ever so slightly to the right as if reaching forward in time. The movement brought her shoulder against his, and neither of them pulled away.

"The box," she said softly. "Should we?"

Aarav set the notebook aside with careful hands. "Together?"

The word floated between them as though they uttered it at the same time. Olivia nodded, and they reached for the box in unison, their fingers brushing against the polished wood. Inside, nestled in faded velvet, they found a collection of letters, their paper softened by time. Each envelope bore both their grandparents' handwriting—notes passed between supposed rivals that spoke of shared dreams and understood sacrifices.

And beneath the letters, a single piece of paper with fresh ink, Micah's handwriting stark against the cream-colored page: *Some mechanisms are designed to bring people together, even across time. Your grand-*

parents understood this. Now it's your turn to wind the spring.

They sat in silence for a moment, letting the weight of the revelation settle around them like reverential quiet in a crowd at a concert. Outside, the city continued its rhythm of traffic and distant sirens, but in Aarav's apartment, time seemed to abide by different rules.

"We should read them," Olivia said finally, her voice barely above a whisper. "But not all at once. Some things deserve to be discovered slowly."

Aarav's response was to reach for her hand, nod, and wait to feel her reach for a beginning letter so that he may reach with her.

The evening deepened around them, the room gradually filling with shadows that softened edges and blurred boundaries. They remained on the floor, surrounded by books and letters and the gentle accumulation of shared moments—both theirs and their grandparents—neither willing to be the first to break the spell that had settled over them like a carefully wound spring, holding potential energy in perfect tension.

In the margin of time between one moment and the next, they had begun to write their own story, one careful annotation at a time.

CHAPTER 10

FALLING BACK

A nemic streams of light cast long, wispy shadows across Aarav's workbench, while outside dark clouds gathered with methodical intention, their presence matching the weight that had settled between his shoulders. The approaching storm made the windows whisper and shudder, while the chorus of clocks seemed to tick with unusual urgency—as if sensing the tension in the air.

When the bell above the door chimed, Aarav didn't need to look up to know it was Olivia. The familiar scent of coffee—her peace offering—drifted through the shop, but today it felt like a mockery of their usual comfort. Her footsteps hesitated halfway to his workbench.

"I brought your favorite," she said, her voice carrying a forced lightness that made his chest tighten. "The Ethiopian blend from that little place on Mason Street."

Aarav's hands stilled over the dismantled pocket watch before him. The brass components gleamed dully under the shop lights, their ancient engineering a reminder of everything he was struggling to preserve. "Thanks," he managed, the word coming out more clipped than he'd intended.

Olivia set the coffee down beside him, careful to avoid the scattered tools and components. The silence stretched between them like an overwound spring, threatening to snap. Outside, the first drops of rain began to tap against the windows.

"Are you alright?" she finally asked, though her tone suggested she already knew the answer.

Aarav's sight was equally hollow and sunken. "My father called this morning. He's found an investor interested in 'modernizing' the shop." His fingers traced the edge of a gear, its teeth worn smooth by decades of steady rotation. "They want to turn it into some sort of boutique watch store. Designer brands. Digital displays. Desperately innovative."

"That doesn't mean you have to—"

"Don't." The word came out sharper than he'd intended, making Olivia flinch. "Please don't try to make this better. I'm failing at everything—this shop, my family's legacy, my own future. I can't even figure out this damned timepiece." He gestured to the mysterious watch they'd been working on together, its mechanism still stubbornly silent.

Olivia's hand hovered over his shoulder before withdrawing. "Maybe we should focus on that for now? Keep things simple?"

"Simple," he echoed, the word tasting bitter. He reached for the timepiece, his movements mechanical. "Fine. Let's work on the escape wheel. You remember how to adjust the pallet fork?"

She nodded, reaching for the tool with careful precision. Her hands trembled slightly as she positioned it, and something in Aarav snapped. "Do you even want to do this, or are you just here because you feel guilty?"

The tool clattered against the workbench. Olivia's eyes, when they met his, blazed with hurt and anger. "Is that what you think? That I'm here out of guilt?"

"Aren't you? Biding time with somethings and someones different until you're satisfied with your slumming it before you head on back to where you have a real place, your own place to be?" The words were poison, and he knew it, but he couldn't stop them as they erupted like a vomit that eases the nausea.

"I'll assume you don't realize what you just said to me," Olivia said, her voice quiet but steady. "It's easier than admitting you're scared. But please do not confuse easy with simple."

Thunder rolled outside, and Aarav stood abruptly, his chair scraping against the wooden floor. Without a word, he grabbed his coat and headed for the door.

"Aarav, wait——"

But he was already stepping into the rain, letting the storm swallow him whole. Behind him, through the shop window, he could see Olivia's silhouette frozen beside the workbench, her hand still hovering over the broken timepiece——a tableau of all he feared to lose, yet couldn't bring himself to keep.

***

The emptiness of her childhood home struck Olivia like a physical presence. Sunlight streamed through bare windows, no longer filtered by her mother's beloved lace curtains, creating stark shadows across floors that had been stripped of their familiar rugs. The walls, newly bare, seemed to echo with the ghosts of picture frames that had traced her family's history.

In the corner, a few cardboard boxes stood sentinel——the last remnants of a life being systematically dismantled. Olivia ran her fingers along one labeled "Dad's Books/爸爸的书" in her mother's meticulous handwriting, then quickly withdrew her hand as if burned.

The unexpected sound of a key in the lock made her start. Her mother's voice drifted in before she appeared: "Olivia? I thought I saw your car outside."

Helen stepped into the room carrying a familiar floral teapot and what appeared to be a worn photo album. Her hair was pulled back in its usual elegant twist, but there was something softer about her today, something almost vulnerable in the way she surveyed the empty room.

"I was just..." Olivia gestured vaguely at the boxes, unable to complete the thought.

"Tracing the outlines no longer here?" Her mother's smile was knowing as she set the teapot and album down on the floor, since there was no furniture left to use. "I brought green tea. And something else I thought you might want to see."

They sat cross-legged on the hardwood floor, steam rising from delicate cups that had somehow survived the great purge of possessions. Helen opened the album with careful hands, and Olivia felt a rush of memories at the sight of the first photograph—herself at six, gap-toothed and beaming, holding up a junior mechanic's toolkit.

"Wàigōng's first gift to me," she murmured, touching the edge of the photo.

Her mother nodded, turning the page. Olivia noticed how she deliberately skipped past certain images, her fingers moving with practiced precision to avoid any that might contain her father. The absence was choreographed, yet somehow more noticeable for its painstaking execution.

"Māmā," Olivia started, then paused, gathering courage. "Are you really sure about selling?"

Helen's hands stilled on the album's pages. Outside, a bird called, its song ricocheting in the empty house. "Actually," she said slowly, "I've been thinking about that." She looked up, meeting Olivia's eyes. "What if I'm making a mistake? Everyone says moving forward means letting go, but..."

"But what if it means holding on to the right things?" Olivia finished, surprising herself with the words.

"Exactly." Her mother touched a photograph of the garden, now overgrown but once her pride and joy. "I keep thinking about Wàigōng. How he held onto that old shop even when everyone told him to sell. I used to think he was just being stubborn, but now I wonder if he understood something beyond the opinions of others, more than the pragmatic."

Olivia thought of Aarav, of the passion in his eyes when he spoke about his craft, of the way his hands moved with such certainty over broken things, making them whole again. She thought of their argument, of words flung like weapons, of her own fear of repeating past mistakes.

"I'm afraid," she admitted, the words barely a whisper.

Her mother reached across the album to take her hand. "Of what, Ā-Xīn?"

"Of getting it wrong. Again. Of trusting too much, or not enough. Of..." she gestured at the empty room, "of ending up with nothing but boxes of memories I'm too afraid to look at."

Helen was quiet for a long moment, her thumb chasing itself on Olivia's hand. Finally, she said, "You don't have to finish every story in the way you thought you would to find meaning in it. Sometimes, it's enough to just keep writing."

The words lept into Olivia's chest like a key turning in a lock. She thought of her grandfather's memoir, of its unfinished chapters and margin notes. Of Aarav's face in the storm-dark shop, fear and longing warring in his eyes.

"How do you know, though?" she asked. "How do you know which stories to keep writing?"

Her mother smiled, turning to a photograph Olivia hadn't seen before. It showed her grandfather in his shop, bent over his workbench, a look of complete absorption on his face. "I think," Helen said softly, "you know by the way it feels when you pause. It's there where you can decide whether to keep going forward."

***

Aarav's apartment bore little resemblance to the orderly sanctuary it usually was. Papers littered every surface like autumn leaves, each sheet bearing the phantom traces of his restlessness—half-finished sketches of watch mechanisms, fragments of calculations, and hasty notes scrawled in margins. The usual precise arrangement of his tools had given way to scattered disarray, technical manuals splayed open at random pages, their neat diagrams a stark contrast to his now chaotic mind.

In the dim light of his desk lamp, he sat hunched over his grandmother's journal, its leather binding worn smooth by decades of similar troubled nights. The pages left agape to an entry from 1982, her elegant script filling the yellowed paper, but the words refused to settle in his mind. Instead, his fingers kept returning to a small component from the mysterious timepiece—a peculiar gear whose teeth bore unusual variations he hadn't seen before.

The piece caught the light as he turned it, revealing subtle marks that might have been intentional or might have been damage.

Like so many things lately, its true substance eluded his understanding. He thought of Olivia's face in the shop, the hurt in her eyes when he'd lashed out. The gear's weight in his palm seemed to grow heavier with each passing moment.

His phone buzzed, startling him. His grandmother's name lit up the screen, and something in his chest tightened. Even after all these years, she had an uncanny ability to sense when he was adrift.

"Nani," he answered, the familiar word carrying a wealth of unspoken emotion.

"Your mother tells me you've been refusing to take her calls," Nani Malholtra said without preamble, her voice carrying across the air with characteristic directness. "And now you're sitting alone in the dark, aren't you?"

Aarav glanced at his reflection in the window—a ghostly figure illuminated by a single lamp. "It's not dark everywhere," he offered weakly.

Her laugh was warm, though tinged with concern. "Ah, my stubborn grandson. Always so precise with your words, yet so imprecise with your heart." There was a pause, filled with the soft ticking of what he knew would be his grandfather's old mantel clock. "Tell me what's troubling you."

He closed his eyes, letting his head rest against the back of his chair. "Do you remember the first watch you ever made?"

"Of course. The 1963 Stellar Movement. It was horrible."

The unexpected answer startled a laugh from him. "Horrible? But you won an award for your early work."

"Oh, not that one. I mean my actual first watch. The one I nearly destroyed in frustration because I couldn't get the balance wheel aligned properly." Her voice softened with memory. "I was so determined to make it perfect that I almost missed the point entirely."

Aarav's fingers tightened around the mysterious gear. "What was the point?"

"That I was trying to create something unique while following someone else's blueprint." A familiar creak suggested she'd settled into her favorite chair. "I spent weeks trying to replicate exactly what my teachers had shown me, becoming more and more frustrated when my results didn't match their examples. Then one day, in a fit of anger, I threw the whole thing across the workshop."

"Nani!" Aarav couldn't hide his shock. His grandmother's steady hands were legendary in the industry.

"Oh, don't sound so scandalized. The interesting part is that when I picked it up, I realized the impact had shifted something in the mechanism. It didn't keep time quite like it was supposed to—it had a slight pause every hour, just a fraction of a second. But that pause..." She trailed off thoughtfully.

"Was it broken?"

"That's what I thought at first. But your grandfather—this was before we were married, mind you—he saw it differently. He said it had character. That sometimes, the mistakes make it unique. And unique doesn't mean broken—it means it's yours."

The words settled into the quiet of Aarav's apartment, mixing with the soft ticking of his own collection of timepieces. He looked at the sketches scattered across his desk—his attempts to modernize traditional designs while preserving their essence. In the corner, one particularly promising drawing lay crumpled, discarded for deviating too far from formally familiar.

"I'm afraid," he admitted, the words barely audible.

"Of what, nātū?"

"Of failing. Of letting everyone down. The shop, our heritage, our future..." He thought of Olivia, of the way she saw beauty in the imperfect, meaning in the breaks between instances. "Of losing something precious because I'm too afraid to let it be anything but perfect."

His grandmother was quiet for a moment, and he could picture her nodding slowly, the way she did when examining a particularly complex mechanism. "You know," she finally said, "the most valuable pieces in our collection aren't the ones that keep perfect time."

"They're the ones with stories," Aarav finished, a memory stirring of her telling him this as a child.

"And stories, my dear boy, are rarely perfect. They're messy and complicated and sometimes they tick a little strangely. But that's what makes them worth telling."

Aarav's gaze fell on the mysterious timepiece component again, seeing its unusual features with new eyes. Perhaps its irregularities weren't flaws to be corrected or excavated but aspects integral to its core with which to understand and flow appropriately. Like the pause in his grandmother's first watch, like the impropriety of his words to Olivia, like the distance between tradition and innovation he'd been so afraid to bridge.

"Thank you, Nani," he said softly.

"Don't thank me. Just stop sitting in the dark." Her tone turned sly. "And maybe call that girl who's been helping you in the shop. The one your mother says makes you smile like your grandfather used to."

After they hung up, Aarav stood and walked to the window.

The city lights blurred in the rain-streaked glass, each droplet catching and transforming the glow into something new and unexpected. Behind him, his collection of timepieces continued their steady performance, each with its own slightly different rhythm, creating a symphony he'd never fully appreciated before.

He uncrumpled the discarded sketch, smoothing it carefully on his desk. In the margin, he began to write, his pen moving with newfound purpose: "There can exist perfection lying between beats that are written...or rather, improvisation can yield beauty if expectation is released."

***

The Heritage Museum's lighting cast a gentle amber glow over the glass cases, lending the collection of timepieces an almost perpetual quality. Olivia moved through the exhibit with measured steps, each display eliciting memories of her grandfather's workshop—the scent of metal and oil, the whisper of tools against brass, the steady percussion of dozens of clocks marking time in their own distinct voices.

The special exhibition, "Masters of Time: The Chén-Malholtra Legacy," seemed both a celebration and a quiet reproach. Her grandfather's tools, laid out with curatorial precision, looked strangely diminished behind glass. She paused before a case containing his workbench lamp, its brass arm forever frozen in mid-reach, no longer illuminating the delicate work it had witnessed for decades.

"It's strange, seeing pieces of your life behind glass," she murmured to no one in particular.

"Like watching your memories become artifacts?" The voice beside her belonged to an elderly gentleman who had approached so quietly she hadn't noticed him. His wire-rimmed glasses caught the light as he studied the display, hands clasped behind his back in a pose that struck her as achingly familiar.

"Yes, exactly like that." Olivia turned to face him properly, noting the way his eyes moved over the exhibits with the appreciation of someone who understood their true value. "Did you know my grandfather?"

The man's smile deepened the wrinkles around his eyes. "Chén Wěi Míng? Oh yes. I was his apprentice for nearly three years in the late seventies. Martin Walsh." He extended his hand, and his grip was firm despite his age. "Though your grandfather always called me 'the impossible student.'"

"Why impossible?"

"Because I was obsessed with perfection. Drove him half mad with my constant attempts to achieve absolute precision." Martin chuckled, moving toward a display that had caught his attention. "Come look at this. I believe you'll find it interesting."

He led her to a case she had initially passed by, containing what appeared to be an unfinished project. Her breath caught as she recognized the intricate sketches spread beneath a half-assembled mechanism—they were preliminary designs for the very timepiece she and Aarav had been struggling to repair.

The museum placard read: "An unfinished masterpiece. In time, it's the potential that makes something timeless."

"He worked on this for years," Martin said softly, "though never to completion. I used to think it was because he couldn't solve some technical problem, but now I wonder if the incompletion was intentional."

Olivia leaned closer to the glass, studying the familiar yet mysterious components. "What do you mean?"

"Your grandfather had a favorite saying: 'A perfect clock might keep time, but an imperfect one tells a story.'" Martin adjusted his glasses, his reflection overlapping with the displayed sketches. "He taught me that, whether we observed, the gaps between gears—the tiny irregularities, the subtle variations—those are where the beauty lives. It took me years to understand what he meant."

Olivia thought of Aarav's hands moving over the timepiece's components, his frustration when they wouldn't conform to expected patterns. She thought of their argument, of the storm, of all the words caught in the breaks of anger and regret.

"There's more here than just technical drawings," Martin continued, pointing to barely visible notes in the margins of the sketches. "See these calculations? They're not just about timing mechanisms. Look closer."

Olivia squinted at the faded pencil marks. Among the technical notations were what appeared to be poetry fragments, philosophical musings, and... "Are those love letters?"

Martin nodded. "Your grandfather believed that time wasn't just something to be measured, but something to be experienced. He was trying to create a device that could capture not just the passing of seconds, but the weight of moments." He paused, studying her face. "The way time feels different when you're with someone you love."

The revelation hit Olivia with physical force. All this time, she and Aarav had been approaching the timepiece as a puzzle to be solved, when perhaps it was meant to be a mirror—reflecting not the precision of time, but its beautiful imperfection.

"He never finished it," she said, understanding blooming like dawn.

"No," Martin agreed. "Because certain stories aren't to be finished. They're to be lived." He reached into his pocket and withdrew a small envelope, slightly yellowed with age. "He left this with me years ago. Frankly, I'd come to donate it when I'd heard they were doing an exhibit on your grandfather. Yet, he said I'd know when it was time to pass it on – and I've a feeling that time is now."

Olivia's hands had a bare tremor as she accepted the envelope. Inside was a single sheet of paper, covered in her grandfather's distinctive handwriting. The note was brief, but its words seemed to pulse with meaning:

My dearest 阿昕,

Time is not a river flowing in one direction, but a dance of moments, each step unique, each pause meaningful. The space amid seconds is where we truly live. Don't be afraid of the gaps—they're what make the you, the life, possible.

With all my love,

外公

When she looked up, tears blurring her vision, Martin had quietly withdrawn, leaving her alone with the revelation. Above the display cases, the museum's clocks continued their steady advance forward, each marking the moments in its own way, their slight discordance creating an unexpected music.

Outside the window, the late afternoon sun painted the sky in shades of pastel, bursting through some sheets of fog while leaving light nestled behind others, and Olivia knew with sudden clarity what she needed to do. The timepiece wasn't just a mechanical puzzle—it was a message, passed through generations, about the beauty of imperfect connections and the courage required to let them tick forward in their own unique rhythm.

She pulled out her phone, fingers hovering over Aarav's number, then paused. Some things needed to be said in person, in a shared space where truth resided. Tucking her grandfather's note carefully into her pocket, she turned toward the exit, her steps echoing with newfound purpose through the halls of frozen time.

Evening had settled over the city like a velvet shroud, streetlights casting pools of amber and blush that gleamed off wet pavement. Olivia stood before Aarav's shop, watching his silhouette through the window—a lonely figure bent over his workbench, surrounded by the steady heartbeat of a hundred timepieces. Her grandfather's letter seemed to pulse in her pocket, its words a quiet encouragement.

The bell above the door felt unusually heavy as she pushed it open, its chime cutting through the metronomic ticking that the air was held. Aarav didn't look up, but his hands stilled over the mysterious timepiece, now partially reassembled on his bench. The words not yet released felt dense with prolepsis.

Three steps in, she hesitated. The shop's familiar scents—brass and oil, old wood and leather—cloaked her like a memory. A week ago, she would have crossed to his side without thought, drawn by the magnetic pull of their shared passion. Now, uncertainty made her footsteps falter.

"I wasn't sure you'd come back." Aarav's voice was soft, almost lost beneath the chorus of clocks.

"I wasn't sure either," Olivia admitted, taking another step forward. The floorboard beneath her foot creaked—the same one that always did, a familiar note in their daily symphony. "But I came to fix things." She swallowed hard, then added, "Not the timepiece. Us."

Aarav finally turned, and the exhaustion etched across his fea-

THE SPACE AMID SECONDS

tures made her heart ache. Shadows pooled beneath his eyes, and his usually immaculate workbench was scattered with tools and components. Their eyes met across the now vast tabletop, and in that moment, the ticking of the clocks seemed to lag, as if time itself were holding its breath.

"I've been afraid," he said, the words emerging with the attentive guard of someone handling something fragile. "Of failing you. Of failing myself. Of failing this—" he motioned to encompass the shop, their shared heritage, the delicate thing growing between them.

Olivia moved closer, drawn by the raw honesty in his voice. "I went to the museum today," she said, retrieving her grandfather's letter. "I learned something about the timepiece. About what it was meant to be."

She placed the letter on the workbench between them, watching as Aarav's eyes moved over the words. The shop's lights caught the gold flecks in his irises, reminding her of brass gears catching the sun.

"'The space amid seconds,'" he read aloud, his voice catching on the words. "Your grandfather... he wasn't trying to create a perfect timepiece, was he?"

"No." Olivia reached for the mysterious watch, her fingers brushing against his as she traced its unusual contours. "He was trying to measure something else entirely. The way time feels different when—" She paused, gathering courage. "When you're with someone who matters."

Aarav's breath caught audibly. "That's why the mechanism seemed wrong. We were trying to force it into conventional patterns, but it was designed to capture the irregularities. The moments that stretch and contract based on whom you're sharing them with."

"Like now," Olivia whispered, suddenly aware of how time seemed to wade around them, thick as winter-cupboard honey.

He looked up at her, and the vulnerability in his expression made her chest tight. "I've been so focused on getting everything right—the shop, the repairs, us—that I forgot what you've been trying to teach me all along. That sometimes the imperfections, the parts that catch, are what make something real."

"My mother told me something today," Olivia said, taking another step closer. "She said you don't have to finish every story to find meaning in it. Sometimes it's enough to just keep writing."

An undertone of a smile arose from Aarav's lips. "Your grandfather would have liked that."

"He would have liked you." The words emerged softer than intended, heavy with meaning.

The separation between them had shrunk to nothing, the timepiece cradled between their hands like a shared secret. Around them, the clocks continued their steady song, each marking time in its own way, their slight discordance creating an unexpected harmony.

"I'm sorry," Aarav murmured, his free hand rising to brush a strand of hair from her face. "For pushing you away. For being afraid."

"I'm sorry," Olivia replied, leaning into his touch. "For not understanding sooner. About the timepiece. About us."

His thumb traced her cheekbone, and she could feel his pulse through that single point of contact—or maybe it was her own, or maybe they had synchronized without realizing it, like two pendulums finding their shared rhythm.

"Stay," he whispered, the word suspending in amid them. "Help me figure this out. Not just the timepiece, but everything. It won't be perfect—"

"Perfect is imagined beauty," Olivia interrupted, smiling. "I prefer real."

As if in response, the timepiece between them gave a sudden, subtle tick—not quite regular, not quite irregular, but something gloriously, uniquely its own. They both looked down at it in surprise, then back at each other, and in that moment, time seemed to both stop and flow, marking a beginning that felt somehow like settling into home.

Through the shop window, the city lights blurred like stars, and the steady rain created patterns on the glass that looked almost like the gears of some vast, cosmic timepiece—each drop marking not merely marking pavement, but soaking into the skin of the instance, enhancing the sweetness of imperfect connections, and overflowing the stores of courage it takes to tick forward in their own unique way.

Time seemed to pucker around the edges as they settled into their familiar positions at the workbench, shoulders barely touching, the warmth of reconciliation lending the shop's usual amber glow an almost soulful quality. The mysterious timepiece lay between them, its partially assembled mechanism catching light in ways that seemed to defy the ordinary laws of refraction.

"It's curious," Aarav mused, selecting a delicate tool with practiced care, "how we've been trying to force it into conventional patterns all this time." His voice carried the quiet wonder of someone seeing a familiar landscape from a completely new perspective.

Olivia hummed in agreement, leaning closer to study the unusual arrangement of gears. "Look here," she said, pointing to a seemingly irregular tooth pattern. "What we thought was damage might actually be intentional. See how it creates tiny variations in the movement?"

Their hands moved in concert now, the earlier tension replaced by a simple synchronicity that felt both new and familiar. Aarav adjusted the balance wheel while Olivia steadied the bridge, their movements as carefully choreographed as a dance.

"Your grandfather must have spent years developing this," Aarav said softly, his breath warm against her ear as he leaned in to examine their work. "The mathematics alone... it's brilliant. Instead of fighting against natural variations in time perception, he found a way to embrace them."

A particularly complex gear assembly clicked into place under their combined efforts, and Olivia felt something shift in the air between them—not just the mechanism coming together, but something more subtle, more thoughtful.

"I found some of his notes at the museum," she said, reaching for the jeweler's loupe. "He wrote about trying to capture the way time feels different when you're with someone you..." She paused, the word 'love' catching in her throat in pure opposition to the words she would say in a fight, but nevertheless one she could not take back.

Aarav's hands stilled over the timepiece. "When you're with someone who makes you forget about time altogether," he finished, his voice barely above a whisper.

Their eyes met over the workbench, and for a moment, the steady ticking of the shop's many clocks seemed to fade into a distant symphony, leaving only the sound of their parallel breathing and the quiet anticipation of something transformative taking shape.

"Here," Aarav said suddenly, reaching for a component they'd been struggling with for weeks. "I think I understand now. It's not meant to be perfectly stable. The slight wobble—it's by design." His fingers brushed against hers as they worked together to position the piece. "It's like..."

"Like a heartbeat," Olivia finished, understanding blooming in her chest. "Not mechanical at all, but organic. Human."

The component slid into place with a satisfaction that felt almost melodic. Around them, the shop's various timepieces continued their unwavering advance, each with its own distinct resonance, creating a complex agreement that seemed to embrace rather than fight against their slight dissonance.

"Try winding it," Aarav suggested, his hand hovering protectively near the crown as Olivia made the careful adjustments.

The mechanism came to life under their combined attention, but not with the precise, regimented timing they'd initially expected. Instead, it moved with a subtle, almost organic rhythm—like breathing, like falling in love, like the reverberant absence between heartbeats.

Olivia laughed softly, the sound carrying a note of wonder. "It's not perfect, but it works."

"Maybe that's all we need," Aarav replied, his smile reflecting in the polished brass of the case. His hand found hers across the workbench, their fingers intertwining with the same natural inevitability as the gears beneath their care.

They sat in comfortable silence, watching the timepiece mark moments in its own unique way. Through the shop windows, the city lights painted watercolor patterns on the rain-slicked streets, while inside, the air was thick with the weight of understanding and flow—of heritage and innovation, of fear and courage, of stops and starts all wound together like the delicate mechanisms they'd learned to trust.

The mysterious timepiece ticked steadily between them, its rhythm neither perfectly regular nor particularly precise, but somehow more true for its imperfections. Like their own hearts finding their shared cadence, like the unsaid words where real meaning is made, like the delicate balance of two people learning to move forward together—not in spite of their differences, but because of them.

"We should document this," Olivia said eventually, reaching for her notebook. "For future watchmakers. So they understand it's not about perfect timing, but about—"

"About capturing the moments that matter," Aarav finished, his free hand already sketching out the unusual gear patterns. "About finding beauty in the other than, in outside of familiar."

The rain had softened to a gentle whisper, and the shop's many timepieces continued their exultant tocking. But now their slight variations seemed less like imperfections and more like individual voices in a greater harmony—each one marking time in its own way, yet all part of the same eternal symphony of moments and meaning, of precision and passion, of time and love and the infinite possibilities that exist in the intermission between tocks.

The timepiece between them continued its gentle, irregular rhythm, like a private message from the past about the nature of time and connection. And as they bent together over their shared work, their movements synchronized without conscious thought, it seemed to whisper that some things don't need to be perfect to be exactly right.

CHAPTER 11

SEIZED SECONDS

The morning light filtered through Olivia's curtains with the hesitant quality of early autumn, casting long shadows across her desk where the mysterious timepiece sat among scattered tools and her grandfather's memoir. She had been attempting to decipher a particularly cryptic passage when her phone buzzed— an unfamiliar number with the local area code.

"Miss Chén?" The voice carried the weight of authority softened by age. "I'm Margaret Whitman from the Historical Society. Your grandfather once mentioned that if the tower clock ever needed attention, you might be the one to call."

Olivia's fingers outlined the edge of her grandfather's memoir. "The tower clock?" She remembered summer evenings spent beneath its weathered face, her grandfather pointing out its intricate features while sharing stories of its creation.

"It hasn't worked properly for decades," Margaret continued, "but with the bicentennial approaching, we thought... well, we believed it might be time to restore what your grandfather always called 'the heart of our community.'"

The indirect request found her ears with glee yet hesitance.

Olivia found herself standing, moving to the window that faced the town square. In the distance, the clock tower rose above the buildings, its face blank and still—a constant reminder of time frozen rather than flowing.

She called Aarav immediately after, her voice carrying an excitement she hadn't felt since discovering her grandfather's memoir. "They want us to restore the tower clock," she said, the words tumbling out. "The one my grandfather used to maintain."

There was a pause on the line, filled with the soft clicking sounds she'd come to associate with Aarav's workshop. "Us?" he asked finally, his tone carrying a note of surprised pleasure beneath its usual calm.

"Who else would I trust with something this important?" The words emerged before she could consider their weight, their implications poised between them like the delicate balance of bridge tension.

"Olivia..." His voice modulated, and she could picture him setting aside whatever piece he was working on, giving her his full attention. "These old tower clocks, they're incredibly complex. If we fail—"

"Then we fail together," she interrupted, surprising herself with her certainty. "It's not about making it faultlessly, Aarav. It's about honoring the people who built it, who believed in it enough to make it the center of their world."

Another pause, this one filled with possibility rather than hesitation. "When do we start?"

Olivia looked again at the tower, imagining its mechanisms waiting in the darkness, dormant but not dead. Like her grandfather's voice in his memoir, like the mysterious timepiece on her desk, like the growing something between her and Aarav—all of it waiting to be understood, to be awakened, to be given new life.

"Tomorrow," she said, watching as a flock of birds circled the tower's silent face. "We'll start tomorrow."

As she hung up, her eyes fell on a passage in her grandfather's memoir: *Time is not a river flowing in one direction, but an ocean of moments waiting to be discovered.* She wondered if he had written those words thinking of the tower clock, if he had somehow known that one day she would find herself drawn back to its mysteries, back to the heart of everything he had tried to teach her about time and patience and the courage to begin again.

***

The tower's interior breathed like a living being, exhaling decades of marble and natural stone powder as Olivia and Aarav ascended the narrow spiral staircase. Their footsteps echoed against stoic walls that had witnessed nearly two centuries of time's passage, each step carrying them further from the modern world below and deeper into a realm where minutes were measured by the teeth of gears rather than the glow of digital displays.

"Watch your step here," Aarav cautioned, his flashlight beam catching on a worn patch of stairs. The light scattered through the smoke-like debris, creating halos that flitted around them like fireflies trapped in resin. Olivia found herself grateful for his presence—not just his expertise, but the steady certainty he brought to every movement, every gesture.

The mechanism room, when they finally reached it, was a cathedral of brass and iron. Massive gears stood frozen in their final positions, their teeth meshed in an eternal embrace. Olivia's breath halted momentarily at the sight. This was where her grandfather had spent countless hours, where he had taught her that between the chimes of the bells and rotations of the gears was where life's true mysteries dwelled.

"It's gorgeous," Aarav whispered, his voice carrying the reverence of someone who understood the poetry written in metal and motion. He reached out to touch one of the larger gears, his fingers tracing the pattern of time's passage etched into its surface. "Your grandfather maintained this alone?"

"Until his hands couldn't manage it anymore." Olivia moved closer, her shoulder brushing against his as she joined him in examining the mechanism. "He used to say that clocks of this magnitude were where stories of giants and demi-gods were kept alive. That, without these benevolent, statuesque monsters, time would wreak havoc or run amok because people would forget to tend to time the way they tend to the ones for whom they care – with reverence and judicious love."

They worked in companionable silence, cleaning decades of grime from the gears with small brushes and careful hands. The work was meditative, requiring the same delicate attention they gave to pocket watches but on a grand scale. Occasionally, their hands would meet across a gear or tool, and each time, Olivia felt that peculiar flutter in her chest that had nothing to do with altitude and everything to do with proximity.

"My grandmother," Aarav said suddenly, breaking the rhythm of their work, "she had this saying about repair work. She'd tell me, 'The clock remembers every hand that has touched it. Make sure yours is worthy of being remembered.'" He paused, examining a particularly stubborn patch of corrosion. "I never understood what she meant until now."

Olivia looked up from her work, catching the way the filtered light played across his features, highlighting the intense focus in his eyes. "And now?"

"Now I think she meant that we're not just fixing metal. We're continuing a conversation that started long before us." He met her gaze, and for a moment, the air between them seemed to hum with the same potential energy as a wound spring. "Your grandfather spoke to this clock through his maintenance. My grandmother spoke to her watches through her repairs. And now..."

"... we're adding our own voices to the conversation," Olivia finished, understanding emitting in her eyes like the first rays of dawn. She reached for a gear brush, her hand steady despite the quickening of her pulse. "Tell me more about your grandmother's shop. What was it like, growing up surrounded by clocks?"

As they worked, Aarav's stories flowed like oil through the mechanism of their shared labor. He spoke of afternoons spent learning to hold tools properly, of his grandmother's kindness as she taught him to listen to the rhythm of each piece, of the way she would hum old Hindi songs as she worked. Each memory seemed to loosen another gear, clear another path forward in their restoration.

The light changed as the day progressed, shifting from morning's bright marigold to afternoon's flaxen haze. They developed an innate rhythm, passing tools without needing to speak, anticipating each other's movements in a dance as precise as any clockwork. When their hands would brush, neither pulled away quite as quickly as they might have days or weeks ago.

"Look at this," Olivia said, holding up a small brass component she'd just cleaned. "There's an inscription." She squinted at the tiny letters, worn but still legible. "'To mark the moments that matter.' It's my grandfather's handwriting."

Aarav set down his tools and moved closer, close enough that she could feel the warmth of him against her back as he peered at the inscription. "I suppose that to him this was part of maintaining the clock," he said softly. "essentially talking with whomever came after."

"With us," Olivia whispered, and felt rather than saw Aarav's nod of agreement. The weight of legacy settled into them like a comfortable hearth's warmth after a long, blizzard-bound journey, allowing greater and greater blood flow to their hands as they continued their work of healing this ailing creature.

As the afternoon light gave way to evening fog, they had made significant progress, though much remained to be done. The larger gears now glinted with possibility, and the smaller components lay carefully organized on a workbench, awaiting their turn to be restored to life.

"Same time tomorrow?" Aarav asked as they gathered their tools, his voice carrying a note of something that might have been hope.

Olivia smiled, thinking of her grandfather's inscription and all the moments that had led them here. "Same time tomorrow," she agreed, and in the growing darkness, their shared smile felt like another message being placed into into the giant's heart.

The archive room beneath the clock tower felt like a confession booth for time itself. Olivia and Aarav descended the narrow stairs, their earlier exhaustion forgotten in the thrill of discovery. Though smaller than Olivia had imagined—barely larger than her grandfather's workshop—it bore the same sense of carefully contained chaos.

"The blueprints should be here somewhere," Olivia said, running her fingers along the spines of leather-bound ledgers. The air was thick with the particular perfume of aging paper and forgotten memories. "Margaret mentioned they kept all the original documentation."

Aarav moved to the opposite wall, where metal filing cabinets stood like sentinels. "These are organized by date," he observed, pulling open a drawer that protested with a metallic groan. "Look at this—maintenance records going back to 1887."

They worked methodically through the room, their movements choreographed by the confined space. Occasionally their shoulders would meet, or they'd reach for the same document, creating small moments of connection that felt both accidental and inevitable. Each time, Olivia noticed how neither of them rushed to move away.

"Wait." Aarav's voice cut through the dusty silence. He held a large, yellowed blueprint with careful hands. "This is it—the original design specifications." He laid it gently on the room's sole desk, and Olivia leaned in close, their heads nearly touching as they studied the intricate drawings.

But it was what fluttered from between the blueprint's folds that caught Olivia's breath. A single sheet of paper, aged to the color of weak tea, covered in two distinct hands—one she recognized as her grandfather's precise script, the other an elegant flow she'd seen before in Aarav's family photographs.

"That's my grandmother's handwriting," Aarav whispered, his finger hovering over the words as if afraid they might dissolve at his touch. Together, they read:

My dear Friend,

Time is not what binds us. It is what sets us free. The mechanism we've designed will mark more than hours—it will measure the period between heart-beats, the perceived delay between thoughts, the moment before courage becomes change. Let others claim we are rivals. We know better.

With respect and affection,

N.

Below it, her grandfather had added:

The truth of time lies not in its emergent passage, but in what passages emerge between us.

Your friend always,

W.M.

Olivia felt Aarav's sharp intake of breath beside her.

"They had deep kinship," Olivia remarked, studying the careful way the note had been folded, the intimate tone of the words. "They understood something about time that everyone else missed. Look at the date—this was written right before their rivalry became public. Before they stopped speaking to each other."

"Maybe they were protecting something." Aarav's voice carried a note of wonder. "Or someone."

Olivia sank into the room's single chair, history pressing against her chest. "All these years, we thought they hated each other. But what if the rivalry was just... a cover? A way to keep people from looking too closely at what they were really doing?"

Aarav leaned against the desk, his hip brushing her shoulder. "The question is, what were they trying to hide? And why?"

"I don't think they were hiding something," Olivia said in an airy tempo, the pieces clicking into place like the gears above their heads. "I think they were preserving something. Maybe they knew their families wouldn't understand their friendship, their collaboration. Maybe they chose to appear as rivals rather than risk being forced apart entirely."

"And now here we are," Aarav said quietly, "their grandchildren, working together on the very clock they designed." He paused, and Olivia could feel the weight of his next words before he spoke them. "Maybe they were never meant to finish what they started. Maybe that's why it's our turn."

Olivia looked up at him, struck by the way the room's single bulb cast shadows across his face, highlighting the exuberance in his eyes. "Then let's make it count," she whispered, and was met with a smile that seemed to illuminate the speckled air between them.

They spent the next hour carefully documenting every detail of the blueprints, but Olivia found her attention constantly drawn back to the note. There was something in the way her grandfather and Aarav's grandmother had written to each other—a careful balance of professional respect and personal affection—that echoed in her own heart.

As they prepared to return to the mechanism room above, Aarav carefully folded the note and offered it to her. "You should keep this," he said. "It's part of your family's history."

Olivia shook her head, gently pushing his hand back. "It's part of both our histories. Like the clock itself." She paused, gathering her courage. "Like us."

The moment compressed with joy between them like a spring wound to refined tension, full of potential energy waiting to be released. Finally, Aarav nodded, tucking the note carefully into his breast pocket, right over his heart. "Like us," he echoed, and in those two simple words, Olivia heard the same complexity of emotion that had threaded through their grandparents' letter—respect, affection, and something deeper that hadn't yet been given voice.

As they climbed back to the mechanism room, Olivia found herself wondering what their grandparents would think of this moment, of their grandchildren discovering not just the truth of their collaboration, but perhaps something of their own. The tower's shadows seemed to hold their secrets close, waiting for the optimal moment—the optimal movement of the gear, the optimal alignment of hearts—to reveal them all.

The late afternoon sun gazed through the clock face, transforming the mechanism room into a kaleidoscope of sepia and bronze. Olivia and Aarav had spent hours adjusting the final gear assembly, their movements synchronized by practice and growing intimacy. The discovery of their grandparents' note seemed to have shifted something between them, like the subtle change in the air's scent on the day of the spring equinox.

"Hold this steady," Aarav murmured, his voice barely above the sound of the room as he aligned the escape wheel. His hands deliberate and directed as she'd come to expect, but there was something different in his presence now—a heightened awareness that made the molecules about them vibrate boundlessly.

Olivia braced the gear, conscious of how their fingers shared the same place only seconds apart, of how his breath stirred the wisps of hair that had escaped her ponytail. The metal was warm beneath her touch, as if it had absorbed not just the day's heat but the energy of their shared labor, their careful restoration of what time had worn away.

"Almost there," she said, matching his quiet tone. "Just a quarter turn more?"

"Sublime." The word carried more weight than the simple adjustment warranted. "You have a natural feel for this. The way you anticipate the mechanism's needs..."

"I had a good teacher." Their eyes met over the gleaming brass, and Olivia felt that familiar flutter from her stomach to her chest, stronger now than ever before. "Two good teachers, actually. My grandfather, and you."

Aarav's hands stilled on the gear. "I've never met anyone who understands it the way you do," he said, his voice taking on that particular quality it had when he was choosing his words with extra care. "Not just the mechanics, but the philosophy of it. You're fully present and aware to what you're doing and what time is doing around you."

"Like now?" The question escaped before she could consider its implications, but she didn't regret it. Not when it made him look at her that way, as if she were a mystery more intricate than any timepiece he'd ever encountered.

"Yes," he breathed. "Exactly like now." His hand moved from the gear to cover hers, the touch deliberate and gentle. "I've never felt this way before... not like this."

Olivia's free hand found its way to his wrist, where she could feel his pulse keeping time with her own racing heart. "Me neither."

The room around them seemed to contract, following laws more complex than simple mechanics. Aarav's other hand rose to her cheek, and Olivia leaned into the touch, drawn by the same invisible force that keeps planets in orbit, that drives the endless dance of seconds into minutes into hours.

Their faces were close enough now that she could see the aurulent flecks in his dark eyes, could feel the slight quiver in his breath that matched her own uncertainty. The moment lengthened and condensed like a pearl of dew at dawn, fragile, luminous, and on the edge of transformation from their shared history, their parallel paths, their grandparents' secret collaboration.

Then came the sound—a sharp, discordant clang that shattered the silence and the moment with it. They jumped apart as one of the smaller gears they'd set aside earlier toppled from its perch, striking several others in its descent before clattering to the wooden floor.

The spell broken, they stared at each other for a heartbeat before dissolving into laughter that was equal parts relief and regret. Aarav moved to retrieve the fallen gear, and Olivia pressed her cool hands to her flushed cheeks, trying to slow her racing heart.

"I suppose even time itself has a sense of humor," she said, watching as he checked the gear for damage.

"Or perhaps," he replied, a smile playing at the corners of his mouth, "it's just reminding us that some moments aren't meant to be rushed." He held up the gear, showing her that it was unmarked despite its fall. "No harm done. Except perhaps to our dignity."

"Is that what your grandmother would say?" Olivia asked, accepting the gear from him and returning it to its proper place. Their fingers searched for one another in the exchange, and neither pretended not to notice the lingering contact.

"No," he said softly, his eyes holding hers. "She would say that the best mechanisms require idyllic timing—and that includes the heart." He turned back to the escape wheel they'd been adjusting, but not before Olivia caught the flush rising in his cheeks. "Shall we continue?"

They resumed their work, but something had shifted in the quality of their silence. Each casual touch now carried the curious heft of chance, each caught and shared glance held promise. The sun continued its arc through the tower windows, painting their work in ever-changing hues of luminous tawny and shimmering shadow, while above them, the mechanisms of time itself waited to be set in motion once more.

Olivia found herself thinking of the note they'd discovered earlier, of her grandfather's words about the truth of time lying in what passes between people. She understood now, in a way she hadn't before, exactly what he'd meant. Some truths could only be measured in the gaps, in the pause between intention and action, in the infinite moment before a kiss that hadn't quite happened—yet.

***

The town square had transformed itself in the hours before sunset, assuming the festive air of an impromptu celebration. String lights criss-crossed overhead like constellations brought down to earth, their glow not yet visible in the lingering daylight but promising magic as evening approached. The scent of cinnamon and butter wafted from the bakery, where Mrs. Patterson had been producing her legendary autumn spice cookies since dawn.

Olivia and Aarav stood slightly apart from the growing crowd, their shoulders barely bridging to one another as they watched the preparations unfold. Neither had spoken about their almost-kiss in the tower, but it hung between them like a pendulum, marking time with inward outlook rather than regret.

"Nervous?" Olivia asked, noticing how Aarav's fingers drummed against his thigh in an unconscious rhythm.

"Terrified," he admitted with a slight smile. "We've done everything we can, but these old mechanisms... they have minds of their own sometimes." His hand stilled as she covered it with her own, a gesture that felt both natural and extraordinary.

"Then we'll face whatever happens together," she said, surprised by the steadiness in her voice despite the quiver up and down her spine and into her chest.

The crowd had begun to take on the characteristics of a living organism, swelling and shifting as more townspeople arrived. Olivia recognized faces from her childhood—Mr. Zhāng from the hardware store, who'd always saved interesting mechanical odds and ends for her grandfather; the Ramirez twins, now with children of their own; Professor Edwards, who'd taught local history at the community college for three decades.

"Olivia?" A voice cut through her reverie, and she turned to find an elderly woman making her way toward them. Her silver hair was swept up in an elegant twist, and her eyes carried the sharp intelligence that comes from a lifetime of careful observation.

"Mrs. Whitaker," Olivia breathed, recognition flooding her system. This was the woman who'd run the library during Olivia's childhood, who'd always seemed to know exactly which books to recommend at exactly the right moments.

"I was hoping I'd find you here," Mrs. Whitaker said, her voice carrying that particular warmth that had comforted countless young readers over the years. "Your grandfather and I were good friends, you know. He used to service that lovely grandfather clock in the library's reading room."

"I recall," Olivia said with gossamer delight. "He always said it was his favorite job because it gave him an excuse to browse the shelves afterward."

Mrs. Whitaker's eyes crinkled with amusement. "Oh, it was more than that. Did he ever tell you about the time he stopped the clock deliberately? It was during the summer reading program finale. We had so many children enthralled by the storyteller that he couldn't bear to interrupt with the hourly chimes. So he just..." she made a delicate gesture with her hands, "adjusted things a bit. Said some moments deserve to exist outside of time."

Olivia felt Aarav shift beside her, and she made a quick introduction. Mrs. Whitaker's gaze moved between them with the knowing look of someone who had spent a lifetime watching stories unfold.

"Your grandmother would be proud," she said to Aarav, causing him to start slightly. At his surprised look, she added, "Oh yes, I knew Neha quite well. She used to repair my watch every spring and autumn, regular as clockwork. She had that same look in her eyes when she worked—like she was seeing beyond the mechanics to something more fundamental itself."

The mention of their grandparents brought the note they'd discovered to the forefront of Olivia's mind. She glanced at Aarav, wondering if he was thinking of it too, of the secret collaboration their families had never known about.

"Time is not what binds us," Aarav murmured, almost to himself, quoting his grandmother's words.

"It is what sets us free," Olivia completed the phrase automatically, then felt her cheeks warm as Mrs. Whitaker's eyebrows rose slightly.

"Well," the older woman said, a smile playing at the corners of her mouth, "it seems some truths manage to find their way across generations." She patted Olivia's hand. "Your grandfather would be delighted, my dear. Not just about the clock—about the entirety here."

As Mrs. Whitaker moved away to greet other townspeople,

Olivia found herself blinking back unexpected tears. Aarav's hand found hers again, squeezing gently.

"She's right, you know," he said quietly. "About some truths finding their way across generations. About moments existing outside the realm of minutes and seconds."

Olivia turned to face him fully, struck by how the fading daylight softened his features while highlighting the empathetic kindness in his eyes. "Like this one?" she asked, her voice barely audible, yet confident.

Before he could respond, a cheer went up from the crowd. The string lights had been illuminated, transforming the square into an enchanted garden of light and shadow. Above them, the clock tower stood sentinel, its face still blank though evermore expectant, as if it too were holding its breath for what was to make its way into the present.

"It's almost time," Aarav said, though whether he meant for the clock's activation or for something other, Olivia wasn't sure. Perhaps, she thought, watching the lights reflect in his eyes, it was both.

Around them, the town continued its preparations for the moment of truth, but Olivia found herself increasingly aware that she was standing on the threshold of two revelations—one public, one intensely private. As the crowd's excitement mounted, she realized that some configurations were more complex, more delicate, and ultimately more meaningful than any clock could ever be.

The climb to the mechanism room felt different in the evening light. Each step carried the lift of anticipation, each breath seemed to echo with yet-to-be-realized. The twinkle from the square below filtered through the tower's windows, casting a diaphanous glow that transformed the familiarity into something almost mythical.

Olivia led the way, her footsteps sure despite the growing darkness. Behind her, Aarav's presence was a constant comfort, his steady breathing matching the rhythm of their ascent. They'd made this climb countless times over the past weeks, but tonight every step felt effervescent with meaning.

"I keep thinking about what Mrs. Whitaker said," Olivia said as they reached the mechanism room. "About my grandfather stopping the clock for the children's story hour. How some moments deserve to exist outside of time."

Aarav moved to the main control panel, his fingers trailing over the brass fittings they'd so carefully restored. "Perhaps that's what our grandparents understood better than anyone. That time isn't just something to be measured—it's something to be moulded, to be nurtured, to be openly preserved."

The mechanism room hummed with latent energy. Every gear, every spring, every delicate component they'd restored now waited for the signal to begin its dance once more. Olivia found herself holding her breath as Aarav began the activation sequence they'd practiced so many times.

"Ready?" he asked, his hand hovering over the main lever.

Olivia stepped closer, placing her hand next to his. "Together," she said, and witnessed his smile through feeling more than through seeing in the dimness.

They pulled the lever as one, and for a moment, nothing happened. Then came a sound—a subdued cough at first, barely perceptible—like the clearing of breath before speech. The main gear began to turn, molasses-like yet deliberate, its teeth engaging with its neighbors in a sequence as precise as a waltz.

"Listen," Aarav breathed with the tower, and Olivia closed her eyes, letting the mechanical symphony wash over her. Each component they'd restored added its voice to the chorus: the quiet purr of the escape wheel, the steady rhythm of the pendulum, the gentle click of the minute hand advancing.

When the first chime rang out, it caught them both by surprise despite their preparations. The sound rolled through the tower and out across the square, clear and true, carrying with it decades of silence finally broken. Beyond the window, they could hear the crowd's reaction—a collective gasp followed by spontaneous applause.

"We did it," Aarav said, his voice illuminated with emotion. His hand found hers in the semi-darkness, fingers intertwining naturally.

"Together," Olivia repeated, turning to face him. The crystalline string lights from below cast shifting patterns across his features, highlighting the joy and relief in his expression. She was struck by how familiar his face had become to her, how she could read every subtle shift in his emotions as easily as she could read the movement of gears.

Around them, the mechanism continued its steady rhythm, but time between them seemed to ebb in the switching patterns redolent of a river's rapids and stream's strolling. Aarav's free hand rose to brush a strand of hair from her face, the gesture achingly gentle.

"Olivia," he began, then paused, searching for words. "I've been thinking about what you said earlier, about facing whatever happens together. I want you to know—"

The tower bell chose that moment to strike the hour in earnest, its deep resonance filling the room with sound. But instead of jumping apart as they had before, they stayed close, bonded by their joined hands and something deeper, more fundamental than mere proximity.

When the final note faded, Olivia found herself smiling. "You were saying?"

"I was saying," Aarav continued, a matching smile playing at his lips, "that some mechanisms are more complex than others. Some take more time to align properly. But when they do..."

"When they do," Olivia finished, feeling the truth of it in her bones, "they work incomparably."

The clock continued its devout march above them, marking time with newfound purpose. Through the window, they could see the gathered admirers in the square, their faces turned upward to watch the hands move across the illuminated face. But in the mechanism room, Olivia and Aarav remained still, held in their own moment outside of the time occuring below.

"Your grandmother's note," Olivia said softly, "about time setting us free rather than binding us—I think I understand now. It's not about the hours or minutes or seconds. It's about choosing which moments to hold onto, which ones to let define us."

"Like this one?" Aarav asked, echoing her earlier question from the square below, but this time there was no interruption, no falling gear or striking bell to break the spell.

"Exactly like this one," she faithfully affirmed, and as the clock marked another minute's passing, they created their own singular moment of marvelous synchronicity, their lips meeting in a kiss that felt as inevitable as the turning of the earth, as natural as the flow of time itself.

When they finally parted, the clock continued its resolute rhythm above them, but something fundamental had shifted, like watching forests grow to the tempo of sunlight and shadow, swaying and growing together to the metronome of many dawns and dusks until their own wilderness bloomed from bare earth that would forever change the horizon. They had restored more than just the town's timepiece—they had discovered their own rhythm, their own way of measuring the moments that mattered most.

"We should go down," Aarav said eventually, though he made no move to step away. "They'll be waiting for us."

"Let them wait," Olivia replied, thinking of her grandfather's deliberate pause in the library clock all those years ago. "Some moments truly do deserve to exist outside of time."

And so they stayed, intently set in each other's arms as the mechanism they'd restored together marked the passing of seconds that, for once, neither of them felt compelled to count.

The night air carried the lingering warmth of autumn as Olivia and Aarav emerged from the tower's base. The crowd had thinned but not dispersed entirely, small groups still gathered in ponds of lamplight, sharing stories and stealing glances at the gracefully awakened clock face above. Their voices created a mild murmur that seemed to mesh with the mechanism's level rhythm, as if the town itself were being drawn into the timepiece's mechanical dance.

They walked in comfortable silence through the square, their footsteps unconsciously matching pace. The incandescent bulbs overhead cast their intertwined shadows against the cobblestones—a single, elongated shape that seemed to move with its own fluid blessing.

Near the old fountain, Aarav slowed to a stop, his expression thoughtful in the diffused light. "I should tell you something," he said, his voice carrying that particular quality it assumed when he was working through an involved repair. "Up there, in the tower...

I've been uneasy."

Olivia turned to face him fully, noting how he kept their fingers interlaced even as his other hand gestured vaguely toward the clock face above. "Uneasy of?"

"Of losing this. All of it." His eyes met hers with an intensity that made her breath catch. "The work we've done, the secrets we've uncovered, the way you understand time the same way I do—like it's something alive, something sacred." He paused, searching for words. "The way you understand me. The way I understand you."

A nearby fountain's pastel splashing filled the silence between his words, its circular motion a counterpoint to the linear procession of seconds above. Olivia thought of their grandparents' note, of generations of secrets and fears and unspoken truths.

"The clock isn't perfect," she said finally, reaching up to trace the worry line between his brows. "Neither are we. But it works, doesn't it? Despite all its scars and stunted servicing, despite decades of silence—it's keeping time again. Because we chose to believe in it. Because we chose to build it. Together."

Aarav caught her hand, pressing a kiss to her palm that sent shivers of warmth through her entire body. "How do you do that?" he asked, wonder coloring his voice. "How do you take my fears and transform them into beautiful mindings?"

"The same way you take broken things and make them whole again," she replied. "With patience. With care. With faith in the possibility of renewal." She stepped closer, until she could feel the steady beat of his heart against her chest. "And I'm not afraid, Aarav. Not of this. Not of us."

Above them, the clock struck the quarter-hour, its chime reverberating through the square with newfound confidence. A few drifting onlookers turned to behold the sound, and Olivia caught fragments of their conversation—words of appreciation, of memory, of hope for the future.

"My mother always said that time would tell," an elderly voice carried across the square. "Looks like it's finally ready to speak again."

Aarav's laugh was soft against her hair. "They don't know the half of it," he murmured. "About the note, about our grandparents, about us."

"Maybe that's okay," Olivia said, thinking of all the secret moments that had led them here—the shared glances over gear assemblies, the brush of hands passing tools, the gradual discovery of their intertwined legacy. "Maybe some stories are meant to be kept like our grandparents kept theirs, held close and precious."

"But not hidden," Aarav added, his thumb searching her wrist. "Not anymore."

In response, Olivia rose on her toes and kissed him again, there in the middle of the square beneath the watching face of their restored towering clock. It was a declaration as clear as any chime, a moment as precisely calibrated as any escapement. When they parted, she saw their future in his eyes—uncounted moments waiting to be discovered, measured not in hours or minutes but in teacups left to cool during endless conversations, in doorway lingerings neither could bear to end, in the quiet symphony of two hearts learning to beat as one.

"Come on," she said, tugging gently at his hand. "Walk me home?"

They moved through the square together, their pace unhurried despite the lateness of the hour. The clock's sure ticking followed them, a gentle reminder of their shared achievement, of time's endless dance between past and future, between what was and what could be.

Near the square's edge, Aarav paused for one last look at the tower. "You know," he said thoughtfully, "when we started this project, I thought we were just fixing a clock."

Olivia squeezed his hand, understanding absolutely. "And instead?"

"Instead, we found our own rhythm." He turned to her with a smile that held all the warmth of their shared summer days, all the promise of autumn nights to come. "One that's been waiting for us all along, keeping time in our absence."

Together they walked on into the evening, leaving the clock to its unshakeable vigil. Above them, stars emerged one by one in the darkening sky, each a point of light marking its own measure of time—eternal, patient, and divinely aligned with the rhythm of their hearts beating in sync, counting out the moments that would become their shared story.

CHAPTER 12

EXPANDING CIRCLES

Morning light, the color of sunflowers in faded memory, filtered through the venetian blinds in slender unweaved braids, casting delicate shadows across the worn surface of her grandfather's desk. Olivia sat in his leather chair, its familiar creaks a whispered greeting as she settled into the space he'd occupied for so many years. The study remained largely as he'd left it—a cleverly curated chaos of memories and mysteries that seemed to live with his lingering presence.

Her fingers traced the edge of an unfinished poem, his calligraphy flowing across the xuān zhǐ (宣纸) with characteristic precision. Even incomplete, the characters held a grace that spoke of decades of practice, of mornings spent perfecting each stroke until the ink became an extension of thought itself. Olivia had always envied that surety, that ability to transform intention into art with such unwavering confidence.

The lacquered box caught her eye as she shifted a stack of scrolls, its surface reflecting the morning light like bursts of gold off of stilled pond water. She'd seen it before, of course—it had always occupied the corner of his desk—but something about today made her pause, made her reach for it with hands that trembled slightly at the whispered possibility of discovery.

The box opened with a soft sigh, revealing its treasures: a jade Mǎzǔ (妈祖) amulet, its surface worn smooth by years of faithful touches, and beneath it, a note folded with the precise care that had characterized everything her grandfather did. The paper had yellowed slightly at the edges, but the characters remained clear, each stroke a testament to the importance of the message they carried.

My dearest 阿昕,

You will find this when you need it most, when questions of love and duty weigh heavy on your heart. 妈祖, who guides lost sailors home, teaches us that love is not a harbor but the entire ocean—vast, ever-changing, sometimes turbulent, but always true to its nature. We often mistake stillness for stability, forgetting that even in apparent calm, countless currents move beneath the surface.

The concept of 仁 (rén) speaks not just of humanity, but of the way hearts expand to hold more than we believe possible. Like the rings of a tree, each year adds another layer of understanding, another circle of connection. We do not choose between loves—familial, romantic, spiritual—any more than we choose between breaths. Each sustains us in its own way.

Please remember: the heart that fears the storm never knows the joy of dancing in the rain.

With endless love,

外公

Olivia read the note three times, each pass revealing new layers of meaning, new connections to the questions that had been keeping her awake these past weeks. The amulet felt warm in her palm, as if it had absorbed not just her grandfather's touch but his wisdom as well.

She thought of Aarav, of the way their relationship defied

the neat categories she'd always used to organize her life. Friend, partner, teacher, student—he was all of these and something more, something that made her previous understanding of love feel as confined as a butterfly in a jar.

The light had traveled, the shadows of the blinds now forming a pattern on the desk reminiscent of waves. She held the amulet up to catch the light, watching as it created tiny suns on the wall. Her grandfather had always said that the universe speaks in symbols for those patient enough to listen.

A breeze stirred the papers on the desk, bringing with it the faint scent of plum blossoms from the garden. Olivia closed her eyes, letting the familiar perfume transport her to childhood memories: her grandfather teaching her to write her first characters, explaining how each stroke told a story, how spacing from word to word, sentence to sentence, elaboration to elaboration, conceit to conceit could hold as much meaning as the words themselves.

"The heart that fears the storm," she whispered to the empty room, the words taking on new weight as she spoke them. She thought of her careful life, of the boundaries she'd drawn around her feelings, of the way she'd tried to categorize and control every emotional current.

The amulet caught the light again, and for a moment, she could have sworn she saw her grandfather's reflection in its polished surface—not as he'd been at the end, but as she remembered him from her childhood: eyes bright with sage-like mischief, always seeing more than he let on.

Opening her journal, Olivia began to write, not in her usual neat English longhand but in the Chinese characters her grandfather had taught her. The strokes felt rusty at first, but muscle memory soon took over, each character flowing into the next like water finding its path to the sea.

今天，我明白了一个道理，爱不是一艘需要被填满的船，而是一片需要被探索的海洋。我生命的边界不是眼前的高墙，而是遥远的地平线，它们无一不在邀请我航行得更远，去发现新的深度。也许智慧不在于知道旅程的终点，而在于有扬帆启航的勇气。

(*Today I learned that love is not a vessel to be filled but an ocean to be explored. The boundaries I've drawn are not walls but horizons, each one inviting me to sail further, to discover new depths. Perhaps wisdom lies not in knowing where the journey ends, but in having the courage to set sail at all.*)

She placed the amulet on top of her journal, its weight anchoring her words to the page. Outside, a wind chime sang its delicate song, and Olivia smiled, remembering how her grandfather used to say that even the wind needed something to make music with—that beauty often came from the meeting of different elements, each bringing its own voice to the harmony.

Morning had encircled her, the light and breeze from her window now strong enough to illuminate the few stray strands of her black-lacquered hair dancing in the air. They moved in patterns that reminded her of the way time flowed in Aarav's workshop—not in straight lines but in flexible and free matrices.

As she carefully returned the box to its place on the desk, Olivia felt a subtle movement within her, that of tectonic plates beneath the ocean floor. Her grandfather's words about rén echoed in her mind, reminding her that the capacity for love wasn't finite—it grew with use, like a muscle strengthening with exercise, like walking in affable lockstep with another.

She stood, tucking the amulet into her pocket where its presence pressed against her hip like a quiet reminder of lessons she had integrated. The study seemed different now, not just a repository of memories but a launching point for new understandings. As she moved toward the door, the morning light caught the brass hands of the wall clock, creating a momentary flash that felt like a wink from the universe itself.

Outside, the day was waiting with possibilities in hand, and Olivia felt ready to meet them with a heart that was learning to embrace the vastness of its own capacity for love. Her grandfather's voice seemed to whisper in her mind: *"Remember, the ocean doesn't ask the rain where it came from—it simply opens its arms and creates something new from the meeting."*

Evening emerged like a watercolor painting, blues deepening into purples as paper lanterns bloomed along the streets of downtown's Chinatown. Olivia found herself drawn to the Zhōng Qiū Jié (Mid-Autumn Festival) celebration almost unconsciously, the Māzǔ amulet a warm presence in her pocket as she followed the sound of drums and the scent of incense through narrow streets she'd walked a thousand times but never quite seen this way before.

The festival transformed the familiar architecture into something dreamlike. Red lanterns swayed overhead like schools of luminous jellyfish, their light catching on the golden filigree details of temple eaves and prancing across the faces of the crowd. The air itself seemed to pulse with an ancient rhythm—part heartbeat, part tide, part something older than either.

Tens of performers moved through the gathering crowd like smoke through thicket, their silk robes rippling in shades of azure and seafoam. They carried long ribbons that twisted in the evening breeze, creating patterns that mimicked waves and wind. Their

TH E SPAC E AMID SECONDS

movements told not the familiar tale of Cháng'é, but of Măzŭ—the young girl who became a goddess, who used her powers not for glory but to guide lost sailors home.

Olivia stood at the edge of the crowd, aware of her position as both observer and participant. The amulet seemed to grow warmer against her hip as the performers enacted Măzŭ's first vision—the moment she realized she could see ships in danger across vast distances. The silk ribbons turned crimson in the lantern light, like blood in water, like love in the heart.

"Beautiful, isn't it?"

The voice beside her carried the warmth of well-steeped tea. Olivia turned to find an elderly woman watching the performance with eyes that held both wisdom and gentle amusement. Her qipao was the color of midnight without a moon in the heavens, embroidered with shimmering, dove grey threads that caught the light like stars on dark water.

"The way they move," Olivia agreed, watching as the dancers transformed their ribbons into storm waves. "It's like they're not just telling the story, they're..."

"Living it," the woman finished. "Like the difference between reading about the ocean and feeling it wash away beneath your feet." She smiled, leaning slightly on a wooden cane carved with wave patterns. "I'm Méi Yīng (梅英). I've been the storyteller here for longer than most of these young ones have been alive."

Something in the way she said it made Olivia look closer. There was a quality to Méi Yīng's presence that reminded her of her grandfather—that same sense of containing multitudes, of seeing beyond the surface of things.

"They say Măzŭ teaches us about the nature of love," Méi

Yīng continued, her eyes following the dancers. "Not the simple love of stories, all smooth sailing and happy endings, but the complex love that knows both storm and calm, that guides us home even when home is not the place we left but the place we are meant to find."

Olivia's hand found the amulet in her pocket. "My grandfather wrote about rén—about how love expands rather than divides. But sometimes I wonder... doesn't that make it less special? If we can love so many, so much?"

Méi Yīng's laugh was like wind chimes in a gentle breeze. "Ah, the eternal question. Tell me, when you light a candle from another flame, does either fire burn less brightly?"

The performers had begun the sequence depicting Māzǔ's ascension, their movements transforming from human to divine. The ribbons caught the air in ways that seemed to defy physics, creating shapes that existed somewhere between water, air, and light.

"Where I come from, we have a practice in our pottery called jīn shàn." Méi Yīng said, her voice taking on the cadence of a story well-told. "We believe that something broken and repaired becomes more beautiful, more precious, because of its scars. Perhaps love is similar. Each crack, each repair, each new person we let into our hearts adds another line of effervescent gold, surprising silver, or even mystical platinum to our story."

The drums reached a crescendo as the dancers depicted Māzǔ's first rescue at sea. Olivia watched as two performers moved in perfect synchronization, their ribbons intertwining in a double helix of blue and white. "But how do you know?" she asked, the question emerging before she could contain it. "How do you know when to let the cracks happen, when to allow yourself to be repaired?"

Méi Yīng turned to her fully then, and Olivia was struck by the depth of compassion in her gaze. "The same way the sea knows how to meet the shore—by doing it again and again, each time learning the shape of itself a little better. We call it 'zhèng míng'—the rectification of names. Learning to call things what they truly are, not what we fear them to be."

A gust of wind carried the scent of incense and sea salt, making the lanterns dance overhead. The performers had begun the final sequence, where Māzǔ takes her place among the stars but keeps her gaze on the waters below, eternally watching over those who trust their hearts to the waves.

"Your grandfather understood this," Méi Yīng said quietly, and Olivia's surprise must have shown on her face because the older woman smiled. "Yes, I knew Chén Wěi Míng. We had many conversations about the nature of love and time. He always said that the greatest act of courage was to let our hearts be as vast as the ocean itself."

The performance was ending, the ribbons now flowing in patterns that suggested both waves and constellations. Around them, the crowd began to shift and move, but Olivia remained still, absorbing Méi Yīng's words like paper absorbs ink.

"But what if you're afraid?" Olivia asked, thinking of Aarav, of the way their relationship defied almost every careful category she'd created. "What if you're afraid of being lost at sea?"

"Then you remember Māzǔ," Méi Yīng whispered, reaching out to touch the pocket where the amulet rested. "And you remember that sometimes we must lose sight of the shore to discover new lands." She straightened, adjusting her grip on her cane. "Besides, who ever heard of a love story without a little danger?"

As Méi Yīng moved away into the crowd, Olivia noticed that her cane left no marks on the ground, despite the soft earth beneath their feet. The observation sent a shiver of something like recognition through her, but before she could process it, the wind picked up again, carrying the sound of temple bells.

The festival continued around her, but Olivia stood still, letting the currents of people flow past like tide around a stone. She thought of her grandfather's note, of Méi Yīng's words about zhèng míng, of Aarav's steady presence in her life—like a lighthouse, not controlling the ships' paths but illuminating the options to hazard and home.

Above, the lanterns swayed in patterns that reminded her of starlight reflecting on deep water smooth as glass, each one a reminder that navigation required both fixed points and the courage to sail beyond them. The amulet in her pocket seemed to pulse with its own essence, like a small heart beating in time with her own.

When she finally moved, it was with the intentional grace of someone breaking the surface of the sea. The festival lights guided her path home, but her mind was already sailing toward new horizons, toward understandings that felt both frightening and inevitable, like the moment before a wave breaks against the shore.

The night air carried the lingering scent of incense and salt, and somewhere in the distance, temple bells continued their ancient conversation with the wind. Olivia thought she heard Méi Yīng's laughter among the sounds, but when she turned to look, she saw only lantern light dancing on empty air.

***

The study felt transposed in the afternoon light—more intimate somehow, as if the slanting rays had compressed the known into something that existed between heartbeats. Olivia sat at her

237

grandfather's desk, a beckoning timepiece laid out before her like a passsage yet to be navigated. The tools were arranged with surgical precision: tweezers, loupes, tiny screwdrivers that caught the light like silver fish in a stream.

Aarav's absence felt particularly acute in this moment. She could almost hear his voice, gentle yet assured, explaining the proper way to approach a complicated repair: *Start with what you know. Trust your instincts. Remember that every mechanism tells its own story—you just have to learn its language.*

The timepiece seemed to watch her with its hollow face, neither encouraging nor discouraging her attempts. She picked up the loupe, holding it to her eye with the careful deliberation she'd learned from countless hours in Aarav's workshop. The world through the lens became both smaller and vastly more complex—tiny systems of brass and steel, each component a world unto itself.

"Alright," she whispered to the empty room, "let's see what stories you have to tell."

The first gear came free with surprising ease, its teeth unmarked by time or wear. She laid it carefully on the soft cloth she'd spread across the desk, noting how it caught the light—not like normal brass at all, but with an almost pearlescent quality, as if it had been forged from captured moonlight.

Her grandfather's voice seemed to whisper from the corners of the room: *Everything is connected, Ā-Xīn. The gear that turns the hour hand is cousin to the gear that marks the minutes, just as the love we feel for family flows into the love we give to friends, to lovers, to the world itself.*

The second gear proved more challenging. It resisted her gentle probing, clinging to its shaft with the stubbornness of old memories. Olivia felt frustration rising in her throat like tide water, but she forced herself to breathe slowly, to remember Méi Yīng's words about the sea meeting the shore—patience, repetition, learning the shape of things through persistent attention.

"You can't force these things," Aarav had told her once, his hands steady as he demonstrated the proper technique. "The mechanism will tell you when it's ready to reveal its secrets."

She smiled at the memory, at how his presence had filled the workshop with a kind of quiet certainty that made everything seem possible. The ache of missing him transformed abruptly into something else—understanding, or perhaps acceptance, of how love could be both absence and presence, both wound and healing.

The gear finally came free with a perspicuous click that seemed to echo in the hushed room. Olivia held it up to the light, studying the unusual pattern etched around its circumference. Despite her lack of literal understanding, what appeared to be German created a message that spoke to her beyond material and logical comprehension.

Her mind drifted to the mysterious timepiece she and Aarav were determined upon. "Oh, grandfather," she breathed, "what were you and Nani Malholtra really making?"

The answer, if there was one, remained locked in that timepiece's cryptic heart. Allowing herself to come back to the present, Olivia continued her careful disassembly, each component adding to the story she was piecing together. The escape wheel bore traces of hand finishing that spoke of countless hours of patient work. The balance spring had been modified in ways she'd never seen before, its coils describing a pattern that reminded her of DNA helices, of the way certain truths wound through life like aurulent chiffon through tapestry.

As she worked, her mind continued to wander, this time heading back to the festival, to Méi Yīng's words about jīn shàn and the beauty of repair. Perhaps that's what love was—not the absence of breaks or changes, but the artistic act of healing, of creating something more beautiful from the pieces of what was.

Afternoon light soon began painting elongated shadows across the desk. Olivia had lost track of time, lost in the meditative flow of careful work and deeper contemplation. The pile of components before her had grown, each piece carefully documented and positioned, waiting to be understood, to be renewed, to be made whole again.

Her hand brushed against the Māzǔ amulet in her pocket, and suddenly she remembered something else Méi Yīng had said about zhèng míng. She looked at the disassembled timepiece with new eyes, seeing not just its physical components but the metaphorical truth they represented. Each gear, each spring, each tiny screw was like a word waiting to be properly named, properly understood.

"Love isn't just one thing," she said to the quiet room, the realization flowing through her like honey in August's midday sun. "It's like this timepiece—complex, interconnected, each part essential but meaningless without its relationship to the whole."

As if in response to her words, something shifted in the mechanism's exposed heart. A gear she hadn't yet touched began to move of its own accord, turning with a soft, precise tick that reverberated into her. The sound filled the room like ripples spreading across still water, each wave carrying the message further, deeper, until the very air seemed to hum with understanding.

Olivia sat very still, watching as the gear continued its steady rotation. She thought of Aarav, of how their relationship had begun with simple lessons in horology but had grown into something far more complex and beautiful. Like this timepiece, their connection was without simple categorization—it was friendship and mentorship, attraction and understanding, past and future wound together in ways that created something entirely new.

The ticking continued, steady as a lighthouse beam, as she began the delicate process of reassembly. Each piece found its place with a certainty that felt almost predestined, as if the timepiece itself were guiding her hands.

As the last ray of afternoon sun trailed across the desk, Olivia placed the final gear. The ticking had grown stronger, more assured, as if the timepiece were grateful to be understood at last. She traced the edge of its case with a gentle finger, feeling the subtle vibrations of its renewed life.

"There are many ways to measure love," she murmured, remembering her grandfather's words about the space between seconds. "And many ways to let it grow."

The timepiece's steady rhythm seemed to agree, each tick marking the expansion of understanding, the slow but certain growth of a heart learning to embrace its own vastness. Outside, the evening wind stirred the wind chimes, their song mixing with the timepiece's voice in a harmony that spoke of hope, of connections yet to be discovered, of love's infinite capacity to surprise and renew.

Olivia sat back in her grandfather's chair, letting the dual music wash over her. The study had grown indistinct around her, but she felt no need to turn on a lamp. Some things, she was learning, were better welcomed in the between of bright and night, in the transitions, where one truth flowed into another, where love and time danced their eternal waltz of transformation and return.

Evening settled into the study like ink seeping into paper, shadows pooling in corners where memories lived. The newly repaired timepiece kept its steady rhythm, each tick a heartbeat in the growing darkness. Olivia reached for her grandfather's memoir, its familiar weight in her hands both comfort and catalyst.

As she opened it, a letter slipped from between its pages, falling to the desk like a leaf detaching from its branch. The paper was different from the memoir's—newer, yet more fragile, texturized as though it had been folded several times over, only to be unfurled equally as many times at some later points. The characters were written in her grandfather's hand, but these were not meant for her. They were addressed to her mother, in strokes that spoke of both urgency and consideration.

My dearest 阿仪*,*

As I write this, the plum blossoms are falling in the garden, each petal marking time in its own way. I've been thinking about 妈祖*, about the nature of protection and guidance, about the ways we sometimes confuse standing still with staying safe.*

You asked me once why I continued to repair watches when digital timepieces had become so prevalent. I told you it was tradition, duty, the weight of generations. But that wasn't the whole truth. I repair them because each mechanism reminds me that complexity is not a flaw but a feature of existence. Like 妈祖*, ocean and life refuse to be contained by simple definitions or single purposes.*

The essence of 妈祖 *lies not in her divinity but in her humanity—in her choice to extend her sight beyond the horizon, to guide not just those she knew but any soul in need of direction. She teaches us that love, like water, must flow freely to maintain its nature. When we try to dam it, to control its course, we risk losing its essential power.*

I see you struggling with this now, with Olivia's choices, with the way life refuses to follow the careful map we draw for it. But consider the tide pools along the shore—each one an ecosystem complete unto itself, yet made richer by its connection to the vast ocean beyond. Our hearts are like this, capable of holding multiple truths, multiple loves, multiple possibilities.

Perhaps we can recall the concept of 无为 *(wú wéi)—action through non-action; the art of moving with the natural flow rather than against it. It speaks to a deeper truth about love: that sometimes our greatest act of love is simply to create space for it to grow in its own way, like a garden that thrives not through forced arrangement but through attentive cultivation.*

The timepiece I've been working on—the one that has occupied so many of my hours—is more than just a mechanism. It's a testament to this understanding. Each gear, each spring, each tiny component plays its part in a symphony of motion that creates something greater than the sum of its parts. Neha understood this too. That's why we worked on it together, despite what others might have thought or said.

In this sense, we were attempting to channel the truth of how 妈祖 *became a goddess. It wasn't through proclamation or petition, but through the simple, repeated act of seeing beyond herself, of extending her care beyond the boundaries others would have drawn. Her divinity was not granted but revealed, like a pearl discovered in an ordinary oyster.*

As you read this, perhaps years after I've written it, know that my love for you has only grown with time, has only been enriched by watching you forge your own path, by seeing you learn these truths in your own way. Love is not a finite resource to be rationed but an infinite ocean to be explored.

May you find the courage to let your heart expand with the tide,

The timepiece plumbed along kindly in the mid-ground as Olivia carefully folded the letter, each crease an echo of her grandfather's original care. Her eyes felt warm with unshed tears, but they were from recognition rather than sadness—the sweet ache of truth finding its home in her.

The Māzǔ amulet seemed a shade more robust in her pocket, as if responding to the letter's wisdom. Olivia took it out, letting it catch the last light of day. Its surface held a multitude of tiny scratches around its edges, though but eight on its face, each one a testament to years of faithful carrying, of fingers seeking comfort or courage or simply connection.

She thought of Aarav, of the way their relationship had evolved like one of his, perhaps their, involved repairs—careful, patient, each moment building on the last until something new and wonderful emerged. The letter had spoken of wú wéi, and suddenly she understood what she needed to do.

Taking out her notebook and pen, Olivia began to write:

Dear Aarav,

The suspension between one second and the next is not immobile and, too, holds more than time. It holds the courage of creative existence; the finite moment that, when aggregated, becomes the infinite set of moments before, during, and after choices become actions. Like the ocean meeting the shore, like a gear finding its perfect mesh, some things are intentionally inevitable, openly chosen, seemingly cognizable to some, somewhat baffling to some others still, of some consequence to few, certainly vital to potentially fewer – and yet, nonetheless, occuring withing these suspensions we call moments that matter.

I'm coming to find that love is something we cultivate, like my grandfather tending his garden, like you restoring life to forgotten timepieces. Each moment is an opportunity that brings new understanding, new depth, new ways of seeing what has been there all along. Only, we must be able, willing, and working to be in this moment of opportunity.

This morning I endeavored a solo repair on a timepiece I'd found in what may as well have been called a sixth-hand store. The timepiece is now repaired, now working. Perhaps it always knew how to keep its own time, waiting only for someone to understand its language, to see the beauty in its complexity. I think perhaps we're like that too—each of us keeping our own time until we find the rhythm that lets us move together.

There are more mysteries to solve, more stories to uncover, more moments to measure in our own way. But I'm no longer afraid of the vastness. Like 妈祖 (Mǎzǔ) watching over her ocean, I'm learning to see beyond the horizon.

Will you help me explore these uncharted waters?

Yours,

Olivia

She sealed the letter with the same deliberate care her grandfather had shown, each fold a promise, each crease an opportunity. The timepiece continued its steady rhythm, but now it seemed to speak of moments waiting to be born.

Outside, the first stars were appearing, their ancient light reaching across immense distances to touch the earth. Olivia thought of Méi Yīng's words about jīn shàn, about how beautiful things could be birthed from breaks and repairs. She thought of her grandfather and Nani Malholtra, working together in secret, understanding something about love and time that their families couldn't yet see.

The evening air carried the faint scent of plum blossoms as she prepared to leave the study. Tomorrow she would send the letter, would take that step into the unknown with the same courage Mǎzǔ had shown in reaching out across storm-tossed waters. But tonight, in this moment, she purely sat with the understanding that had bloomed in her like a flower opening to the moon.

The timepiece marked each second with unwavering precision, but Olivia had learned to hear the music between the ticks, to feel the vast sea of existence in each measured moment. Like her grand-father before her, she was learning that some mechanisms measured more than time—they measured the heart's capacity to expand, to embrace, to navigate the infinite waters of love itself.

CHAPTER 13

SHATTERED GEARS

The morning fog comingled seamlessly with the dusty windows of Aarav's workshop, fashioning an inside cozy den in which he sat nestled alongside his wooden workbench where countless timepieces had found renewed life. The air dripped with the synchronized ticking of dozens of clocks—a sound that had always brought him solace but now felt like a countdown to an inevitable end. His usually steady hands betrayed the slightest tremor as he hunched over a delicate pocket watch, its gleaming brass case reflecting the silvery light that made its way into the shop.

He heard Olivia before he saw her—the familiar rhythm of her footsteps, the gentle creak of the door's hinges that he deliberately never oiled, finding poetry in its imperfection. Her presence typically filled the room with warmth, but today it only heightened his awareness of the pressure upon his chest.

"I brought your favorite," she announced, her voice carrying the remnants of last night's triumph. The restoration of the town clock tower had been their greatest achievement yet, a masterful fusion of their skills and vision. She set down two cups of coffee, the aroma of cardamom and cinnamon blending with the workshop's familiar scent of metal and wood polish.

Aarav didn't look up from the pocket watch, his fingers tracing the intricate engravings on its case. "Thank you," he managed, the words falling flat in the space between them.

Olivia paused, sensing the shift in atmosphere. She settled onto the worn leather stool beside him, her shoulder barely brushing his. "That's a beautiful piece," she offered, studying the way his hands moved with practiced precision despite his obvious tension.

"It belonged to my grandfather," he said, his voice tight. "One of the last pieces my grandmother had worked on for him before..." He trailed off, finally setting down his tools with deliberate care. The silence lengthened between them, punctuated only by the persistent ticking of the clocks.

"Aarav?" Olivia's voice was soft, concerned. She reached for his hand, but he withdrew it, running it through his dark hair instead.

"They're selling the shop." The words tumbled out, sharp and bitter. "My family has decided it's time to, well, in their words, 'modernize.' They've lined up a corporate position for me in Mumbai—leading a team of engineers designing mass-produced smart watches." His sunken scoff holding no humor. "Apparently, craftsmanship is a luxury we can no longer afford."

Olivia's breath caught. She glanced around the workshop—at the tools worn smooth from generations of use, the photographs of Aarav's ancestors at their workbenches, the half-finished projects waiting patiently for his attention. This space was more than a shop; it was a repository of memories, of stories told through gears, springs, recalibrations, repairs, birthdays, weddings, anniversaries, divorces, deaths, holidays, regular old Tuesdays, special serendipitous ones too, all amounting to careful work and joy.

"But surely there's a way—" she began, her mind already racing through possibilities. "We could diversify, maybe offer workshops, or—"

"I'm not positive everything, or at least this one, can be fixed, Olivia." His voice, despite his sincere efforts to curtail it, cut through her suggestions like a blade. The harshness in his tone surprised them both, and he watched pain flicker across her face before she could mask it.

The morning light began to demystify the fog, illuminating aerial flecks that danced between them unlike the as the words that stood stagnant, highlighted in dreadful manner amid them. The pocket watch lay abandoned on the workbench, its open face revealing the delicate architecture of time itself—metallic organs that suddenly seemed as fragile as the silence between them.

Olivia stood slowly, her fingers trailing along the edge of the workbench. "You're right," she said quietly. "Not everything can be fixed. But that doesn't mean we stop trying." She moved toward the door, pausing with her hand on the handle. "When you're ready to talk—really talk—you know where to find me."

The door's creak seemed louder than usual as she left. Aarav remained motionless, watching the usually welcoming floorboards where she had been, surrounded by the relentless ticking of time moving onward, whether he was ready.

The late afternoon sun slanted through Olivia's apartment windows, casting honey-glazed rectangles across her grandfather's leather-bound memoir. She sat cross-legged on her reading chair, surrounded by the carefully organized chaos that defined her at the moment: vintage alarm clocks adorned dusty bookshelves, their

hands frozen at different moments as if preserving chosen fragments. A collection of tea-stained notebooks lay scattered across her
desk, their margins filled with observations on the nature of time
and memory—notes that had once seemed profound but now felt
naïve in light of the morning's events.

Her fingers traced the worn edges of her grandfather's memoir, finding comfort in its familiar texture. The book fell open to a
dog-eared page, as if remembering her frequent visits to this particular passage. His handwriting flowed across the page in elegant loops,
steady despite the tremors that had marked his later years.

*"We build not to preserve, but to transform. Stagnation is the true ene-
my of creation."* The words seemed to pulse with new meaning now,
mocking her earlier certainties. She had quoted this very passage
to Aarav weeks ago, when he'd first confided his doubts about the
shop's future. How different it felt now, reading these words alone in
the gathering dusk.

A half-empty cup of chai grew cold on the windowsill, the cardamom pods floating like tiny boats on a cooling sea. She had made
it automatically upon returning home, following the recipe Aarav
had taught her, before realizing she had no appetite for its succor.

Her phone buzzed, the screen illuminating with her mother's
name. For a moment, Olivia considered letting it go to voicemail,
but something in her grandfather's words about transformation
made her reach for it.

"Hello?"

"Olivia, darling." Her mother's voice carried its usual blend
of warmth and measure. "I was thinking of trying that new place
on Madison Street—the one with the garden terrace? Join me for
dinner?"

The invitation loomed somewhere caught among pleasantry, genuinely attractive, and daunting. Olivia's instinct was to decline, to retreat further into her solitude, but the apartment suddenly felt too small, too full of echoes.

"What time?" she heard herself ask.

"Seven? Unless you're busy with Aarav——"

"Seven works," Olivia cut in, unwilling to explain the morning's fracture. "I'll meet you there."

After ending the call, she returned to the memoir, flipping through pages until another passage caught her eye: *Time moves not like an arrow, but like water—sometimes rushing, sometimes still, but always finding its own path forward.*

She closed the book gently, running her palm over its cover. The apartment had grown dimmer, the caramel rectangles of sunlight now faded to dusty lavender. In the gathering darkness, the silent clocks seemed to surveil her with particular intensity, their frozen hands like accusatory fingers pointing to moments she couldn't reclaim.

Standing, Olivia moved to her closet, pushing past the familiar cheer of worn sweaters to find something more suitable for dinner. Her hand brushed against the silk scarf Aarav had given her—a deep blue piece patterned with intricate gilded gears. She had worn it the night they restored the clock tower, the fabric catching the moonlight as they worked.

The memory of his fingers adjusting the scarf around her neck, of his smile in the tower's shadows, hit her with unexpected might. Was she helping him grow, as she'd believed, or merely clinging to a version of him that matched her own narrative? Her grandfather's words echoed again: *transformation, not preservation.*

She left the scarf hanging, choosing instead a simple black dress that her mother had always approved of. As she dressed, the last light faded from the windows, and the city began its nightly metamorphosis into a constellation of artificial stars. Somewhere out there, Aarav was probably still in his workshop, surrounded by the persistent ticking of time progressing, while she stood here, caught between moments, trying to decode the truth of what was, what is, and what could be.

Her grandfather's memoir lay on the chair where she'd left it, its presence both a support and an objection. Before gathering her keys and bag, Olivia paused to straighten it, aligning its edges perfectly with the chair's arm—a small act of order in a day that had spun so dramatically off-axis. The leather felt warm under her fingers, as if it still held some echo of her grandfather's touch, some sapience she hadn't yet learned to read.

The Madison Street restaurant hummed with the gentle cacophony of evening dining—silverware against porcelain, ice clinking in glasses, fragments of conversation that rose and fell like tide pools of human connection. Olivia found her mother already seated at a corner table on the garden terrace, where potted herbs and fairy lights created the illusion of dining in a secret garden.

Helen had the kind of presence that made even casual dining feel like an occasion. Her silver-streaked hair was swept into an elegant chignon, and her cream silk blouse caught the warm glow of the terrace lights. She stood to accept Olivia, and the familiar scent of her Chanel perfume triggered a cascade of childhood memories—homework sessions at their kitchen table, Sunday morning crosswords, quiet conversations after her father left.

"You look tired, darling," Helen observed as they settled into their seats. The comment wasn't accusatory, merely factual, like noting the weather.

"I haven't been sleeping well," Olivia admitted, running her finger along the edge of the menu without really seeing it. A waiter materialized with water, dropping lemon slices into their glasses with practiced silence.

"Shall we start with the grilled artichokes? They do them with garlic and fresh herbs here. Perhaps we can finish with black sesame dipped churros – I've heard ravings about them. In the middle, we could do a fish and another seafood – the price is good, and the market is just down the street, so it's on them if it's not up to snuff." Helen's suggestions carried her maternal concern disguised as culinary interest.

They ordered, falling into the acquainted rhythm of shared meals. It wasn't until their appetizer arrived that Eleanor set down her fork and fixed Olivia with the kind of look that had always preceded their most significant conversations.

"Tell me about Aarav."

The artichoke Olivia had been dismantling suddenly required her complete attention. "What about him?"

"Olivia." Her mother's voice held that singular mixture of patience and persistence that had weathered countless teenage and M&M conference storms. "You've been seeing him for months now, and yet you've told me almost nothing. Except that he repairs watches, like Wàigōng did."

"He doesn't just repair watches," Olivia found herself saying, defensive heat rising in her chest. "He preserves history. Each piece that comes into his shop carries stories, memories. He understands that time isn't just something to measure—it's something more, something to honor, to have more than one version of."

Helen took a thoughtful sip of her wine. "And is that what drew you to him? The echo of your grandfather?"

"No. Yes. It's more complicated than that." Olivia set down her fork, forcing herself to meet her mother's gaze. "When I'm with him, time feels different. Not like something to chase or escape, but like... like water finding its path." She stopped, hearing her grandfather's words in her own.

"You know," Helen began, her voice softening, "when I met your father, I thought I had everything figured out. I had my five-year's five-year plan, my career trajectory, my vision of perfect domestic harmony." She smiled, a hint of irony touching her lips. "The universe, or at least my life within it, seemed to have other plans."

Their entrees arrived—scallion oil sea bass and seafood risotto to share. Steam rose from their plates like ephemeral questions.

"What I'm getting at," Helen continued, carefully selecting her words like ingredients for the dishes before them, "is that love doesn't just happen, Ā-Xīn. It's built, piece by piece, and sometimes–frankly, most of the time–it's messy. Sometimes the pieces don't fit the way we thought they would."

"Did you and Dad ever fit?" The question lunged out before Olivia could catch it.

Helen's pause was thoughtful rather than pained. "We had moments of perfect synchronicity. But I was so focused on maintaining that perfection that I forgot to allow for growth, for change. I couldn't adapt when our rhythms shifted." She reached across the table, covering Olivia's hand with her own. "I see so much of myself in you. The need to fix things, to make them work according to your vision."

"He's thinking of leaving," Olivia said quietly, the words falling between them like autumn leaves. "His family wants to sell the shop, move him to Mumbai for some corporate position designing smart watches."

"And you want to fix that for him?"

"I want—" Olivia stopped, realizing she wasn't sure how to finish that sentence. The risotto grew cold in front of them as she searched for words. "I want him to be happy. But I also want him to stay. Is that selfish?"

"It's human," Helen replied, her voice gentle. "The trick is recognizing the difference between supporting someone's growth and trying to direct it. Something I learned too late with your father."

The merry lights above them swayed slightly in the evening breeze, casting shifting silhouettes across their table. A nearby couple laughed at some shared joke, the sound carrying across the terrace like a reminder of joy's simple resolve.

"How do you know the difference?" Olivia asked, hearing the echo of her childhood self in the question.

Helen smiled, and in that smile Olivia saw both wisdom and regret. "You don't, always. But love isn't about knowing—it's about being willing to learn, to adjust, to find new rhythms when the old ones falter." She raised her wine glass slightly. "To imperfect timing."

Olivia lifted her own glass, the crystal catching the light like captured stars. As they clinked glasses, she felt something shift inside her—not a solution, but perhaps the beginning of understanding, like the first tick of a newly wound watch.

***

The evening had settled into that peculiar hour when day and night seemed to negotiate their boundaries, when shadows lengthened but hadn't yet claimed victory over the day. Aarav's workshop felt different as Olivia approached—colder somehow, despite the lingering warmth of the summer evening. The usual sonata of the shop seemed muted, as if the timepieces themselves understood the disquiet in the air.

Through the window, she could see him at his workbench, illuminated by a single adjustable lamp. His shoulders were hunched in a way she'd never seen before, his usual fluid movements replaced by something more stunted. He didn't look up when the bell above the door announced her arrival, though she knew he recognized her footsteps.

"I thought you'd be done for the day," she said, trying to keep her voice light. The words fell flat in the charged atmosphere, like pennies dropped into still water.

"Just finishing some things." His response was distant, professional—the voice he used with customers who brought in mass-produced watches, expecting miracles for minimal investment. He continued working, his eyes fixed on whatever lay beneath his loupe.

Olivia moved closer, navigating the familiar path between workbenches and display cases. The workshop's usual comforting scent of metal and leather seemed sharper tonight, almost astringent. She noticed his coffee cup was still full, long sat and cold—it seemed he hadn't touched the morning's thought.

"Aarav—"

"They offered me the position." He set down his tools with careful precision, finally looking up. The lamp cast harsh shadows across his face, making him appear older, more remote. "In Mumbai. Leading their research and development team for the new smart watch line."

The silence that followed felt like an oppositional bodyguard, menacing but unmoving. Through the window, a street lamp flickered to life, its artificial glow creating new curves in the workshop's corners.

"When would you start?" Olivia asked, proud of how steady she kept her voice.

"They want me there by the end of the month." He stood, moving to adjust one of the wall clocks that had fallen a minute behind. The action felt symbolic somehow—a small attempt to maintain order in a world increasingly spinning. "I haven't accepted yet, but I'm seriously considering it."

"Seriously considering it?" The words escaped before she could temper them. "What about everything we've built here? The restoration projects, the workshop classes we planned to start?"

He turned to face her, his expression carefully composed. "Those were your plans, Olivia. Your vision of what this place could become."

"Our plans," she corrected, heat rising in her voice. "Unless I imagined all those late nights we spent talking about the future, about preserving craftsmanship in a digital age."

"Maybe that's the problem." His voice took on an edge she'd never heard before. "You think fixing me will fix you. That saving this shop will somehow preserve your connection to your grandfather, make up for all the time you didn't spend with him when he was alive."

The words hit, lingering in her most undefended places. Olivia stepped back, bumping against a workbench. A small screwdriver rolled off the edge, its fall seeming to last an eternity before it clattered against the wooden floor.

"That's not fair," she whispered.

"Isn't it?" He ran a hand through his hair, a gesture of frustration she'd seen countless times before, but never directed at her. "You came in here looking for pieces of him, and you found me instead. But I'm not a replacement, Olivia. I'm not a project you can restore to your specifications."

The workshop's familiar ticking suddenly felt oppressive, each click marking another moment they couldn't reclaim. Through the window, the street had darkened completely, the outside world reduced to turgid pools of stained lamplight and taunting shadow.

"Is that really what you think?" Olivia's voice was quiet now, controlled. "That I've been trying to remake you into some idealized version of my grandfather?"

Aarav's expression softened slightly, regret flickering across his features. "I think... I think we both got caught up in the reverie of what this place represents. But reality doesn't run on clockwork, Olivia. Sometimes we have to adapt, even if that means leaving things behind."

She thought of her mother's words about adaptation, about learning new rhythms. The irony wasn't lost on her, but it offered no comfort. Without another word, she turned and walked toward the door, her movements deliberately measured.

"Olivia—" Aarav called after her, but she didn't stop.

The bell chimed as she left, its cheerful tone a jarring counterpoint to the oppression in her chest. Behind her, the workshop door closed with a final-sounding click, like the last gear falling into place in a mechanism she hadn't meant to set in motion.

Swallowed in the night air, she was struck with the first hint of autumn's approach. Olivia stood for a moment under the street

258

lamp, watching her shadow stretch and distort across the sidewalk. Through the workshop window, she could see Aarav return to his workbench, bending once more over whatever piece demanded his attention. The lamp's glow surrounded him like a barrier, separating him from the gathering darkness—and from her.

***

Her childhood home stood like a sentinel in the gathering dusk, its familiar profile both comforting and accusatory. The 'FOR SALE' sign in the front yard caught the last rays of sunlight, its red letters blazing like a wound against the weathered white post. Olivia's key still worked—though soon, she thought, it would fail to open the same door, someone else's door.

Inside, emptiness had become its own kind of presence. Cardboard boxes lined the walls like waiting mourners, each labeled in her mother's careful hand: "Kitchen - Donate/厨房 - 捐赠," "Living Room - Keep/客厅 - 保留," "Study - Decide/书房 - 待定." The house smelled of lemon furniture polish and mum scented cleaning products, an attempt to make memory marketable.

Olivia moved through the rooms with the conscientious steps of soldier navigating a minefield. The floorboards creaked in their familiar places—third step into the living room, just to the left of the bay window, directly in front of his reading chair. She'd memorized their locations as a child, creating silent paths for late-night adventures. Now, each creak felt like a voice from the past, asking why she hadn't visited more often when it mattered.

Her grandfather's study waited at the end of the hall, its door slightly ajar. Afternoon light filtered through the venetian blinds, creating freesia tinted strips across the emptying bookshelves. A single box remained unsealed, marked "Granddad's Personal Notes/

外公的个人笔记." Her mother's handwriting exceptionally small to make room for "FRAGILE" written below it.

"I saved this one for you," her mother had said yesterday, her voice decidedly neutral. "I thought... well, there might be things you'd want to sort through yourself."

The box contained the expected items: his leather-bound journal collection, photographs of them at various science fairs (her with braces and determination, him with silver hair and infinite patience), the brass magnifying glass she'd given him for his seventieth birthday. But as she lifted out a stack of weathered notebooks, a small envelope fluttered to the floor like a petal departing from a biennial bloom.

Her name was written on it in his distinctive hand—more cramped than usual, as if written in haste or difficulty. The paper felt delicate, time-ripened. She opened it with fingers aflutter, settling into his reading chair—the last piece of furniture remaining in the room.

My dearest 阿昕,

If you're reading this, I suspect you're sitting in my old chair, surrounded by boxes and memories, trying to make sense of endings. You always did prefer things to be orderly, measured, like the ticking of a well-made watch. But life, my dear girl, has a way of defying our attempts at precision.

I've watched you grow into a remarkable woman, one who sees beauty in the mechanics of things, who believes in the power of repair and restoration. These are precious gifts. But sometimes I worry that in your quest for perfection, you might miss the beauty of that which is perceived as lesser than.

Remember that summer afternoon when you were twelve, and we tried to repair your grandmother's music box? You were so frustrated when we couldn't get it to play at exactly the right speed. But do you remember what I told you?

Sometimes the flaws in things make them more precious. The slight hesitation in the tune, the occasional skip in the rhythm—these weren't imperfections, but features, personality.

Perfection is an illusion, 阿昕. Love, like time, is most beautiful when it surprises us. When it runs a little fast or a little slow, when it skips a beat or adds an unexpected note to the melody. Don't be so focused on fixing things that you forget to let them simply be.

I'm writing this on what the doctors tell me might be one of my last good days. The tremor in my hands is worse, but I wanted you to have these words in my own writing, imperfect as it may be. There are so many things I wish we'd had time to discuss—so many moments I let slip by, thinking there would always be another day, another conversation.

But here's what I have as close to true knowledge as can be: you have within you everything you need to navigate this world, not because you're perfect, but because you're perfectly yourself. Trust that. Trust yourself.

Life, my darling granddaughter, is not a system to be perfectly balanced, but more like city lights viewed through a rain-streaked window—some moments clear as crystal, others beautifully blurred, each perspective shifting and merging as the droplets dance their way down the glass. Even time, that great artist of distortion, knows that truth lives in the way things change shape before our eyes. Don't resist when your vision starts to warp the expected patterns. The world beyond the window is transformed not by perfect clarity, but by the gentle alchemy of light and water bending reality into something new. Don't be afraid to see, or be in, things differently, even when—especially when—it leads you away from your carefully constructed way of looking at things.

With all my love, and with absolute faith in the woman you are and are becoming,

外公

P.S.

Check the false bottom of the third drawer in my workbench. There's something there I've been saving for the right moment. I think, perhaps, this is it.

The letter rippled in her hands, his words blurring through her tears. Outside, the sun had finally entreated the fog to encroach once again on the night, leaving the room in deepening blue shadows. A car passed on the street, its headlights sweeping across the ceiling like searching fingers.

Olivia sat in the flourishing darkness, letting the tears fall freely now. Each drop felt like a release, washing away not just grief but the rigid expectations she'd built around herself like armor. Her grandfather's words echoed in her mind, mixing with her mother's wisdom about adaptation, with Aarav's accusation about trying to fix him to fix herself.

The house settled around her with familiar sounds—the tick of the old radiator, the distant hum of traffic, the whisper of wind through trees that had watched her grow up. In this moment of vulnerability, surrounded by the physical evidence of endings and beginnings, inside her she felt a recasting. It wasn't acceptance, exactly, but perhaps its precursor: the understanding that some things needed to break before they could be rebuilt into something new, something true.

***

The Fig Café had been their spot once, back when friendship seemed as simple as shared flat whites and synchronized class schedules. Now, five years later, Olivia sat at their old corner table, watching Toshi through the steam of her untouched coffee. The café had changed—edison bulbs replaced the old fluorescents, succulents dotted the windowsills where textbooks once sprawled—but the essential rhythm of the place remained: the hiss of the espresso machinc, the murmur of conversations, the steady pulse of alternative music just beneath awareness.

Toshi looked different and exactly the same—her blonde hair shorter now, professional, but she still fidgeted with her necklace when nervous, a habit Olivia had forgotten she remembered. They'd spotted each other at the farmer's market that morning, a collision of past and present that left them both stammering through an impromptu coffee invitation.

"You look good," Toshi offered, her smile careful, measured. "I saw the article about the clock tower restoration. That must have been amazing."

"It was." Olivia traced the rim of her cup, wondering how they'd arrived at this moment where their once-fluid conversation had crystallized into small talk. "Though now it feels like another lifetime."

The silence that followed felt miry with unspoken histories. Through the window, afternoon light painted patterns on their table, shifting like the years between who they were and who they were now.

"I'm sorry," Toshi said suddenly, the words tumbling out as if she'd been holding them back. "Not just for... everything back then. But for never trying to fix it. For letting five years pass because I was too proud, too scared to admit I'd been wrong."

Olivia's hand stilled on her cup. The last time they'd spoken, really spoken, had been in this same café. Toshi had just accepted the internship they'd both competed for—the one Olivia had helped her prepare for, not knowing they were rivals. The betrayal hadn't been in the competition, but in the silence that preceded it.

"Why didn't you just tell me you were applying?" The question that had haunted her for five years finally found voice.

Toshi's fingers worried at her necklace. "Because you were always the brilliant one, the one with the perfect plans and the unwavering focus. I thought... I thought if I told you, you'd help me succeed, like you always did. And I needed to know I could do something on my own." She laughed softly, but the sound held no humor. "I've always envied that about you—your ability to pursue what you love with such certainty."

"Certainty?" Olivia repeated, the word tasting bitter. "Toshi, I haven't been certain about anything since the day my wàigōng died. I've just gotten better at pushing forward – or so I'm told, upward."

The confession touched down between them like an uneasy honeybee at a picnic. In the background, the café's antique wall clock ticked steadily, marking time in a rhythm that felt suddenly marked.

"I saw the 'For Sale' sign outside his house," Toshi said softly. "Mom mentioned they finally convinced your mother to sell. Are you okay?"

The question, simple and sincere, cracked something in Olivia's mindfully maintained composure. "No," she admitted, surprising herself with her honesty. "No, I'm not okay. Everything's changing, and I keep trying to hold onto pieces of the past like somehow they'll anchor me, but..." She stopped, hearing the echo of her own words.

"You know what I remember most about your grandfather?" Toshi leaned forward, her voice gentle. "How he used to say that broken clocks were just timepieces waiting to tell a different story. I never understood what he meant until I broke my mom's antique watch last year. The repairman said he could fix it to keep perfect time, but it would lose the slight pause it had developed between ticks—to me, this was the aspect that made the watch special to her."

Olivia looked up sharply, meeting Toshi's eyes. "What did you do?"

"I left it as it was. Some things aren't meant to be fixed, just accepted." Toshi reached across the table, hesitating before laying her hand over Olivia's. "I know we can't go back to who we were and what we had before, but maybe... maybe we can figure out something for us now?"

The touch was unexpected, a bridge across years of silence. Through the window, clouds shifted, changing the patterns on their table. The café's wall clock chimed the half-hour, its sound both familiar and new.

"I'd like that," Olivia said finally, turning her hand to squeeze Toshi's briefly. "Though I should warn you—I'm distinctly less certain about everything these days."

Toshi smiled, genuine this time. "Good. Certainty was always your least interesting feature."

They both laughed then, the sound shattering the last pane of the tension between them. As they settled into easier conversation, Olivia took stock of something inside her—a recognition that perhaps growth wasn't about perfect restoration, but about finding value in the ways we change, even when those changes lead us away from who we thought we needed to be.

Later, walking home in the swelling pale violets and corals, Olivia thought about Aarav, about how she'd been trying to preserve something that perhaps needed space to transform. Her phone weighed heavy in her pocket, full of unsent messages and unspoken candors. The city hummed around her, its rhythm neither perfect nor predictable, but persistently, defiantly alive.

***

The workshop felt different that night. Shadows hid in corners where sunlight usually played, and the usual chorus of ticking took on an almost accusatory rhythm. Aarav sat alone at his workbench, the single desk lamp creating a pool of harsh clarity in the surrounding darkness. Before him lay the mysterious timepiece he and Olivia had been restoring together—its brass case gleaming dully, its internal workings exposed like an open heart.

The evening pressed against the windows, transforming them into polar, black mirrors that reflected his hunched form and the scattered tools-of-trade. He'd been sitting here for hours, since Olivia's swift departure had left the air laden with missed opportunities. His coffee had gone icy, untouched, next to a stack of papers from the Mumbai firm—their corporate logo gleaming with all the soulless efficiency he'd once disdained.

His hands moved with mechanical fidelity over the timepiece's delicate mechanism. Each component had a purpose, a place, a perfect trajectory of motion that contributed to the whole. It should have been simple: identify the flaw, make the correction, restore proper function. He'd done it countless times before. But tonight, something felt different.

The spring beneath his fingers was a marvel of engineering—a strip of metal that had once been alive with potential energy, waiting to be released in careful, measured increments. Now it lay still, its purpose interrupted by age or accident or perhaps simply the inevitable entropy that claimed all things eventually.

"Come on," he muttered, adjusting his grip on the jeweler's screwdriver. "Just need to—"

The snap was barely audible, but he felt it reverberate through his entire body. The spring had broken, its ends curling away from each other like lovers after an argument. The sound died slowly in the air, mixing with the workshop's persistent ticking until he couldn't tell which was louder—the chronicle of his failure or the reminder that time moved forward irrespective.

He set the broken piece aside with trembling fingers, suddenly aware of how tightly he'd been holding himself. The lamp's glare caught the spring's fractured end, creating a prism of light that scattered across his workbench like escaped moments.

His phone buzzed—his grandmother's name illuminating the screen. For a moment, he considered letting it go to voicemail, but something in him needed to hear her voice, to connect with the judgment that had guided him since childhood.

"Nani," he answered, his voice rougher than he'd expected.

"I knew you'd still be at the shop." Her voice carried across the miles with familiar warmth, touched with knowing concern. "The lights are visible from the street, nātū. Like a lighthouse for lost souls."

He managed a weak laugh. "I'm not lost, Nani. Just working."

"Mm." The sound underpinned by decades of maternal skepticism. "And how is Olivia?"

The question caught him off guard, though it shouldn't have. His grandmother had always possessed an almost supernatural ability to read between his words, to find the truth he was trying to hide even from himself.

"She..." He glanced at the broken spring. "We had an argument. About the Mumbai position."

"Ah." A pause, filled with the freedom of understanding. "And what did you break?"

"What makes you think I broke something?"

"Because you are your grandmother's grandson," she said simply. "I too would retreat to my workbench when my heart was troubled, focusing on mechanisms I could control until something inevitably snapped."

Aarav looked at the scattered components before him, seeing them suddenly through new eyes. "The spring," he admitted. "In the piece Olivia and I were restoring together. I thought I could fix it myself, make it perfect again, but..."

"But some things resist perfection," his grandmother finished softly. "Do you remember what I taught you about broken gears, nātū?"

"Every gear has its purpose," he recited, the lesson rising from memory like smoke from incense, "even the broken ones. Sometimes they teach us where the real strength lies."

"Yes." He could hear the smile in her voice. "But do you understand what it means?"

Aarav picked up the broken spring, letting it catch the light again. "I thought I did. But lately... everything feels out of alignment. The shop, the Mumbai offer, Olivia..." He trailed off, the names of his uncertainties hanging in the air like planetary satellites with willingness to work in brilliant tandem or rip from orbit in search of new gravities.

"When Wěi Míng passed," his grandmother said after a moment, "with the help of Olivia's mother, I visited his workshop alone. There, I found a box of broken watches in his workshop. Each one had a note attached—the story of its damage, the owner's name, the date it stopped. At first, I thought he'd kept them as reminders of failures, of repairs he couldn't complete. But then I read his journal."

She paused, and Aarav found himself holding his breath, waiting.

"He kept them because each broken piece taught him something about resilience, about the beauty of imperfect things. Some watches, he wrote, aren't meant to be fixed—they're meant to remind us that even broken things can be precious, that sometimes the flaw becomes the feature we love most."

Aarav looked at the timepiece before him, almost as if his eyes had physically refocused, he saw past its mechanical failure to what it represented—the hours he and Olivia had spent bent over it together, theorizing about its origin, celebrating small victories in its restoration. Even broken, it held something valuable, something that transcended its function.

"Nani," he said quietly, "I think I've made a mistake."

"The question isn't whether you've made a mistake, nātū. The question is whether you're brave enough to learn from it." Her voice softened. "Not everything that's broken needs to be fixed. Sometimes it just needs to be accepted, and then we promise to ourselves to work within and on that accepted in earnest."

The workshop's chorus of ticking seemed to change then, becoming less an accusation and more a reminder—each click a heartbeat, a moment, a chance to choose differently. Outside, the night had deepened, but somehow the darkness felt less an inquisition, more a curiosity.

"Thank you, Nani," he whispered.

"Go home, nātū. The watches will wait. They're good at that."

After ending the call, Aarav remained at his workbench, the

broken spring cool against his palm. Each tick of the surrounding timepieces seemed to whisper his grandmother's wisdom: *Sometimes the flaw becomes the feature we love most.*

He carefully gathered the scattered components of the broken timepiece, placing them in a small wooden box. The Mumbai papers he left where they lay, their corporate sheen dulled in the lamp's glow. Tomorrow would bring its own decisions, its own challenges. But for now, in the quiet of his workshop, surrounded by the steady heartbeat of time moving forward, he allowed himself to acknowledge a simple truth: sometimes the most valuable repairs begin with accepting that perfection isn't the goal.

Midnight found them separate, yet linked by the same impulse to translate feeling into words. In her apartment, Olivia sat at her desk, surrounded by the silent timepieces that had once seemed like faithful companions but now felt more like witnesses to her transformation. Across town, Aarav remained in his workshop, the single lamp still burning, but his tools set aside in favor of paper and pen.

Dear Aarav,

I'm writing this letter in the space between ticks, in that moment of suspension where anything feels possible. The irony isn't lost on me—using paper and ink to reach you when we've spent months surrounded by far more sophisticated mechanisms of time and connection.

Today I found a letter from my grandfather, hidden away like so many of the truths we keep from ourselves. He wrote about the beauty of imperfection, about how life defies our attempts at precision. I've been thinking about that, about how I've approached our relationship like one of your watches—something to be calibrated, adjusted, perfected.

You were right. I have been trying to fix things, to impose order on chaos, to make the world run according to my carefully wound expectations. But what I'm realizing, sitting here surrounded by frozen clocks and fading light, is that perhaps I've been trying to fix the wrong things.

When you said I was using you as a replacement for my grandfather, it hurt because there was truth in it. But not the truth you think. I wasn't looking for him in you—I was looking for the certainty I felt when I was with him, that sense that everything had its place and purpose. What I found instead was something far more valuable: someone who understood that time isn't just something to measure, but something to experience.

I don't want to fix you, Aarav. I want to accept you – the you that was, that is, and that will be. I want to learn the rhythm of who you are, not who I think you should be. If Mumbai is where your path leads, then I want to know that version of you too—not because it fits my plans, but because all your versions matter to me.

There's a space between what we plan and what we live, between the tick and the tock, between who we think we should be and who we are becoming. I'm learning to live in that space, to find beauty in its ambiguity.

Yours,

Olivia

Dear Olivia,

The workshop feels different without you here. The ticking of the clocks, once a symphony of order and purpose, now sounds more like questions without answers. Or perhaps I'm finally hearing what they've been saying all along—that time isn't just a progression of measured moments, but a river that carries us places we never planned to go.

Tonight I broke the spring in that mysterious timepiece we've been restoring. My hands were steady, my tools precise, but something went wrong anyway. I've been sitting here staring at the broken pieces, thinking about how much of my life *has been spent trying to fix things, to maintain the illusion of control.*

My grandmother called. She told me about your grandfather's collection of broken watches—timepieces he kept not as reminders of failure, but as lessons in the beauty of imperfect things. It made me think of all the times you've looked at a damaged watch and seen not just what it was, but what it could become. I used to think that was about restoration, about returning things to their proper function. Now I wonder if it's about transformation—about finding new ways to be valuable, to be beautiful, to be true.

The Mumbai position sits on my desk with the weight of a reputed milestone, promising a future of precision and progress. But what keeps drawing my eye is that broken spring, curled like a question mark, asking me what I really want. Not what my family expects, not what tradition demands, not even what logic dictates—but what makes my heart tick in time with the something beyond myself.

I accused you of trying to fix me, but maybe I've been trying to fix myself into someone else's idea of success. The truth is, when I'm with you, I don't feel like something that needs fixing. I feel like something that's becoming.

The other day, I read about the Chinese concept of jīn shàn (金缮), and I thought of you – in truth, I thought of us. Maybe that's what we've both been learning, in our own ways. That the real art isn't in hiding our breaks and imperfections, but in letting them show us new ways to be whole.

Yours,

Aarav

Neither letter was sent that night. Olivia's remained on her desk, bathed in moonlight that turned the paper silver. Aarav's stayed folded beside the broken timepiece, waiting like a held breath. But something had altered during the act of writing them—as if by acknowledging their fears and hopes on paper, both had taken the first step toward making that which currently wasn't, into is and hopefully was.

The night nestled around them, the city's rhythm slowing but never quite stopping. In her apartment, Olivia finally slept, her grandfather's letter tucked beneath her pillow. In his workshop, Aarav dozed in his chair, the broken spring still in his palm, its edges relaxed by his warmth.

Between them, the unsent letters held their truths like sages holding history—waiting for the right time, the right courage, the right understanding to set them in motion. Outside, the world continued its eternal dance of light and its absence, unconcerned with human measures of time and timing, while inside two separate shelters, two hearts began the delicate process of finding their way back to synchronicity, not through perfection, but through the honest acknowledgment of their beautiful, necessary, authentic breaks.

CHAPTER 14

THE SPACE AMID SECONDS

Dawn crept through Olivia's window like a hesitant thief, radiating shivering shadows across her grandfather's aged desk where she sat, pen hovering over paper. The letter to Aarav lay before her, its edges crisp and white against the burled wood—a stark contrast that seemed to mock the messiness of her thoughts.

She read over her words again, each line an exercise in vulnerability that made her chest tighten:

Aarav,

I've started this letter seventeen times. Each attempt feels like trying to repair a watch with trembling hands—precision lost to fear.

Remember when you told me that time isn't linear but layered? I didn't understand then. But sitting here, surrounded by my grandfather's unfinished memoir and half-wound watches, I think I'm beginning to. We're all just moments layered over moments, each tick forward carrying the weight and height of what came before.

I've been thinking about that first day in your shop, how you nearly quoted my grandfather's words back to me when referring to how handwriting and watchmaking both were "capturing time between movements." I was too caught up in my own rhythm then to truly notice how our stories were already inter-twined, like gears meant to mesh but slightly out of alignment.

My grandfather's final chapter remains unfinished, and maybe that's fit-ting. Because this isn't about endings, is it? It's about the courage to leave space for what comes next, even when we can't see the full mechanism.

Olivia paused, her pen making a small dot on the paper as she held it there, suspended between thought and action. The morning light had strengthened, illuminating the steam that rose from her osmanthus oolong tea to dance above the desk like scattered reflec-tions, each one precious and impossible to grasp.

She thought of Aarav's hands, steady and sure when working with the most delicate watch parts, yet trembling slightly that eve-ning in the park when he'd almost reached for hers. The memory kindled something in her, and she lowered her pen to add one final line:

Time is imperfect, and so am I. But maybe that's where we begin.

The words felt right—raw and honest in a way that perfectly polished sentences could never be. She folded the letter with unhur-ried care, each crease sharp and intentional, but stopped short of sealing the envelope. Instead, she placed it beside her grandfather's memoir, its worn leather cover absorbing the morning light.

Her fingers traced the embossed title, feeling the subtle notches and nicks in the leather. Opening it to the next unfinished chapter, she found herself drawn to a passage she'd read dozens of times before, but now it seemed to carry new weight:

Time, her grandfather had written, *is not a river flowing in one di-rection, but an ocean of moments. We don't move through it; we swim in it, each stroke changing the current for those around us.*

Olivia glanced at the letter, then back to the memoir. The parallels weren't lost on her—both pieces of writing suspended in the delicate balance between completion, hope, and possibleness of being, whether supportive. Her grandfather had always said that the most important parts of a story happen in the margins, beyond that which is written and that which is yet to be.

The gentle tapping of the wall clock—the only timepiece she'd kept running since that day in the shop—marked the morning's movements. Each click seemed to whisper, *not yet, not yet*, until suddenly, she understood. She stood, leaving both the letter and the memoir open on the desk. Words, like the millions of individuals in the city gradually finding their places in the morning light, needed time to settle and soak into their rhythms.

Today's city's rhythm was not dissimilar from the mechanical precision she'd once clung to. Somewhere in that urban symphony, in a small shop filled with the heartbeats of countless timepieces, Aarav would be beginning his day too.

The thought brought a smile to her lips—not the polite, measured expression she'd perfected over years of social conditioning, but something real and slightly crooked, like the imperfect circles they'd discovered in her grandfather's hand-drawn watch designs.

Tomorrow, she would seal the letter. Or perhaps she wouldn't. For now, she was content to exist in this undefined domain, where the possibility of what might be felt more true than any painstakingly crafted ending.

The morning light in Aarav's shop fell differently now, as if the air particles themselves had learned new channels in which to guide newcomers in the weeks since Olivia's last visit. He stood at his workbench, calibrating a Victorian pocket watch whose ornate case reminded him of the way she would trace patterns on his desk while thinking—unconscious geometries that seemed to mirror the intrigues of their relationship.

The bell above the door chimed, its tone slightly off-key. Aarav didn't need to look up to know who had entered; his mother's perfume—jasmine and sandalwood—announced her presence before her footsteps did. But there was another scent too, familiar yet unexpected: his grandmother's cardamom tea.

"Mulagā," his mother's voice carried the forced lightness he'd come to associate with difficult conversations. "We thought we'd stop by."

Aarav set down his tools with subtle bracing, each movement measured and precise. When he turned, he found himself facing not just an intervention, but a study in contrasts: his mother, Isha, dressed in crisp business attire that spoke of her real estate success, and his grandmother wrapped in a hand-woven shawl whose patterns echoed the intricate workings of the watches that surrounded them.

"I brought fresh pakoras," his grandmother said, holding up a paper bag that had already left translucent spots of oil on its surface. Her smile carried the weight of decades spent in this very shop, though her eyes held something more—a glimmer of conspiracy that made Aarav's tension ease slightly.

"I have meetings later," Isha began, surveying the shop with the appraising eye that had made her notorious in Mumbai's property market. "But we need to discuss the logistics of—"

"Of having breakfast with your son," his grandmother interrupted, already clearing a space on the workbench. She shooed away Aarav's protests about oil spots on the wood. "Some stains are worth keeping. They add richness."

The edges of his grandmother's silver hair refracted the light much the same as watch crystals at precisely the right angle to create a new worlds of color as she moved about the shop. These momentary halos reminded Aarav of the way time seemed to bend around her. She had always existed somewhat outside of its normal flow, operating on what the family jokingly called " NST - Neha Standard Time"—a rhythm that somehow always led to exactly where she needed to be.

"Before we eat," his grandmother offered, reaching into the folds of her shawl, "I brought something for you to see." She withdrew a small wooden box, its surface worn smooth by years of handling. The hinges protested mildly as she opened it, revealing a watch that Aarav had never seen before, despite having grown up surrounded by his family's collection.

"My first repair," she explained, lifting it carefully. The watch was unremarkable in its appearance—a simple women's timepiece from the 1950s—but the way his grandmother held it raised it to something precious. "It stopped working years ago, but I've kept it."

Isha shifted, her designer heels clicking against the floor. "Aai, we're here to discuss the future, not—"

"The future is built on the foundation of the past," his grandmother cut in, her voice gentle but firm. "Just like every watch Aarav repairs carries the history of its previous owners, every decision we make is shaped by the moments that came before." She turned to Aarav, holding out the watch. "It no longer ticks, nātū, but it's still a part of me. Not everything needs to work to have value."

Aarav took the watch, feeling its weight—lighter than expected, yet somehow dense with meaning. The crystal was scratched in a pattern that reminded him of the marks on Olivia's grandfather's workbench, the ones they'd spent an afternoon trying to decode like a mysterious language of time itself.

"I remember when this shop was just a dream," his grand-mother continued, her words meant for both of them now. "Your grandfather thought I was mad, wanting to learn repair work when we could barely afford to buy the tools. But he understood something that took me years to learn: sometimes the most valuable things we possess are the dreams we haven't realized yet."

The morning light had given way to an ethereal, pewter cloud cover tempered by occasional sun bursts, permitting long shadows to stretch across the workbench like the hands of an enormous clock. Aarav studied the watch in his hands, noting the slight irregularities in the case that marked it as hand-finished. His mother's silence held its own dissension, all but uproarious with unspoken arguments about progress and practicality.

"It's beautiful," he said finally, looking up to meet his grand-mother's knowing gaze. "Even now."

"Especially now," his grandmother amended, reaching for the bag of pakoras. "Now, let's eat before they get cold. Cold pakoras are like unlived moments—a waste of perfectly good potential."

As they settled into their impromptu breakfast, Aarav noticed how the cloud-bound light caught the auric-dappled parts of his grandmother's and even his mother's eyes, turning their gazes into miniature constellations that danced between past and present. His mother's phone buzzed insistently in her bag, but for once, she let it ring.

In the quiet that followed, broken only by the hum of chatting timepieces that filled the shop, Aarav found himself thinking of Olivia's words about the brief but somehow everlasting gaps between the ticks and tocks. Perhaps that's where they all were now—suspended between the tick and the tock, waiting for the mechanism of their shared story to align.

Autumn had painted the park in shades of aged copper and light caramel, though Olivia barely noticed the seasonal shift until a maple leaf spiraled down to rest on her grandfather's memoir. She sat on what she'd come to think of as her bench—the one furthest from the walking paths, where the morning light filtered through the canopy in ways that reminded her of the way it did in Aarav's shop.

The crisp air carried the scent of fallen leaves and distant wood smoke, so different from the oil-and-metal perfume that had become familiar during her hours of watch repair lessons. She traced the edge of the letter she'd written to herself months ago, back when the loss of her phone had felt like an amputation rather than the liberation it had become.

Dear Future Self, it began, the words slightly smudged from handling, *I wonder if you'll recognize the person writing this. The one who measured worth in LinkedIn connections, Instagram likes, reciprocal tags with people at new, and often soon to be old, places, calendar invites to creditable things, unexplored opinions...*

A melody drifted across the park, pulling her attention from the page. Someone was playing violin near the stone fountain—not the usual busker's fare of popular songs, but something that made her think of clockwork and constellations. The musician, barely visible through the trees, swayed with each phrase, his body becoming part of the music's being.

The tune was hauntingly familiar, though she couldn't place it. It reminded her of something Aarav had said during one of their lessons, when she'd grown frustrated with a particularly delicate repair: "Sometimes the beauty isn't in the precision, but in knowing when to let the imperfections exist."

She returned to her letter, reading further:

I keep thinking about what Dad used to say before he left—that time is the only truly democratic resource. We all get the same twenty-four hours. But sitting in Aarav's shop, watching him bring dead timepieces back to life, I'm starting to think Dad had it wrong. Time isn't democratic at all. It bends and stretches, runs and crawls, dances and stumbles. Maybe that's why we try so hard to measure it—not to control it, but to understand our place within its flow.

The violin's melody shifted, incorporating what seemed like intentional dissonances that resolved in unexpected ways. Olivia found herself holding her breath during the pauses between phrases, those perfect moments of anticipation that reminded her of the contrasting from one antecedent tick to its consequent tock in a masterfully calibrated watch.

Her eyes fell on a passage she'd underlined in her grandfather's memoir: *The greatest fallacy of watchmaking isn't technical, but philosophical. We pretend we're measuring time, when really we're measuring our relationship to it. Every watch tells two stories: the one on its face and the one in its owner's heart.*

The writing continued onto the next page, but a loose sheet fell from between the pages—notes in her grandfather's cramped handwriting, mathematical formulas interspersed with what looked like poetry:

In the space amid seconds
Where pendulums pause
And gears catch their breath
Lives the truth we forgot:
Time is not linear

But a dance of moments
Each step both precise
And gloriously wild

The violin music swelled, and Olivia realized why it had seemed familiar. It was Vaughan Williams' "The Lark Ascending"—the piece that had been playing in Aarav's shop the first time she'd successfully completed a repair on her own. She remembered how he'd smiled then, not his usual careful smile but something raw and genuine that had made her hands tremble as she'd closed the watch case.

A breeze stirred the leaves around her feet, carrying with it the scent of approaching rain. The violinist had reached the piece's climax, where the solo line soared above the implied orchestra, free yet somehow still connected to the underlying rhythm. It was like watching someone walk a tightrope while dancing—technical precision and wild abandon perfectly balanced.

Olivia gathered her papers, tucking them carefully into her grandfather's memoir. The sky had given way to an ethereal, pewter cloud cover, but she remained, watching the violinist draw the piece to its close. As the final notes soaked into the autumn air, she understood something that all her years of rigid scheduling and hypervigilant planning had never taught her: structure existed not to constrain, but to create tolerance for freedom, for being.

Standing, she felt the weight of the memoir in her hands, the letter to Aarav in her pocket. The violinist had begun to pack away her instrument, her movements as deliberate as a watchmaker's. Behind her, the fountain's water caught what remained of the morning light before being clasped by the clouds, breaking it into countless strings of glittering could-be's.

It was time to visit the shop. Not because it was scheduled or expected, but because sometimes the distances between seconds and souls demanded to be filled with something more than waiting.

The afternoon light poured through the shop windows like cooled honey, catching the brass and silver of the timepieces, transforming Aarav's workbench into an altar of faint-edged metallics. He bent over a 1940s pocket watch, his movements direct yet tender, as if he were handling not just machinery but memories themselves. The watch's case bore an inscription so worn it had become illegible—a love letter reduced to shade and suggestion.

The bell above the door remained silent when Olivia entered; she'd learned months ago exactly how to open it to avoid the chime. But Aarav knew she was there nevertheless. Perhaps it was the minute change in the air, or the way time itself seemed to lengthen its breath when they were present together. His hands floated over the pocket watch, though he didn't immediately look up.

Olivia moved through the shop like water finding its level, navigating around displays of restored chronometers and perpetual calendars until she stood before his workbench. Without ceremony or explanation, she placed her letter beside his tools, the cream envelope stark against the wood's almost burnt patina. The paper still held warmth from being carried in her pocket, as if the words inside were alive and breathing.

Aarav finally raised his eyes from his work, and Olivia caught her breath at what she saw there—not the careful distance of recent weeks, but something raw and honest that reminded her of unticking watches: mechanisms waiting to spring back to life.

"The inscription," he said, gesturing to the pocket watch before him, his voice carrying the slight roughness of long silence. "It's been worn away by years of handling. Someone loved this watch so much they slowly erased their own message."

"Maybe the message served its purpose," Olivia replied, thinking of all the words they'd left unspoken. "Like a letter you write but never send."

Aarav set his tools down with deliberate care, each piece finding its predetermined place in the leather roll. The routine looked like meditation, or perhaps prayer. When he finished, he pushed the pocket watch aside but didn't reach for her letter.

Instead, he began to speak, his words carrying the load of extensive cogitation: "I've been thinking about something my grandmother said this morning. About value not being tied to function." He paused, fingers tracing an invisible pattern on the workbench. "I've spent so much time trying to fix things—watches, expectations, myself—that I forgot sometimes broken things are just..." He searched for the word, and Olivia found herself holding her breath. "Complete," he finished. "In their own way."

The confession defied gravity in the air between them, as tangible as the dust motes indifferently frolicking in the lambent afternoon light. Olivia thought of her grandfather's memoir, of all the unfinished chapters that somehow told a more honest story than a polished ending ever could.

"I'm afraid," Aarav continued, each word measured like the tick of a chronometer, "of losing the shop. Of disappointing my family. Of letting go of everything I thought I needed to be." His eyes met hers. "But mostly I'm afraid that in trying to preserve everything, I've already lost what matters most."

Olivia felt the truth of his words resonate with something in her own heart—that the moments between the moments, where what is attended to and what is not, is where fear and hope danced like binary stars, each defining the other's orbit. She thought of the violin music in the park, how it had found beauty in its imperfect resolutions.

"When my phone disappeared," she said, "I thought I was losing my connection to the world. But really, I was just learning to connect differently." She gestured to the letter on the bench between them. "Nothing started or stopped any differently - not universally. But... I stopped, and, at the same time, started, differently for certain. Some things need to be done in a way that takes time. In ways that leave marks on paper and wood and memory."

Aarav nodded, finally reaching for the envelope. But instead of opening it, he reached into his desk drawer and withdrew another letter, the paper slightly creased as if it had been taken out and returned many times. "I wrote this days ago," he admitted. "But the timing never seemed right."

"When is it ever?" Olivia asked, a smile tugging at the corner of her mouth as she remembered their first meeting, how she'd all but demanded an immediacy and he'd made her wait, teaching her patience along with horology.

The shop filled with the sound of their shared silence, punctuated by the synchronized ticking of dozens of timepieces—a chorus of mechanical heartbeats marking the moment. Through the window, the late afternoon light painted shadows that looked like the teeth of gears across the floor, slowly turning as the Earth spun beneath them.

Neither reached for the other's letter yet. Instead, they sat together in the warm light, letting each unmarked space stretch and breathe around them. Sometimes, Olivia realized, the most import-

ant steps forward happen in absolute stillness, in those precious moments between intention and action and back again are where all
possibilities exist simultaneously, like the perfect tension of a butterfly pausing so long on the edge of its chrysalis before taking flight.

The mysterious timepiece lay between them on the workbench,
its components arranged in a scattered nebula of brass and steel that
caught the gilded autumnal afternoon. Each piece seemed to hold its
own story: the slightly worn teeth of the escape wheel, the patina on
the balance cock, the hairspring that curved like a galaxy in miniature. Olivia noticed how the parts had been laid out in a pattern that
echoed the way her grandfather had drawn his designs—function
flowing into artistry.

"No pressure this time," Aarav said softly, his voice carrying
the same gentle authority he'd used during their first lessons. "We're
not trying to prove anything." He paused, selecting a loupe from his
tools. "Or maybe we're proving something different."

Olivia felt the weight of their letters in her pocket, still unread.
Like Schrödinger's correspondence, their words existed in all possible states until observed, and somehow that possibility felt more
precious than certainty. She reached for her own loupe, the familiar
motion bringing back memories of countless hours spent learning to
see the nuances.

"Your grandmother said something interesting about value,"
she ventured, examining the balance wheel. "About how things don't
need to work to matter."

Aarav's hands stilled over the movement. "She has a way of
saying exactly what you need to hear, even when you're trying not
to listen." He smiled, the expression softer than she'd seen in weeks.
"Like someone else I know."

They worked in comfortable silence for a while, their movements synchronized like well-matched gears. Olivia found herself remembering the violinist in the park, how the music had seemed to exist in the period amid notes as much as in the notes themselves. Their repair work had that same quality now—each action measured not by its accuracy but by its fidelity.

"I went to the museum in Tokyo," she said, cleaning the pivot jewels with practiced hand. "The one where your family's watches are displayed alongside my grandfather's." The memory surfaced like a photograph developing: glass cases filled with timepieces, each one a chapter in their shared history. "There was this one piece, a chronometer from 1952. The curator said it was unique because it had parts from both our families' workshops."

Aarav looked up, his eyes catching the light. "The collaboration piece? The one they made during the trade festival?"

"They worked together," Olivia continued, "during a time when everyone said they were rivals." She held up the mainspring they were about to install. "Like this one—it's not original to the movement, but somehow it fits perfectly."

A memory seemed to pass across Aarav's face like a cloud across the sun. "My grandmother told me that story this morning. About how some things need to break before they can become something new." He reached for the movement, his fingers brushing hers as they aligned the components. "She kept her first repair job, even though it no longer works. Said it reminds her that everything has its own time."

They continued working, each step a confidential play of mutual understanding. The mainspring coiled into place with a satisfying click. The escape wheel found its home, its teeth catching errant beams of autumn like moments waiting to be released. When they reached the balance assembly—the heart of the watch—they both paused.

"In Tokyo," Olivia said, her voice barely vibrating her vocal cords, "my granfather's old master showed me something. A notebook of your grandmother's, from when she was learning repair work." She smiled at the memory. "She wrote that every watch has two hearts: the one we build from gears and springs, and the one we create from hope and memory."

Aarav's hands were steady as he held the balance cock in place, but Olivia could see the emotion in his eyes. "The first heart keeps time," he said. "The second one makes time worth keeping."

Together, they lowered the balance into place. The motion required four hands working in unified coordination—an intimacy of purpose that spoke louder than words. As the final screw turned home, they held their breath together.

For a moment, nothing happened. The workshop held its collective breath, dozens of timepieces clicking around them like a mechanical Greek chorus. Then, almost imperceptibly at first, the balance wheel began to swing. The escape wheel caught, released, caught again. Time, held suspended for so long, began to flow.

The timepiece's tick was distinctive—not the precise, clinical beat of a modern watch, but something more organic. It reminded Olivia of the pulse between heartbeats, of the pause between violin phrases, of the elysian pressure before dawn when the world braces for breath.

"It's not perfect," Aarav observed, listening to the slightly uneven rhythm. "The beat's off by a fraction."

Olivia thought of her grandfather's unfinished memoir, of letters written but not yet read, of all the beautiful imperfections that made life worth measuring. "Maybe that's exactly right," she said, and felt Aarav's smile more than saw it.

Amber encased them, casting long shadows across the workbench. Outside, the city continued its eternal recreation of meetings and consequent movements, each second marking both an ending and a beginning. But here, in this sanctuary of measured time, Olivia and Aarav sat in companionable silence, listening to the slightly syncopated heartbeat of their restored timepiece—a rhythm as singular and imperfect as the breaks between beats where they had found each other.

***

Dusk painted the town square in watercolor hues, the restored clock tower rising above the gathering crowd like a sentinel marking not just time, but memory. String lights crisscrossed overhead, their warm glow mixing with the last rays of sunset to create an atmosphere that existed somewhere between reality and dream.

The repaired timepiece rested in its velvet pouch against Olivia's hip, its weight familiar now, like a secret shared between friends. She watched Aarav moving through the crowd, stopping to speak with elderly craftsmen whose hands bore the same distinctive calluses as his own. Each conversation seemed to weave another thread into the tapestry of their community's history.

"It's quite something, isn't it?" A voice beside her made her turn. Mr. Yang, the antiquarian whose shop bordered Aarav's, gestured toward the clock tower. "When they first proposed the restoration, I thought it was foolish. Why spend so much effort preserving an old mechanism when digital would be more precise?" His eyes crinkled with self-deprecating humor. "But precision isn't everything, is it?"

Olivia's hand drifted to the velvet pouch. "No," she agreed, thinking of the slightly uneven tick of their repaired timepiece. "Sometimes the imperfections are what make something true."

The square had transformed into a living museum of horology. Display cases showed the evolution of timekeeping in their town, from sundials to atomic clocks. Children pressed their faces against the glass, pointing at the intricate mechanisms while their parents shared memories of grandparents' pocket watches and first wristwatches. Near the base of the tower, a local historian was explaining how the community had once synchronized their daily lives to its chimes.

Aarav appeared at her side, his presence changing the quality of the air around her like a shift in atmospheric pressure. "They want us to donate it to the permanent collection," he said quietly, nodding toward the museum curator who was arranging the displays. "Our repaired piece. They say it's the perfect bridge between our families' histories."

The velvet pouch seemed to grow heavier. Olivia thought of all the hours they'd spent working on the mysterious timepiece, how each repair attempt had brought them closer to understanding not just the mechanism, but themselves. "It belongs there," she said finally. "Like your grandmother's first repair job—some things are meant to be preserved, even if they're not perfect."

Around them, the crowd began to shift, moving closer to the tower as the hour approached. The curator was explaining the significance of the restored mechanism, but Olivia found herself focusing instead on the way Aarav's hand had drifted closer to hers, not quite touching but occupying the same space, like parallel lines that might, against all mathematical logic, eventually meet.

The first notes of the quarter-hour chime rang out across the square. The crowd fell silent, collectively holding their breath as the historic bells marked time in the same voice they had used for generations. Each tone seemed to ripple through the gathering like waves on a pond, touching everyone with memories both personal and shared.

"We did this," Olivia said softly, feeling the truth of it in her bones. "All of it. Together." She didn't just mean the timepiece in her pocket or even the tower restoration, but something larger—the preservation of moments, the acknowledgment that time was something to be experienced rather than merely measured.

Aarav's hand found hers as the hour strike began, his fingers intertwining with hers in a gesture that felt both inevitable and surprising. "Here's to imperfect timing," he said, his smile visible more in his eyes than on his lips.

The final bell tone faded into the evening air, leaving behind a silence that felt like faith. Around them, conversations resumed, but with a different quality—somewhat quenched, more reflective. Children ran through the square trailing sparklers that wrote ephemeral starscapes in the darkening sky. The lights overhead seemed to shine with greater purpose, creating pools of gathering that turned strangers into neighbors and neighbors into friends.

Olivia reached into her pocket with her free hand, feeling the smooth velvet of the pouch, the solid presence of the timepiece within. Tomorrow, they would donate it to the museum, adding their chapter to an ongoing story. But for now, it remained their secret, ticking away in its slightly syncopated rhythm, marking time in a way that was uniquely their own.

The night air carried the scent of beautiful death—fallen leaves and woodsmoke, spiced cider from a nearby vendor, the metallic tang of approaching rain. Above them, the restored clock tower stood silhouetted against the deepening mauve of the sky, its illuminated face a reminder that even in darkness, we find ways to measure our passage through the world. Not to control time, but to celebrate our place within its flow.

They stood together at the base of the tower, their joined hands forming a connection as tangible as the gears and springs they'd repaired together. Around them, the community continued its kind celebration of preserved history and renewed connections, but in that moment, they existed in their own world amongst another—a pocket of time as precious and imperfect as the timepiece they'd brought back to life.

The evening had settled into Aarav's shop like the city itself after rain, quietly transformative yet teeming with life ready to brave the next, whatever that may be. The celebration's distant murmur filtered through the windows, mixing with the suddenly jazz-like performance of timepieces that had witnessed their story from the beginning. The repaired timepiece sat between them on the workbench, its tick adding its voice to the groove—slightly off-beat, yet somehow perfect in its divergence.

Olivia settled into what had become her chair, a worn leather piece that had belonged to Aarav's grandmother during her apprenticeship. Steam rose from their tea cups in rudderless spirals, carrying the fragrance of cardamom and memories. The unread letters lay before them like bridges waiting to be crossed.

"I've been thinking about what you said after Tokyo," Aarav began, his fingers tracing the edge of his letter to her. "About how time isn't just what we measure, but what we make of the measuring." He picked up her letter, the paper catching the lamplight. "May I?"

Olivia nodded, cradling her own cup of tea like a talisman. The shop's familiar scents—metal and oil, leather and wood, tea and time—wrapped around her like a well-worn shawl. She watched as Aarav opened her letter with the same care he showed to century-old timepieces.

His voice, when he began to read, gave her words a rhythm she hadn't known they contained:

"Aarav,

I've started this letter seventeen times. Each attempt feels like trying to repair a watch with trembling hands—precision lost to fear..."

As he read, Olivia found herself watching his expressions change like light through stained glass. Each word seemed to land differently in the growing that was being ever-made between them, transformed by his voice, by the evening's gentle darkness, by all the moments that had led them here.

When he reached the final line—*"Time is imperfect, and so am I. But maybe that's where we begin."*—his voice carried a quiver that had nothing to do with uncertainty.

The silence that followed felt like the weightless moment before a stone dropped into still water sends out its first ripple, full of potential energy. Then Aarav reached into his desk drawer and withdrew his own letter, written days ago but held back by the same fear that had kept them orbiting each other like binary stars, always connected but never quite touching.

"I wrote this the night after we argued about modernizing the shop," he said, unfolding pages that showed signs of frequent handling. "When I realized that preserving the past doesn't mean refusing the future."

He handed her the letter, then reached for the repaired timepiece, cradling it in his palms like a living thing. As Olivia began to read, its tick seemed to align with her heartbeat:

"Dear Olivia,

Time, my grandmother always said, is not a river but a dance. We don't move through it; we move with it. I've spent years trying to preserve something I thought was slipping away, only to realize that nothing truly preserved remains alive.

You came into my shop demanding essentially immediate service, wearing time like armor. Now you've taught me that the flow of moments between one and the ones that are yet to come are where we truly live. That precision without purpose is just motion, not meaning.

I keep thinking about your grandfather's memoir—how the unfinished chapters tell a more honest story than any polished ending could. Perhaps that's true of us as well. We're all unfinished chapters, marking time in our own imperfect ways.

The watch we're trying to repair... I finally understood what makes it unique. It's not meant to measure time as it passes, but time as we experience it. The slightly irregular beat, the way it seems to pause between ticks—it's not a flaw but a feature. Like the finite pause between a conductor's motion and the played notes, or the moment before nightfall, or the breath between words when everything that matters levitates, suspended in what may be.

I'm afraid of many things: of losing the shop, of disappointing my family, of watching our craft fade into history. But most of all, I'm afraid of missing the moments that matter while trying to measure the ones that don't.

You once asked me why I became a watchmaker. I told you it was family tradition, which is true but incomplete. I chose this path because I believed time could be contained, controlled, understood. You've shown me that its real beauty lies in the way it escapes our attempts to capture it—like love, like memory, like the space amid seconds where we find ourselves truly being alive..."

The letter continued, but Olivia found her vision blurring. She looked up to find Aarav watching her with an expression that reminded her of the moment their repaired timepiece had first begun to tick—wonder mixed with vulnerability and a touch of fear.

The shop's collected timepieces paced around them in their various rhythms, creating a mechanical tide that ebbed and flowed like breathing. Outside, the celebration was winding down, the sound of bells marking the hour carrying across the quieting square.

"Your grandmother was right," Olivia said finally, her voice serene and fond. "Not everything needs to work perfectly to have value." She reached out to touch the repaired timepiece, her fingers brushing against Aarav's. "Sometimes the imperfections are what make something irreplaceable."

They sat together in comfortable silence, letting time, in all its variable flows, wash about them. The letters lay open on the workbench, their words no longer trapped in possibility but released into reality, like the steady tick of a well-loved watch marking not just time, but the moments that make time worth measuring.

Through the window, the clock tower stood illuminated against the night sky, its face a reminder that even time itself is measured not exclusively in mechanical precision, but in the stories we create between its beats. The repaired timepiece continued its distinctly minute syncope, marking their shared presence in its own particular way—a mechanical heart beating in time with their human ones, each imperfection a note in their ongoing philharmonic.

CHAPTER 15

TIMELESS

The rolling, restrained clacking of a hundred timepieces filled the walls of the Heritage Museum's main gallery, their synchronized rhythm creating a near-palpable atmosphere as genial light spilled through the towering windows. Olivia stood before the central display case, her fingers tarrying a few centimeters above the glass. Inside, nestled on midnight blue velvet, lay the mysterious timepiece that had changed everything.

"It's strange," she murmured, more to herself than to Aarav beside her, "seeing it here, behind glass. Like watching a bird in a cage after knowing it in flight."

Aarav's shoulder brushed against hers as he leaned closer, his presence as steady and grounding as ever. "But now everyone can see its beauty," he replied, his voice carrying that benevolent lilt that still made her heart skip. "Not just us."

The curator, Dr. Li, approached with measured steps, her heels clicking against the hardwood floor in perfect time with the assembled clocks. She carried a leather-bound book with present reverence – Olivia's grandfather's memoir. The sight of it made Olivia's throat seize.

"If you're ready?" Dr. Li asked, glancing between them.

Olivia felt Aarav's hand find hers, his callused fingers intertwining with her own. The touch anchored her, just as it had that first day in his workshop when he'd guided her hands through the delicate process of dismantling a pocket watch.

The gathered crowd hushed as Dr. Li opened the memoir to a marked page. Olivia spotted her mother in the front row, standing beside Aarav's grandmother. The two women had developed an unlikely friendship over the past months, bound together by their shared hope for their children, their poetically indelible past, and their mutual love of strong chai.

"'Time isn't just what we measure,'" Dr. Li read, her clear voice carrying to every corner of the room, "'it's what we live through, together.'" She paused, letting the words settle. "These words, written by Chén Wěi Míng in his final year, capture the essence of what we celebrate today – not just the mechanical mastery of timepieces, but the human stories they contain eternally."

Olivia felt tears prick at her eyes as Dr. Lǐ continued reading. Her grandfather had always said that time was the only true liberty – that it passed equally for everyone, regardless of wealth or status, and we had no say in whether it passed. Standing here now, however, she understood something deeper than she had previously: that time wasn't just passing, it was accumulating, building layers of meaning like sediment forming stone. By being bound by the same master, we could all master ourselves – being unrestricted to experience timing not only as we wanted to some degree, but being granted power to experience timing as we needed to certain degree.

Nani Malholtra approached them after the reading, her eyes bright with unshed tears. She reached up to cup both their faces, one hand on each cheek. "He would have been so proud of you both," she whispered in Marathi, a language Olivia had begun learning, the words now familiar and warm. "Your grandfather, Olivia, and me, Aarav – we see in you what we always hoped for: that love could bridge what pride once broke."

Olivia's mother joined them, slipping an arm around her daughter's waist. The four of them stood there, a living bridge between past and present, their shadows merging on the burnished floor beneath the vibrant glow of gallery lights.

Behind them, the mysterious timepiece ticked on, its sound barely audible yet somehow filling the pulses between their heartbeats. Its rhythmic undulation seemed to whisper of all the moments that had led them here – of chance meetings and careful choices, of broken gears and mended hearts, of time lost and found and transformed into something precious.

The afternoon light released to dusky sun and diaphanous fog, painting the room in cadmium hues that caught the brass and silver of the displayed timepieces. Each one reflected a different facet of the light, creating an array of tiny suns that gamboled across the walls. Olivia watched them move, remembering her grandfather's words about how light behaved like time – how it could bend and stretch and sometimes, in rare and beautiful moments, stand perfectly still.

She turned to look at Aarav and found him already watching her, his dark eyes holding that mixture of certainty and wonder that had first drawn her to him. In that moment, surrounded by the unshakable heartbeat of a hundred timepieces, Olivia felt the truth of what they'd created: a love that existed in the domain amid seconds, where time itself seemed to pause and gather, waiting for them to write their story into its margins.

The private corner of the museum felt like stepping into another century. Antique clocks lined the walls, their faces catching the late afternoon light that filtered through leaded glass windows. Olivia traced her finger along a mahogany display case, leaving no mark on the immaculate surface but feeling the weight of history beneath her touch.

Aarav led her to a tucked-away alcove where a grandfather clock stood watch, its pendulum swinging in hypnotic arcs. The even rhythm reminded her of waves rolling onto a beach absent of matter, held in existence by only sand, of the way time seemed to wash through their veins now – no longer was it adversary to fight but a companion with which to travel.

"I've been thinking," he began, his voice carrying that particular tone she'd come to recognize – the one that meant he'd been turning something over in his mind for days, examining it from every angle like one of his more enthralling repairs. "About the workshop."

Olivia felt her breath break. She knew how much the family business meant to him, how it represented not just legacy but identity. She'd watched him struggle with the pull of tradition and the push of progress, much as she had struggled with her own inherited expectations.

"I'm keeping it," he continued, a smile lifting at the corners of his mouth, "but not exactly as it is. I want to transform it into something new – a place where the old and new can coexist. Classes on traditional watchmaking, but also modern repairs. A space where stories can be shared, where time isn't just measured but accepted, possibly understood."

The relief and joy that flooded through her must have shown

on her face because his smile inclined, became more certain. She reached for his hand, remembering how these same fingers had taught her to handle the delicate inner workings of watches, how they'd helped her find that fastidiousness and faithfully feeling weren't mutually exclusive.

"I have news too," she said, pulling him closer to the grandfather clock, its ticking creating a private rhythm for their conversation. "I've been writing. Not just organizing Grandfather's memoir, but weaving our stories together – his, mine, yours, our families'. It's becoming something larger than I expected, something about how time doesn't just pass but accumulates, how it carries forward the echoes of every moment we choose to make meaningful."

Aarav's eyes became imbued with understanding. "Like layers of sediment forming stone," he said, echoing her earlier thoughts in that uncanny way he had, as if their minds had begun to tick in synchronicity.

They stood in serene silence for a moment, watching particles of time's remnants in the slanting light. Each particle seemed to hold motionlessly suspended for a nearly unobservable moment, defying force and time itself, before continuing its graceful descent.

"Do you ever wonder," Olivia asked, her voice barely above a whisper, "if we're failing them? By not doing things exactly as they did?"

Aarav's response was thoughtful, measured like the beats of the grandfather beside them. "I used to. But I've realized that the greatest honor we can pay to their legacy is to let it grow, to let it adapt and evolve. Like time itself – constant yet ever-changing."

She leaned against him, feeling the steady rise and fall of his chest. Through the window, she could see the town square where their journey had begun, where he had first written her that quote about choosing your tides wisely. How far they'd come since then, how many tides they'd created with their own choices and chances.

"Besides," he added, a hint of playfulness entering his voice, "I think they knew something we're only just learning – that the best traditions are the ones that leave room for innovation, for surprise, for love."

The clock struck the hour, its deep baritone chimes filling the alcove. Olivia closed her eyes, letting the sound wash over her. In that moment, she understood with perfect clarity that their fear of failing their respective legacies had been transformed into something else entirely – not an end, but a beginning, a chance to build something that honored the past while embracing the future.

As the final chime faded, Aarav pulled her closer, his warmth a contrast to the cool air of the museum. "Come on," he whispered, "I see there's dancing in the square, and I think it's time we added our own rhythm to this day."

They left the alcove hand in hand, their steps falling naturally into sync. Behind them, the antique clocks continued their steady count, marking not just the passage of time but the growth of something timeless – a love that, like the best traditions, knew how to both honor its roots and reach for the light.

The town square bloomed with life as evening settled in, festive lights crisscrossing overhead like a tapestry of stars brought down to earth. The restored clock tower stood as a silent protector, its illuminated face casting a genial glow over the gathering crowd. Each hour chime seemed to resonate with something deeper than time – perhaps memory, perhaps creation.

Aarav's grip on Olivia's hand tightened almost imperceptibly as they emerged from the narrow street into the square. The air hummed with violin strings and piano notes, a small ensemble having set up near the base of the tower. Their music drifted through the cooling air like autumn leaves, each note carrying its own artifact of meaning.

"Do you remember," Aarav began, asking her, without words, to a stop at the edge of the impromptu dance floor, "what you said to me that day in the workshop? About how we spend so much time measuring moments that we forget to live them?"

Olivia smiled, recalling the frustration in her voice that day, the way she'd thrown down her tools in exasperation at another failed attempt to regulate a particularly stubborn design. "I believe I was being rather dramatic about a chronograph at the time."

"You were right, though." His eyes held that particular volume she'd come to associate with his most honest moments. "We get so caught up in precision that we miss the beauty of imperfection." He gestured to the musicians, who had begun a waltz that seemed to weave through the evening air like silk. "You're always saying you want to live in the moment. I also want to live in the moment. Dance with me?"

The invitation stalled between them like held breath as the magician vanishes from the stage before reappearing in the crowd somewhere. Olivia felt the familiar flutter of anxiety – the same she'd felt when he'd first asked her to try repairing a watch movement. "I don't really dance," she started, but even as the words left her mouth, she knew they weren't quite true. It wasn't that she didn't dance; it was that she'd always waited for the perfect moment, the perfect partner, the perfect song.

"Neither do I," Aarav admitted with a grin that transformed

his usually serious face. "But maybe that's the point. Sometimes the most beautiful movements are the ones we haven't measured first."

Within an instant of her careful nod, he had already stepped backward into the dance space, drawing her gently with him. Around them, other couples moved with varying degrees of grace, some clearly practiced, others charmingly awkward. The diversity of their motion created a kind of living timepiece, each pair marking time in their own singular manner.

Their first steps were hesitant, a stumbling attempt to find rhythm in chaos. Olivia couldn't help but laugh as Aarav nearly stepped on her toes, his usual exactness replaced by endearing clumsiness. But then something set— perhaps in the music, perhaps in them. They stopped trying to count beats and instead began to feel them, their movements becoming more fluid, more natural, more one.

"You know," Aarav said as they turned beneath the canopy of lights, "I've been thinking about what time really is. We measure it, track it, try to control it, but maybe it's more like this. It's not about getting every step perfect; it's about moving through, being together, creating something new with each moment."

The violin soared above the other instruments, carrying a melody that seemed to speak of longing fulfilled, of distances bridged. Olivia leaned closer, breathing in the familiar scent of metal and sandalwood that always clung to him. "Is that your way of apologizing for almost crushing my feet?"

His laugh rumbled through his chest, and she felt it in her own. "Maybe. Or maybe it's my way of saying that I've learned something from all this: time doesn't move us; we move through it. And I want to keep moving with you."

The words settled over her like evening dew, each one perfect in its simplicity and depth. Around them, the square continued its dance, a whirl of color and motion and joy. The clock tower chimed the quarter hour, its sound mixing with the music in a way that made time itself feel like a tangible thing, something they could carry between them.

Other dancers had begun to notice them, creating an ever-swelling section about them as if recognizing something special unfolding. Aarav's grandmother watched from the edge of the square, her eyes shimmering in rejoice, while Olivia's mother stood nearby, no longer trying to hide her smile.

As the waltz drew to a close, Aarav pulled her closer, their steps slowing until they were barely moving at all. In that moment, suspended between one song and the next, between one heartbeat and another, Olivia understood something fundamental about time and love and the superficial abeyance that exists between measured moments. It wasn't about perfect timing or carefully planned steps. It was about finding someone whose rhythm matched yours, even in the stumbles and missteps.

The musicians began another piece, this one slower, more contemplative. But Aarav and Olivia remained still, creating their own island of calm in the midst of motion. Above them, the stars had begun to emerge, their ancient light traveling across vast distances to witness this simple moment of connection.

"So," Aarav whispered, his forehead resting against hers, "was that moment worth living?"

Olivia's words were lost in the music, and in this sort of wandering her answer was found – yes, noted the music. So too did her body affirm as it defied the forces that would pull her away from the moment, while her mind surrendered to the forces that would pull her closer to it.

***

Bright white morning light streamed through the workshop's windows, throwing long rays across the workbenches and setting ablaze motes of dust that danced in the air like tiny galaxies. Over the past months it had transformed subtly, much like its occupants. Vintage tools still lined the walls, though now they coexisted with modern equipment and carefully framed photographs that told the story of two families, once rivals, now intertwined.

Olivia sat at her usual bench, the one by the eastern window where the morning light landed with grace for proper, detailed work. Her grandfather's loupe lay beside a scatter of components, each piece catching differently – brass warm and yielding, steel cool and exacting. Across from her, Aarav worked with the focused intensity she'd come to love, his hands moving with practiced fluidity over their latest project.

The town square clock commission had come as a surprise, though perhaps it shouldn't have. After the previous night's celebration, the mayor had approached them with the idea: a timepiece that would mark not just hours and minutes, but the heritage of their community. It would be their first true collaboration, a melding of their different approaches to both time and craft.

"What if we incorporated elements from both our families' designs?" Aarav mused, looking up from the preliminary sketches spread between them. "Your grandfather's escapement design was revolutionary for its time, and my grandmother's method of jeweling..." He trailed off, his fingers tracing the outline of a gear train.

Olivia smiled, remembering how once such a suggestion would

have seemed impossible. "A fusion of traditions," she said, reaching for her notebook where she'd been drafting ideas. "Like us."

Her eyes drifted to the mysterious timepiece they'd restored together, now temporarily back in the workshop for reference. Its steady ticking provided a backdrop to their work, a reminder of where their chronicle had begun.

"I used to think precision was everything," Aarav said, setting down his tools and coming to stand behind her. His presence was warm, familiar. "That there was only one right way to measure time, to live life." His hands settled on her shoulders, and she leaned back into his touch. "But I'm coming to truly know that it's the imperfections that make true meaning."

"Like us," Olivia repeated, but this time it wasn't a question or a comparison. It was a statement of fact, as extant as gravity or the passage of time itself.

They worked through the morning, their movements synchronized without conscious effort. Ideas flowed between them like water – her artistic vision complementing his technical expertise, his precision balancing her innovation. The design took shape under their hands: a clock that would honor tradition while embracing change, much like the love that had grown between them.

On the walls, their history watched over them. Photos from the museum opening hung beside sketches from their grandfathers' journals. A candid shot from their dance in the square had already found its place, the joy on their faces captured in eternal suspension. Each image marked a moment when time had seemed to pause, to gather itself around them like a protective embrace.

As the sun climbed higher, casting new shadows across their work, Olivia found herself studying Aarav's profile. He was focused on calculating gear ratios, his brow furrowed in concentration, yet there was a contentment in his posture that spoke of belonging, of finding one's place in the universe.

"What are you thinking?" he asked without looking up, somehow sensing her gaze.

"About time," she answered honestly. "About how we try to capture it, control it, understand it. But maybe it's simpler than that. Maybe it's just about being present in the moments we're given, and creating something meaningful with them."

Aarav set down his calculator, turning to face her fully. The late morning light caught in his dark eyes, turning them to brewed chai. "Is that what we're doing? Creating something meaningful?"

The question swayed in the air between them, weighted with more than just their current project. Olivia looked at their shared workbench – at the blend of old and new tools, at the sketches that combined their different styles, at the home they had created together.

"I think," she said slowly, choosing her words with the same care she used when handling delicate PCBs in their new smart watch repairs, "we're doing something even more important. We're showing that meaning isn't found in unmarked measurements or flawless executions. It's found in the way we choose to spend our moments, and with whom we choose to spend them."

Aarav's smile was slow and warm, like sunrise over distant mountains. He reached for her hand, his callused fingers cuddling perfectly between hers. Together, they turned back to their work, to the creation of something that would mark time for others while celebrating their own journey through it.

The mysterious timepiece continued its steady count behind

them, its ticking a sensible reminder that some measurements go beyond mere mechanics. In the gaps from mark to mark, in the pause between tick and tock, they had found something timeless – a love that didn't need to be perfect to be absolutely right.

***

The clock tower's observation level offered a different perspective of the city, one that made Olivia think of her grandfather's words about how distance changes what we see without changing what exists. The celebration below had dwindled to a gentle murmur, the string lights now competing with the emerging stars that seemed close enough to touch.

Aarav sat beside her on the ancient wooden bench that generations of clockkeepers had used during their vigils. Between them, a bottle of wine they'd been saving – a Bordeaux from the year both their grandparents had briefly visited Switzerland, though at different workshops on different days. The symbolism wasn't lost on either of them.

"Do you remember," Olivia began, watching the town lights flicker like earthbound constellations, "that first day at the farmers' market? When I was so lost in my own thoughts I barely seemed to function?"

Aarav's laugh was warm in the cool evening air. "You mean when you were looking for something honest." He reached into his jacket pocket, pulling out a worn piece of paper. "I still have the quote I wrote for you that day. Well, not the one I gave to you, but the one I wrote after you had already left."

The paper was creased from frequent folding and unfolding, the edges soft with wear. In the gentle light from the tower's lanterns, his handwriting remained clear: "Time isn't a river rushing past us -

308

it's the process of our becoming. Each moment is both sculptor and clay, shaping who we are while being shaped by who we choose to be."

He blushed with sentimentality. "I keep it with me still. It reminds me that sometimes the most important moments are the ones we co-create."

Olivia leaned against him, their shoulders touching in a way that had become as natural as breathing. Below them, the town square clock they'd helped restore marked the quarter hour, its chime carrying clearly in the night air. Each note seemed to hang suspended before dissolving into the darkness, like memories transforming into something more insubstantial.

"I found something today," she said, reaching for her own bag. "The last entry in my grandfather's memoir. I hadn't been ready to read it until now." She withdrew the leather-bound journal, its pages still carrying the faint scent of his pipe tobacco. "Listen to this: 'True connection isn't found in the moments ticked offed but in the moments we choose to tick off with purpose, with awareness, with love.'"

The words seemed to expand between them, filling the observation level with an almost tactile presence. Aarav turned toward her, his movement causing the ancient bench to creak slightly. In the dimness, his eyes held the same intensity they had when he was focused on his most intricate repairs, but now that focus was entirely on her.

"Olivia," he began, his voice carrying a weight she'd never heard before, but then he stopped, seeming to realize that this moment transcend the need for words.

Their kiss, when it came, was like time itself came to attention.

Not their first kiss, but somehow more profound – unhurried and perfect in its imperfection, like the slight asymmetry in a handcrafted watch face that makes it uniquely beautiful. The clock chimed again in the distance, but neither of them counted the strikes.

When they finally parted, the stars had shifted faintly overhead, continuing their ancient recreation across the sky. Olivia thought about how many lovers had sat in this very spot over the centuries, each feeling as though they were the first to discover this particular magic.

"You know," Aarav said softly, his fingers betwixt with hers, "I like time this way – like us. Something to be experienced, embraced, even when we can't predict exactly where it's leading."

The night air carried the shadowy scent of late-blooming jasmine from the garden below, mixing with the metallic tang of the tower's mechanisms and the woody notes of the wine. Olivia closed her eyes, letting herself fully inhabit this moment, knowing it would soon join all their other memories, like the careful accumulation of seconds that make up a life.

"Maybe that's what they were trying to tell us all along," she mused, thinking of their grandparents, of all the seemingly random events that had led them here. "That time really is the something that connects. Like an constitutional thread running through everything, binding past to present to future."

Aarav pulled her closer, and they sat in comfortable silence, watching the town below prepare for sleep. The clockwork beneath them continued its steady count, but up here, in their private observatory, time was not in rigid measurements, but in heartbeats and shared breaths and the potentially infinite between moments.

The stars wheeled slowly overhead, telling their own story of time's passage. Yet in their , Olivia and Aarav had found something that existed outside and without – a connection that, like the most precise chronometer, needed no external reference to know its own truth.

They stayed there until the wine was gone and the night air grew too crisp to ignore, each lost in private thoughts that somehow met in the middle, like the hands of a clock marking the new hour.

As they finally rose to leave, Aarav paused at the top of the spiral staircase. "You know what's strange?" he said, looking back at the bench they'd shared. "I've been up here hundreds of times, maintaining the clock. But I never really saw it until now."

Olivia understood. Sometimes it took a different perspective – or the right person beside you – to see, to accept, and, if fortunate enough, to understand.

Morning arrived with the fateful certainty of a well-maintained timepiece, light spilling through the workshop windows in measured increments. The mysterious timepiece sat on the counter, its glass face catching the stirring rays and transforming them into tiny rainbows that pranced across the worktop.

Olivia moved through this acquainted space with deferential steps, aware that this morning marked a transition. Soon, the timepiece would take its permanent place in the museum, becoming part of the town's collective memory rather than their private mystery. The thought carried both melancholy and rightness, like the bittersweet experience of a box of chocolates gifted to you from a friend longer immediate.

Aarav was already there, carefully preparing the custom-built display case they'd designed together. His movements were unrushed and nurturant, each gesture carrying the weight of understanding that this was more than just another piece to be preserved.

"It's strange," he said without looking up, somehow sensing her presence behind him, "how something can become so much more than the sum of its parts."

Olivia approached the counter, her fingers trailing along its edge until they reached the timepiece. Her own light caught its brass surface, warming it like a living thing. "Like us?" she suggested, echoing their conversation from yesterday.

His smile was answer enough.

As they began the process of preparing it for collection, Olivia noticed something she hadn't seen before – a small irregularity in the metal of the back casing. "Wait," she said, reaching for her loupe. "There's something here."

Aarav paused in his work, moving closer as she cautiously turned the timepiece over. There, barely visible beneath years of careful handling and kind wear, was an inscription. The letters were tiny, clearly carved by a master's hand, requiring both the loupe and the perfect angle of morning light to read:

To those who measure love by moments mutual

The words seemed to oscillate in the air between them, carrying echoes of their grandparents' wisdom and their own journey of revelation. Aarav's hand found hers, their fingers intertwining with the same adoration that marked their work together.

"Do you think they knew?" Olivia asked softly, thinking of the two who had crafted this piece, whose rivalrous companionship had somehow contained the seeds of this moment. "That someday we would find this? That we would understand?"

The workshop filled with the close yet far away sounds of ticking – not just from the mysterious timepiece, but from all the clocks and watches they'd repaired together, each adding its notes to this point. The cacophony should have been chaotic, but instead it felt like a kind of music, a symphony of measured moments.

"Maybe that's what makes it beyond knowledge," Aarav replied, his voice carrying that blend of technical devotion and poetic understanding that had first drawn them together. "Not that they knew, but that they hoped. They created something that could only be fully understood when the right moment arrived – when the right people found it."

Olivia thought about time then – not as the rigid progression of seconds they'd both spent years measuring, but as something more fluid, more alive. How many moments had this timepiece witnessed? How many hands had held it, never seeing the message it carried? How perfect that it had waited for them, revealing its secret only when they were ready to understand it.

The morning light continued its divine advance across the workshop floor, touching each tool and timepiece in turn, transforming this habitually understood place into something almost sacred. The inscription caught the light with purpose now, the letters seeming to glow with an inner fervor.

"It's like a blessing," Olivia said, running her finger over the words one last time before they would be sealed away in their museum display. "Not just from them, but from time itself."

Aarav nodded, understanding as he always did the layers of meaning in her words. Together, they began the final preparations, each movement designed as only those that accept without full understanding can, preserving not just the physical object but the story it contained – their story, their families' story, the story of time itself and how it brings the right people together in the right moments.

The mysterious timepiece ticked on, marking each second with the same steady precision it had maintained through decades of silent waiting. But now its sound carried something more – a reminder that some measurements go beyond mechanics, beyond the countable.

As they worked, the morning light caught them both, casting their shared shadow on the workshop wall – two figures moving in synchronization, their movements akin to clockwork, yet beautifully, boundlessly alive.

The town square shimmered in the crisp morning air, dew still clinging to the cobblestones like scattered diamonds. A crowd had gathered despite the early hour, their excited murmurs creating a gentle susurration that reminded Olivia of the sound of sand running through an hourglass. Above them, covered in cream-colored fabric, waited their creation – the new clock that would mark not just time, but the intersection of past and future, tradition and innovation, two families once divided now united.

Aarav stood beside her, his shoulder brushing hers in that familiar way that still sent electricity through her skin. He wore his grandfather's waistcoat, carefully restored, the silver chain of a pocket watch – his father's – catching the morning light. Olivia touched the pendant at her throat, her own grandfather's loupe transformed into a piece of jewelry that married function with aesthetics.

"Ready?" he whispered, his breath warm against her ear.

The mayor had insisted they unveil it together, a symbolic gesture that wasn't lost on anyone present. Olivia saw Nani Malholtra in the front row, dabbing at her eyes with the edge of her sari, while her own mother stood tall and proud beside her, their shoulders touching in unconscious mirror of their children's stance.

The crowd hushed as they stepped forward. The fabric rippled in the morning breeze like a sail about to catch wind. Olivia's fingers found the cord at the same moment as Aarav's, their hands overlapping in a gesture that felt both casual and profound.

"This clock," Olivia began, her voice carrying across the square with unexpected strength, "is more than a timepiece. It's a testament to the way time flows not just forward, but also between people, between generations, between hearts."

Aarav squeezed her hand, taking up the thread of her words with the seamless synchronicity they'd developed. "It carries elements of traditional craftsmanship passed down through both our families, while embracing unconventional techniques and ideas. Because that's how we honor the past – not by freezing it in place, but by allowing it to grow, to evolve, to find new expression in each generation."

Together, they pulled the cord. The fabric fell away in a graceful sweep, revealing their creation to the gallant morning shine. A collective gasp rose from the crowd, followed by spontaneous applause.

The clock face gleamed, its surface a masterwork of brass and silver, with intricate patterns that seemed to shift and flow as the light moved across them. Olivia's artistic vision had transformed traditional geometric patterns into something organic and alive, while Aarav's technical brilliance ensured that every element served both function and form. The hands, crafted from metal salvaged from both their grandparents' workshops, moved with improbable fluidity across the face.

But it was more than just beautiful. Hidden within its design were elements that told their story – the slight asymmetry in the hour markers that mimicked the arrangement of stars on the night they'd danced in the square, the subtle engraving around the edge that incorporated words from both their grandparents' writings and marginalia, the way the light caught and held in certain angles, creating patterns that echoed the mysterious timepiece that had brought them together.

As the clock began to strike the hour, its sound was both familiar and entirely new – a voice that carried echoes of all the timepieces that had marked significant moments in their lives, yet spoke with its own distinct tone. Each strike seemed to resonate with an aspect within each person listening in a means deeper than time, something that existed in the world but only fleetingly, in the pause between when your being asserts the truth and when your intellect, emotions, lips, and limbs begin to fabricate it.

"We did it," Olivia whispered, feeling tears well in her eyes despite her smile.

Aarav turned to her, his face illuminated by the same light that made their clock as radiant as a second sun. "And," he said softly, his dark eyes holding that mixture of equanimity and excitement that still made her breath catch, "we're only merely beginning."

The crowd's chatter resumed around them, people pointing out different elements of the design, taking photos, posting videos, and sharing their impressions. Yet, without care for the actions or reactions of others in any meaningful manner at that moment, Olivia and Aarav remained still in their own moment, their fingers still intertwined, watching their creation mark the opening of a new hour.

Above them, the hands moved with intended grace, each second precisely measured yet somehow transformed into something more meaningful than mere duration. As the last of the remaining morning fog caught on the metal surfaces obscuring certain elements of the design, certain others were underscored to create patterns that allowed those that wished to pause to connect with everyone present in a web of shared moments and collective memory.

In that distance between back then and when, where past and future met in an eternal present, the clock continued its tried and true count above them, its voice clear and even truer in the momentarily unencumbered air. As they turned to walk away, their steps naturally connecting into sync, the square filled with the sound of their clock marking time for all. Yet beneath its measured rhythm, in the moments missing ticks that had become their private domain, a different kind of time flowed. But now its measurement wasn't just of minutes and hours – it was of moments shared, of choices made, of love that had grown in the pauses between talks, in the breaks between decisions, in the silent moments when two hearts learn to beat as one.

The morning sun continued its arc across the sky, casting their shadows before them like arrows pointing toward a future that, while unmarked on any calendar, promised to be more generous, humane, and elaborate than either of them had imagined possible. Together, they stepped into that future, carrying with them the understanding that some things – like love, like time, like the extent and expanse of meaning – can never be fully measured, only fully lived.

CHAPTER 16

THE RHYTHM WITHIN US

The pre-dawn fog refused to retreat with the late autumn cold front that beseeched the city to welcome winter. The resultant light inside the workshop burst through in wispy, sterling beams catching the brass pendulums and crystal faces of countless timepieces. Their collective musical rhythm soothed Olivia much the same as when her head laid atop Aarav's chest. She navigated the familiar path between workbenches, two coffee cups warming her hands, their rich aroma mingling with the shop's perpetual metallic and earthy hints.

Aarav looked up from his workbench, his dark eyes crowing at the corners as she approached. A half-finished sketch lay before him, pencil lines capturing the essence of what would become their newest creation. Without a word, she placed his coffee beside him— black, with just a whisper of cardamom, the way his mother had taught her to make it during their days in Mumbai.

"You're earlier than usual," he noted, his voice carrying the warmth of appreciation rather than surprise. One of the sun bursts caught a few of the, now more developed, silver threadings through his black hair, evidence of the passing since their first encounter in this very shop.

Olivia settled into her spot beside him, breathing in the familiar scent of coffee and outlook. "The words wouldn't wait," she replied, pulling out her notebook. The leather cover was worn now, its pages filled with the careful observations and raw confessions that would soon become her book. "Sometimes I think they have their own timing."

Aarav's hand found hers briefly, a gesture so natural it felt like the movement of a well-oiled gear. "Like everything else worth waiting for," he said, turning back to his sketch. The blueprint before him was unlike anything they'd created before—a timepiece that married the classical elements of his family's tradition with innovations that would have made his grandmother ever the more joyous.

They worked in companionable quiet, the kind that comes only after learning to read the agape between words. As the final breathes of autumnal light shifted across the floor, Olivia's pen moved across the page, crafting the preface that would invite readers into their world of measured moments and measured love.

The shop's bell chimed in a darling manner as the first customer of the day entered, but neither of them rushed to move. This was their ritual now—these precious morning meetings when time seemed to lag with patient understanding.

"You know," Aarav said suddenly, his voice thoughtful as he added another line to his sketch, "I think this shop has finally found its rhythm." He paused, his eyes meeting hers. "And so have we."

Olivia felt the truth of it snuggle in her chest, heating her even beyond the coffee between her palms. "It only took us a few broken gears to get there," she replied, her laugh fond with memory.

"The best mechanisms often do," he said, and in his smile she saw echoes of all the moments that had led them here—the frustrations, the fears, the unexpected joy of finding someone who accepted and understood that love, like time, wasn't meant to be perfect, but present.

The morning continued its smooth progression, marked by the steady tocking of the clocks and the glorious scratching of pen against paper. Through the window, Olivia watched the city rise, its rhythm syncing naturally with their own. In the placidity of their shared space, she felt the truths of what her grandfather had tried to tell her in his memoir.

She looked down at her coffee cup, now half-empty, and smiled at how such a simple thing could hold so much meaning. It wasn't her old blend anymore, nor the blend that was once new, or even the blend the where she might think it useful to demarcate a, no her, former life. This mixture, like all else in her world now, was an evolution, an as-perfect-as-she-could-configure blend of what was and what could be.

***

The bookstore broke its seconds into its own parts in anticipation, every creak of its wooden floors a susurration of history. Olivia stood at the small podium, her fingers tracing the embossed cover of her book—*The Space Amid Seconds*. The familiar scent of paper and binding glue wrapped around her like an old friend's embrace, reminding her of countless hours spent here finding solace in others' words before learning to trust her own.

The crowd before her was intimate but significant: faces that had witnessed her transformation from a woman bound by routine to one who had learned to dance with uncertainty. Her mother sat in the front row, love shining in her eyes. Beside her, her new partner who steadfastly demonstrated to them both that love could arrive in unexpected seasons. A few rows back, she spotted Mrs. Jia from the café where she used to hide behind her laptop, now genuinely smiling instead of offering concerned glances over coffee cups.

The invisible wings of her grandfather's memoir fluttered against her heart from where it rested on the stool next to her—her constant companion throughout this eternal, beauteous voyage. Its pages, dogeared and annotated, had become a map leading not just to his wisdom, but to her own voice.

"Time," she began, her voice finding its power in the stillness of the room, "is not what I once knew it to be." The words flowed now, natural as breathing, so different from her first stumbling attempts to capture the philosophy that had transformed her life. "We cannot control it, but we can, through our senses, perceive it. This perception can be acute, obtuse, or not at all, with reverence, with joy, with disdain, with indifference, with sadness, with disgust, with awe, with envy, with pride, with surprise, with anticipation, with empathy, with shame, with hope, with guilt, with fear, with awkwardness, with confusion, with gratitude, each with purpose or, possibly, without, and each with love or without. Within this perception we can choose how to measure it. Within those measurements, we find meaning – bound to the measurements that have occurred, or not, and bound to the measurements that will come, or not, in whatever manner you provide, or not – in acceptance, or not, in understanding, or not."

As she read, she felt rather than saw Aarav's presence at the back of the room, unwavering and reassuring as the ticking of his beloved timepieces. He stood near the antique grandfather clock that had witnessed their first real conversation, when she had still been too afraid to admit that what she was seeking wasn't just answers about time, but about herself.

The passage she chose spoke of between seconds, of where life neither halts nor hastens—where measured intervals given way to the joyfully laboring pauses between them. Her voice carried the weight of hard-won wisdom, of nights spent questioning everything she thought she knew, of mornings waking to find that uncertainty could be beautiful if you learned to embrace it.

"In the end," she read, her voice sure despite the emotion threatening to break through, "it's not the standard measures of hours or minutes that define us, but the breaks—the moments in which we choose whether to fill and then how to fill time, making timing authentically ours."

The applause that followed felt like a release, a collective exhale of understanding. As she signed books afterward, each interaction became its own measured moment—a shared smile, a whispered thank you, a story offered in exchange for her own.

When the crowd had thinned, Aarav approached, carrying something wrapped in simple brown paper. Their fingers brushed as he handed it to her, sending familiar sparks dancing across her skin.

"For all the unwritten chapters still to come," he said softly as she unwrapped an antique pen, its surface etched with her initials. The craftsmanship was unmistakably his—each letter carved with the same precision he brought to his watchmaking, but with an artistry that spoke of something beyond mere skill.

Olivia ran her finger along the engraving, feeling the stories yet to be told embedded in its surface. "How do you always know?" she asked, the question encompassing far more than just this perfect gift.

His smile held the wisdom of someone who had learned to

read time in all its forms. "The same way you knew to walk into my shop that first day," he replied. "Sometimes the heart keeps better time than any clock."

In the mellow hum of the evening, Olivia, enveloped by a warm circle of light across her desk, sat creating shadows that danced along the edges of her grandfather's old pocket watch. The antique pen Aarav had gifted her lay beside an empty notebook, its metallic surface catching the light like a promise waiting to be fulfilled. Beyond her window, the city had settled into that peculiar quietude that comes after midnight, when the hours bend to flow with greater ease.

Her fingers strolled on the edges of Aarav's unopened letter, feeling the substance of the words contained within. She had carried it with her for weeks, like a talisman against uncertainty, afraid that reading it might somehow break the delicate balance they had found. But tonight, with the success of her book launch still humming through her veins and his gift reminding her that courage often comes in small moments, she felt ready.

The paper whispered as she unfolded it, releasing a faint scent of his workshop—ferrous, oak, osmanthus, and something indefinably him. His handwriting cascaded across the page in precise strokes, each letter formed with the same care he brought to his craft.

My beloved Olivia,

There's an irony in how long it has taken me to write this letter, considering how much of our togetherness has revolved around timing and time keeping. At this point, I've started and stopped a hundred and three times in my mind, each attempt feeling inadequate to capture what I want to say. Perhaps that's fitting— we've always found our truest connections in the designs less forced, in the repose when we are not bound by over thinking, under doing, or watching ourselves.

I recall the day you first walked into our shop, looking for a recovery for your phone. Even then, I would like to think that I could sense you were seeking something deeper. We both were, though neither of us could have named it. You looked at me with eyes that seemed to be measuring something beyond time, agreeing, beyond my comprehension, to my proposal of learning more about horological artistry, and I found myself wanting to understand what you saw. You were, and are, remarkable.

These past months you, and in concurrent fashion we, have taught me that precision isn't always about perfect alignment. Sometimes it's about finding beauty in the slight imperfections, in the way two seemingly misaligned pieces can create something unexpected and wonderful. You've shown me that tradition doesn't have to be a cage, that innovation doesn't mean abandoning what came before. You've helped me see that life truly happens amid our designs, holding them to truth as we see them unfurling, how others receive that unfurling and how they may find their own truths, and how we can amend it in endless, tenseless, joy – together.

I carry your grandfather's sentiments with me now, too. Time is not a master to be served, but a companion to be understood. I think I finally grasp what he meant. In watching you navigate your own journey, in seeing you transform pain into purpose and confusion into clarity, I've learned that time is not just what we measure, but how we mark the measurements and what we make of them.

I don't know what tomorrow holds. The future, with all its uncertainty, still sometimes terrifies me. But I do know this: I want to keep choosing you, every second, every moment. Not because it's safe or certain, but precisely because it isn't. Because love, like time, is not about perfect synchronization but about finding our own rhythm together.

There are so many mysteries still to solve, so many watches to repair, so many stories to write. I want to face them all with you, in all the spaces between seconds that we can find.

Eternally yours,

Aarav

The lamp's light blurred as tears gathered in Olivia's eyes, but her hands remained steady as she reached for the pen he had given her. The notebook opened to its first blank page, and she began to write, her words flowing as naturally as time itself:

My dearest Timekeeper,

You once told me that every watch tells two stories—the one marked by its hands and the one held in its heart. As I sit here, reading your words, I realize that we, too, have always told two stories: the one visible to the world, and the deeper truth that lives in the quiet moments we've shared...

Her pen moved across the page, filling it with all the words she had held back, all the truths she had discovered, all the love that had grown in the stops and starts between what they shared, what could be called their own. Outside, the city continued its gentle nighttime rhythm, but in the circle of lamplight, Olivia had found her own exquisite measure of time—not in seconds or minutes, but in the inking of her heart as she wrote their story anew.

***

The workshop thrummed with the untroubled intensity of focused minds, each student bent over their respective workbenches in various stages of concentration. Pale crystalline ribbons of light streamed through the thin, floor to ceiling windows that became partial skylights, catching temperately busy fingers that danced like time made visible. Olivia moved between the workstations, her steps confident now where they had once been hesitant, pausing to offer guidance or encouragement as needed.

At the front of the room, Aarav demonstrated the adroit process of balance wheel adjustment, his hands moving with the aplomb of someone who had turned craft into poetry. "The beauty of watchmaking," he was saying, his voice carrying the gentle authority of experience, "lies not only in the precision, but in understanding why that precision matters."

Olivia caught his eye across the room, sharing a private smile at the echo of their own path forged together in his words. She recalled her first lesson here, how her hands had intuition but were rendered frustrated by hang-ups of questioning purpose and positioning. Now, watching a young girl carefully place her loupe with the same determination Olivia had once felt, she saw their legacy taking shape in unexpected ways.

The class continued its advance, punctuated by occasional questions and the soft clicks of tools against metal. Near the window, Mrs. Patel—who had initially come only to appease her grandson but had discovered an unexpected value and delight—worked with methodical care on a pocket watch, finding an inscription marking a birth that spoke to her of her own rebirth.

After the students had filed out, leaving behind the lingering energy of shared purpose, Aarav beckoned Olivia to his private workbench. "I have something to show you," he said, pulling out a leather folio she hadn't seen before. As he opened it, she recognized the precise lines of his technical drawings, but these were different from his usual work.

The design that emerged was breathtaking in its complexity and meaning. At first glance, it appeared to be a clock, but as she studied the details, she saw how he had woven elements of both their families' histories into its mechanistic integrity. The escapement incorporated motifs from her grandfather's signature exacting construction, while the case bore the distinctive experimental materials and lines that had made Aarav's grandmother a force for innovation.

"It's part of our story," he explained, his finger still searching the whimsically complex patterns. "Told from a time that was and, once we build it, in a time that will be."

"Historical preservation through patterned advance," Olivia murmured, recognizing in the design all the themes they had wrestled with in their time so far together. "Like us."

"I thought we could install it here," he said, gesturing to the central wall of the workshop. "As a reminder that the best traditions are the ones that grow and morph, while keeping their mettle intact."

She leaned against him, feeling the steady rhythm of his breathing align with hers. The workshop around them held the whispered promises of hundreds of timepieces, each marking moments in their own unique way. But none would tell a story quite like this one—a story of two people who had learned that love, like time, was well measured not in grand gestures but in small, precious moments of choice and change.

"Your grandmother would love this," she said softly, knowing how much that approval still meant to him.

"And your grandfather would have appreciated the comedic charm," he replied with a gentle laugh. "The so-called rivals' grandchildren, creating something new together."

Through the windows, they could see the square preparing for evening, its pace slowing like a well-regulated pocket watch winding down for the night.

"We should get ready for tomorrow's advanced class," Olivia said eventually, though she made no move to step away. "Mrs. Yang is determined to master chronograph assembly."

"Time enough for that," Aarav replied, his arms tightening

around her slightly. "Right now, I just want to exist in this moment with you." And so they did, as all around them, time marked its eternal transition in tick, in tock, and in love.

***

Their footsteps echoed off the museum's walls, each sound reverberating through the quietude like ripples in an ocean comprised of flexible glass. Olivia and Aarav moved with unhurried purpose toward the exhibit they had visited countless times before, their fingers decorated by one another's. The late afternoon light filtered through the windows on high, casting sprawling shadows that seemed to reach for the memories held within these walls.

In its glass case stood proud their timepiece, its off-kilter, yet steady, ticking heartbeat pronounced among the other, silent artifacts. Around it, yellowed letters and sketches told a story of public rivalry and private esteemed companionship transformed into legacy—their grandparents' correspondence arranged with careful reverence. Olivia's eyes traced the familiar words etched on the plaque: "To those who measure love by moments shared."

"Strange to think it'll be gone tomorrow," she murmured, her free hand lifting to rest against the glass that felt more like warm skin than cold case. The timepiece clasped the light, its brass and silver surfaces gleaming with the same vitality that had drawn them together all those months ago. "Like starlight in our memories," she whispered, "still shining long after its source has vanished. We've seen it, touched it, felt its warmth – and yet, we know that we're reaching for something that's already gone."

Aarav stepped closer, his presence warm and steady beside her. "Not gone," he corrected gently. "Merely making space for new stories. Like we did."

328

She studied their reflection in the glass—her shimmering, raven colored hair touching his shoulder, their bodies angled naturally toward each other like compass needles finding true north. Behind them, the exhibit's diffused lighting caught the subtle threads of silver in his hair, the laugh lines around her eyes. Time's gentle markings of their journey together.

"Do you think they'd be proud of us?" The question flew from her lips before she could catch it, carrying all the weight of their shared history.

Aarav was quiet for a moment, his thumb drawing thoughtful circles on her palm. "I think," he said finally, "they'd remind us it's not about pride. It's about what we've built—and what we'll keep building."

Their eyes met in the reflection, and Olivia saw in his gaze the same understanding that had first drawn them together—that time was not just a measurement but a medium, kindred to light passing through stained glass, transforming ordinary moments into something sacred.

She turned slightly, taking in the full scope of the exhibit. Their grandparents' tools lay in careful arrangement—the same tools that had later found new purpose in their own hands. Sketches showed the evolution of their craft, from rigid tradition to flowing innovation. And everywhere, in the margins of letters and concealed compartments of display cases, lay the evidence of love's patient work.

A museum guide appeared at the far end of the hall, keys jingling softly—a friendly reminder that closing time approached. But neither Olivia nor Aarav moved immediately. They stood there, letting the moment stretch like taffy, adoringly observing their timepiece mark the precious between what had been and what would be.

"It taught us well," Aarav said finally, his voice carrying the quiet certainty that had become his hallmark. "About time, about patience—"

"About love," Olivia finished, squeezing his hand.

They turned away slowly, their steps measured and unhurried. Behind them, the timepiece continued, its ticking following them down the hall like a benediction. Tomorrow, new artifacts would take its place, telling different stories to different hearts. But its lesson would remain with them, engraved into their shared understanding.

Outside, the evening was settling over the city like a tenderly placed blanket, streetlights beginning to twinkle like early stars. They paused on the museum steps, letting the transition from past to future wash over them. Above, the first true stars were appearing, eternal timekeepers marking their own vast scales.

"Ready?" Aarav asked, and both knowing he meant more than just leaving the museum.

Olivia nodded, feeling the weight of what they called them set comfortably into its place alongside their dreams of what may come. "Always," she replied, meaning every moment, every possibility that lay ahead.

They descended the steps together, their shadows merging in the gathering dusk, while behind them, inside its glass case, their timepiece kept its steady count of seconds that mattered only because they meant something to someone, someones, them.

The clock tower's rooftop opened to a the inky sable sky painted with terraced fog clouds being punctured by a single, signaling star every so often – each one a celestial marker of universal rhythms. Olivia and Aarav sat surrounded by the gentle glow of paper lanterns, their picnic spread across a worn Persian carpet that had once graced his grandmother's sitting room. Laid before them, the city breathed in its evening silence, punctuated only by the deep resonance of the sentimental underneath them marking each quarter hour.

The night air carried the lingering warmth of a day well-lived, touched with the sweetness of jasmine from the climbing vines crawling along the tower's edge. Olivia leaned back against the parapet, a glass of wine catching starlight in her hand, while Aarav sat cross-legged beside her, his attention focused on something hidden from her view.

"Close your eyes," he said softly, the words carrying that particular exuberance that emerged every few months from him—the one that meant he was about to shift her world slightly on its axis.

She complied, feeling the night air dance across her skin. The sounds of the square below seemed to fade, leaving only the steady rhythm of their inhales and exhales. Something that had both hefty lift and tensionless friction pressed into her palm—metal warmed by careful hands, intimate as a heartbeat pressed another.

"Open them."

In her hands lay her grandfather's pocket watch—the one she'd believed would never tick again, its mechanisms too damaged by time and grief to repair. But now it sat whole and beautiful, its silver case polished to a gentle gleam, its face clear as moonlight. As she held it, she felt the subtle vibration of its movement, a pulse as dependable as love.

"How did you...?" The question trailed off as she opened the case, revealing the enchanting design of gears and springs within. The craftsmanship was unmistakably Aarav's, but there was something more—tiny modifications that spoke of hope and progress even if undetectable by others.

"I wanted you to have a piece of him with you," Aarav said quietly, his hand coming to rest over hers where she cradled the watch. "Not just as a memory, but as something living and growing."

Tears magnified her vision as she traced the case's familiar engravings—her grandfather's initials intertwined with a pattern that had always reminded her of flowing water.

"Though I can't say it was easy, the mechanism was actually simpler than I'd thought," Aarav continued, his voice gentle with understanding. "It wasn't broken so much as... waiting. Like some stories do, until the right moment comes to tell them."

Olivia leaned into him, feeling the steady rhythm of his heart against her shoulder. The watch in her hands ticked in perfect harmony with both, finding its own place to exist in the symphony of time.

"You're my timekeeper," she whispered, the words carrying all the weight of their shared journey. "You always will be."

He turned to her then, his eyes reflecting starlight and something deeper—the same recognition that had drawn them together from the start. "And you're my story," he replied. "The one I choose to live in for each space between seconds."

They sat in the homes they had built in one another, sharing bites of baklava from his mother's recipe and sips of wine that tasted of summer evenings yet to pass. The watch rested between them, its steady ticking a reminder that some moments, though fleeting, imprint themselves forever on the heart.

Midnight approached and the giant beneath them roused in joy to sound its twelve solemn notes, Olivia found herself thinking of all the ways time could be measured—in heartbeats and breaths, in shared glances and gentle touches, in the words offered in love, in the willingness and actuality to purely be present, in the try and the triumph. The watch in her hands had once marked her grandfather's days; now it would mark hers and Aarav's, keeping time not just in minutes and hours, but in moments of love chosen and renewed.

The clock began to toll, its deep tones rolling out across the sleeping city. Aarav drew her closer, and together they counted the chimes, each one a beat in the continuing rhythm of their shared story. As the final note faded into the star-and-grey-strewn night, Olivia felt the true alignment of past and present, of ending and beginning, of time measured and time lived.

In her hands, her grandfather's watch ambled on in precision, marking not just the passage of ambulation of the world about her, but the presence of love that transcended from out, to in, to out again, everlastingly.

Dawn painted the square now before them in hues of gilded rose and muted azure, the first light catching on the polished surface of the clock they'd built together. Olivia and Aarav stood hand in hand before it, watching as their masterpiece prepared to mark its first waking hour in its permanent post.

The square began to stir with early risers—the baker whose warm scent of fresh bread had been part of their morning ritual, the newspaper vendor who had watched their story unfold in episodic installments, the cafe owner who had witnessed their earliest, public conversations. Each nodded in recognition as they passed, their presence adding to the weight of the moment.

As the minute hand approached twelve, Aarav squeezed Olivia's hand gently. "Ready?" he asked.

She nodded, feeling the beatific weight of her grandfather's watch in her pocket, its ticking now pulsing with and nearly for the beating of her heart. "Together," she replied, the word carrying all their shared promises.

The first chime rang out across the square, clear and true as a lover's vow. Each subsequent note built upon the last, creating a melody that spoke of time not as a master, but as a companion in the toil and pass and prevail and indistinct of life. As the final tone faded into the morning air, the town seemed to hold its breath—then release in collective exaltation.

Olivia felt Aarav's arm slip around her waist, drawing her closer as they watched their creation continue its eternal task of marking moments measured and meaningful, or otherwise. The morning light caught the inscription they'd carved along the clock's base: "For those who find love in the spaces amid seconds."

Time moved forward in its regular rhythm, marked now by their own timing. The square began to fill with the usual morning bustle—children rushing to school, partners silently consoling themselves as their lovers depart for their respective days, shopkeepers preparing for the day of service, phones ablaze on faces carrying all sorts of emotions, elderly couples taking their morning walks, the city as electric and mechanical and organic as human chaos creates. Each person who passed seemed paused to admire or acknowledge the protector of time stood still – their acceptance like water transporting materials downstream to build a bridge of understanding love and being a scant amount deeper.

Aarav turned to her, his eyes holding all the warmth of their shared tomorrow. "Shall we open?" he asked, though they both knew he meant so much more the shop.

"Yes," she replied as seriously and swiftly as she could muster.

As they walked toward their shared future, Olivia felt the truth of it all settle in her. Their footsteps fell naturally into their own entrancing rhythm, and she found herself thinking of all the ways they had learned to measure love—in careful adjustments and patient repairs, in morning coffee and evening stars, in the gentle space between tick and tock where two hearts learn to beat as one.

The clock chimed the quarter hour, its notes carrying across the awakening town like a blessing, and Olivia understood at last what her grandfather had tried to teach her all along. Her voice, when it came, was soft but certain, carrying the weight of every moment that, guided by their earnest decisions, had led them here:

"Time is not a straight line, nor a perfect circle. It is a series of moments—messy, fleeting, and timeless. And in those moments, we find love created and shared, again and again."

Made in the USA
Las Vegas, NV
21 December 2024

15038441R00198